The CARMICHAEL File

S. J. Garrett

Other Titles by S.J. Garrett

CHRONICLE Series
Chronicle of Destiny
Chronicle of Summer

ETERNITY Series
Ghost Eyes

DESCENDANTS Series
Shadow on the Sea

3rd DISTRICT Series
The Shaughnessy File
The Carmichael File

Dedicated with love to Sia, the real life Audra. I wish that true love could have saved you as well. I miss you.

PROLOGUE

There was a place known as the 3rd District.

When viewed from a plane, it resembled a small triangle located in the edge of New York City, New York. From space, it could not be seen. It was not a landmark. It was not a place of great historical import. It was, for all intents and purposes, a backwater area in a bustling city of hundreds of thousands of people.

It was also the place where magic lived. If your life crossed the roads of 3rd District, it was said, then you would find true love and live happily ever after. You would find a true faerie tale story.

This story is one of them.

Folder One
RAYNA

CHAPTER ONE

Seventeen years ago. . .

When the father arrived at Enforcers Headquarters, he was pale and drawn. He was also nearly inconsolable as he desperately tried to explain what was wrong to the lobby receptionist. Finally, at a loss, the young woman simply called up to the top floor. She relayed what she knew and listened to the answer. She hung up and said only, "Mr. Mason will be down in a minute."

Lucas Carmichael found himself unable to sit as he paced back and forth through the lobby. All eyes watched him in concern. Though he was only part of 3rd District by marriage, he was a member nonetheless. Everyone in the District stuck together.

A tall and distinguished man walked into the lobby a minute later. His calm ice-blue eyes missed nothing. The sharp sensation of fear stung his skin, but it came only from the outside and not within. He walked over and firmly got in Lucas' path, forcing the other man to pull up short. "Sit down."

No one had ever refused to listen to an order from Eric Mason, particularly when he spoke in the firm tone of command. Lucas sat down. He gripped his shaking hands together and stared at the floor. "You protect everyone in 3rd District," he finally blurted. "You and Ms. Taber have gifts. You can—you can forcefully interfere with outside forces and powers."

Eric sat down beside him and lifted an ash colored brow. "Yes," he conceded. He offered nothing further. "What happened?"

As before, Lucas could not stop the words from spilling out.

"You know my wife and I have two daughters."

"Rayna and Mika." Warmth filled Eric's voice. "They are well loved by those who meet them. Mika should be nine now, and Rayna four?"

"Someone wants them dead."

The words dropped like bombs into the lobby. Everything came to a halt. All eyes shifted. Horror filled some gazes. Fury filled others. The young receptionist immediately left her post and went to fetch a glass of water. When she brought it over, Eric took it without looking away from Lucas. "Drink this," he ordered.

Lucas shook his head. "Why would anyone want my girls dead? They're so beautiful. So giving." The glass was firmly pushed against his mouth and it was drink or choke. He drank. As the water slid down his throat, it brought a cooling sensation that helped to steady his mind and emotions.

The receptionist watched him critically for a moment before going back to her post. Eric set the glass aside and braced his arms on his legs as he leaned forward. "How do you know someone wants them dead?"

"I saw it." He drew a ragged breath. "Neither girl has a lick of modesty. When I told them they could go swimming if they got their suits on, they were pulling off their clothes before they got to their room. And I saw it." His voice dropped so low even Eric almost couldn't hear him. "The Bloody Check."

"Son-of-a-bitch." Eric raked a hand through his ashy hair and stirred the white streaks over his ears. His mind automatically attuned itself to his partner's, and her rage almost shook the building. Almost at the same time, they both calmed and began to think logically. There was only one course. The details would be tricky, though.

Rhianna Taber walked into the lobby a few minutes later. A folder was in her hand. She walked over to the two men and inclined her head. "Let's go into a conference room." She gestured across the hall.

The two men stood. Lucas went first, still almost dazed despite the water of clarity. Eric gestured Rhianna to go before him, like the old-world gentleman he still pretended to be. She arched a red brow and then just shook her head and went into the conference room. He went in behind her and shut the doors firmly.

"Mr. Carmichael," Rhianna began as she sat down, "you know your wife was prophesized to give birth to two exceptionally powerful beings. Two very special children that we of the Enforcers fully intended to recruit eventually."

"What are they?"

"I don't know," she admitted. "My touch on the future is vague at times. Impressions and hunches mostly. All I know definitively is that Rayna and Mika are critical to the peace of the entire world, let alone the peace of our District."

"Is," his voice broke for a moment, "is that why someone would issue a Bloody Contract for them?"

"It's a strong likelihood." Eric leaned back in his chair. "But we're going to have no way of knowing why someone is so afraid of what are clearly powers of good until the girls are at least twenty-one. Their powers should fully manifest at that time. It won't be sooner. They are only half-3rd District. We just need to be sure they make it to that age."

"I'll do anything!" Lucas vowed.

Rhianna and Eric exchanged a long look before he took the folder from her and opened it. He pulled out the stack of papers inside and slid them to Lucas. "Here is what we are offering. It is a two-fold deal. When the person who ordered the Bloody Contract makes an attempt for Rayna, she will emerge miraculously from a mere accident . . . except she will be asleep. She will remain in a coma until her twenty-first birthday, cared for at a strictly controlled Enforcers' hospital. Once she awakens, her powers will combine with ours to nullify the Bloody Contract."

Lucas drew a bracing breath. "And Mika?"

"We can't use the same contract for both." Eric rubbed the

bridge of his nose. "It would be too obvious. Hers will have to be slightly different. She will survive however many accidents necessary for her to reach twenty years of age. At that age, one of the accidents will place her within a matching coma. She will remain asleep until Rayna awakens. And the same will happen for her that happens for Rayna."

A little chill went down Lucas' back. "They could sleep for . . . for years! They won't know anything of the world they enter! And what if something happens when they are children? How will they grow and learn?"

"Enforcers have been investigating the possibilities associated with subliminal learning," Rhianna offered. "We have learned, conclusively, that things heard while asleep can remain. It may be a shot in the dark, but we could use these study results to formulate learning tapes for the girls. If their minds can learn, then they will wake with only a few hang-ups to their development. Reading would be a big one, but not insurmountable."

"I'll take care of the details of the tapes if needed," Eric promised quietly.

Lucas took a long, bracing breath. The idea of his babies being stuck in a coma for potentially years was terrifying, but it was more terrifying to think they might die. Without letting himself think, he signed his name across the bottom of the contracts. Eric and Rhianna signed as well, and the girls' safety was officially in Enforcers' hands.

Outside the building, it almost seemed as if something screamed in fury. Rhianna's eyes didn't waver though something came and went in Eric's eyes. Something that sent a chill down Lucas' back and yet simultaneously reassured him. If his girls were to be saved, then only these two could do it.

A few days later, only just arriving back from a trip, his daughters were happily riding with their mother and aunt in a car zooming down a freeway; neither had any idea of the danger and their parents had no intention of telling them unless necessary.

They had gone out of town to visit the girls' uncle and give him support in the family's difficult times. Lucas had nearly lost the family company. At a loss for what to do, he had turned the reigns over to his brother in the hopes that a fresh start would pull them back from the brink. Thankfully, it seemed to be working. The entire family was relieved.

Aunt Yvonne was Lucas' sister-in-law. She had picked up the girls and their mother and was now bringing them home. Rayna and Mika both liked her a lot. She always smelled like cookies, and if there was anything better to smell like, neither girl could envision it.

It was late at night but they still hit a snarl of traffic. As they continued along, bumper to bumper, Rayna pressed her nose to the window to look at New York City. It glowed and sparkled with millions of lights.

Her attention was diverted when she saw shadows moving along the side of the road. Frowning, she tried to see better. She was an exceptionally small girl, and she was still in a toddler's car seat at four years old. Her height in no way detracted from her mental growth. Her mind was much further along than her young age indicated. With precise clarity, she said, "I see people."

"On a freeway?" Yvonne's voice was warm. "At night? I hope they don't get hit."

Mika tried to lean over to see what Rayna was watching. She was in a special seat for older children, but she was also small for her nine years. She was also quite nimble and smart, and she wiggled out of her harness to scoot over to her sister. "Let me see!"

"Mika!" their mother ordered sharply. "Get back in your seat, young lady!"

"You sure she isn't Houdini reincarnated?" her sister-in-law groused.

The two girls peered out the window. The people were doing something. They seemed to be acting weird, too. They weaved back and forth as if dizzy, and they staggered up onto the freeway. A chill went down Rayna's back as the car began to move faster, the traffic *finally clearing. "Mommy . . ."*

At the note of fear, both adults glanced back at her. Something, no one would ever know what, made Yvonne jerk her gaze back around to the road. With a shriek, she slammed on her brakes as she saw the figure crossing the freeway on foot.

The car went out of control and careened across the lanes, causing horns to blare and brakes to screech. Miraculously, no other cars were hit. Not so miraculously, the uncontrolled car hit the side of the embankment . . . and went into the air over the side.

By the time the ambulance arrived, a crowd had already gathered. Motorists had pulled over to rush to the wreck to provide help. The mother had been killed on impact. Yvonne was only alive because one of those who had stopped knew CPR. The quick thinking motorist relinquished her position to the paramedics and jumped into the on-going search. Yvonne had tried to say something about her nieces before losing consciousness.

The car was a mangled mess, but it was clear where a car seat had been torn free. Flashlights illuminated the area as did floodlights when copters arrived. People called for the girls, but there was no true hope of finding them alive.

When Eric arrived on the scene, he joined in the search as well. He made his way down the steep slope of grass as he headed for the gully at the bottom. It was the line marker between private land and state highway. He didn't cross over as he moved down the gully with confidence. The wind shifted and it led him swiftly to a slightly hidden shallow that most eyes would have passed over.

He found Rayna in that shallow. She had been torn out of her car seat and was lying like a broken doll. Though he knew she would be fine, his fingers trembled slightly as he checked for a pulse. It was there. Unsteady but strong. A quick look told him that she had only bruises and scratches from the ordeal.

He shrugged out of his jacket and gently wrapped her up. Almost possessively, he lifted her into his arms and kept her close. She was truly tiny, her Faeriekin blood evident. He softly rubbed his cheek over her white hair. "It's okay, sleeping beauty," he murmured softly. "You'll be fine now. I promise."

He made his way back to where the paramedics were located. He nearly had to force himself to let her go so that she could be examined. There was just something about her that had grabbed onto his heart and not let go. He watched her be taken away to the Enforcers' hospital and then turned his attention to finding Mika. Oddly, he wasn't entirely surprised she could not be found, even as dawn approached. There was no such thing as coincidence.

He went to the hospital as soon as the search party disbanded for sleep before trying again. He said nothing to them of their futile efforts. In truth, it always warmed his heart that so many strangers would pull together to give help where it was most needed.

He found Lucas sitting outside Rayna's room. Grief had aged him within a matter of hours. Eric walked over to kneel in front of him. "I am sorry," he said quietly, "but we are not gods. We can't stop everything. If we could, we wouldn't even have needed the contract that has likely saved her life."

"She'll wake as a four-year-old in an adult body." Lucas looked at him with dull eyes. "How will she ever cope?"

"She will be an adult," he disagreed. "I will arrange for the subliminal tapes to cover everything from regular schooling to modern events to pop culture to as much as she might have learned simply being in school. She will be completely innocent," he warned, "and trusting, though. Some things simply cannot be taught by anything other than experience."

Lucas said nothing. What could he say? He had no control over anything, not even his own life. Not even the precious lives of his babies or his beloved wife. "Will they find Mika?" he asked faintly.

Eric gave him the truth though it was a painful one. "No. But she will live. You will see her again. I swear it." When there was no response, he got to his feet. His eyes drifted to the room where Rayna slept. Heart aching, he went inside and shut the door.

She was pale and still. She breathed on her own but she was

not awake. Once the hospital was sure she would not wake, she would be hooked up to other machines to provide nourishment for her growing body. It seemed almost obscene, the thought of a little girl confined to a hospital bed for years.

Something about her felt achingly lonely. Her world had fallen silent. Even when she listened to her tapes, her world would be alone. It broke his heart. He pulled the visitor chair over and sat down beside her. Gently he covered her hand with one of his. "Hey," he said softly. "I know you're scared. But you're not alone. I'm here with you now. I won't let anything happen to you. You like flowers, don't you? Well, when you wake up, I know a garden I can take you to see. It grows against a castle in the mountains, covered by clouds and sheltered from even the harshest snow and rain . . ."

One year ago . . .

Eric walked in the hospital room with a bouquet of flowers in his hand. It was Saturday at two. Every week, at that exact time, he always came to visit Rayna. He had never missed a single day. He came on holidays too. Her birthday and Christmas. Any day that she deserved more than usual to have someone by her side.

As he sat down beside her, he gently covered her hand with his. He talked to her of anything and everything in the world. He told her some of the funny moments of trying to upgrade all the computers in Enforcers, and of the world events that might interest her. For fifteen years, she had grown like a flower in a greenhouse. He told her of that too, describing how her face had matured and her hair had grown. He laughingly told her that she still wasn't tall. At twenty, she might be five-foot even but likely no more.

There were times where he felt as if she was listening to him. He felt as if she truly heard him. His powers of the mind, the abilities that picked up on the signals of the minds of other beings, always seemed to hum louder when he talked to her. And he talked to her of everything he could. It felt as if he could tell her anything, even things he had never told anyone else.

It would be another year until she awoke. Another long, lonely year. He so badly wanted to see her smile, to hear her talking back to him. She seemed to be a light in the darkness to him. He brought her hand to his cheek and closed his eyes. "I wish you could wake up, Rayna," he murmured. "This world needs you. There's so much you have to do and see. You never deserved this future. I just wish . . ." His voice trailed off. Wishes were useless. Her contract bound her.

Her hand moved. Shocked, he stared at her face, sure he had imagined it. Her hand moved again, distinctly more deliberate than a muscle twitch. The machines monitoring her began to record the signals of a waking mind. In his own mind, he could feel the feathery brush of a strong presence reaching out. She was waking up, but it should have been impossible!

He leapt to his feet and rushed out into the hall. "Doctor!" he barked, and the tone of command made everyone leap to do his bidding.

When Rayna opened her eyes a few minutes later, her gaze was blurry at best. Odd images swam above her with faces distorted like a funhouse mirror. One of the faces looked like her father but he seemed much older. Another face was attached to a body in a white coat; a doctor, probably. No other faces looked down at her. "Who .. ." Her voice broke against her will.

"Easy, little one," the doctor soothed. He was already checking her pulse and examining her eyes. "Your voice and eyes haven't been used in a long time. It will take a while for the nerves to come up to speed."

She drew a deep breath and focused. She could see and understand hundreds of dozens of things in her mind. She had no memories to associate to her knowledge. It was just there. She remembered going to preschool and learning about numbers. Suddenly here, in her mind, she knew how to multiply and divide complex equations. She knew what an equation was.

There was more than that, though. Something more important. A garden near a castle in the mountain. It had been described so clearly that she felt she had already been there. She drew a breath and concentrated. "Who?" she asked again, stronger.

The doctor and Lucas exchanged a look. They knew what she was asking. Carefully, Lucas asked, "Who what, Rayna?" Firm orders still rang in his ears.

"With me. Who? Talked." Her lashes fluttered closed. "He called to me . . . So lonely . . ."

"There was no one here, Rayna," he lied softly. "It was just a dream."

She didn't doubt her father but she also didn't entirely believe him. A dream didn't leave her hand tingling with the warmth of being held and it didn't leave her heart aching with the loneliness for another being.

Present . . .

Everyone in New York City knew Rhianna Taber on sight. She was the face on the front of Enforcers that handled day-to-day tasks and oversaw the usual meetings and business problems that came with running one of the biggest companies in America.

The opposite was true of Eric Mason. Only his name was known by many since it was on everything she signed. They were equal partners and co-owners, but he never attended meetings and never handled the casual business. His duties were more detail oriented. If he showed up at a business owned by Enforcers, then it was because someone had screwed up, and everyone knew it.

He and Rhianna had a give and take relationship. They gave each other hell and at the same time took care of each other. They were the same age with only a few months separating them (with Rhianna being older). They denied a familial connection, but anyone who met them knew that they were more like twins than partners. They worked seamlessly together.

It was why, when she tapped a scarlet fingernail on the document in front her, he was already reaching for it before her finger was done moving. Both were sitting at her desk going over

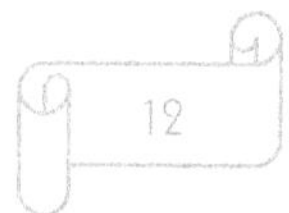

some . . . interesting developments. "Look," she offered. "A coincidence."

A wry smile crossed his handsome face. "Rhi, there's no such thing as coincidence around people from the 3rd District."

"Still blame me for that?" she asked idly.

"Yes."

"At least you're reliable in your opinions."

He shook his head slightly and then raked a hand through his hair in agitation. "So let me get this straight. Budgets Inc. has gone on along merrily without a single restructure or reorganization for several years. Now, when they have at their fingertips one of the brightest minds around, they don't want to promote her up through the ranks?"

She regarded him with a smile. "Riku," she used the nickname with the affection of a longtime friend, "you're going to worry the rest of your hair white."

He glowered at her. "The streaks are not because I'm old," he reminded her. "It's genetic."

"Yes, but we *are* old, Riku."

"Shut up, Rhi." He leaned back in his chair and studied the report intently. "Something smells rotten and it's not that perfume you're wearing."

"Audra's idea of a crank gift. I had to wear it at least once." She swiveled to face her computer and began to type quickly despite her long red nails. "I got my hands on the personnel data for Budgets. From the day she started there, mysterious accidents have kept occurring. They're documented, but it's as if no one wants to see a pattern. But that isn't surprising considering the *other* thing."

He glanced up at the note in her voice. "What other thing?"

"I got into the manager's email."

"Do I want to know how?" he asked ruefully.

"No." Her black eyes snapped with the sparks that meant her temper was on the rise. "This manager is the one that works directly over Rayna. In his inbox and trashcan, I've found emails dating back to the beginning of her employment six months ago. Every single email is a litany of the same. Harassment. Her coworkers seem to be taking vicious delight in terrorizing her. She attached any relevant emails and attachments to her emails to her manager, and since the latest was as of this morning, I'd have to say he's done absolutely shit."

That alone told him that it was severe: she never swore. Eyes narrowed, he leaned forward to look over her shoulder. A little electrical hum filled the air around him, evidence of his own growing anger. "And we've received no report. How nice. What kind of harassment?"

"Well, several of the emails are lists of statistics on coma victims. The percentage of who wake up, the amount of mental damage, the erosion of mental and motor skills." Her voice reflected her disgust. "There are photographs of CAT scans of coma victims' minds, showing the places where brain matter deteriorated. It's *disgusting*. And then there are those who make snide comments about her not being a miracle and how it must be a scam because no one could wake from a sixteen-year coma without a lick of damage."

"So she's being harassed," he said quietly, "and there are mysterious accidents occurring. Nearly fatal accidents that everyone is turning a blind eye to. Why does she stay there?"

"No one else would hire her," she admitted simply. "And it was the only one of our companies that had an opening we could get her into without the experience most other places demand. The girl *is* brilliant, Riku. But she's very innocent and that puts her at a big risk. These accidents should *not* be happening. Her contract was solid."

"She woke up too early," he murmured, an unknown note of wistfulness in his voice.

"And whose fault was that?" She lifted a brow.

He sighed and got to his feet. "Mine, yes, I know. It's not like I intended to wake her up," he added defensively. "Hell, Rhi, you know I'd never do anything to hurt that girl! I'd sooner drown myself."

"You can't drown, Riku."

"It was a metaphor, dear." He raked a hand through his hair again and ruffled the aforementioned white streaks. There really was no other option than to go and take a look at the company and find out not only what the hell was going on, but also to find out what was happening around Rayna Carmichael. Her contract was not completed until her birthday arrived, and she was not safe from the death that she had been marked for. It was a week to her birthday. He could take care of things for a week.

"I'm going to head over there tomorrow," Rhianna said suddenly and caught his attention. "It shouldn't be a problem."

"No."

"Pardon?"

He cleared his throat. "Sorry, it slipped out. Sometimes I forget to be tactful and erudite. What I meant to say was, I'll go instead of you. Your face is far too well known. I'll get a feel for the layout, the people and such, and keep an eye on our sleeping princess. If I go in undercover then no one will tense up and put forward their best face. I'll be able to see things as they really are."

She watched him head through the connecting door into his office, and she covered a smile as she turned back to the papers on her desk. She had no doubt that he would indeed see everything clearly. He would be with Truth, and Truth always laid bare everything to the light.

CHAPTER TWO

She was known as the Miracle Girl of the 3rd District, but as Rayna Carmichael hurried down the sidewalk toward the front door of the office where she worked, she didn't feel much like a miracle. It was another of those days where her coordination was sketchy at best and she couldn't quite get a grip on her depth perception.

The physical problems were the least of her worries. She felt lost mentally, slightly adrift in a very weird world. She couldn't even watch the news or read the paper. She didn't understand anything happening, so why try to torture herself? Thankfully, it had also become a good excuse for her ignorance. Sometimes she felt like she was still asleep.

But there really was no denying she was a medical miracle. She had survived a horrendous car crash without a single broken bone, survived a sixteen-year coma, and then within a short time of her awakening as a twenty-year-old, she had been on the same level mentally as her peers. Most who met her couldn't tell she had never gone to school. In fact, it was impossible to tell, especially because she had a gift with computers.

The only thing that gave her away was her lack of an ability to communicate in writing. Her reading skills were minimal; she always carried a dictionary. Her writing skills most closely resembled an elementary school student. She was trying to teach herself, but it was a painfully slow process when she constantly had to look things up.

As always, her shoulders were braced when she reached her

desk. The humiliation was to be brief that morning, though, since only one or two nasty notes had been left for her. She tore them up and shredded them without reading them. She immediately straightened up her area to remove any other evidence. She hated her desk to be messy, and others messed it up just to torment her. She had the receptionist desk, and it always looked bad to clients if she had clutter around.

She logged onto her computer after dumping the shred bin. Her desktop appeared, and she discovered it had been changed to a graphic image of the damage done to a coma victim's brain. She promptly changed the wallpaper to the cutest, fluffiest kitten she could find and then began to trace the residue the culprit had left behind. She had quickly learned how to manipulate the internal server the company ran on, and she used it to take a small measure of justice for herself.

She opened her opponent's email, carefully read through a couple, found what she wanted, and forwarded it to the woman's husband. She would be so busy trying to explain to her husband why she was calling a coworker 'love nuggets' that she wouldn't bug Rayna again for a while. It certainly didn't sound like something she ought to be calling an associate.

A financial advisor going past her desk stopped to eye her menacingly. A great number of people in the company disliked her purely because no one else ever did. She was beautiful and kind, and she had an innocent trust that let her see the good in mankind. She took delight in the smallest things. Everyone who met her loved her, and because of it, she brought out the worst in people who embraced crueler emotions.

Rayna looked up at the woman beside her desk and lifted her chin slightly in an almost dare. The woman opened her mouth but shut it as the front door opened. She scuttled away swiftly instead. Rayna clenched her hands together under her desk and found a smile for the old man that had entered. The smile softened her face and made her violet eyes light up the entire room. When she smiled, everything was right with the world. "Good morning!"

"Good morning!" He smiled back. The highlight of his entire week was coming in to Budgets Inc. to go over his retirement stocks. Every visit, rain or shine, Rayna was there to greet him. Her smile was his sunshine. "How are you, my dear?"

"Awake." She smiled as she said it. She got to her feet and made her way carefully around her desk, moving slowly to avoid hitting things. She tried to keep them in the same places, but her coworkers moved them to torment her. "Here, have a seat." She helped him into one of the chairs. "You're always early," she teased. "You need to find someone to budget your time!"

He gave a cackle that turned into a cough. She immediately got him a cup of water, and he smiled at her. "You're an angel, Rayna."

Her cheeks turned bright pink. "Not me." She got to her feet and went around behind her desk again. Shoulders tensed, she picked up her phone and dialed a number. When the other side was answered, she said, "Mr. Meadows here to see you."

"I told you not to buzz me when people are early!" was the snapped response. "Don't you have any working brain cells, or were they all killed in the coma? Call me when it's actually nine o'clock, you idiot!"

She winced as the phone slammed down on the other side. She slowly hung up her own phone and fought the tears rising to choke her. "It's my job," she whispered softly. She drew several deep breaths and ignored the fact that Mr. Meadows was watching her. She didn't want him to worry, but it was so hard to keep calm when all she wanted was to curl up and cry. Being an adult could be nothing but a frustration.

The bell chimed over the door. Relieved, she turned with a smile. "Good morning," she started to say, only to have the words slowly die and fade away. Her eyes widened and red color swept up her cheeks. The sudden breathlessness was entirely foreign but oddly familiar.

She had never truly been able to understand the concept of

attraction. Some of the kinder women had tried to helpfully point out what they felt were attractive men, but she simply hadn't gotten it. She had finally decided that she simply wasn't mature enough to be attracted to anyone yet, or perhaps she might just not be capable of attraction at all.

Apparently, she had been wrong.

The newcomer standing just inside the doorway made her feel flushed as she looked at him. He was tall and broad shouldered with a lean and beautiful strength. It was a strength well displayed in his short-sleeved shirt and blue jeans. His arms were corded with muscles that hypnotized her. She wanted to touch them, just to see if they were as strong as they looked.

She couldn't guess at his age, but he was definitely an adult. A bone-deep calmness in his ice-blue eyes seemed to say he had done, and seen, it all. The youth to his features made her guess he might be in his late twenties, and he was more perfectly beautiful than any TV star. His ashy brown hair *begged* to be touched, and the little white wings of hair over his ears just added to the temptation.

Without looking away from him, her fingers flew over the keys of her keyboard as she sent an email to one of the few coworkers she liked and trusted. *Attractive men? The short word for them?*

Her eyes flickered to her monitor as the response came back quickly. *??? You mean 'hot'? ☺ Should I be coming up there, Rayna?*

The man cleared his throat and smiled a little. Rayna blinked and realized he was holding out a clipboard to her. He was also wearing a hip holster that held gardening tools. "Oh!" She leapt to her feet, blushing brightly. "I'm so sorry; I was busy staring at you." Her eyes popped wide. "I mean . . ."

Eric barely hid a second smile. She was so wonderfully sweet! And lovely as well; she was lovelier than he remembered. Her silvery dove hair had been cropped closely around her face and nearly resembled fine feathers. Her eyes were colored the delicate violet hue of morning glories just beginning to wake. Soft and fair skin without blemishes covered her entirely. Not an ounce of makeup touched her skin but she didn't need it. Nature itself had given her an untarnished beauty.

As she took the clipboard from him, his eyes sparkled. Even in her low-heeled shoes, she didn't quite reach his shoulder. More than her height made her small, though. She possessed an overall deceptive fragility thanks to fine bones and supple curves. She could not be mistaken for a teenager, though. It was a curious magic.

His faerie princess. He couldn't stop the delight at seeing her again but kept his voice casual as he said, "Enforcers sent me out. The front area is in some desperate need of maintenance. I thought I'd sign in and get to work. Does everyone come through here?"

"Umm-hmm." She was studying the clipboard. The paperwork had been written as simply and plainly as possible, and it was very easy for her to read. "I'm the receptionist. And, sir, your figures are wrong. You undercharged us." She handed him the clipboard back. "Based on your estimated hours of work and pay per hour, we should actually owe you close to three hundred dollars more at the end of your job. Two hundred ninety-five dollars and twenty-six cents, to be precise."

He stared at her for a moment. He had known she was brilliant, but she had managed to surprise him. She had absorbed her subliminal tapes with a hungry attention, her attention fixated powerfully enough that the machines recording her brainwaves had almost busted. Now she had just done long multiplication and division in her mind faster than a lot of scholars could do it with a calculator. She needed to be tested, and soon, so that she could get at least the high school degree she deserved. "You must have studied a lot in school," he said, putting admiration in his tone as he fixed the clipboard. "Why aren't you a financial advisor?"

"Good question!" Meadows harrumphed. "Rayna is the nicest, sweetest girl in this building!" He thumped his cane on the floor to add emphasis.

"Yes, she's *such* a miracle," one woman concurred snidely as she went past. "Rayna never went to school and yet she's so smart!

20

She doesn't have a high school diploma let alone a college degree. Used to be we'd call people like that either stupid or lazy. Or both. "

Rayna didn't respond. She stared at Eric's collar because she was too humiliated to meet his eyes. Fiercely she clenched her hands into fists at her sides and bit down on her lower lip. The urge to cry faded, and she took a quick breath before looking up at him with a smile that didn't reach her eyes. "She's right. I don't have an education. I never went to school. I was in a coma. They gave me subliminal tapes that taught me everything."

The pain in her eyes tore at him. He fought to maintain his self-control and not fry that self-righteous bitch to a crisp with lightning. He never harmed weaker beings, but the violent urge was strong. *No one hurt his faerie princess.* "I see." He kept his tone deliberately light. "Well, I don't think someone without a degree is an idiot. I don't have one either."

"Oh." She blinked and then smiled genuinely. Her eyes sparkled. "No wonder your math is bad. Oops!" She covered her mouth with a hand. "Sorry. I sort of tend to say what's on my mind. I'm trying to learn not to."

"Don't change," he suggested. He took the clipboard back when she had signed it. "You'd make a lot of people, including me, very sad."

"And me!"

She smiled at Meadows. "Thank you, and you, sir." She heard the phone ring and quickly sat back down to pick it up. "Budgets Inc., this is Rayna. May I help you?" She waved a little as Eric left and then again as Meadows finally headed back to his meeting. The call was a long one, and she tuned out the rest of the office as she walked the caller through one of the company's customer spreadsheets. It wasn't a requirement, but why should she turn him over to someone who didn't care and would be rude? Besides, spreadsheets were numbers and she definitely knew numbers where she might never know words.

It was only when she hung up the phone that she realized a

bunch of women had gathered at the window in front of her desk. It faced the front of the building where the sorely neglected front lawn and landscaping were located. She frowned. What on Earth were they all doing there? Since when did they care about the lawn?

She got her answer as one woman purred, "Look at that ass. That is one fine piece of flesh."

"Look at his *arms*." Another woman sighed. "That is one first class body wasted on such a low class job."

"Think he'd ride a woman as competently as a lawnmower?" another asked slyly.

"I don't know, but let's have that mower bronzed if it manages to rip his shirt off."

Rayna's frown deepened as she got to her feet and moved closer to see outside. Sure enough, Eric was outside and he was fighting with the lawnmower. The jeep-like device had decided to resist his control, and his shirt had snagged on the fender. It definitely looked like it was in imminent danger of being torn off.

She studied him for a long moment. He really was beautiful. Something wild and free clung to his presence. If he answered to anyone, it was whatever gods he might believe in. He could not be bound by rules and regulations; if he followed them, it was because he genuinely believed in them. Anger simmered in her heart at the disrespect the other women showed. No one deserved to be treated that way, especially not him.

She knew she would get the sharp edge of someone's fury, but she couldn't stop herself from stepping up in his defense. "You know," she said softly, "if it was a bunch of men standing here saying these things about a woman, you would accuse them of harassment."

There was a collective gasp as all ten women turned to look at her. Outrage rose swiftly. "How dare you accuse us of harassment!" someone snapped.

She linked her hands behind her back and her nails dug into her palms. "I didn't say that. I simply stated a fact. You chose to blame yourself because you knew I spoke the truth."

Knowing she was right—both times!—only made the horde angrier. Most stomped off in furious and indignant huffs. The ringleader, one of the higher-level managers, pinned Rayna with an icy glare. "You know, it doesn't surprise me that you stick up for him." Her voice sounded as bitter as winter. "You're nothing but a nobody. An uncultured little idiot from that backwater 3rd District. Frankly, you're probably not even human. *Less* than human. You should have stayed asleep. No one wants you in our world."

As she turned on an ice pick heel and stalked down the hall, Rayna bit down hard on her lower lip. It was only when she tasted blood that her tears subsided. The pain choked her for long moments. She started to sit down at her desk again when someone going outside opened the front door. A waft of furiously hot air slapped her. Her eyes went to where Eric was digging in the ground. Sweat gleamed visibly across his skin, and a quick look revealed no water cooler nearby. Concerned, she got to her feet.

Outside, Eric swiped an arm across his forehead. It was hot, his back was killing him, and he was in heaven. Gardening was more of an obsession than a hobby. If he couldn't feel the dirt between his fingers, catch the scent of flowers . . . he would stop existing. Hell, Rhianna had put him in charge of the Enforcers Headquarters' gardens just so he would have something to do and stop pestering her. At least there he didn't have to deal with a temperamental mower, he thought crossly. Stupid thing had to be possessed.

His mind could not wholly focus on the job. He had seen the altercation at the window. He didn't know what had been said, but the body language had spoken volumes. He would have ignored the entire scene if he hadn't seen Rayna intervene. If she had been hurt . . .

"Sir?"

He straightened in surprise at the sound of her voice. She stood just a foot away, and she had a frosty bottle of water in her hands.

In a violet sundress with a white vest, she looked as fresh and pure as any of his orchids. Her shoes, he saw then, had been specially made to help her balance and were fastened on with straps. They should have made her look younger, but they only emphasized the graceful lines of her legs—and those were pure, one hundred, glorious, percent adult woman.

He cleared his throat as he realized where his mind seemed determined to wander. "Yes?"

"I thought you might be thirsty. It's so hot out here." She held the bottle out to him with a smile. "My name is Rayna Carmichael. What's yours?"

"Riku." He used his nickname without compunction. He gratefully took the bottle and opened it. "Thank you, Miss Carmichael."

She shook her head. "It's just Rayna. I'm not comfortable with formality, and besides, you're old." She went pink as he lifted a brow. "I meant older than me. I'm sorry. My language skills are very bad at times. I never know how to say what I want." Her eyes flickered back toward the office. "They're always horrible but I never say anything. And whenever I find the courage to say something, they say something worse. I'm not sure why I try."

He removed his glove and reached out a hand to run his thumb lightly over her lower lip. It looked slightly bruised and swollen, and he could see where she had bitten hard enough to draw blood. "Biting your lip?" he asked softly.

"Yes. Trying not to cry." Her eyes searched his face. There was something about his touch that was familiar. His soft, almost velvety, voice seemed to be imprinted in her ears. "Where did I meet you?" she asked softly. "I'm sure I have. I recognize your voice."

The fact that she had no idea her words could be taken as flirting was just another part of her charm. He didn't think she even knew what flirting was, and it made her utterly refreshing in such a superficial world. "I'm sure I'd remember if we'd formally met. You're beautiful."

"Really?" A blush touched her cheeks. "Thank you."

"You sound surprised."

"I guess I never thought about it." She tilted her head. "People are so focused on beauty that I assumed I had none. It's as if . . . beauty is all that can make people special. But it's not right." Something faraway seemed to move in her eyes, something that shifted and flowed like feathery power. "There is always right and wrong in the world. Black and white. You just have to know how to push aside the shadows."

A little chill rippled down his back as he began to understand her slowly growing power. She had the power of Truth. How it would manifest, he didn't know, but she saw with such childlike innocence that she could use her powers without tearing herself apart. Perhaps the coma had been more of a salvation than anyone had known.

It was still a painful power. His heart ached at what she would go through. He wanted to protect her from her own gifts. Carefully, he said, "I think you're right. About being wrong." He grinned sheepishly as he realized how it sounded. "Right?"

She giggled softly. The sound was pure enchantment. "Right!" She glanced at her watch and winced. "I have to go." She reached out to touch his hand with hers. "If you need anything," she told him, "ask for me. I'll help however I can."

As he watched her run back toward the entrance, he slowly lifted his hand to look at it. How could *anyone* treat a creature so open and giving with such cruelty? His fascination and near obsession with her over the years just seemed to be growing. Come hell or high water, he would keep her safe.

When her birthday was past and her contract was complete, he was taking her to Enforcers where her mind and skills could be used properly. A flower would die without room for its roots to grow, and he refused to see her wither. Enforcers was the perfect garden for her, and he fully intended to be there to tend to her and make sure she blossomed.

His obsession, however, was beginning to be a little alarming.

He was attracted to her. Well, who wouldn't be? He told himself fiercely, over and over again, that it was simply a natural reaction to the fact that she was beautiful. He had not even *once* considered kissing away the hurt on her lip. Never. Not once. Hadn't been in his mind.

A soft laugh fluttered through that same mind. *Liar*, came Rhianna's voice teasingly.

Shut up, Rhi, he muttered mentally. *Go away, damn it.*

Mental bonds were more hindrance than help when it came to his 'sister', so he ignored her as he always did when she was being a pest. He focused his attention on his work and kept his ears always alert to the people coming and going. People talked frankly as they walked past him, as if he was part of the scenery. His head began to pound under the litany of complaints he heard.

By the time the workday was ending, he was ready for a shower and a strong drink. It wasn't the heat, it was the humanity! Humans could be such bastards. Muttering under his breath, he pulled his gloves off and slapped them against his leg. Dust promptly rose. He coughed and muttered more distinctly. He heard a soft giggle and turned his head to see Rayna standing next to him. A jacket sat around her shoulders and her bag was in her arms. "Hi," she said. Her eyes twinkled.

"Whoops." He grinned. "You didn't hear me, did you?"

"Just a little." Her eyes sparkled all the more as she crouched beside him. "Your day was as long as mine, so it's okay." She pulled a tissue out of her pocket and began to wipe at the smear of dirt on his cheek. "You really like your job, huh?"

He could not move or think properly as she cleaned his cheek. She was so open and giving that it almost drove him mad. He found himself craving those very qualities, but his knees shook with the terror of protecting her. He wanted her hidden behind arbors and garden walls where she couldn't be found by anyone else. "Yes, I do." He found a smile. "Do you like your job, Rayna?"

"It's boring." She shrugged one shoulder. "I always get done

with my work quickly and no one else wants to give me anything. I work on my reading in the downtimes by looking at the contracts and agreements and so on."

"You don't read?' he asked softly, hurting for her.

"I do, but not well. Hazards of being in a coma when you're a child," she said with a false sort of cheerfulness. She got to her feet and pushed her hair back as it tried to blow into her face on a warm breeze. "I'll see you tomorrow, Riku." She smiled more naturally. "At least, I'd like to. You're a good person." She bent and kissed his cheek before hurrying away down the walkway.

He reached up and touched his cheek, smiling to himself. Then, gathering his equipment, he began to pack up for the evening. She lived in 3rd District. She was safe there. He wouldn't need to worry about her again until tomorrow. For now, he was going home and getting cleaned up, and pretending that he hadn't wanted to turn his head and meet her lips with his own.

He was in *deep* trouble.

CHAPTER THREE

Eric was never one to give less than his all when he was on a project, and his project was two-fold since he really did feel compelled to do the landscape. So, bright and early the next morning, he was heading for Budgets Inc. He wanted to be there when people first arrived so that he could see how things were at that time.

To his surprise, he wasn't the first one there. Rayna was sitting in the break area under an umbrella, her head tucked on her arms as if she was asleep. Several books lay open around her, and he walked slowly closer, wondering what she was reading.

One of the books was about art. Another was on computers. A third was on grammar and sentence structure, and a dictionary lay just under it. His heart ached for her. He quietly knelt beside her and studied her sleeping face. Seeing her here was so much better than seeing her in the hospital. A flush of life clung to her cheeks, and her beauty looked as soft and ethereal as her Faeriekin blood implied.

The sun had not raised high enough to bring the summer heat, and a chill still infused the air. He didn't want her to get frozen, so he softly touched her shoulder. "Rayna?" He kept his voice gentle. The last thing he ever wanted to do was frighten her.

Despite his care, there was a trace of pure terror and panic when her eyes opened. Her eyes focused on him, and she blinked drowsily as the fear faded. "Riku?" She carefully sat up and a shiver roughened her skin.

He immediately removed his light jacket and put it around her shoulders. He bit back a smile; it was almost three times too big. "What're you doing out here?" He couldn't stop himself from brushing her hair out of her eyes. "I thought the office didn't open for another hour. Why are you sleeping out here?"

"It's quiet." She rubbed at her eyes with a soft yawn like a child. "I don't sleep well so I end up napping in places." She shivered despite the jacket and drew the edges further closed. "I accidentally napped in the break room once. I've been careful not to do it again."

Anger carefully hidden, he eased onto the bench beside her and studied her face. "Why don't you just spend more time at home?"

"I live alone." She picked at the paint peeling on the table. "My father lives in the Bronx."

"That's a fair distance away from here. And, aren't you only twenty?" The law lifting the age of majority to twenty-one had been a large spot of trouble for many people over the last few years, but he had always, and would always, stand by it. Some kids needed those few extra years. Others, like Rayna, were too advanced for their age.

"I am but . . ." She lowered her gaze. "I asked for independence. My father was smothering me. I love him, but I couldn't live that way. I couldn't blink or breathe or do anything without him there. I wanted to go to school," her voice was wistful, "but he refused to even let me out of the house. So I got my legal freedom and moved back to the 3rd District where I was born."

"I would think," he said carefully, "that a man who lost his wife and a daughter would be desperate to hold onto his other daughter, especially if she had been asleep for sixteen years."

Her smile was sad. "I know he loves me. And I love him. But I just didn't fit into his world. I don't have a world of my own. My life is like my apartment. Small and cold. At least out here, I feel a little less out of my depth."

It took every single ounce of two thousand years' worth of self-control not to pull her into his arms. He knew the complex where she lived. She had one of the smallest apartments. The simple fact was that she couldn't afford more on her current salary. She barely made over minimum wage.

Unaware of his thoughts, she offered him a genuine smile. "Anyway, I like being here early. This way I'm at my desk when the office opens."

"Let's get some coffee," he offered. "There's a truck around back. I saw it as I was coming in. Want to come with me?"

"Sure." She swung her feet around and stood up. She nearly bumped her head on the umbrella, but she ducked in the nick of time. Despite the mishap, she moved with a startling grace. Aware he was staring, she blinked at him. "Is something wrong?"

"You must have worked so hard," he murmured. "Physically, to be able to coordinate as well as you do."

"It hurt," she admitted with a child's candid honesty. "My muscles had never been moved. I only stopped using a cane or walker about seven months ago. It was five months of almost constant pain before that. And I still have trouble with my height perception. And my eyes." She rubbed at them again. "If I can get the money, I want to go see an eye doctor. My doctor from the hospital said that because my eyes were not used when I was growing, they never developed as they should."

"You'd be very cute in glasses," he told her gravely. In the back of his mind churned unformed plans for getting her in to the best eye doctor in town. If she didn't want glasses, there were plenty of laser surgery technologies.

She considered the idea of wearing glasses. A lack of vanity meant her only concern was, "I hope I can get them in a color I like." She fell into step beside him as he began walking around the side of the building. She snuggled further into the coat, intrigued by the way it had absorbed his warmth. "How old are you?"

"Old enough I feel it," he said with emphasis. He gestured to the white wings in his hair. "Don't let these fool you. They're genetic. All the men in my family get them. Women get black streaks, unless

they have black hair. My aunt had very dark hair, and her streaks appeared with an almost red hue."

"I like it on you," she decided. "It's nice. It makes you look . . ." Frustration crossed her face as she tried to find the word she wanted. "Like . . . a gentleman. No." She rubbed her forehead. "What's that word? The one meaning refined or unique, or something?"

It dawned. "Distinguished?" he murmured, once more feeling his heart ache for her. Truly, it seemed as if the ache never went away. It just changed between sympathy to pain to enchantment to obsession.

"Yes!" She gratefully took the cup of coffee he handed her, and she was completely oblivious to the longing looks from the young man selling the coffee. "I spend hours on Wikipedia," she confessed. "And I read dictionaries. But I never know *what* word I need, so I can't look it up. I've thought about memorizing the entire darn thing."

"You're one hell of a woman, Rayna Carmichael. I don't think I've ever admired anyone more." It was nothing less than the absolute truth.

She blinked at him, then smiled. "Thank you. To be honest, I kind of admire you."

He lifted his brows in surprise. "Me?"

"Sure. You do what you love without caring how others perceive it." She sat down on the edge of a picnic bench and swung her feet lightly.

"What makes you think I love my job?" he asked her curiously.

She frowned at him. "Well, why do it if you don't?" She fell silent for a few moments and studied the ground. "Sorry," she finally said. "Guess I'm childish. I forgot adults don't always get to do what they want."

"What do you want to do?" He eased onto the bench beside her and angled his body so that his knees brushed hers. He noticed her fingertips were slightly whiter than usual and picked up her hands to warm them between his.

"I want to go to school." She stared at their hands but didn't seem to be seeing anything. "I want to learn about computers. I've been teaching myself, and I've learned it quickly. I mean, it's mostly numbers, and I'm really good with numbers." She looked around and saw no one else, but she still lowered her voice. "I can hack into most systems," she confessed. "And I once made Mr. Oppenheim's computer run only in binary."

He burst into laughter. "I'd have paid to see the look on his face!"

Her smile lightened her face and the entire area. "It was funny! He looked like a pink cabbage, all wrinkled and mad! He hopped around for hours until someone came and fixed it." She slipped her hands deeper into his. He was so warm and strong. He was much bigger than she was but she felt nothing except kindness inside him. He made her feel safe in a way she never had before. No matter what he said, she was sure she had met him somewhere. And she was sure she had missed him. "You're a good man." His brows lifted and she tilted her head. "No one's ever said that?"

"Ah, no. I think the nicest thing I've ever been called is intimidating. The worst things . . . well, you're too young to hear them." He paused briefly. "You know, I think *I'm* too young to hear them."

He was rewarded with a giggle. "Then they're all wrong." She slipped her hands free and got to her feet. She removed his jacket and held it out to him. "I have to go now. And Riku . . . thank you. You don't treat me like I'll break, and you don't treat me like I'm some sort of freak. I can just be me." She bent to kiss his cheek softly and hurried away toward the front of the building.

Silence lingered until he heard the coffee seller clearing his throat. Startled, he looked over. "Yes?" He could barely see the man inside the truck so he got to his feet and walked over. "Is something wrong?"

"No." The other male was attractive and probably in his late twenties. He was also slightly uneasy as he mumbled, "You, ah, have a thing for Rayna?" When Eric slowly lifted a brow, he flushed. "Thing is," he said earnestly, "I really like her. She's sweet and innocent and so pretty. I'd love to ask her out sometime but she has no clue I'm attracted to her, and I don't want to make her stop visiting. I've been trying to get my courage up but . . ."

Something shook inside Eric. It was dark and violent, nearly calling up his powers over the elements. As it was, clouds swept briefly across the sky. Before he could stop himself he said, "Rayna belongs to me. Don't waste your time, kid."

"Lucky bastard," he sighed sadly.

Suddenly realizing what he had said, Eric swiftly left the area and headed for the front where his work was waiting. What the hell was wrong with him? He had no claim to Rayna other than where her safety was related. Even that was sketchy at best. Why had he warned off someone who seemed like a decent guy? He put it out of his mind as he got out his tools. It was time to get his mind off Rayna and focus on the other part of why he was there.

He kept his eye on the people coming and going. After a while, he moved closer to the building and worked right under the front window where Rayna's desk was situated. She opened it after a few moments to let in the morning air, and he was able to perfectly hear everything that went on. It took only a few minutes before he realized how good she truly was at her job.

She handled every customer that came to the desk with the same friendly personality, and it was clear all of them would have preferred to deal with her than anyone else. He counted at least ten people she helped at the desk rather than referring them back; her knowledge of policies and procedures was absolute.

She was the same on the phone, patiently walking people through lengthy documents without ever once losing her composure. She repeated herself as needed, and her voice was always warm and friendly. Her skill was underscored for Eric by the fact that she had probably never *read* the documents; she had learned solely on listening and observing. He could barely imagine what she might be like with better reading comprehension.

Why the *hell* was a woman like that working a front desk? Annoyance gnawed inside him at the utter waste of talent. Damn it, they could just train her up the ranks and take advantage of her natural learning ability!

He got to his feet and yanked his gloves off. He stuffed them in the back pocket of his jeans as he headed down the walkway toward the parking lot. He pulled his cell phone out and punched speed dial. When the other side was picked up, he said without preamble, "I want the monthly employee appraisal reports."

"Okay." Rhianna went through her files and tucked the phone between her ear and her shoulder. "Any reason why in particular?"

"I want Rayna's reports. Rhi, she's even more brilliant than we thought. She handles herself like a queen and has the warm and open manner of a real lady. She's also good with customers and probably knows as much about this place as the accountants themselves. The clients even have a real preference for her." He kept an eye on the building as he spoke, not wanting someone to overhear.

"Then why is she still a secretary," she murmured, and it was mostly to herself. She was reading Rayna's reports, and her brows slowly climbed. "I see nothing at all mentioning that in here. Her reports are just good enough to keep her, but not so good as to have her recommended for promotion. Average, average, average." She snorted rudely. "Needs improvement on her ability to read instructions. What a surprise. They *know* she can't read well. They give her written instructions just to give her a chance to screw up."

"I think it's jealousy," he said flatly, and described what he had seen the day before. He could all but hear the steam coming out her ears from temper, and knew the sparks were in her eyes again. "They don't like that someone without any degree is better than they are. I miss the old days," he muttered in frustration, "when people didn't need those damned pieces of paper."

"Now you really sound old." She drummed her nails lightly on the top of her desk. "With reports like this, we can't hire her from her current position. She'd have to be fired or leave the job first so we can pick her up as a new employee entirely. Find out whatever you can and I'll start a workup for a restructure. Once we have names, we'll go from there."

"Okay." He saw Rayna leaving the building for a break and his attention splintered. "Later, Rhi," he murmured and hung up on her knowing chuckle.

Rayna glanced to where Riku usually was but didn't see him. It was disappointing as she walked slowly down the path that went around the building. She had been completely aware of his presence outside her window. Her skin still tingled and she felt warm from the inside out for once. She had the curious feeling that she was holding her breath until she saw him again.

A familiar hand holding a clutch of wildflowers suddenly lowered in front of her face. Startled, she turned her head to find herself looking into Eric's smiling blue eyes. "You surprised me, Riku." She looked back at the flowers. "They're lovely. Are these the ones you're planting?"

"I think they might be for you," he told her gravely.

"Me?" Her eyes widened. "No one's ever given me flowers." As soon as she said it, she frowned. "No . . . someone did. On my birthdays. I think." She gave him an apologetic frown. "Sometimes I could swear I know things from my coma, but it doesn't make sense. My father swore he was the only one who visited me."

The lost note in her voice broke his heart. His determination to keep his identity secret suddenly seemed to pale compared to her confusion. He couldn't tell her now, though. It was already too late. He had to play things through until she was safe. "Maybe he didn't know," he offered. "But, regardless, these are for you."

She took the flowers and buried her nose in them. They smelled wonderful. "Why?"

"Because they reminded me of you," he told her simply. He

had seen the flowers growing in a bed of roses and hadn't liked the idea of just getting rid of them. There was a lot of courage in growing so beautiful in a place where beauty took a different shape, just like Rayna.

"Oh." She regarded him for a few moments before smiling. "Can I spend my break time with you?"

"Of course." He waited until she sat down on the curb, and then sat down beside her and stretched out his legs. He noticed she was doing the same and smiled because the capris she wore revealed a nice length of leg. He wasn't surprised she'd had trouble with her height perception; her legs were beautifully long and shapely. It was hard to fight the urge to run a hand down them.

There was a peaceful quiet for a few moments. A sort of buzzing began to skim across his mind, and he realized it was coming from her. She seemed to be nearly vibrating with frustrated anger and confusion. "If you need to vent," he offered idly, "be my guest. Your coworkers giving you issues again?"

She said nothing for a few moments, somehow unsurprised that he had guessed, then she sighed and drew her legs up to wrap her arms around them. "Well," she hedged, "I don't want to be a tattletale but . . ." The frustration that had been bubbling up finally spilled over. She had never had a friend to talk to about work before. "It's making me crazy!" she finally blurted.

"What is, sweetheart?" The endearment was out before he could stop it, but she either didn't notice or didn't mind.

"Everyone!" She got to her feet to pace back and forth. "The manager is sleeping with one of the advisors." She blinked. "Well, not sleeping I guess but they're, well, you know." Blushing, she waved it aside and ignored his quick grin. "Because of it, he gives her preferential treatment and she's an *idiot*. I don't care how many degrees she has.

"Nobody listens to the clients, and they all end up leaving frustrated and angry. I've had to talk dozens into not changing companies because they were so upset. And the people who do know what they're doing are left underappreciated because they're too new to be mean."

She whirled and looked at him with vivid violet eyes. "Why?" she demanded. "Why do people have to be mean in order to get anywhere? Why can't someone be nice and be able to do just as well? What makes people lie and cheat? I don't understand it!"

He felt the ground tremble under his feet and a strong gust of wind whipped her silver hair around her face. He let out a little breath and curbed his power. She had pulled a very deep, almost instinctual, response from him. "I don't know," he admitted quietly. He got to his feet and gently tucked her hair behind her ear. As he did, he spotted a bruise on her cheek. He frowned darkly and bent to see it better. "What the hell is this? Did someone hit you?"

"No." Her color rose as he stood so close to her. His breath smelled like peppermints, as if he had eaten some candy. His skin smelled like fresh grass and rich dirt. It smelled wonderful, wild, and earthy like summertime. It had always been her favorite season. "I . . ." She tried to catch her scattered thoughts as her pulse thudded in her body. "I'm clumsy," she whispered. "Weird accidents happen."

"Like what?" She smelled sweet and fresh like wildflowers. It was shredding his control to bits, leaving him with a wild urge to carry her down to the grass and see if she tasted as pure as her soul felt. He warily eased back a step, not trusting himself. It didn't help any that he could see the sudden awareness in her eyes, a sort of startled desire as if she didn't even understand her own body. Did she want him as badly as he wanted her? The thought gnawed happily on his aching body and hormones.

She took a quick breath and told herself to get a grip as he stepped back. What on earth was wrong with her? Her entire body ached, and she felt as if she was a magnet helplessly drawn to him. Her hands literally burned to feel his hair and skin. She wanted . . . she had no idea *what* she wanted. "Well, I, uhm." She took another breath. "Well, strange things happen."

"What sort of things?"

"Ladders almost fall on me, books and such. Someone accidentally put rat poison next to the sugar. I almost put it in my cup but one of the nicer men stopped me. I also almost fell down the stairs once when someone bumped into me. Just stupid things." She tried to smile. "If it'll happen, it happens to me."

"Your name isn't Murphy," he murmured, anger in his stomach. She looked frightened and lost as if she had no friends in the world.

"Huh?"

He shook his head. "Sorry. Murphy's Law joke. Look it up on your Wiki. So what happened this morning?" He lightly touched her cheek.

"There was a computer monitor sitting on top of a shelf." She shrugged one shoulder. "I walked under it and it decided to fall. One of the janitors yanked me out of the way in time and the cord whipped around and hit my cheek. Considering it almost flattened my head, I don't mind."

"I see. Well, I'm glad you're okay," he told her softly. "It would upset me if you were hurt." That was an understatement. If he found someone who had deliberately harmed her, he would unleash floods that put Hurricane Katrina to shame.

"Thank you." She looked at her watch and gasped. "Whoops. I'll be late getting back. Can I join you for lunch too?" Her eyes sparkled. "I like being with you."

"I'd be honored." He gave her a courtly bow and enjoyed listening to her giggle. With a smile, he watched as she began to jog lightly back toward the building. He even got a moment to admire the curve of her bottom as she knelt to re-lace her sneakers. Small, yes, but she was one of Mother Nature's most glorious creations.

Wind gusted across his face, and he turned his head sharply as he heard a cracking sound. There was an immense tree branch over Rayna's head, likely as big as she was, and it was beginning to break off the tree. "Rayna!" he shouted as he lunged toward her.

She stood and turned only to muffle a shriek as he slammed

into her and sent them rolling several feet away, just as the branch crashed to the ground right where they had been. Shaking from head to heel, she burrowed against his body. Somehow his arms around her made her feel safe and secure. "Oh god," she whispered. "Why me?!"

He didn't answer, and he kept one arm around her waist and the other hand under her head to protect her from striking it. Tension lined his body, and he stared intently at the tree as he sought its spirit. There was no response. It was, as far as could be seen, just a near accident.

Her shaking registered finally. He looked down to see tears seeping under her lashes and falling down her cheeks slowly. His heart broke. "Rayna," he said roughly. "Don't cry. God, don't cry."

"Why, Riku?" She curled her fingers into his shirt and held onto him for dear life. It felt as if she had no anchor anywhere. "Why is this happening to me? I should have stayed asleep! Maybe I should have just died!"

"No!" he countered fiercely. "I'm not going to let *anything* happen to you!" Their eyes met and he couldn't fight the battle any longer. Not when she looked like she had nothing left. She had *him*. She would never be alone again. He lowered his head and hungrily took her lips with his, pure fire burning through his body at the taste and feel of her.

Her eyes went wide, red color climbing her face. He realized, belatedly, she had never been kissed before, let alone kissed by a man who wanted her, and almost lifted his head. But then her hands came up to frame his face with innocent trust. Something slumberous filled her eyes as her body shifted instinctively to be closer. On a tortured groan, he sank into the kiss once more and drew her as close as he could.

Hot. She was burning up. A strange pleasure rushed through her body, every nerve ending alive. Everywhere she felt his skin, felt his weight, her body sent out wild messages of pure delight. Each touch fueled her hunger for more. She didn't know what was happening but she didn't fear it. She trusted him to teach her.

When his head finally lifted, she felt unnervingly cold and lost, wishing only for the feel of his kiss once more. "Riku," she whispered, studying his face. "You kissed me."

"Yeah." His voice was a rough caress. If she didn't stop looking at him with that innocent desire in her eyes, he was going to do it again, and again, until she was kissing him back, needing him as he needed her. His sleeping beauty was waking in more ways than one, with her body now waking as a woman. And he knew, beyond a doubt, that he could not bear the idea of anyone else waking her. "I liked it."

"Oh." A shy smile touched her lips. "I've never been kissed before," she whispered. "But I liked how you kissed me."

He gave a soft groan that turned into a laugh. He had never known honesty could be so dangerous. "Rayna, sweetheart, saying something like that to a man is hell on his hormones." He sat up carefully and pulled her up as well. She was covered in dirt and grass and there were scratches all over her calves. Someone was going to pay deeply for putting marks on her. "If anyone hassles you," he said with steel in his voice, "tell me."

"Why would they . . ." Innocent, yes, but she was quick. Her cheeks slowly turned red. "You mean they might think we . . . that you . . . that I . . . Oh no. But you just kissed me because I was crying!"

"No." He rubbed his thumb gently over the bruise on her cheek. "I kissed you because I want you." He helped her to her feet and caught her hands when she started to brush the dirt off. "Don't. I'll walk you back and explain what happened."

"Okay." She was limping slightly, but when she felt his concern, she tried to hide it. She thought she might have pulled something in her ankle because it didn't quite want to support her weight without pain. "I'm okay."

He pushed the door open and called, "Anyone have an ace bandage? A tree branch tried to crush Rayna." Not to his surprise, no one came running with concern except for the janitor. "Here," Eric said, and helped ease Rayna onto her chair. "I'll leave her to you," he told the janitor when he saw he was armed with a first aid kit. Over the other man's head, he winked slightly at Rayna and smiled when she blushed prettily. "Don't worry about lunch," he told her. "I forgot my, uh, boss wants to see me. I'll be back tomorrow. Lunch then, definitely."

"Okay." She winced as the antiseptic burned her leg. "Ow." Distracted by the process, she didn't even see when he left the building. When the janitor had finished and wrapped her ankle, she used a bottle of water and a tissue to wipe away the dirt. She just ignored her coworkers when they smirked as they went past.

At lunch, she decided to eat at her desk and went onto the internet. You could find anything on the net, including information on men and women, relationships, and sex. She wanted a definition for what she was feeling and figured it was related to all three. She found her answer shortly. *'Passion - a powerful emotion, such as love, joy, hatred, or anger. Ardent love. Strong sexual desire; lust. The object of such love or desire.'*

That was interesting, she decided, and looked up 'lust.' It was even more fascinating. *'An intense or unrestrained sexual craving.'* Remembering the word Eric had used, she looked up 'want' as well. *'To desire greatly, to crave.'* So he wanted her in a sexual manner. He felt desire for her. She thought she might feel the same, and wondered not only how to find out, but if she had the courage to even try.

CHAPTER FOUR

The door blew open on a powerful gust of wind. Being as it was the top floor of the building, and the window was shut, Rhianna didn't bother to look up from the email she was reading from her adopted daughter. "Hello, Riku," she said calmly.

Eric stalked into her office, over to her desk, and leaned over to plant both hands on the top. The resulting thump made her paperweight rattle. "Rhi!" he snapped in annoyance. "Stop it at once!"

She lifted a brow. "What am I being accused of now?"

"The Shaughnessys," he retorted succinctly, "were a bad influence on you!"

The family he referred to was a family that Rhianna had issued contracts on for more than one hundred and fifty years. The final one had been completed about five years prior. A former Enforcer member had also been under contract, and had been assisting the Shaughnessys to fall in love as part of her deal. She, herself, had married the last one and was expecting her second child soon.

Rhianna idly propped her cheek on her hand as she studied her best friend. "I take it," her voice was amused, "that you're having a wee bit of trouble with our young princess." Since it wasn't a question, she didn't really expect an answer.

He answered anyway. "Yes, damn it!" He straightened and stalked away and raked his hands through his hair. "Damn it to hell, Rhi, I want her so badly I can taste it! And it's *worse* because I'm falling over my own feet for her!" Literal flames flicked from the white wings in his hair, evidence of his unrestrained emotion for Rayna and his lingering frustration. "I kissed her."

She began to read her letter again. "Why blame me then? You're the one who followed his hormones and discovered more than he expected. How does Rayna feel about things?"

"I don't think she really knows. Hell, Rhi, she'd never been kissed before." Frustration simmered inside his voice and eyes. "It wouldn't be so bad if I could convince myself that's all the more reason to let her go."

"Instead you want to teach her all about men and the mysteries of being a woman." She quirked a brow slightly. "Well, if you're having this much trouble," she began as she got to her feet, "I'll just call in someone else."

"No!" He saw her raise one elegant brow and cursed softly. He raked his hands through his hair again. "Hell." He glowered at her as she laughed at him. "Stop gloating," he muttered as he stalked into his office. "It's rude!"

She winced good-naturedly as he slammed the door, and then bit her lip to hide a chuckle. Things were progressing nicely. Nicely indeed. It probably wouldn't even hurt to send Rayna an email. Anonymously of course. If the girl was half the hacker she seemed, she might even trace it back to Rhianna. She looked forward to the challenge of stopping her.

The next wave of harassment began the next morning. Rayna got to work to discover that someone had been leaving little notes all over her desk and in all her folders. Some just had words. Others had disgusting and disturbing images. Even though her mind did not understand entirely what she was looking at, she did understand the intent.

She destroyed all the notes that she found and booted her

computer. The wallpaper had been changed again. She changed it back quickly, her fingers beginning to tremble. Anger simmering under her pain, she once more traced the route back to the person who had gotten in. She contemplated her options before deciding to use remote access to get into the man's iPhone. She then proceeded to erase everything and reset it to factory default.

That done, she got into her own computer's protocols and erected password protection for everything. If anyone tried to get into her computer without a password, they would lock the system down entirely.

She knew it was futile, but she reported the emails to her manager. She promptly got a response that said she was blowing things out of proportion and would be suspended if she tried to cause trouble again. Rayna, not knowing the legalities or policies of Enforcers, who owned the company, believed him. With nothing else she could do, she began to count the time until break and lunch when she could see Riku again.

An hour later, she was surprised to receive a random email. She hesitated but went ahead and opened it. There was no return address and no subject. The body of the email read, *Ask him about his family*.

Trying to trace the sender only brought a string of useless information. She sat back in her chair with a frown. She would have to try later to see if she could break through. In the meantime, her mind was occupied by the message itself. She could only assume it was referring to Riku.

It made her begin to wonder. She hadn't asked anything about him yet. It felt a little startling as she realized how deeply she wanted to know everything. She had asked Remy, and her older friend had gently cautioned her against confusing lust with love, but she was still somehow sure she was falling in love and not just lust.

When her break arrived, she quickly locked her computer and got to her feet. She rushed out of the building and down the sidewalk. Eric was at the end trying to operate an edging machine.

He saw her and stopped the machine as he turned with a smile. "Hey there." To his utter surprise, she leapt into his arms and clung on tightly, her feet dangling as she held onto his neck. "Rayna, what's wrong?"

She just shook her head and pressed her face against his shoulder, feeling safe again. He went with his instincts and wrapped his arms around her to hold her closer. He walked over to where there was shade under an oak tree and sat down on the bench with her held safely on his lap. "It's alright," he murmured, pressing his lips to her hair. "Tell me."

"They were at it again this morning," she whispered. "They had put notes everywhere, and someone had changed my desktop. There were emails too . . ." She shuddered lightly. "I told my manager but he said if I bothered him again I would be suspended. I just . . . I just really wanted to see you. I knew you'd make me feel better."

His arms tightened for a moment against his will. He carefully relaxed them and eased her back to frame her face with his hands. "Listen to me," he urged quietly. "If the manager won't listen, contact Enforcers directly."

She gave him a sad smile. "Why would they listen to me?"

His eyes narrowed slightly for a moment. Enforcers was dedicated solely to protecting those of 3rd District. How could she not know that they would move heaven and hell if she was being tormented? Heads were going to roll when he found out who had deceived her. "Try calling," he suggested softly. "Ask for Rhianna Taber and give your name."

"Why would she know *my* name?" She shrugged one shoulder. "It's okay. I don't mind it so much." She rested her head on his shoulder with a little sigh. "It's okay as long as you're here. I'll miss you when you're done with the landscaping."

"Rayna . . ." He closed his eyes and held her closer. The idea of never seeing her again, never holding her in his arms, was a nightmare.

"I was wondering . . ." She ran a finger over the chain of the necklace he was wearing and wondered what was on it. It was under his shirt somewhere and she wasn't brave enough to go looking, no matter how much she was tempted. "Would you tell me about your family?"

"Ah . . . hmm." He thought about things for a few moments. He hadn't really thought about his family in a very, very long time. "It was," he said slowly, "a difficult family to live in. A difficult time. I'm from 3rd District, too," he added with a smile. "So you know the stigma." He nuzzled his nose into her hair softly. "I fell into the family tradition, learned some special skills. Things happened and I lost my family. My best friend and I both did."

"I'm sorry." She lifted her head and frowned. "It must have hurt so much. I . . ." She looked down at her hands. "The car accident . . . it killed my mother and I lost my big sister. My family is just my aunt and uncle and my father now. I don't see my aunt or uncle much. They're normal."

In other words, not 3rd District. "I'm sorry, Rayna. It must still hurt since it's like yesterday for you."

She looked at him in surprise. "Yes, yes it is. You're the only one who has ever seemed to understand that." She clenched her hands into fists in her lap. "I went to sleep one night and woke up sixteen years later. I was four and woke up almost twenty. Sixteen years . . . it feels like a single night."

"No wonder you have trouble sleeping." He gently covered her hand with his.

"Yeah." She looked up at him and studied his face. "I was looking up things," she blurted suddenly. "I, uhm . . ." She began to blush. "You said," she whispered, "you wanted me. I think I want you, too."

"I see. You only think you do?" He kept his voice teasing with effort. A tremor was starting from his soul outward, the quake rumbling in his body. He could barely keep his hands off her to begin with without having her so honestly admitting her emotions.

"Well, I'm not sure. I've never wanted anyone before. Would .

. ."

"What, sweetheart?"

"Would you kiss me again?" she whispered. "I liked it." She looked up at him with a shy smile. "Teach me how to kiss."

The quake gathered fury, straining at its bounds. He forced his hands to be gentle as he smoothed her hair out of her face. Their skin brushed lightly and he nearly felt light headed. His gaze dropped to her lips, his pulse throbbing everywhere at once. "Do you have any idea," he asked roughly, "how badly I want you? I'm terrified of hurting you."

"You would never hurt me." She was sure of it. She lifted her hands to lightly touch his face, and her skin tingled with sheer delight. He was so hot and strong. Her fingers moved unconsciously, caressing his skin. "Please, Riku. I want to know why you're so different for me." She slowly drew her touch away though it was hard. The way he was looking at her stole her breath.

He took a deep breath and cupped her cheek warmly. "Knowing you've only ever wanted me . . ." A shudder rippled through his powerful body. "I'll fight anyone who tries to take you from me." He knew he didn't deserve her, but he craved her more than life. She was like the elements that made him up. Critical. Essential.

"Really?" she whispered in return.

"Really." He lightly touched her lips with his and tasted the curve of her smile. Her lower lip had a slightly metallic taste and he knew that she had been biting it again. "Rayna . . ." His voice was aching as his tongue touched the sore and soothed it. Surprise filled her morning glory eyes and he brushed her lips with his again. "Yes?"

"You . . . I mean . . . tell me what to do," she finally finished simply.

"I can't." His lips curved. "Kissing has a tendency to prevent speaking. That's okay, though, because demonstrating is so much better." Her lips had curved as well and he cupped her chin and tilted her head back slightly. The sunlight filtered across her face and his breath caught. "Rayna."

Her eyes closed as his mouth settled on hers, and everything seemed to fade away into the background. His tongue glided over her lips and the feeling made her breath catch. She wondered what he was doing.

Open your mouth.

It was his voice in her mind, and she didn't question how she had heard it. Hesitantly, she did as he asked, and a searing wave of heat flooded her as he deepened the kiss, his tongue surging into her mouth to tangle with hers. Her skin flushed, and she felt her breasts throb with a pleasure that was almost pain, almost as if they were begging for his touch. Trying to stop it, she pressed against him and unconsciously deepened the kiss further.

A shudder went through his body. His jeans felt too tight and confining, all of his clothes abrading his skin. He wanted nothing between them. He wanted to savor her soft skin against his. And when she tentatively returned the kiss, his control shook violently. He carefully eased back until there was a breath between their lips. "Got it yet?" he asked huskily. "Or should I kiss you again?"

"Yes. Please." She shivered as he did as asked, his mouth moving on hers with a hunger she instinctively recognized. Delight streaked through her, and she clung to him tightly as he deepened the kiss, his hands moving over her back in caressing sweeps that spread the heat through her entire body. His hand slid around her body and softly cupped her breast. Her nerves awoke with a vengeance and she gave a little gasp of fright at the sharp longing that went through her body. The pleasure was intense and shocking. "Riku," she managed to say when he released her lips.

He knew. He gently ran his hand down her ribs and around to her back. Holding her against him, he held his breath and counted to ten. Then he counted to fifty. Even counting to one hundred didn't tame his raging hunger. At that point, he was fairly sure nothing ever would. Some fires were never meant to go out. "Are you sure," he managed to ask, his voice like rough silk, "you haven't done that before?"

A shyly pleased smile lit her face, and she nuzzled against his neck. "Yes." Joy spread through her as she recognized the craving and hunger inside herself. If this was passion, then no wonder it was considered so dangerous. "Riku . . . I want you," she whispered.

A shudder wracked his body. "Don't say that," he muttered into her hair.

Horrified, she jerked back. "It's wrong?" she asked. "Did I say something wrong?"

"It's not wrong, Rayna! It's just hell on my self-control!" She blinked at him, and he said bluntly, "I want to make love to you." Her color rose instantly and he found a smile. She had been *very* busy with Wikipedia's cross-reference system. "Admitting something like that makes it very hard to keep my hands to myself."

"Should I . . . should I not have lunch with you?" She held her breath.

He saw the naked longing in her eyes and ran a hand through his hair to make sure he wasn't giving off flames. Sure as hell he was hot enough to do it! "No," he said. "I want you to have lunch with me." His grin turned wolfish for a moment. "I wouldn't mind having you *for* lunch." He lowered his head to teasingly nibble at her lower lip so she couldn't mistake his meaning.

She got it. Blushing, but smiling, she ran her fingers down his cheek. She couldn't stop herself. "Good." She slid off his lap and regarded him for a few moments. She leaned forward and kissed him lightly and then straightened and ran toward the office building.

He touched his lips and considered the merits of turning the garden hose's cold water on himself full blast. Letting out a long breath, he leaned back against the tree and stared at the blue sky overhead. Rhianna was right, though he hated to admit it. He didn't need her meddling in his affairs. He was falling in love without anyone's help at all.

He didn't see Rayna again until lunchtime, which was to his advantage because it gave him a chance to lurk beneath her window again, and listen to the goings on. His hand tightened around his spade at one point, as he listened to the sly remarks of a few of the women. Rayna would be biting her lip again. It made him furious, furious enough that he decided to take a walk down to the other side and work over there. It removed the temptation to throw thunderbolts.

To his cynical amusement, a woman leaving the building spotted him and started over toward him deliberately. She was, he observed objectively, really quite stunning in appearance but could not hold a candle to Rayna in his eyes. She was also walking with the slight sway to her hips that indicated she was a veteran of sexual affairs.

He wasn't impressed. Even if he hadn't been aware that she was acting out of an attempt to hurt Rayna, he wouldn't have been impressed. Her thoughts were open and un-jumbled, completely without complication to anyone let alone a mental master such as Eric. He gave her a once over and then turned back to his flowers without a word.

"Ahem." She cleared her throat distinctly.

He turned with a slightly lifted brow. Though she couldn't have been that close to thirty, he couldn't resist saying, "Yes ma'am?"

The slight emphasis in his voice made something in her eyes flicker. It disappeared quickly and she bent down to see the flowers better. "I just love flowers," she cooed. She shifted her weight, giving him a clear view of her generous bust. "Don't you just love roses?"

"I love all flowers, but roses aren't my favorite. They're common. I prefer wildflowers that grow against everybody's wishes." His smile was as cool and deliberate as his words. "Wildflowers are much more radiant. There's an honesty in them that makes them irresistible. And they don't have thorns."

Her cheeks flushed an angry shade of red. "I'm not surprised you prefer that little . . . nobody! You're nothing but a gardener and she's uncultured and completely unsophisticated! Sure, she's pretty enough, but she doesn't even know how to dress herself properly!"

"Odd." He turned back to his flowers, a little infuriating smile on his lips. "She looked as if she knew what she was doing when she got dressed." He deliberately sighed wistfully. "I wish she could wear shorts to work."

She gaped at him for a moment. A hiss of fury slipped past her lips and she stalked a few feet away.

Sensitive to Rayna as always, Eric knew when she started to approach. He stood and turned around to see her jogging toward him. When her eyes met his, he gave her a slow and masculine smile. It was a deliberate statement of intent. It said clearly that he had found the woman he wanted and looked forward to having her in his arms again. He wanted the message clear to the roses in the area that he had made his choice.

The message was adorably lost on Rayna, but she still knew his smile was completely for her alone. She glowed softly with happiness as she stopped in front of him. Her arms were wrapped around a large lunchbox. She was slightly flushed as well, and he skimmed a finger down her cheek. "Don't run in this heat."

"I didn't want you to get hungry," she protested.

"I'm always hungry around you." He put a possessive arm around her waist as he began walking. He knew that the 'rose' was shortly going to be spreading more rumors, but that was fine by him. He would make his move soon and remove Rayna from their clutches forever. His wildflower needed a new garden and gardener.

"I, uhm, I hope you don't mind," Rayna mumbled, peeking up at him, "but I sort of *made* lunch."

"You made lunch?" He looked at her in surprise as she set the box down on a table underneath several large trees. Curious, he watched as she removed the lid and let the tempting smell inside waft out. His mouth began to water. "If it tastes even remotely as good as it looks," he said with feeling, "I'll be your slave forever."

She giggled softly and sat down beside him. "I wanted to do something nice for you. I don't know if anyone has ever taken care of you before and I kind of wanted to." She leaned her head on his shoulder. "You make me feel as if I'm needed, even just a little. It's a nice feeling. And . . . I need you a lot too, I guess," she admitted in a soft rush. "You make everything seem like it'll be okay."

He closed his eyes as a wave of emotion rushed through him. There were different levels of need. This was the first time in his life anyone had ever simply needed him to be there. Just him. There with her. She didn't know what he was or where he was from or the power he held, and she needed him anyway.

She had made him lunch. The simple gesture was the final straw. He couldn't even determine when it had begun. When he had found her in the woods after a terrifying car accident? Over the years when he had spent all his free time with her, keeping her company when no one else would? When he had walked into an office and his sleeping beauty had smiled at him with morning glory eyes? It didn't matter when. The truth was there in front of him. He was in love with her. Had always been in love with her.

"Rayna." His voice came out strained. "I want to kiss you again."

"Oh." A shy smile lit her face and she moved closer to him. She tilted her face up invitingly. She had been hoping he would. She had discovered that when she wasn't around him, she felt as though a part of her soul was missing.

The innocent action made his control shudder but his hands were gentle as he framed her face and lowered his head. He kept the kiss tender, lingering over the flavor that was so uniquely her own. She knew what to do now and met the lazy surge of his tongue with her own, tentative but unafraid.

Wind began to blow, swirling around them, and he pulled himself under control with effort. Easing back slightly, he stared down into her face and studied her flushed cheeks and swollen lips. The lower one had been bitten again, and he gave in to the urge to soothe the sting with his tongue. "Don't do that," he murmured.

"But if I cry, they get worse," she whispered.

"Don't cry. You're far better than any of them. Hold your head high, Rayna." He nuzzled his nose into her hair and felt something cool touch his skin. He looked closer and began to slowly smile. "Well, well," he murmured.

She gasped and went furiously red as she lifted a hand to cover her ear. With a laugh, he caught her wrist and pulled it into her lap. He pulled her hair back with his free hand and smiled all over again as he saw her ear. She had triple-pierced ears, the third ring nothing more than a little silver cuff around the top edge of her ear. Her silvery hair hid it almost entirely from view. "What brought on the urge for multiple piercings, love?"

Horribly embarrassed, she mumbled, "I was trying to 'act my age.' I liked it so I kept it. But I was worried someone might think it was weird or something. Does it look okay?"

"It's enchanting." He nibbled on the rim of her ear and listened to her take a quick breath of combined surprise and desire. His. She was going to be his. He would make his move the very next day and then take her away where he could protect her from everybody. And once everything was done, he was going to dedicate all of his attention to capturing her heart and claiming her as his wife. He had a nice castle with a vast garden that his sleeping princess would simply love.

CHAPTER FIVE

Lunch consisted of baked chicken, homemade bread, salad, and a slice of purely decadent peach cobbler. Eric ate his share with gratitude and delight. Contented, he sighed deeply. "Honey, you are one hell of a cook." He wistfully eyed what was left of her slice of cobbler. "You can cook for me anytime. I can't believe you can cook like this when you've only been mobile for seven months!"

She gave him what was left of her cobbler with a smile. It was a smile that turned into a giggle when he didn't even pretend to look guilty. "I like to learn," she said happily. "I can't learn enough to be content. Some of the easiest books to read are cookbooks, so I've read all of them. And I like it. It's fun."

"And you're *good* at it." He helped her pack the containers away. "As if you couldn't tell by me licking the plate."

She glowed softly with happiness as she smiled at him. "I could cook you dinner some time."

Temptation swirled through him but he firmly leashed it. He could wait. There was time. "I'd love that. How about this weekend?" He picked up her hand and kissed her fingers. Her fingers tenderly touched his lips in turn, and he pressed her palm against his cheek, just wanting to savor her touch. "Lunch is almost over. I need to return you to the greenhouse."

"Greenhouse?"

"You remind me of my beautiful flowers," he admitted.

Her eyes softened until they were the color of morning glories in glorious bloom. She didn't want to go anywhere. She wanted to sit

with him in the summer sun and simply pass the time. She had always felt as if she had time to make up for, but now she wanted nothing more than to make time stop entirely.

He eased a hand into her thick hair and tugged her closer so that their lips met. He lingered for a moment until he could release her with a tender smile. He deliberately licked his lips. "Cobbler." When she giggled, he skimmed a thumb over her delicate cheekbone. "Let's go. Don't let them bring you down."

"If I have you, it's okay." She got to her feet and her heart thudded powerfully in her chest as he took her hand and entwined their fingers. He was so much bigger that she should have been afraid, but she wasn't. She felt safe and cherished as if she was the most important thing in his world. Her heart reveled in it.

When they were halfway down the sidewalk, he squeezed her hand and let go so she headed toward the building alone. There was a package outside the door and she knelt to scoop it up. The hair on the back of his neck stirred and he looked up sharply to see a large stack of roofing tiles teetering on the edge of the roof.

"Rayna! Move!" He shot forward using his wind magic to propel him faster. His hand closed around her wrist and he jerked her up into his arms. He leapt backward just as the tile crashed to the ground where she had been. The tiles shattered and bits of rock flew everywhere.

She was shaking, he noticed. That was fine; he was too. He buried his face in her hair and held her fiercely. "That scared me to death," he muttered. "I see what you mean about weird things." He looked up at the roof and let his eyes glow with the gold color that marked his powers visibly. The menacing presence faded. Turning back to Rayna, he asked, "Are you okay?"

"Yeah." She gulped air. Tears and panic were held as tightly inside as possible. "You looked really cool," she said, trying for humor. "I could have sworn you were commanding the wind." She frowned suddenly. "You're 3rd District born. Was it you after all?"

That much he could tell her. "Yes. Do you know what you can

do?" He knew what her powers were made *of*, but not precisely what they could *do*. If she had a better idea, then it would help him and Rhianna immensely.

"I dunno." She shrugged one shoulder. "My mother was the one from 3rd District, but I don't think she got a chance to tell me or my sister before the accident. I have very few memories at all, really. It's like I have no memories before waking."

His heart aching, he cuddled her for a moment before gently putting her on her feet. "Report the incident," he told her. "Trust me, even if the manager doesn't report it himself, something *will* be done."

She smiled. She trusted him without question. "Okay. I believe you." She stepped around the debris and walked into the building. Eric, his deepest instincts on the prowl, went back to his work under her window. He didn't want her to be far from his sight or hearing.

The roses were looking for blood again. He didn't say anything but he let a soft wind blow in the window—despite it being closed. He heard a soft giggle and smiled, his mission accomplished. He also took a few minutes to call Rhianna but shortly returned to work.

The window opened suddenly "How," came Rayna's voice over his head, "did you do that?"

He looked up to find her leaning on the windowsill. "Do what?" he asked innocently.

"I reported the incident and my manager told me to not worry about it. A few minutes later he's contacting me full of apologies with the promise the building would be checked for safety hazards." She poked him in the nose. "I know you did it."

"Who, me? I'm just a gardener with a little special ability." He caught her hand and nipped at the pad of her finger gently, just for the sheer delight of hearing her breath break and seeing her color rise.

She slipped her hand free, quickly, and went back to her desk before he made her forget her own name. She didn't notice it, but everyone else did shortly, that she was visibly happy. His unwavering

support and love gave her a self-confidence that made her radiantly beautiful.

And, for some reason, the women couldn't snipe at her. It was harder and harder to even look at her, as if she was making them uncomfortably aware of their own shortcomings. It had always been that way, as if they had to face the truth around her. Before, it had driven them to be cold and cruel. Now, they couldn't even bear it.

Rayna had to work a little late that day because of a letter she had to finish typing, and she was sure that Eric had already gone home. She felt oddly lonely and disappointed. But maybe it was better, she decided as she headed out of the building. Now she wouldn't go home to a lonely house after having just been in his arms.

To her surprise, he stood at the end of the walkway with his hands tucked in his jacket pockets. He smiled at her, and emotion welled up inside her in a long, vibrant wave that choked her. She rode on it without hesitation and ran down the sidewalk toward him. He expected her this time, and as she leapt into his arms, he caught her close and spun her around.

She laughed and wrapped her arms around his neck tightly. "I wanted to see you," she said happily. "I was worried you'd left already."

"What sort of man would I be if I didn't walk you to your car?" he teased as he set her down gently.

She flushed slightly. "I don't own a car. I ride the bus." Embarrassed, she said, "I don't know how to drive, let alone have the money to take lessons. I can afford to live, but that's it."

"Well, allow me to be your chariot then," he offered with a courteous bow. He straightened and smiled. "I saved for a long time to afford my car." It was a lie, but there was no other way to explain how a gardener could afford the sleek little sports car. Rhianna had laughed at him for months after he had gotten it but, damn it, if she could have a screaming red motorcycle, then he could have his car.

"Okay." She stayed close to him as they walked across the

parking lot, and she felt for the first time as if she wasn't alone anymore. The sound of tires squealing made her frown, and she wrinkled her nose as the smell of burning rubber filled the air. "Lead foot."

"Where'd you learn that term? Wiki?"

She grinned suddenly. "My friend Remy. She says she has one."

He laughed. As he swung an arm around her shoulders, he saw a car barreling toward them across the lot far faster than was safe.

It was aimed at Rayna.

Reflex kicked in. He tackled her and sent them both tumbling across the asphalt so that the car shot past where they had been. The car slammed on the brakes and did a donut to swerve around and come back at them.

He wrapped Rayna safely in his arms and quickly rolled them between two parked cars. The driver aiming for them missed entirely, and seemed to sense a third attempt would be too risky. They drove out of the lot as fast as he or she had arrived. Eric tried to get a glimpse of the license, but it was gone before he could focus.

Rayna was shaking so hard her teeth were chattering. Terror flooded him and he sat up quickly. He ran his hands over her to make sure she hadn't broken anything; her bones were too delicate to endure that much trauma! She was scraped and bleeding from nicks, but she was otherwise fine. "God," he said roughly, and pulled her into his arms. "If I hadn't been here . . ."

"All these accidents . . ." she whispered, and there was a soft whimper in her voice that ripped at him.

He framed her face with hands that were still trembling. "It wasn't an accident, sweetheart. That car was deliberately aiming for us. For you. They couldn't care less about me." He got to his feet and lifted her up into his arms. "I'm taking you home where you're safe."

"Please!" she blurted. She grabbed his arms as he put her in his car. "Will you stay with me just a little while? So I'm not alone."

He ran his hand through her hair. "Alright," he murmured. He knew beyond a doubt how the night was likely to end. It was inevitable. She was, as yet, too innocent to understand, but he did. The emotion between them was too powerful to be restrained for much longer, and as there were never any coincidences around those in 3rd District (he *still* blamed Rhianna for that), he knew that what bound him and Rayna could not be stopped. "Where do you live?" he asked. He had to ask. She would wonder how he knew where she lived, otherwise.

She gave him the directions and settled back in her seat. "It looks a little rundown," she warned him, "but it's safer that way. We keep the residential areas looking like they're beyond hope so outsiders don't try to take over."

He smiled at her. "I'm from 3rd District, too, remember? I know what it's really like." Ruefully, he added, "Considering the rumors that fly, I'm glad I'm from there so that I understand the truth."

She knew what he meant. Rumors were all over New York, and even beyond, about the old-fashioned place known as 3rd District. It wasn't like Manhattan or the Bronx. It wasn't even like a small town within a city. It simply was what it was, and it had been that way even long before the time when New York had been New Amsterdam.

In appearance, the District held fast to the historical styles that had built it and grown within it over the periods. The most modern looking building besides Enforcers Headquarters still looked as if it had been built in the mid-1800s. Yet there was more to the District than its historical value. There was magic. Everyone whispered of the people who were different. And everyone knew that if you were drawn to the District, eventually your dreams would come true.

The apartment building she lived in wasn't very big and neither were the apartments. There were bigger places but, as she had said, she couldn't afford them. Eric parked the car outside her place and followed her in as she unlocked the front door.

Apartment was too big a word. It was more like a studio: one giant room and a bathroom. The tiny kitchen was enclosed behind a counter and she had put her bed behind a series of folding screens to give her a semblance of having a bedroom. Her furniture consisted of a table and two chairs, a well-used beanbag chair next to a bookcase, and a couple of lamps. No more.

"It's very small," she apologized. "I'm sorry. It's also really cold at night and hot during the day." She shrugged one shoulder. "I can't afford to turn the heater or air conditioning on. I usually just take a hot shower and get into my pajamas and robe."

He ran a knuckle down her cheek. "It's fine, Rayna." He glanced around the room again and this time his eyes fell on a painting hanging over the kitchen sink. His breath caught as he walked toward it slowly. It was an exquisite representation of the sun setting behind Enforcers Headquarters. "My god," he breathed. "How did you manage to afford this?"

She cleared her throat. "I didn't."

"It was a gift?" He couldn't tear his eyes away.

"No. I," she coughed lightly, "I painted it." When he looked at her in shock, she blushed and looked at the floor. "I painted it. I could only afford one canvas, so I've only done this one." Impulsively, she took it down and held it out to him. "Here."

"Rayna," he said, stunned. He had never known anyone like her. So open and giving. And brilliant. Dear god, she was stunningly brilliant and talented. He would make sure she had it all, he thought fiercely as he took the painting and set it safely on the counter. She would have the time for schooling and the money to buy as many canvases as she wanted. He would love to have her help redecorate his office. Hell, he would set her loose on the entire building.

Silence fell between them as they watched one another. Tension grew stronger and stretched as two bodies, two hearts, and two souls stirred with growing hunger. She drew a quick breath, sensing the odd atmosphere, and it frightened her a little. She had never felt anything like it before. She took a wary step backward and whispered, "I'm just going to take a shower."

He watched her flee into the bathroom and took several long breaths to grab for composure and control. He wanted her so bad that even his teeth hurt. He heard the shower running and went

around the counter to get himself a cup of coffee. It was cold, and he nuked it in the microwave before taking a bracing sip. Resigned, he studied his cup. Even a day old, her coffee was delicious.

She stood under the pouring water and tilted her face into the spray. The scratches stung as the water hit them but she ignored the pain. Her mind was buzzing, refusing to settle down. Over and over again, her memory flashed to the moment she had seen the car coming at them. The tires squealed in her ears. The downside of her ability to memorize things she learned was her inability to forget other things, especially things she really wanted to forget.

A new memory flashed across her eyes suddenly. Tires squealing, her mother screaming. The sense of a jarring impact and then flying through the air. Then . . . nothing. She covered her ears on a terrified cry.

Instants later, Eric jerked the shower door open. "Rayna?" he asked in worry. "Are you hurt after all?"

She didn't even heed her nakedness; she threw herself into his arms on a soft sob. "I heard it!" she said into his shoulder. "I could hear the tires from the accident! I remembered what happened when I was four! I thought it was happening again!"

"It's okay, sweetheart. I'm here." He grabbed a towel and wrapped it around her gently, removing temptation from sight even if not from memory. Dear god, she was stunning. Long legs and graceful curves, slim as an orchid and twice as lovely. There wasn't a blemish on her body but for the single mark over her left hip. Just seeing it filled him with anger.

When a contract for death—a Bloody Contract—was made on a member of 3rd District, their body showed the contract as a small red check known as a Bloody Mark. Her Mark would disappear on her twenty-first birthday, providing he could keep her alive that long.

He gathered her up in his arms and carried her out of the bathroom. He moved around the screens and gently set her down on top of her bed. It was a plain twin bed, only just big enough for her. He figured his feet would hang off the end. "No more tears," he soothed. He rubbed another towel over her hair softly. "It'll be alright. You're here, everything's fine."

"Riku." She turned her face into his hand when he cupped her cheek gently. "I'm so much trouble," she whispered. "All those stupid accidents and then that car . . . I should have just stayed asleep forever." Tears slid down her cheeks. "It's better than being so alone."

"You're not alone," he insisted fiercely, his heart breaking. "I'm here." Tears continued to glide down her cheeks, and on a soft groan, he scooped her up onto his lap. His lips rushed over her face to steal the tears. "Don't cry," he whispered. "God, Rayna, how can you think you're alone? I can't make myself leave you no matter how much I know I should!"

A powerful, bone deep sense of conviction filled her, and she wound her arms around his neck. "I don't want you to go. Stay with me. Teach me how to love you." Her lips trembled. "Unless you don't want me anymore."

He caught one of her hands, brought it down his body, and pressed it against his erection straining against his jeans. She blushed brightly and tried to jerk her hand back but he held her gently. "A man can't lie about this," he teased her softly, his breath hitching slightly as the heat of her skin burned him.

Warmth gathered inside and pooled low in her belly, making her ache curiously. She was suddenly vividly aware of the differences in their bodies and felt infinitely feminine and . . . powerful. It was power to know that he wanted her. This man who could have any woman he wanted had chosen *her.* "Riku," she whispered, looking at him with naked longing on her face.

"Are you sure?" He drew her hand up to rest over his heart.

"Very sure. Please, love me."

She leaned up and kissed him softly, briefly startling him, but he caught his balance and deepened the kiss, lazily curling his tongue around hers. When she was truly secure in being his lover, she would be a force to be reckoned with. It made his knees weak with delight.

She trembled softly and he eased back enough to ask, "Frightened?"

"No." She slid her arms around his neck and held on as he slowly lowered her to the top of her bed. She wasn't afraid. Anticipation was filling her. She felt hot and feverish, and a restless sensation of pleasure, that rushed through her blood, made her quiver beneath him.

He sensed it with relief. He had been afraid her nerves would be stronger than her heart and body. He gently skimmed his fingers over the curves of her breast above the towel, savoring her soft skin. Her nipples tightened and passion flushed her skin as her eyes closed in surrender.

"Rayna," he murmured, softly running kisses over her face and down along her neck and shoulder. She trembled softly and her fingers moved convulsively in his hair. Impatience churned, and he held tightly to his control as he began to unwrap the towel slowly. She deserved all the tenderness he could find for her. They could explore desperation later. "Let me see you."

"And you." She slid her hands down to the buttons of his shirt. "I want to know everything." She slowly opened the buttons, fascinated by the golden skin she revealed and the hard muscle beneath. The chain he wore had a pendant at the end, and she reached for it curiously.

It was a flat disc of some strange metal with the symbols for all the elements etched into it. She could feel the age and the power, and it made her skin prickle in recognition. Lying against his chest as it did, it was somehow a stark reminder of how powerful he was, both with the wind and physically. Instead of frightening her, the knowledge comforted her, and she threw her arms around his neck.

He held her a moment and then slowly released her and laid her down again. The towel was open now and revealed her beauty, brilliantly. Her skin was soft peach and her breasts were curved perfectly for his hands. Her hips were delicately shaped, and her stomach trim.

His lips slowly curved as he saw something else. "Well, well," he murmured, and lightly touched the little silver hoop she wore as a belly button ring. "Hiding this, were we?"

She smiled shyly, completely unembarrassed and not bothering to question why. "It would be out of place at work."

"So it would." He didn't bother to resist the temptation. He slid down her body and pressed kisses to her soft stomach before teasing where the hoop rested. Her breath caught and her fingers curled into the material of his shirt. He impatiently shrugged it off and ran his hands slowly over her sides.

She quivered again as his wandering hands sent fire licking right to her core. She wanted more: more of his touch and to touch him more. She started to say so, but his lips closed over the point of one breast and the lash of pleasure was so shocking she couldn't stop a soft cry.

She tasted like fresh river water, pure and clean. He felt ravenous for her taste and could barely keep his hands gentle as they ran over her without stopping. He caressed her breast with lips and gentle teeth and then lavished the same attention on its twin.

She began to shake in his arms like a plucked string and her breath was only a soft pant as he slid his hand slowly down her body, ruffling the soft silver curls shielding her most vulnerable flesh. The scent of her was rich, like wildflowers in full bloom. Trying to soften the shock, his mouth covered hers just as his fingers slipped between her legs.

Her startled gasp was muffled by his mouth and a quiver rippled through her body. He deepened the kiss further until it was almost out of control, and his fingers carefully parted the folds protecting her. A shudder went through his body. She was hot and wet, her desire for him as complete as his for her. "Rayna," he said thickly, burying his lips against her throat and tasting her pulse.

She couldn't answer, caught in a suspension between pleasure and pain, her body demanding something she couldn't recognize let alone name. Desperate, she clutched at him, her head pressing back against the pillows as he slowly slid a finger inside her. "Are you okay?" he murmured huskily, watching her face with rapt attention.

"Yes," she managed to whisper. "Riku, please!" She didn't know what she wanted, but she knew beyond a doubt he would be able to help. She trusted him with her body as completely as she had with her heart.

His thumb shifted, pressed against nerves she had never known were there, and her senses came apart in a blinding rush of light and color. She would have cried out with ecstasy but his mouth was on hers again and he was kissing her deeply.

The waves went on and on until she thought she might faint from the pleasure. It ebbed then, and she gulped air as her body relaxed in his arms. "Riku." It was barely breathed in wonder.

The lazy purr to her voice felt like a physical caress. His eyes raptly memorized her face. He had looked his whole life for her. He had been waiting for her for so long. His other half. The one element he had never been able to truly master. His light.

She felt drowsy and satiated, and dimly flabbergasted at how powerful desire could be. None of her reading had mentioned that. It also hadn't mentioned it wasn't long satisfied. She strangled a gasp as she felt his fingers slowly caressing her. The tension rushed back wildly on a surge of pleasure and she could only manage to say, "What are you doing to me?"

"Did you think that was all?" His mouth rushed over her face hungrily. "There's more. So much more. Let me have you, Rayna. Please. We belong together."

Certainty filled her. "Yes." She returned his kisses eagerly and pressed her body against his. With a hungry sort of pleasure, she ran her hands over his shoulders and chest, learning the feel of his skin. She wanted to taste him, too, to see if he tasted like peppermints everywhere. "Can I . . . can I touch you?" she whispered.

He shuddered. "Later," he promised huskily. "Right now I need you too badly." He gave her another kiss before rolling off the bed to remove the rest of his clothes.

She watched him intently, her color rising as she saw how aroused he was. A shiver of fear rippled through her. She knew the mechanics, knew what was going to happen, but didn't see how it would possibly work. It seemed a little frightening, but this was *Riku*. He would never hurt her. He watched her as well, waiting for her response. If she was afraid, then he would stop and she would never know what it meant to be complete. She wanted him, and she shyly smiled at him in welcome.

He returned to her on a hoarse sound of need that might have been her name, and his weight sank them into the mattress. He buried his hands in her hair and tilted her head up as he kissed her deeply. Her arms wrapped around him, holding him tightly, and a shudder went through his body. "Hold me," he muttered. "Tightly. God, I need you!"

Her breath hitched as his hands slowly drew her legs apart until there was room for him to rest between them. She could feel him, hard and hot, at the entrance of her body, but he didn't move. He just kept kissing her with a desperate sort of hunger that had her passion flaring wildly to life. Helplessly, her hips arched against him as the ache spread.

His control holding by thin threads, he braced his weight on his hands and slowly entered her. Sweat broke out on his skin. She was hot and tight and fit him perfectly. Tears slid under her lashes and he knew he was hurting her, but he couldn't stop. A tortured groan rumbled in his chest as he surged into her fully, burying himself to the hilt.

She gave a startled yelp and clutched at his shoulders. There wasn't really any *pain* as much as a startling sense of being stretched and filled. It was both oddly foreign and yet just as oddly familiar and wonderful. His entire body trembled as he fought to stay still for fear of hurting her. She took a deep breath and savored how it felt. It was beautiful. "I'm okay." She breathed it into his ear as she wound her arms around his neck. "We fit."

His control cracked. Fit? They *belonged* together. "Hold onto

me," he urged roughly. "Just hold on and I'll protect you!" He slowly withdrew from her body and then sank in again, his lips seeking hers eagerly. He slowly slid a hand down between them and caressed the bundle of nerves he had found before.

She could only cling onto him desperately as he began to move faster, driving deeper. His knowing fingers added to her pleasure as it churned and surged through her body. It grew hotter and hotter, stronger and stronger, and she couldn't contain a whimper as her desperation began to border pain.

His hands cupped her hips and dragged her against him tighter as he surged into her a final time, and she gave a wild cry as the tension broke and sent her body careening through ecstasy without restraint. His low groan echoed in the air as his own release claimed him, and she held him fiercely, refusing to ever let go.

The silence afterward was soft and welcome as they rested and found their breath again. The apartment no longer seemed cold, but a chill finally touched his sweat dampened body and he knew she would feel it even more acutely with her smaller size. He thought she had fallen asleep—which was adorable as hell—but she tightened her hold when he tried to ease away from her. "No," she mumbled into his shoulder. "I don't care if everyone does it."

He wondered where her mind had gone this time. "I'm not leaving," he reassured her, and he couldn't keep the note of possession out of his voice. She was his completely. He had never wanted any woman like that, and he had never been wanted the way she wanted him. Even then, his pulse barely normal, he wanted her all over again. "Everyone?" he thought to ask.

"I read somewhere," she nuzzled her nose against his shoulder, "men usually leave after."

He thought for a moment to find a suitable way to explain. Slowly, he finally said, "There are different levels of desire. When it's just a superficial feeling, once the 'itch is scratched' it goes away and, yes, the person visiting usually leaves. Men are the stereotype, but it's not gender specific. On the other hand, when the desire is deep and real, when you can't breathe for wanting someone," his voice deepened without his control, "when you're consumed with so much emotion it overwhelms you . . . that's a feeling that doesn't leave. And if it's there, the owners of it don't want to part."

"Oh." She tilted her head back to look up at him, picking out the details of his face in the lamp lit room. "Is that what the true meaning of a lover is? Are we lovers?"

"A lover," he ran a hand through her hair, "is one who loves. So, yes, we are lovers. And not even wild horses are dragging me from this bed."

She hid a smile. "It's too small for you." She wiggled her feet against his leg, well aware his feet were dangling. "We could make a bed on the floor," she suggested. She lowered her gaze. "That is, if you want to spend the entire night."

"I want to," he said with regret, "but my clean clothes are at home. I do need to leave early enough for a shower and such." He studied her face intently and picked out the features with a feeling akin to awe. He had a feeling that he would die without her. "Would you move in with me?" he asked suddenly.

Her eyes widened with surprise. "What?" She clung to his shoulders tightly as he got off the bed and swung her up into his arms. "Move in . . . with you? But why?" She sat on the edge of the beanbag as he pulled blankets and pillows down to the floor to make them a soft nest.

When it was complete, he lifted her into his arms again and settled her gently in the bed he had made. He joined her quickly, rolled them in the blankets, and then settled back with her sprawled over the top of him. She adjusted herself a bit, clearly unused to using a person as a pillow, but shortly snuggled closer. She fit perfectly in his arms as if she had always belonged there. "I want," he told her softly, "to have you with me always. I want to be able to wake in the morning and see your face. And," he added with warm amusement, "my bed is bigger."

She giggled at that and then sobered. "I'd like to live with you,"

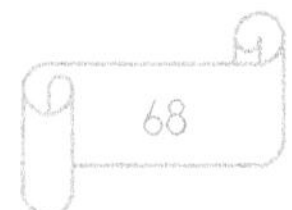

she admitted, "but my father might object. I know I'm not under his guardianship, but I don't want to hurt him."

He smiled internally. Lucas would never object to the safety and happiness of his daughter. "Well, I'll meet him, and then ask you again. I won't let you get away from me now, Rayna."

"Okay." She let out a little sigh and cuddled against him. The pendant he still wore pinched her skin, and she wiggled a little until she could grab the disc and lift it. "Where did you get it?"

"It was made for me when I was born." Impulsively, he slipped the chain off and slid it over her head. "Here. I want you to have it." A deep sense of delight filled him as she sat up slightly and the pendant fell to rest against the top of her stomach. A tempting image filled his mind of her swollen with his child, and his breath caught. It could have already happened. Ah hell. That went onto the list of things he would need to talk to her about if she hadn't already Wiki'ed it. "Rayna . . ."

She inexplicably smiled at him, almost as if she could read his mind. "Would you believe that the one thing that never unnerved me about waking as an adult was the, uhm, *interesting* thing that happens every month?"

He began to smile as well. "I had half expected that to be the thing that unnerved you *most.*"

She shook her head. "I got lucky. I started one before I was released from the hospital. One of the nurses sat me down and told me everything. I had already picked up some of it from my 'birds and the bees' tape. It came up again recently while I was looking up desire and sex." A hint of pink touched her cheeks. "I can count much better than I can read, and I'm regular. We're safe."

"It's not foolproof," he tenderly told her.

"It's not?"

"Nature is a very fickle thing, love." He skimmed a knuckle over her belly. "I wouldn't mind it if we weren't safe."

She thought of being a mother, and while it deeply appealed, she was practical enough to admit, "I don't know anything about babies." She smiled shyly. "I wouldn't mind learning, though. If you were there."

"I'm not going *anywhere*." He started to draw her toward him, his lips seeking hers, when he caught trace of a familiar scent.

Fire.

He jerked her down against him just as the window shattered and a gas canister already ablaze was hurled inside. "Shit!" He leapt up and jerked on his jeans. She scrambled up after him, and he yanked his shirt on over her head. He scooped her up into his arms and raced for the door.

The thick wood burst into wild flames as someone outside set it on fire as well. It took only seconds to choke them both on the smoke. Fury lined his face and a low snarl emerged from his throat. Flames licked through his hair as he held Rayna with one arm. He lifted his other hand and aimed at the flames. "Open!" he barked.

The flames obeyed the command and pulled back from the door. One hard kick opened it, and he carried her out into the night amid the sounds of people screaming and sirens blaring as fire trucks arrived.

There was enough of a fire break between apartments to keep the flames from spreading, and people flooded the area as they banded together to control the blaze until firemen arrived. Eric carried Rayna away from the crowd and leaned against the hood of his car as he held her fiercely in his arms. His heart thudded in his chest with terror. If he hadn't been there . . . "Are you okay?" he asked her.

She was shaking so hard that her teeth rattled. "Yes. Th-they tried t-to kill us." She burrowed against him on a low sound of fear. "When will it stop?! What did I ever do?!"

He heard the sound of a familiar motorcycle and looked up to see Rhianna arriving. The fact that she wore street clothes and no makeup told him that she had been yanked from a sound sleep—she never went out without her 'armor'. Her face was white as she looked for him. When she spotted him, he gave a slight nod, and she visibly blew out a breath. She immediately turned and began snapping out orders that everyone leapt to obey.

Rhianna would handle everything, so Eric put Rayna into the car and drove to the inn a block away. It was *very* well defended, and only a fool would try to touch her there. When they arrived, he wasn't at all surprised to see a very pregnant woman with black hair standing on the front steps. "Hello, Audra," he said as he got out of the car.

"What the hell is going on?" Audra Shaughnessy demanded. Her eyes fell on Rayna, and a brow slowly lifted as she recognized her and the possession in Eric's touch. Her nose flared softly as she caught the combining of their scents. "Well," was all she said.

Rayna was oblivious to the byplay. She could only stare at Audra with something akin to awe. She felt positively tiny next to the tall woman, and there was a predatory sensation to Audra that was oddly comforting. She was a protector. Rayna was certain.

They all heard a loud explosion and turned sharply to see Rayna's apartment going up in a mushroom cloud. Audra cursed softly in another language and blocked the doorway with her body as a little boy holding a wiggling wolf cub in his arms approached the door. "Go inside," she said quietly, steel in her tone. "Find your father and uncle. Have your mother prepare a room for our guest."

The little boy ran to do her bidding, shouting for his parents, but Rayna didn't hear him. Her eyes were fixed on the blazing building. The explosion sounded over and over in her ears until she was hearing screams as well, echoes of the present and the past overlapping and blurring.

It wasn't just her immediate past. It was a further past. One her mind could not comprehend. Something slimy and evil slithering toward her, rising over her with brutal menace. It wanted her dead. It had approached her with a waver to its steps, as if it was dizzy or drunk.

Before her mind could try to process the ancient memory, other memories intruded. The car accident. The people who had been watching the traffic. The person who had staggered in front of the car as if dizzy or drunk. *It was the same people*!

A choked scream emerged from her throat, and she clamped her hands over her ears. Voices. She could hear so many voices. Physical voices of those going past overlapped with their voices in her mind. Their voices said it was tragedy. Their minds said they were grateful it wasn't them.

She only distantly became aware of Eric shouting her name. Her eyes lifted to his but she couldn't quite focus on him. She couldn't hear the voice of his mind. The pain in his voice was truth. "The accident . . ." Unable to withstand any more, her eyes closed and she slumped against him.

"Rayna!" He pressed his hand against the pendant she wore and used it to connect to her mind. It was alive and wild, nearly reading as static with its fury. Even Eric, as powerful as he was, had to fight to find out what was happening. He had to peel away layers and layers until he finally saw, at last, what it was that she could do.

For all intents and purposes, she had become a human lie detector. She could hear the truth amid myriads of lies. Her powers of Truth were awakening too soon. Her birthday wasn't until Saturday. Two days. She shouldn't have awakened. He painfully buried his face in her hair. She was always waking too soon, pushing past safety. And when she woke, no matter what he said, she would know the truth of him.

Audra studied him intently. "I've known you for over a century," she said mildly. "I've never seen you like this."

"I hadn't found Rayna." He lifted Rayna fully into his arms as he turned to look at his friend. "Audra, I must ask for your help. Please guard her."

"Bring her inside, Riku," Madelyne Shaughnessy said softly from behind her sister-in-law. "She'll be safe here." She smiled at Audra. "You go rest."

"Damned overprotective den mothers!" Audra stalked off with a mutter, her stride still lengthy and graceful despite the eight-month

curve of her stomach. "Kalin," she ordered the wolf pup, "stop chewing on your cousin's ankle." Content her son would obey, she went into the guest room she and her husband were using.

Eric smiled and followed Madelyne as she headed toward another room. "I appreciate this, Maddie."

She gave him a teasing smile. "It's just a little odd to think I might have a sort of stepmother who is younger than me." He had played as big a role in raising her as Rhianna had; she had always seen them equally as her adopted parents. Her heart ached a little to see the emotion on his face as he gently placed Rayna on the bed, but it was a good ache.

"Protect her," he said in a quiet voice as he walked to the door. His eyes moved to the tall man standing behind Madelyne, his hand resting possessively on her hip. "Kienan, I'm trusting you as well."

"She'll be safe," Kienan Shaughnessy assured him firmly. He grinned slightly. "We get to go to the wedding, right?"

"Hush," his wife scolded.

Knowing Rayna was in good hands, Eric headed for the door with long and determined strides. He was going to join Rhianna in bashing heads together and then he was going to go home and plan for the next day. It was going to be a bitch. His only salvation lay in Rayna's truth ability allowing her to see why he had deceived her. He could not lose her now.

CHAPTER SIX

When Rayna awoke, it was to the early morning light streaming in through gauzy curtains. She sat up with a jerk and looked around wildly, terrified because she didn't know where she was or how she had gotten there. How much time had passed?!

The door opened and a rather plain looking young woman peered around the edge at her. The first thing out of her mouth was, "It's the morning after the fire."

Rayna's shoulders relaxed and she slumped over. "Thank you," she whispered. A thought made her look up and glance around. "Where am I? And where's Riku?"

Madelyne searched her eyes but saw no understanding for her lover's true identity. Mentally wincing, she walked into the room. This was not going to be easy for Rayna *or* for Eric. "You're at the Gentle Brook Inn, and Riku said he would see you at work if you want, but he would prefer you stay here and rest."

"Oh." She picked at the top of the blanket, a soft blush warming her cheeks as she remembered the events prior to the fire. "He's . . . we're . . ."

"I know." Madelyne smiled as she opened the window to let in the fresh air. "He loves you very much." She walked over and sat on the edge of the bed. "My name is Madelyne Shaughnessy. I run the inn."

"Oh. Of course." She had heard all about the Shaughnessys. Mel Shaughnessy was one of two owners and operators of the Shaughnessy-Tavoularis Conglomeration and had a wonderful reputation as a brilliant CEO and generally decent guy. His wife was a computer sciences teacher at a college. Madelyne would have to be his sister-in-law, married to Kienan, the youngest Shaughnessy male. "It's nice to meet you." She smiled. "My name is Rayna Carmichael."

"It's nice to meet you too, Rayna." Madelyne glanced at the door as it opened and her sister-in-law stepped into the doorway. "Mel better have done that shopping," she scolded as she saw the bag Audra held.

Audra snorted. "Brian's shop is barely down the street. Don't be silly." She walked over and set the bag down before easing herself carefully onto the side of the bed. "So." She studied Rayna. "The princess is awake."

Rayna ducked down slightly and pulled the blanket over herself more tightly. She felt positively outclassed between the calming Madelyne and the brilliantly stunning Audra. "Yes. I . . . I woke a year ago."

Audra's brows shot up and then lowered quickly. "I see. Excuse me, I have a call to make." She got to her feet and walked out of the room.

"Did I . . . did I offend her?" Rayna asked warily.

"No, Audra's always like that." Madelyne snagged the bag with a smile. "Here, she went and got you some clothes."

"Oh. Thank you. I'll pay you back."

"Sure, we can figure that out later." *She doesn't need to worry about it.*

Rayna blinked as she heard Madelyne's voice on top of itself. There was no delay between them yet somehow she could hear both phrases clearly and distinctly. Slowly she said, "You don't want me to repay you." When Madelyne lifted a brow, she rubbed her forehead. "I . . . I can hear the truth over a lie. I remember. My mother told me that once."

"That is not an easy power. Have a shower," Madelyne offered gently. "Get dressed and come have some breakfast." She got to her feet with a smile. "If you insist on going to work, Kienan said he'd give you a ride."

"Oh. Thank you." Rayna waited until she had left the room before opening the bag and looking inside. Underwear, bra, comfortable cotton pants, and a cute sleeveless shirt with cherries all over it. Audra knew how to shop. There were even shoes in the bag.

She took a shower first to wash away the smoke and grime. She also blushed vividly as she washed away the evidence of making love with Riku. If she hadn't done so much reading, she might have been alarmed by the mess. Instead, it just made a warm glow bloom inside her. She belonged to someone, and he to her. It was wonderful.

The clothes felt strangely soothing to wear and helped settle her nerves more. But, then, she knew about the maker's gifts. Just another 3rd District miracle worker. She stepped out into the hall and looked around. A little boy with brown hair already going gray shot past being chased by a little black wolf cub. She saw a man with dark golden brown hair grinning at the sight as well and asked, "His pet?"

"His cousin." Mel Shaughnessy straightened and offered a hand. "My son no less. I'm Mel. You must be Rayna."

"Yes." As she took his hand, she suddenly felt the same predatory sensation from him as she had felt from Audra. It was a sensation that made her feel safe and protected. She spotted an amber rim around his pupils, and it dawned on her at last that Mel and Audra were werewolves. No wonder they felt so safe to be around! "Nice to meet you, Mr. Shaughnessy."

"Mel." He smiled. "Too many Shaughnessys around here. You'll get confused." He led the way toward the kitchen and said over his shoulder, "Kalin, leave your cousin alone." He smiled wryly at Rayna. "He's learning to hunt."

"Oh." Bemused, she went into the kitchen ahead of him and found Audra in a lively argument with another man who bore a striking resemblance to Mel. She could only assume she was looking at Kienan Shaughnessy. "Good morning," she said hesitantly.

"Good morning!" Kienan gave Audra a firm glare. "Sit down, damn it." Assuming she would obey, which she did with a curse, he walked over to smile at Rayna. "Well, you're Rayna. Maddie was right; you are cute."

"Stop embarrassing her!" Madelyne nudged her husband aside and escorted Rayna to a chair. "It could be worse," she consoled her. "Aenya and her husband are off on a trip to England, and Taegan is teaching today while Kally walks a boardroom." She thought about that. "Stalks. She stalks a boardroom, and with a three-year-old on her hip."

Rayna watched them without shame. It was an amazing whirl of life and color. A complete family unit. A little black haired toddler tried to climb onto her lap and she picked him up, recognizing Mel's eyes and assuming he was the wolf child. She *really* wanted a child too. Hers and Riku's. Maybe they would be lucky and Nature would be in a fickle mood.

She was a few minutes late to work and had to brace herself as she walked in the front door. Luckily for her, the first person she saw was Remy Germaine. Her friend eyed her intently and then nodded decisively. "You look good," she said.

"Despite the incident, I feel good," Rayna admitted. She waved Remy closer after a quick look around. When the taller woman leaned down, she whispered, "I have a lover."

Remy grinned. "Well, duh, hon. You're *glowing*. I'm insanely jealous," she added woefully. "My ex-husband never made me glow."

"That's why he was your ex." Rayna sat down at her computer. "How's Nicole?"

"Madly missing you. She wants me to bring her here to see you." Remy leaned on the counter. She loved Rayna as much as she loved her sisters and daughter. She was glad that Riku had come along to bring such joy to her. She deserved the best.

Several women came hurrying over. Remy bristled distinctly, something dangerous flickering in her eyes. The other women paid her no heed as they clustered around Rayna. "Are you okay?" one asked with genuine concern. "Everyone's heard about the fire."

"I'm fine," Rayna told her.

"Well, it's a good thing you weren't hurt!" another female said. *She should have been scarred! Then she wouldn't so beautiful anymore!*

Rayna booted her computer without looking up. "I don't need your false pity. Be quiet or go away."

Remy's brows lifted and she nearly cheered. The other women were more taken aback. "Well!" one said. Snidely she added, "I see the gardener put steel in your spine. You're not better than us now, honey. You're just another woman who spread her legs." *Lucky bitch.*

Rayna smiled. "Jealousy isn't flattering to you. And besides, I can have a fling if I want. I'm an adult. And it's . . ." Her voice stopped. Literally stopped dead, her vocal cords freezing. Startled, she pressed a hand to her throat. She had tried to say it was just casual, but the words wouldn't come out. Because it was a lie?

She tried a second time, but again the words wouldn't come out. What then, she wondered. If it wasn't a fling, wasn't an affair, what was it? The frustration welled and she blurted, "I'm in love with him!"

The other women could think of nothing to say. Silent, they all walked away. Remy coughed and leaned on the counter again. She studied the shocked expression on Rayna's face. "Didn't notice, did we?" she asked gently. "Hell, kid. I noticed it the first day."

"I'm in love," Rayna whispered. Blinding joy rose inside her and she leapt to her feet. "I have to tell him! Is he outside?" She hurried to the window.

"Nuh-uh. Haven't seen him this morning. He might be dealing with paperwork related to the fire. He's the type who would want you protected." Remy ruffled her hair. "You bring him over for dinner, okay? If Nicole has him wrapped around her finger within five minutes, he's worth keeping."

Before she could answer, Mr. Oppenheim rushed into the area.

"Everyone!" he barked. "Look sharp and get everything in order! Enforcers is on their way over! Eric Mason himself is coming down to discuss a reorganization of the company as well as to discuss company policy!" He turned and leveled a finger at Rayna. "Your complaints did this! I want you out of sight when he arrives!"

The entire office went into a flurry of panic, especially when they saw that the limo had already arrived outside. Remy rushed to prepare a conference room. A crowd gathered, and Rayna was rudely shoved to the back. As short as she was, she couldn't see a thing, even when the door opened. There came a loud gasp and a few women gave strangled shrieks. Rayna, frustrated, jumped up a little in an effort to see.

Someone planted their elbow sharply in her side and sent her tumbling. "Ow!" She landed with a thump on the floor and rubbed her side. It belatedly dawned on her that a stark silence had fallen and she turned her head to discover that the crowd had parted. There was a man in a suit standing in front of her.

She looked up and all the color drained from her face. Spots swam before her eyes as she stared at Eric's face, certain it was all some big mistake. It couldn't be possible. Riku couldn't be Eric Mason, he couldn't! He was a gardener! "R-riku?" she whispered.

"Riku is a nickname my friends gave me," Eric told her calmly, fighting the violent urge to pull her into his arms and promise it would be alright. She looked lost and adrift, and he felt her pain as if it was his own. "My name is Eric Mason. I believe I'm your boss."

There was an uncomfortable silence, and Oppenheim stepped forward with a false smile. "Mr. Mason, shall we go into the conference room? I'll have a secretary join us. Let's see . . ." He looked over the crowd.

"Bring Rayna." Eric didn't bother to look to see if his order was followed. He started walking down the hall with a stride that made light bounce off his well-tailored suit and broad shoulders. "She'll do a fine job."

Rayna scrambled to her feet to escape, but Oppenheim

ushered her down the hall as well. Terrified, in a panic, she instinctively turned her abilities off, too afraid to hear what Eric had to say. The action was pure self-preservation and she had no idea she had done it. She simply couldn't bear to hear whatever his heart might have to say.

The conference room was used for larger meetings but Eric walked in as if he owned it—in fact, he technically did. He set his briefcase on the table before the seat at the head and gestured for Oppenheim and Rayna to also sit. She did so, warily, and well down the table from him. It broke his heart. "Let's get started," he suggested, and sat down.

"Mr. Mason," Oppenheim began, "I don't understand how this meeting is called for."

"Silence." Eric cut across his words with a steely look. "I've been watching the company for days now, posing as a gardener, and I am highly disappointed with what I have seen here. Rhianna Taber and I have decided it's time for changes. Long overdue changes."

He began to remove documents from his briefcase. "I have compiled a list of names and positions. You can see for yourself what changes I intend to make. Recognition for hard work is always to be encouraged, and you are personally aware of this. You wouldn't be a manager at all without our recognition program. This company has fallen to the wolves." Mentally, he sent an apology to Mel and Audra. He would work with wolves like them any day. "Customer service suffers and the manner of the department is disgusting.

"We've pulled all of your past emails. Harassment, Mr. Oppenheim, is not an amusing matter. You had an employee who was being threatened, emotionally and mentally abused, and you did nothing to stop it. You told her she would be suspended for complaining. Clients have continually reported complaints of snobbishness and rudeness." He drummed his fingers lightly on the table. "I experienced the derogatory nature firsthand. If my orders are not met, I will completely erase the company of the dead weight and begin anew."

Oppenheim was turning an interesting shade of red and green like a Christmas tree. Red with shame, and green with fear. Rayna couldn't help but enjoy it. Served him right, the bully. At least what Eric was doing was for the good of the hard workers. He had believed everything she told him. It was a small comfort.

Oppenheim swallowed hard and looked over the organization chart in front of him. Seeing Remy Germaine's name at the top in what was currently his position was sickening. Other obvious changes stood out, but one in particular was distinctly glaring. "I, uh, don't see Rayna Carmichael's name on this chart."

Rayna's head jerked around, and Eric smiled coolly. "Yes, because she's being fired." Her color drained and he once more fought the urge to go to her. As soon as this was done, he was going to take her away and make up for all of it! "Rhianna and I have discussed things and we wish her to be hired on at Enforcers HQ. She's too good a worker to be wasted here. As you're aware," he added in a hard tone. "The false appraisals make that clear. Were you afraid to have her possibly promoted over you? As it stands, we have to fire her here, and hire her on new at Enforcers because of this."

Rayna stared at Oppenheim in shock, and he refused to meet her eyes. "She, well . . . she's . . ." Lacking a defense, he went on the offense. "How do I know you're not doing this because you're screwing her?" he asked bluntly. "Your actions, Mr. Mason, speak of impropriety and favoritism!"

Eric, trusting Rayna's ability to hear the truth, lied, "It was always purely business for me. Why would I want her for a wife?"

Rayna recoiled as if struck. Nausea bubbled up and she shot to her feet. "Excuse me," she whispered thinly, and ran out of the office. She wanted to cry and to scream, to rage against fate. How *could* he?! She had *trusted* him!

"Serves you right," one woman laughed as she saw Rayna. "Got yours, didn't you?"

The fury welled up and Rayna turned on her without warning. "Yes I did! I'm sure it amuses you to no end! You're all nothing but narrow-minded bitches who can't accept their own faults when they're flung into your faces! If you don't like facing your shortcomings, then never look into a mirror again! Until you speak the honest truth to yourself, mirrors will crack when you gaze upon them!"

The women recoiled away from her in fear as they sensed the power in her. She didn't notice. She gathered her bag and bolted from the building. "I quit!" she shouted over her shoulder. "Tell Mr. Mason he no longer has to fire me!"

When she got outside, she saw a familiar car at the curb in front of the limo. Her uncle was just getting out. "Uncle Larry?" On a little hitch of breath, she ran toward him and leapt into his arms. "Take me with you!" she pleaded. "I need to get away!"

Larry Carmichael caught her in surprise and patted her back. "Of course!" He ushered her into the car. "I caught wind of what happened," he explained. "It frightened me, so I came to make sure you were all right. I'll take you home and it'll be fine."

Eric sensed her leave the grounds only when he felt the sudden sharp stretching of the lines of power between his soul and the pendant she wore. "Shit!" He leapt to his feet. Her ability must have turned off, he realized in terror. She wouldn't have left without him otherwise. Dear god, how he must have hurt her! "Oppenheim," he snapped, "get started on these plans! I have to go find Rayna!"

Leaving Oppenheim gaping, he tore down the hall and came to a sharp stop in the lobby as he saw the women staring horrified at a broken mirror. "What the hell?" He went around them and toward the door. "Rayna!" he shouted. "Rayna!!"

Remy walked up and grabbed his arm. Her green eyes were icy. "Come with me." She stalked outside and dragged him with her. Once out the doors, she rounded on him. "You *idiot*!" she shouted. "Do you have any idea what you just did?!"

He felt the warning sensation of her power and knew she was truly pissed. He also knew who she was; he knew everyone in the District. "Rayna can hear the truth over lies," he told her swiftly. "She turned off her ability and heard me tell a lie that hurt her. You have to tell me where she is!"

Her eyes missed nothing. The suffering and fear on his face was real. "Her uncle picked her up," she said curtly. "He lives in Manhattan."

"How would he . . ." The color drained from his face. "What kind of car does he drive?"

"A blue Taurus."

The same kind of car that had almost hit them. A lump of ice settled in his stomach. Had Rayna walked right into a den of snakes, certain she was safe? "I have to find her," he shouted over his shoulder as he ran down the sidewalk. If anything happened to her, he would destroy everything in his path!

As the car headed down the freeway, Rayna closed her eyes and curled up as small as she could. "Thanks," she whispered.

"Any time. What happened, anyway?" Larry demanded.

"Someone's trying to kill me, and I took a lover, but he only did it to find out about the company." She swiped at her eyes. "I just want to curl up and die. My father will have a heart attack if you tell him."

"Ever since he almost lost the company," he said quietly, "it's been hard on him emotionally, especially with your coma and all. I won't tell him about all this, promise."

"Thank you." When they got to the large house, she followed her uncle inside and sent a little wave toward her aunt who was cooking in the kitchen. "I'll just stay a few days," she promised. "Long enough to find a new apartment."

"That's fine, you know we're glad to have you." Yvonne leaned in from the kitchen. "Have some lunch and go take a nap. It'll be better afterward, honey."

"Okay." She didn't feel much like eating, but she worked her way through a bowl of chicken soup, not wanting her aunt or uncle to worry. To her surprise, she began to feel sleepy shortly thereafter. "I guess I am tired," she admitted over a yawn. "It was an eventful night." Her cheeks flushed faintly as she remember how eventful.

"Go upstairs and rest then," her uncle soothed. "We'll wake you for dinner."

"Okay." She got to her feet and headed upstairs to the guestroom, rubbing her eyes sleepily. She didn't know if she would sleep well or not, but she was certainly tired. With a little sigh, she kicked her shoes off and curled up on top of the bed. Maybe just a little nap would help make everything better.

Hours passed. She didn't know what time it was, but she became aware of someone shouting her name in her mind, over and over, demanding she wake up. She forced her way up through the layers of sleep, dimly terrified at how hard it was to wake herself up. She had to literally force her eyes open, and her entire body felt like lead. When she did manage to open her eyes, it was to find her uncle standing over her with a knife in his hand.

Shock reverberated through her soul, and her mind instinctively gave a wild mental cry, shouting Eric's name as she saw the muscles in her uncle's arm tensing. *Riku! Please!* Her mind screamed his name over and over again, reaching for him blindly the way he had reached for her.

The window shattered in a blinding rush of snow and wind. The blizzard swept into the room, slammed into Larry's chest, and flung him violently into the other wall. Eric swung in the window and landed like a large cat on the ground, the black cloak he wore flaring around his body in the wind. Flames licked down along the white locks in his hair and lightning crackled around his left hand. "Stay away from my woman!" he snarled gutturally.

Rayna fought for control of her body. She had no strength and her muscles refused to obey. There was an odd taste in her mouth, mingling with the remnants of the taste of the soup. Her innocent mind didn't want to accept that she might have been drugged, but she was far too smart to truly discount it.

Her eyes fixed on Eric as he straightened and stood in the center of the blizzard. He commanded it as skillfully as he had commanded the meeting. But, here, he was beautiful. "Riku," she managed to whisper.

"Rayna, for god's sake, wake up!" He didn't take his eyes off of Larry. "You turned your abilities off, sweetheart! If you hadn't, you would have known!" He took a ragged breath. "Your uncle has been trying to kill you!"

"No!" Larry shouted. "It was all *his* doing! He forced me to do it! He was using me like he used you! I'm family, Rayna! Listen to me!"

"Rayna." Eric didn't look at her but his mouth was dry with terror. "Please."

She got her feet under herself and staggered forward a step. She felt betrayed and used by everyone, but she knew something with bone deep certainty. She still trusted Eric. She wore his pendant. He had called her his woman. She trusted him more than her uncle! "Riku!" She flung herself at him with her remaining strength, and his arms closed around her, fiercely.

A shudder went through his body as he held her tighter. His mind sought hers, pinpointed the wall she had made, and erased it. She couldn't exist with that wall in her mind, not and survive. It was nearly midnight, and when it was, it would be Saturday. It would be her birthday. She would be twenty-one. She shuddered in his grip, her eyes opening wide, the color turning white. Her power rose wildly as the seconds ticked mercilessly toward midnight.

Larry lunged forward and closed his hands around her wrist. "Rayna!" he pleaded urgently. "Please listen to me!"

A clock began to toll loudly somewhere, and her powers unlocked with a vengeance. It didn't matter whether she heard the lie or touched someone who lied. She would hear the truth. She *was* Truth. Larry's truth poured into her through his hands just before Eric flung him away with a lightning bolt to the chest.

"The truth," she whispered softly, her voice echoing eerily, "will set you free."

The command was the deepest and greatest of her abilities.

Larry screamed in terror and horror as his body mutated into a shape echoing his deepest inner soul. Eric held Rayna closer and his stomach churned as Larry melted into the shape of a deadly, venomous, cobra.

The cobra lunged forward, and Eric pushed Rayna one way as he went the other. Fire swirled down his arm and flung the cobra away violently. It began to slither off, realizing it was outmatched, and he started to go after it. "Come back, you bastard!"

Rayna began to sway on her feet and her vision grayed at the edges as her mind rushed into overdrive and then simply shut down. "Riku, I love you," she whispered, and tumbled to the floor in a curtain of silver hair.

"Rayna!" Terrified, he abandoned the cobra and lifted her into his arms. Was this from the drug . . . or also a result of the incomplete contract?

Rhianna found Eric sitting in the lobby of the Enforcers' hospital and staring blindly at the floor. She softly eased onto the seat beside him and wrapped her arms around his shoulders tightly. After a few moments, he asked in a strained voice, "Well? The doctors got the drug flushed of her system, but she won't wake. Tell me, damn it!"

She closed her eyes for a moment and then sighed and released him. "She doesn't want to wake up," she admitted quietly.

His head jerked toward her. "What?"

"She's scared." She raked a hand through her tangled hair. It was wild from her race to the hospital. Her surrogate brother had given her too many scares these last few days. "When I tried to link to her, all I got was wild static, like the kind that stems from fear."

"Do you think the contract has anything to do with this?"

She was silent for long moments. "No," she finally said.

"Today's her twenty-first birthday."

He began to curse softly under his breath. Pressing his face into his hands, he whispered, "She turned her ability off. She thought I was telling the truth when I said I was involved with her for business reasons."

She gently rubbed a hand over his back. There was nothing she could do for him that she had not already done. "Talk to her," she suggested softly. "Tell her everything. Tell her the full truth. You have to wake her, Eric, like you did before."

"I don't know how I did!"

"Then kiss her goodbye," she said simply. "I'm sorry, Riku." She pressed her lips to his cheek, got to her feet, and walked out of the lobby.

He stayed there for several minutes before he finally got to his feet and walked slowly down the halls toward the room where Rayna was resting. The guard outside stepped to the side to let him in and shut the door softly behind him.

Rayna was lying as she had for so long, motionless and still in a hospital bed. Machines beeped softly, reading her vital signs as normal. She almost looked as if she was merely taking a nap.

He drew the visitor chair closer to the bed and sat down. He picked up her hand and pressed it to his cheek. His eyes closed as he prayed in a way he had never prayed before. "Hey," he said softly. "I'm so sorry, Rayna. I never meant to hurt you. I was so certain that you would hear the truth, so I lied. I shouldn't have done it, I know. I hurt you and put you into danger. It took all my power to find you again."

He was silent for long moments. She deserved the full truth. "My name is Eric Mason but my birth name was Erikulen. That's where my nickname of Riku came from. I'm co-owner of Enforcers. I have been since the year 333BC when I and Rhianna helped build 3rd District and established Enforcers to protect it.

"I'm an elemental master. I was born to a family of what you would call warlocks who specialized in elements. I got a full dose of them all, and I had them mastered by the time I was your age. The pendant I gave you was made as a symbol of my power. It connects us, you know. I'm surprised it didn't tell you about me.

"Before 3rd District was built, there was nowhere for people like Rhianna and I and our families to go for safety. We lived as nomads, wandering the East Coast. At that time, the East Coast was a large network of united indigenous people. The people were the ancestors of the Native Americans that met English settlers.

"In the year 334BC, I was training to be a warrior with another tribe in another village. Rhianna showed up one day, in a terror, and demanded I return to our village. When we got there it was a sea of fire and blood." He closed his eyes. "We couldn't save anyone. All we could do was flee to the north, gathering as many people of power as we could, bringing them away from those who hated them.

"Rhianna and I knew there needed to be a safe haven for our kind, no matter what form they took. We built 3rd District as our own tribe and formed Enforcers. As the area grew, so did Enforcers. When each new form of government came along, they saw we didn't care if they were in charge, so long as they gave us protection if we needed it. Once they knew that, they were content to let us be. By the 1700s, Enforcers was a power to rival the king overseas. He worried until he saw that we had no care for anything but protecting 3rd District. His support continued. When the country was revolutionized, the congress and new president offered their support. It's stayed ever since.

"Over the years, 3rd District became a legend. We let it, kept cultivating it, making sure that just enough mystery remained to keep the wrong people away. Nowadays, people can accept, fairly easily, our existence as nothing but conjecture and rumor."

He stopped talking again. He closed his eyes for a moment and rubbed his cheek against her hand. It was so cold. "I'm over two thousand years old," he murmured. "People have come and gone, in my life, for centuries. I've made friends and I've made enemies. I've never been in love . . . until you.

"When your father approached the Enforcers, saying you and your sister had been marked for death, and he didn't know why, Rhianna and I were outraged. We agreed on a contract for both of you. For you, instead of dying in an accident, you would be put into a coma until your twenty-first birthday.

"The accident occurred, and I joined the search. I found you under an oak tree." He gave a soft laugh. "You were so tiny! You're still nothing but a little thing, but back then even more so. And beautiful even then. It killed me to think that something like this had to happen to any child, but most especially to you.

"I couldn't stay away. Every weekend, every year, I visited you, just to talk like this. I talked about the weather and things that were happening. I talked about you, described how your face and body were maturing. I kept hoping my voice was reaching you, so you weren't alone. I guess it was, because you woke too early."

Pain filled his eyes. "I'm sorry, Rayna. I never meant to put you in so much danger. If you'd slept until today, none of this would have happened. But because you were awake, we knew we needed to protect you. We made sure you had a job, and place to live, when you left home.

"We realized a week ago just how terrible things were at Budgets. Rhianna decided to go in and check things out and protect you. I volunteered to go in her place. I told her it was because she was too recognizable, but that wasn't the truth, though I didn't know it until later. The truth, Rayna, is that I've loved you in some way or another since I met you.

"I denied it, hid it, and fought it. But I loved you. How could I not? You're the other half of me. For all my mastery of the elements, light always eluded me. You brought the light with you. Until I met you, I never knew what it meant to be complete. Without you, there's nothing but loneliness. You once said you needed me. I need you, too, more than anything else."

He got to his feet and looked down at her peaceful face. He lifted his hand and gently cupped her cheek to skim his thumb over her cheekbone. "I know how scary it is out here. Your powers must terrify you. If," his voice broke, "if you want to stay asleep, then I won't stop you. If you're happier where you are, then stay there. I'll come and visit you, talk to you, and wait until you're ready to come back to me. I'll be waiting." He leaned down and touched her lips lightly with his, and the tears he couldn't stop slid down his cheeks to land on her skin. "I love you," he whispered. Before his control crumpled entirely, he straightened and turned to go to the door.

"Riku?"

He froze with shock. His heart began to pound, and he looked down to find her eyes opening. Shaking, he eased onto the bed beside her. "Rayna?" he managed to ask.

"I heard you," she whispered. "It was you all those years. You brought me back."

His trembling hands lifted and framed her face as she sat up in the bed. "I can't live without you," he whispered, and the words not only rang true, but his deepest emotions poured into her through the contact. "I love you," he added softly and drew her closer until their lips met in a tender kiss.

It was the only truth that had ever mattered.

CHAPTER SEVEN

Rhianna was reading a file when Eric walked in through the connecting door. "What are you still doing here?" she asked. "Don't you have a flight to catch?"

"Not just yet." He sat down on the edge of her desk and waited until she looked up. "I thought you'd like to know what Rayna found by hacking through the computers of her father's old company."

She smiled. "That girl is dangerous. Get her pregnant so she stays busy and out of my databases."

He grinned. "I'm working on it, but it won't stop her." He sobered quickly. "It seems Larry Carmichael was not happy his older brother had inherited the company. He laid a trap and baited it so well that his brother couldn't get out. When the dust settled, Larry stepped in and saved the company, and Lucas turned it all over to him, convinced that it had been his fault."

"Then why the contract for death?" she murmured.

"We won't know until we find Mika Carmichael. Is there any sign of her at all? We both know she survived. She had to. I haven't heard of any other young women entering inexplicable comas, let alone waking when Rayna did, so something must have gone wrong somewhere."

She held up Mika's contract. "Something is happening, that's for sure."

He took the contract and lifted a brow as he saw the words 'In Progress' across it. "Well." He dropped the contract back onto the desk. "Keep us informed."

"You bet. Have a good honeymoon and send me photos. I love that old castle."

"You got it." He walked back into his office and shut the door behind him. A smile instantly lit his face as he saw Rayna sitting on the edge of his desk. He immediately crossed to her and drew her into his arms for a kiss. His wife. It still thrilled him.

She melted against him with a little sound of pleasure and smiled as he eased back. "Keep it up and we'll miss the flight. And Rhi might be irked at us again."

"It's not like that couch is uncomfortable. At least, you weren't complaining at the time. And the doors are soundproof." He skimmed a hand through her hair. "We don't know," he said quietly. "We're looking."

"Okay." She trusted him to do whatever he could. She got to her feet with a steadily growing grace. Her eyes had recently been mended through advanced laser surgery, and it had a dramatic impact on her movement. Thoughtfully, she glanced at the closed door. "She's waiting," she murmured. "Do you know who for?"

"No. I've never really known." He slid an arm around her shoulders.

"I hope she finds him." She closed her eyes. "We all deserve a happy ending."

Listening from the other side of the door, Rhianna could only smile. Rayna was perfect for Eric, just as she had always thought. She walked back over to her desk and picked up Rayna's contract in time to see it sign as 'Complete.' She added a few notes and slipped it into the folder on her desk. She slid it into one of her drawers where she then wrote 'Carmichael' across the front.

What Eric didn't know, she thought impishly, wouldn't hurt him.

Status: File Begun
Analysis: A sleeping princess dreams of love, and only a man who loves her can waken her.

Folder Two
GWYN

CHAPTER EIGHT

When the car accident happened, Mika was flung far from the car because she wasn't wearing her seatbelt and harness. She went sailing clear over a gully and to the other side, where she hit with a painful impact. Something in her arm crunched frighteningly as she found herself tumbling head over heels for several feet.

She skidded to a stop and began to cry with fear and pain as she realized her arm wasn't moving right. She called for her mom and her aunt, and her sister too, but no one could hear her over the sirens.

She tried to get up to go find them, but a rustling in the bushes made her freeze with terror. She turned her head and watched as a pack of snakes slithered out of the bushes and steadily advanced toward her. Terrified, she whirled and ran, scrambling as hard as she could with a broken arm.

She broke through some foliage, and found herself in the air as the ground gave way. She dropped and went rolling down the hill before finally coming to a stop against the side of a cabin. The blow knocked her unconscious, and she couldn't see the snakes as they drew closer.

"Hey!" a young man snapped as he yanked the door open. "Who's out there?" When there was no response, he looked around and saw the snakes closing in on the girl. "Give me my gun!" he barked into the house, and his youngest brother scrambled to give it to him. The man quickly shot at the snakes, and they took off in fear.

"What's going on?" The second eldest peered around the door as his older brother rushed over to the figure on the ground. His eyes

widened. "Oh holy hell, there's a kid out there!"

"Whaaat?!" There was a veritable stampede as five other brothers came rushing to the door and tripped over one another.

The eldest ignored them as he knelt beside the little girl. He could tell on a single look that her arm was broken, and she was scraped and bleeding from her multiple falls. He gently eased her into his arms and carried her toward the house. "Get me some hot water!" he ordered. He saw the youngest goggling and glared at him. "Joseff!"

"Oh!" Joseff, at nine, was the baby in the family and quick to follow orders because his brothers loved giving them. He got the hot water and towels, and then hovered nearby as he watched his oldest brother removing the girl's clothes to get to the wounds. "Who is she? Is she okay?" In his hovering, he actually began to hover. His feet lifted off the floor entirely.

The second oldest caught him and put him down. "Joseff, calm down. Heul," he addressed the oldest, "is she alive?"

"Yeah." Heul gently began to clean the wounds. "Poor baby must have fallen down the hill."

"How old is she?" The question came from identical eleven-year-old twins.

"No clue. She's so tiny!" It startled Heul. Even Joseff wasn't that little! The faerie princess who had fallen into their house was no bigger than a minute, looking like a five-year-old in size. At least Joseff looked his age at nine. In fact, he was unusual in his family because he was normal sized. Everyone else was very tall.

"Can we keep her?" This time the question came from the thirteen-year-old sitting on the kitchen table.

"She's not a pet!" the fifteen-year-old felt compelled to jump in. "Right, Arian?"

Arian, the second oldest, was busy rummaging in a clothes trunk so his voice was muffled when he said, "She probably has a family."

"She can't go back." Heul's voice was flat with fury.

"Why not?" Arian walked over with a frown, one of Joseff's shirts over his arm. He saw instantly what Heul had and sucked a sharp breath in. "Shit. Shit shit shit. She's 3rd District."

"What's that got to do with anything? We're from there too," Joseff demanded. "And that's my shirt!"

"Look."

Everyone crowded around the couch to get a better look, and the three oldest all understood what they were looking at. The little girl was marked for death. Right over her left hip was the glaring red checkmark that meant someone had contracted for her death. "A Bloody Check on a kid. Someone wants her dead," the thirteen-year-old muttered. "That's way not cool."

"So we protect her!" The fractionally taller of the twins was usually the spokesperson. "We'll make her our sister! But, how old is she? Owen, can you see?"

Owen was the fifteen-year-old. He lifted a hand and gently touched the girl's cheek to seek her mind with his. He received a wild whirl of static . . . then nothing. Startled, he yanked his hand back. "She's really powerful, whatever she is. Her mind locked me out. But I think she's nine or so."

"My age!" Joseff's face lit with delight.

"Let's get her arm set." Heul gently tucked the girl into the shirt Arian handed him. "Someone bring me a slat of wood." The thirteen-year-old had already been at it and was holding out a small plank. "Thanks, Gavin."

"But . . . what if she doesn't want to stay?" Arian leaned on the edge of the couch. "She has a family, I'm sure."

The little girl began to stir, a little whimper coming from her throat as her arm throbbed painfully. Heul murmured softly to her, his heart hurting. It killed him to see a baby so hurt. He lifted her onto his lap and cuddled her, rocking gently as she began to wake up. His brothers climbed around him, gathering closer, wanting her to know she was safe.

"I hurt." She whimpered and clung onto Heul with her good

arm. "I hurt!"

"I know, I know. Shh. It's okay, you're safe." He smoothed her tangled white hair back from her face. "Can you tell us your name?"

She opened her mouth but nothing came out. Tears welled up in her eyes. "No. I don't remember."

"What!" The twins almost fell off the couch.

Owen was levelheaded. He leaned further over the couch so she could see him. "That's okay," he told her softly. "If you don't remember, we'll be your family. All of us will be your big brothers."

She sniffled and rubbed her eyes on Heul's shirt. "Really?"

"Yeah!" Joseff grinned at her. "You can be like my twin, okay, 'cause we're the same age and all." He frowned suddenly and looked at Arian. "Where's she going to sleep?"

"We'll build a bunk bed for your room for now," Arian promised. He leaned on his arms on the back of the couch. "I'm Arian Trahern. That's Heul, the eldest. Then there's Owen, Gavin, Tomos, Seisyll, and Joseff. He's the baby, like you."

"I'm not a baby!"

The little girl smiled but it wobbled at the edges and broke all their hearts. Giving in, she turned her face into Heul's shoulder and began to cry as she held onto him as tightly as she could. He said nothing. He just rocked her gently back and forth, trying to comfort and soothe. After a while, she slipped into an exhausted sleep, simply too worn out from the trauma to remain awake when she knew she was safe.

"Girls cry a lot," Tomos mumbled.

"You cried when you fell off the roof," Seisyll reminded him.

"Did not!"

"So what do we call her?" Arian asked Heul.

Silence fell on the entire room. Eyes and feet shifted. Finally, Joseff said, "She has hair as white as snow, like Grandma did. So . . . Gwyn?"

"That's nice." Heul smiled. "Gavin, you up to some computer B&E?"

"Ooh, with permission? Sweet!"

Present . . .

The words were splashed across every headline. 'Miracle Girl Gets Married.' Gwyn Trahern stared at the newspaper picture of the happy couple as they stood outside the Gentle Brook Inn and exchanged vows. The young woman . . . there was something very familiar about her beyond the eerie fact that they were damn near enough alike in appearance to be mistaken for twins.

"What are you reading?" one of her older brothers asked as he peered over her head.

She set the paper down where he could see. "This." She frowned deeply. "I think I know her." She saw the worry on his face and smiled. "Oh, don't scowl, Gavin, you'll wrinkle."

"Gee thanks." He regarded the paper intently and watched his baby sister's face from the corner of his eye. "Do you think it's from before you came to us?" he finally asked when the silence got to him.

"Don't know." She smiled at him. "It doesn't bother me. I like the family I have. Even if," she added impishly, "they are over-protective."

"You're too little!" he complained good-naturedly as she got up and went to the stove for coffee. "We feel like . . . like giants!"

She muffled a soft giggle. Her brothers, with the exception of her twin, were all over six feet in height. She was five-one. She weighed slightly over one hundred pounds. Her brothers felt like giants; she felt like a faerie! She was completely dwarfed by them. Then again, she was also the youngest. Height seemed to scale downward with age.

Heul was the oldest, at thirty-six, and a height of six-seven. Arian was next oldest, at thirty-four, and the two years had taken away two inches. Owen came after him with another loss of two years but only about half an inch. Gavin followed at thirty, but he was shorter by just a single inch. Identical twins Tomos and Seisyll were two years younger than Gavin, but actually stood at Owen's six-four height.

Joseff, Gwyn's own twin, blamed their elder twin brothers for the fact that he *should* have been six-foot but was instead a mere five-seven. It was a height well used, though, as he was proportionately not that much smaller than their brothers. He and Gwyn weren't blood related, which accounted for her delicate frame, but they were somewhat linked mentally and might as well have been born twins. They even celebrated their birthdays together.

Gwyn had given up being vexed by being the baby in terms of age and size. She was actually bemused by the entire thing. Her brothers looked perfectly at home on a construction site; she could only imagine the hilarity if they were like bakers or something. "Can I go with you to the site?" she asked.

"No!" Gavin glared at her. "Not a chance."

She considered throwing her coffee mug at him. "Oh come on!" she complained. "It wasn't even my fault, and Joseff saved me, and no one got hurt!"

"No." Heul took her mug from her as he went through the kitchen. "And don't drink the coffee, sprite. You'll get hyper."

"Hyper!" She glowered indignantly. "Well, see if I cook dinner for you again! Find a wife and make her do it!" She took endless delight in needling Heul about being single. Well, all of her brothers really, but especially Heul. "I think all of you are spoiled," she announced. She crossed her arms and set her chin in a mutinous line. "You're so used to having me around that you can't take care of yourselves. I think I'll move out."

Heul choked on his coffee and Gavin fell out of his chair. Owen, walking into the kitchen, could only say in a complaining tone of voice, "Great, there goes dinner. Nice, guys. Real nice."

CHAPTER NINE

The phone rang as she was fastening her pearl necklace on. Smiling wryly, Gwyn picked up the phone without looking at the ID. "Rice cooks for an hour, and make sure it's covered with water first or it'll burn."

"You're an angel," Tomos said with feeling. "And if we all get on our knees and beg very prettily, would you please, please, please make us a cake?"

She muffled a giggle and slipped her earrings on. "You guys are horrible! You act like I'm five million miles away, and I'm only just down the street!"

"It's too far," he retorted with feeling.

His sister sighed. She had lived with her brothers for seventeen years. At twenty-six, she had no reason to stay with them any longer, other than her love for them. They had lived on private land for the first three years of her life with them, and then they had all moved into an abandoned building in the 3rd District. They had turned it into a company and a home alike. The company, Driven Snow Architecture, now had one of the best reputations in the country.

While her brothers were the contractors and construction workers equally, she was an interior designer. She was also the voice for the company and took on the tasks of arranging contracts, working with clients, and doing the actual design of the buildings. She had dual majors in Architecture and Design, and Interior Design.

She knew one of the reasons she was in charge of meeting clients was the same reason her brothers were terrified to have her

out of their sight: everyone who met her loved her, and she made friends with all she met. She didn't think it was a *bad* thing, but her brothers sure did! They just didn't listen when she told them she was also a good judge of character.

"Caaaaake," Tomos intoned in her ear.

She burst into laughter. "Oh alright! I'll bake a cake for you!" She sighed fondly. "Are you sure you love me because I'm your sister, or do you love me because I can cook?"

"We'd love you even if you burned water," he assured her. "But I won't deny that we *really* love your cooking." The grin was in his voice as he added, "At least you don't have to worry about cleaning up behind us anymore. Unless you want to, of course."

"Ha!" She hung up on him. She was smiling as she did, though. She loved her brothers.

There was a surprising summer storm falling outside so she shrugged into the jacket for her suit. She wasn't sure how she would juggle an umbrella and a briefcase, but she was willing to give it a go. She had an important meeting that she refused to be late for.

The call had come through a week prior. A company that made and produced computer video games was looking to move into a larger building. They wanted to hire Driven Snow. She was on her way to meet with the owner to discuss a contract. Joseff and Gavin, diehard game players, were ecstatic.

She liked Memories' games herself. They were well built and well designed, and they always had such beautiful art and stories. She cried her way through a lot of them, which was okay because Tomos did too.

Because she didn't own a car, she caught a taxi and settled back for the ride. Unfortunately, it was morning rush hour and traffic was brutally heavy. The taxi got stuck mere blocks from her destination. "I'm sorry, Miss Trahern," the driver apologized over his shoulder. Since his car covered her area, he often provided her ride. He didn't mind. She was a delight to have around.

"It's not your fault." She smiled. "I don't mind walking. In fact," she rummaged in her purse for the payment, "I'm paying you for the full trip. The extra is a tip. Buy your wife something pretty."

He laughed. "You're an amazing young woman, Miss Trahern."

"Ha. Tell it to my brothers!" She opened the taxi door and then opened her umbrella. Traffic was at a standstill, and she hustled through the cars to the sidewalk. Moving as quickly as she could, she made her way down the sidewalk around busy passersby. Much to her chagrin, her umbrella was stolen in a gust of wind and she stepped right in a puddle. Oooh. She hated it when days acted like that!

Taylor Vincent was not a patient man by nature but he had learned the art of waiting over his thirty-two years. For most of his life, he had wanted to own his own business. Now he did. For most of his life, he had wanted to make the art and stories in his brain something to be enjoyed by all. Now he did.

Owning and operating Memories was no small feat. He worked twice as hard as any of his programmers and developers. He had to write the stories, draw all the concept art, and provide the backgrounds. He then had to review everything and make sure any changes flowed with his original idea. He always listened to suggestions from his employees, too. After a 3D animator had once suggested he change a male lead to a female lead, the game had ended up even better than he had hoped. He now made sure everyone got a copy of the script before it went in for production.

He didn't run things solo, though. So he had more time to focus on his art, he had an administrative assistant. He gave her free reign to make decisions as long as she kept him up to date. Since she knew her way around business, he had never had to worry about anything. Except for his distressing lack of patience.

Tired of pacing his office while he waited for the architect from

Driven Snow, he headed down to the lobby of the large building that Memories shared with other companies. Ten minutes might as well have been ten hours. And, anyway, the rain outside was very inspiring so he brought his sketchpad with him.

The security guards in the lobby were used to seeing him with his sketchpad. Much to the bemusement of the guards and his employees, the artist often won out over the businessman in Taylor Vincent.

He tuned everything out around him, only vaguely listening to the doors opening and closing. He had been trying for a week to design a faerie princess for the next game he was working on. He just couldn't picture her in his mind. Kind and beautiful but spirited. Waving a wand, he thought with humor, but not to cast magic. She was horrible at magic. A fireball might turn into an inferno or fail to light even a candle.

A feminine giggle cut across his thoughts and instantly stole his attention. His heart gave a wild clench in his chest and then kicked into overdrive. He looked up, in shock, to see the security guard offering his arm to a young woman trying to put her shoe back on. The guard was smiling widely and said something that had the young woman giggling again. The sound seemed to dance teasingly through Taylor's heart and soul.

As if sensing his gaze, she looked right at him and gave him an impish smile. The entire world went away from around him in a wash of color. There she was. His faerie princess, smiling at him in a rain-splashed suit the color of fresh snow.

Her hair was the same, a wild tumble of white curls that framed a face too beautiful to be real. Her eyes were an unusual shade of purple-gray, like the storm clouds that brought thunder and lightning. She was tiny, only barely over five feet in height, and had a slender frame and gently curved figure. She was stunning. Breathtaking. If she had sprouted faerie wings, he wouldn't have batted a lash.

He moved closer helplessly. He had to know who she was.

Where she was going. Where she was from. He needed to know everything.

"I'm Gwyn Trahern," she was saying to the guard. "I'm the architect from Driven Snow Architecture. I'm here for a meeting with Mr. Vincent." When the guard pointed at Taylor, she glanced over and smiled, her eyes crinkling mischievously at the corners. "Oops." In a soft voice, she whispered to the guard, "I thought he was the artist!"

"He's both," he whispered back.

"Oh. Oops."

Hopelessly enchanted, Taylor walked closer. When he got close, he realized in delight that she was truly faerie sized and barely reached his shoulder. He felt immensely bigger despite the leanness of his build. It brought up a sudden urge to defend and protect. He should have kept that sword one of his employees had given him as a prank gift. "I am indeed Taylor Vincent," he told her. "It's a pleasure to meet you, Miss Trahern."

She shook her head and made the pearls she wore at each ear glimmer softly. "Gwyn, please."

"Gwen as in Guinevere?"

"Gwyn as in G-W-Y-N." She smiled. "It means 'snow' in Welsh."

His eyes moved over her soft skin and white hair. "Good call on your parents' behalf." Something pained flickered in her eyes before it disappeared. "Did I say something to hurt you?" he asked softly.

"Just a little, but it's okay. My parents died a long time ago. I never knew them. My eldest brother Heul has raised me and our other six brothers. We own Driven Snow together. It's a family thing."

He tucked his sketchbook under one arm and offered his other. Her hand settled lightly on the crook of his elbow as he escorted her toward the elevator. "Eight siblings," he murmured ruefully. "And you're the only girl?"

"The one and only *and* the baby." She giggled when he winced. "It's not that bad," she reassured him. "Most of the time they don't try to lock me in a tower. Well, they've threatened it, but they know I could get out. I'd cry." She nodded sagely. "My brothers are suckers for tears."

"Most men are."

"If you men cried more yourself, you wouldn't be such babies about it." When they stopped on the second floor, another man got on board. She was quick to move when she saw the stack of boxes he carried was unstable. She caught the top one before it fell. "Whoops! Here, I have it."

"Thanks!" He gave her a grateful smile. "Just stick it back on top."

"It'll just fall again." She smiled. "I don't mind carrying it. Which floor?"

"Fifth." He ran his eyes over her with a masculine appreciation that annoyed Taylor. "Are you new?"

"Me? No." Her eyes sparkled. "I'm the architect from Driven Snow. Mr. Vincent is looking to hire my company. I'm hoping to charm him into signing over a fortune," she added gravely, but the twinkle in her eyes belied her words. "Lacking that, I'm going to wow him with my amazing architectural talents."

As the doors on the fifth floor opened, the man took the box back and got off the elevator. Wistfully, he watched as the doors shut again. Taylor Vincent was one lucky bastard, and he would be an idiot if he didn't hire the lovely faerie with the mesmerizing smile.

By the time they made their way to the twentieth floor and down the winding halls toward his office, Taylor was more enchanted than ever. Gwyn seemed to have absolutely no idea of her impact on people. She had a smile for everyone, a giggle for just the wonder of living, and her eyes sparkled merrily at an inner joke the universe might never get. She was truly as kind as she was beautiful, and he craved the opportunity to sketch her.

"Before we sit down," he offered impulsively, "would you like to see everyone at work?"

Her face brightened. "I'd love to! I've always wondered what went on behind the scenes! The credits are always so long and I know everyone is important!" She giggled. "You even gave a credit to the people who deliver pizza!"

Overhearing her, one worker called, "That pizza guy is a *life saver* when we're on a deadline." He peeked over the top of a cubicle. His blue eyes looked woebegone behind thin-rimmed glasses. "Can I have an office? Please? That way if I work through the night, I can have a couch to sleep on."

"You can have a red stapler," someone else called.

"Ha ha ha. You're such a riot." He slunk back down into his cubicle.

Taylor sighed. "Welcome to Bedlam. Really, we do work here." The affection was clear in his voice. "The smartass is Marie. She does battle scenario programming. The geek with glasses was Blake. He's a text input processor. I.e. he checks for typos."

"BIG typos," came Blake's voice. "'Cause Veronica can't type."

"Bite me, four-eyes!" a woman's voice retorted from across the room.

"And that's Veronica," Taylor offered, trying not to smile. "In case you couldn't tell, she's also a scenario builder."

By that point, Gwyn was giggling without stop and the hand covering her mouth could not hide it. No matter how big the company was, it was clear that everyone worked together as if they were family. She felt perfectly comfortable and natural there, as if she belonged. It made her more determined than ever to win this contract. These people deserved an amazing new building all their own.

Taylor showed her around and let her see the programming and building going on. She was fascinated with the 3D capture and delighted by seeing a landscape built one layer at a time. As she leaned over the modeler's shoulder, she said, "It might be my A&D degree, but I think you've accidentally got a 16th century style on a 12th century building."

"Aw, hell. Bless your degree. You're right." The young woman made a few mouse clicks and fixed the offending roofline. "You want to try? Ever used a CAD program?"

"Yes." She looked at the computer wistfully. "But I'm better with modern design." She smiled. "I'll leave this stuff to the experts. You're much more talented with it than I am."

"Keep her!" someone whispered loudly from across the room.

"We're quitting if you don't!" someone else called.

Taylor laughed. "And on that note, let's go talk business." He once more offered his arm and led her through the maze of cubicles toward the conference room. "And just think, this is just one of our three floors. There's two times this amount of smartass talent running around."

"We don't run," an older man countered as he peered around his cubicle wall. "You said we couldn't be trusted to not be carrying scissors."

"Neither can I," Gwyn admitted in a stage whisper. She smiled up at Taylor as she heard the laughter behind her. "I like your employees. They're wonderful. And you're pretty wonderful too. You know them all by name. I think that's why your games are so wonderful. Everyone loves their job and it shows."

He had nothing to say to that. He felt humbled. When he glanced over his shoulder, he could see all of his employees peering over and around their cubicles, looks of fascination and delight on their faces as they watched Gwyn. He didn't blame them.

And, therefore, he was doubly astonished when they reached the conference room and found his assistant glaring fiercely at Gwyn. "This is our architect?" she snapped. "Taylor, are you an idiot? What does someone like her know about design? All she's good for is using her looks and batting her lashes to get a deal!"

Gwyn recovered from the attack before he did. She offered a hesitant smile. "Maybe you should reserve judgment until you see my work. I'm actually quite good, and it has nothing to do with my appearance." She smiled then, with genuine friendliness. "Thank you, though. My brothers say I'm too pretty, too."

Taylor cleared his throat. "Gwyn, meet Melissa Washburn. She's my assistant." He very rarely reminded Melissa that she had no real position of power. He only did it when he wanted to remind her that his word was law.

Melissa's eyes flashed angrily as she got the point. She gave Gwyn a once over. "I hope you're as good as you say you are, else you'll never get anywhere."

Gwyn kept her smile. "Well, you can join us and find out for yourself." She winced as Melissa whirled and slammed into her office. She frowned at Taylor. "I didn't intend to offend her."

It didn't take a genius to recognize a woman's jealousy. He wasn't entirely surprised by it. Melissa had always been exceptionally proud of being the most attractive female in the company. In every way, Gwyn trumped her. "She's just cranky today," he finally said. He smiled, offering to share the joke. "She got up on the wrong side of the wrong person's bed."

"If she'd gotten up on the right side of the right person's bed, she'd have been smiling." Her eyes twinkled. "I'm glad it's not personal. I don't like offending people." She went into the conference room and set down her briefcase while he shut the door. She was momentarily startled as he held a chair for her, but she sat down with a smile that flashed the dimples at the corner of her eyes. "Thank you."

He sat down across from her. "Before we get started, I have something I need to say." She tilted her head and he smiled. He wanted to capture that expression too. "I absolutely have to sketch you."

"Me?!"

"Yes. If you don't mind."

"Oh." Flustered, she felt her cheeks heat. "No, no, I don't mind. It just surprised me." She smiled suddenly. "I wasn't expecting you to be the artist for the games as well as the producer. No wonder you have such beautiful eyes." She went red and covered her mouth as he lifted a brow. "Oops. I meant you've got an artist's eyes."

She hadn't, however, been wrong with the first statement either. Her new client was deadly gorgeous. His hair had a fascinating shade of smoky gray, almost as if he should have had black hair but it had never darkened all the way. His eyes had the full hue of black, but it reminded her of obsidian with the way it seemed to possess a rainbow of colors inside the darkness. They seemed both dreamy and suave, as if he saw beautiful things that he had the intelligence to grab. He was lean and muscular with a sort of predatory grace that no amount of tailored suits could hide. He should have been a model, not an artist.

He had an earring. The little gold hoop seemed so out of place at first that she wasn't sure she had seen it clearly. She looked again and then smiled to herself as she opened her briefcase. A rebel, she decided, and thought she liked him all the more for it. "Well, Mr. Vincent, shall we get started?"

"Taylor, if you don't mind." He watched her with elemental male hunger in his eyes. She had a way of moving that had every hormone he possessed sitting up at attention and wanting to howl at the moon. Her lack of awareness of her own appeal was just part of her charm.

"Taylor, then." She pulled folders out of her case and spread them out. "Because Memories is growing quickly," she began, "it needs to be a building bigger than your immediate need. Also, it needs to be something new and unique, because otherwise it will get lost in the shuffle. I've provided for a game lobby as well."

"A lobby." He leaned back in his chair. "What for?"

She smiled. "A place on the first floor where people can come in and demo your games and buy merchandise. In the interior design plans, I've arranged to have the lobby decorated with no images but original sketches, ones like the kind that recently sold on eBay for two thousand dollars."

He coughed lightly. His rather sadistic employees had taken great delight in posting the listing everywhere. He had nearly had a heart attack. "It was a giveaway," he explained. "I didn't expect that,

I assure you!"

She giggled softly. "Most don't." She flipped open the top folder and slid it across to him. "The basic blueprints are already included care of Owen Trahern. He's the one who takes my sketches and makes them feasible."

He stared in stunned disbelief at the pictures in front of him. She had done a full drawing, showing the building from all possible angles, and every image was as good as a photograph even though it was rendered in blue pencil and black ink. 'Talented' was not the word for her.

The building she depicted was five stories in height. It sat on the corner of a street and took full advantage of the western/northern view in order to catch the sunset in the windows. It was marble and glass with a water fountain surrounded by a brilliant garden in the front. "This is . . . amazing," he managed to say.

"The garden is already plotted as well. Tomos Trahern is our landscaper." She flipped through another folder. "He's already laid out the groundwork, for lack of a better word, and has a list of suppliers for what he needs to make our image a reality. Also," she slid across another folder, "here are the interior design plans. I wanted to avoid the worn effect of so many buildings where they're all the same inside."

He opened the folder eagerly, more and more delighted with everything he saw. "This is stunning. Really, really stunning. I've dreamed and imagined having my own building and company, and you've made the first a reality. You managed to capture exactly what I wanted. You're hired."

She laughed at him. "We at Driven Snow like to give a customer their full money's worth. As time goes, if we discover impracticalities we weren't able to plan for, we'll adjust the designs as needed. You'll likely see me at the site before construction but not often during."

"Why not?" He frowned.

She sighed. "I could give you a line about not being needed but it's actually just stupid family dynamics."

His frown became a grin. "Overprotective brothers?"

"Yes!" She pouted when he laughed at her. "When I was twenty, there was almost an accident. I and my brother Joseff were surveying a site and a piling came loose. It would have knocked me off the second floor but he got me out of the way. Ever since, they've panicked if I go near a site."

"Is it only overprotective brothers, or do you have an overprotective boyfriend as well?" he asked casually. She hadn't mentioned one, but he thought it better to double check.

"Just brothers." Her eyes danced merrily. "They scared all potential candidates away."

"You sound so crushed." He said it dryly, but a mingled relief and delight inside told him that he might be getting too far in over his head already.

"Well, I figure if I find one who can't scare, he's worth keeping. The rest weren't." She began to gather up her folders. "You can keep these copies for yourself. I have the originals. If you decide to make changes, let me know, and we'll sit down and hash them out."

"Give me just a moment to get the contracts you emailed me the other day." He got to his feet to step into his office across the hall, and he wasn't very surprised to find Melissa in there seething. "Yes?" he asked as he got the paperwork from his files.

"Well?" she demanded.

"Yes, I'm hiring her." He turned and gave her a bland look. "Jealousy is unbecoming on you, Melissa. Just because she's more beautiful doesn't mean you have to be snide to her. She treated you with genuine kindness and you snapped at her."

She drummed her fingers on her arm. "You think she's more beautiful than me?"

"To quote another faerie tale, she's the fairest in the land. And, FYI, that's not just applicable to her looks. It applies to her heart, too. She doesn't judge on appearances, unlike someone else around here. She's also damned talented, just as promised." He turned on his heel and walked out without anything more.

Gwyn was still waiting for him in the conference room, but she was peeking at his sketchbook. She jumped guiltily and dropped it on the table. She tried to look innocent, and he grinned. "Help yourself."

She didn't need to be asked twice and scooped up the book to begin actually skimming through the pages. The absolute delight on her face made him feel as if he was Rembrandt, or Michelangelo, or Da Vinci. As if he was the greatest artist known in the world. "You like it?" he asked softly as he sat down.

"It's amazing! Oh!" She giggled. "I love the werewolf! He looks like he'd eat me for lunch, but he's got a kitten on his shoulder! And look at the soldier! He's so handsome!" She looked at him, eyes merry and guileless. "He looks kind of like you."

He winced sheepishly. "Guilty." He would have liked to take it as a flirtation but she seemed blissfully oblivious to how her words sounded. It was refreshing and wonderful at the same time. "You don't think it's a bad thing for a soldier to fall for a faerie princess?"

"Why should I?" She smiled at him as she handed the sketchbook back. "Love is love, no matter what shape it takes." She laughed. "I'm from 3rd District, though, so I guess it's little wonder I'd think that, right?" Her eyes sparkled with merry mysteries. "Magic comes to us with our breakfast."

Delight filled him. Was his faerie princess truly a faerie? He would have been ecstatic if he could find out it was true. "Will you have lunch with me today?" he asked as she signed the contract. He hated the idea of not getting more time to spend with her. "We could discuss the building some more."

"I'd love to, but I have another site I need to visit. Another hopeless dreamer like you." Her mischievous smile took the sting out of the words as she stood and picked up her briefcase. "Driven Snow is very glad to have you hire us. And so am I," she added softly. "You're a good person, Taylor Vincent."

By the close of business, the entire building, and not just Memories, was aware of her beauty and gentleness. The security guards were visibly smitten with her, and any person who had spoken to her was in awe. She truly was the faerie princess of the company, and she had woven spells with a simple smile. Half a dozen people called Taylor and told him personally that he would be an idiot to lose her—professionally or personally.

He wasn't an idiot. He intended to keep her as long as he could. She brought fresh air and a renewed sense of life with her. She also turned out to be a wonderful muse. Within minutes of her departure, he was in his office and sketching madly.

Melissa was in his office, too, and pacing with anger. He only listened with half an ear, but she didn't notice it as she walked around furiously. "They told me I couldn't even hold a candle to her!" she fumed.

"Mm-hmm."

"They dared compare us!" She found it outrageous. "Me, compared to that unsophisticated little nobody from that backwater district! I went to the most prestigious schools in the country and my shoes cost more than her entire suit!" She stopped for a breath and finally realized he wasn't even listening. "Taylor!"

"What!" He looked up, startled.

Annoyed, she reached over and took his sketchpad. "Now what are you on about?" To her dismay and disgust, she found herself looking at a picture of Gwyn Trahern depicted as a faerie princess. She had an adorable look of disgruntlement on her face as she stared up at the bird perched on her head. "Jesus, this is unbelievable."

He took his sketch back with dignity. "Try some graciousness," he suggested to her curtly. "And perhaps you might be able to compete with Gwyn. Now, good night. Lock the door as you leave."

She seethed to herself but left the office and the building. Somehow she refrained from slamming doors as she did so. She was still pissed, and it was worse knowing Gwyn truly was as talented as she was beautiful. Even though Melissa didn't want to, she loved the designs. She wouldn't have minded teaching the little upstart a thing or two, though!

A slithering sound echoed behind her as she was unlocking her car, and she felt a chill. When she turned, there was nothing behind her. Disturbed, she started to get into her car when sharp pain exploded in her leg as if something had just bitten her. She crumpled to the ground unconscious, the venom gliding through her veins even as the cobra glided away from the scene.

CHAPTER TEN

It was midnight before Taylor gave up on trying to sleep. Nerves and excitement coiled so tightly inside him that he felt like a rubber ball let loose in a rubber factory. He hadn't felt that way in six years. Not since he had first formed Memories with a handful of workers—including Blake and Veronica—and set out to grab his dream. Now he stood on the cusp of realizing the next big step of his dreams. His own building.

He had saved and saved until he could afford the land. His employees had helped. Each had willingly taken a five percent pay cut to pour more funds into the land. In return, he had offered each some stock in the company. Now the land was his, outright, and the building was going to be paid for with a loan. As long as he kept his company going strongly for the next twenty years, eventually the building would be his, entirely, too.

Full of restless energy, he got out his sketchpad and began drawing. He normally only did concept art that was turned into full designs by other artists he employed, but the images were so strong in his mind that he found himself drawing more than concepts and sketching full scenes and character depictions.

It wasn't until dawn crept in that he realized he had drawn dozens of sketches of his faerie princess. His white haired, stormy eyed, faerie princess. He softly traced a finger over the line of her face. It was imprinted in his memory. He knew, no matter how long he lived, that he would never forget it. He was definitely smitten.

He wasn't due at the office that day. Unless they were under a short deadline, everyone took Saturdays and Sundays off. Unfortunately for him, that meant he had two whole days to pace and fidget with nothing to do. He cleaned up the apartment, made breakfast, and sketched a comical image of his werewolf being turned into a frog by the magically inept faerie.

He gave up around seven in the morning. There was no law against visiting his own land, and that's what he wanted to do. He wanted to see the site where his building would be going up and pretend it was already done. He had a good imagination.

He drove to the site eagerly, not sure what to expect to see after a day of having Driven Snow on board. When he parked at the site, though, he found himself unsurprised. Supplies and equipment had already been delivered and the foundation was nearly completely dug. A large stack of pilings and steel beams sat facing the foundation, and he headed for it. It would be a perfect perch for studying his kingdom.

As he rounded the edge of the stack, he got a swift surprise as he discovered he wasn't the only one there. Gwyn was perched on the pilings, a morning wind ruffling her hair and pulling out the curls before letting them spring back.

The punch of lust was so staggering that he put a hand out to brace himself. It seemed to rip from his soul outward, a silent detonation of hunger that made his body ache and burn. The longing to touch her, to taste her, was breathtaking and powerful. He wanted nothing more than to know if she tasted as pure as her name implied.

She wore a pair of pale blue jeans, faded from many washes, and a soft, peach-colored camisole. His hands burned to find the softer flesh under the cotton. Smitten? Had he thought he was smitten? He was enthralled. He walked forward slowly, not wanting to startle her. "Good morning."

She still jumped a little, her head swinging around toward him quickly. When she saw him, her eyes lit from within with delight. "Good morning!" Her eyes sparkled. "Come to survey your kingdom, m'lord soldier? I admit, I couldn't stay away, either." She returned her gaze to the empty ground as if already seeing it built.

The déjà vu stunned him. He stared at her, astonished that she would quote his faerie princess in the game without ever once knowing the script or plot. "I thought I might view the land." He leaned against the stack beside her. "I never thought I'd find a faerie here viewing it, too."

"A faerie!" She giggled softly. "Well, I can't confirm or deny it, sadly, but my brothers have nicknamed me 'sprite' because I'm so little and quick to get into trouble."

"You admit it?" He grinned at her.

She grinned back. "To everyone but them." She stretched largely, oblivious to his hungry gaze following the ripple and movement of her curves. "And you better not tell." She spotted movement and held up her hand. To his wonder, a bluebird flew over and landed delicately on her fingers. She brought it down to rub her cheek against its feathers. "Hi there."

He mentally photographed the image; it needed to be drawn as well. "How did you get into this business?" he asked. He couldn't control his hunger to know everything about her. "I know it's family owned, but still."

"They wouldn't let me learn to build, so I had to go into the planning stages." She giggled softly. "Like I said before, I have seven brothers. All bigger, all older. My twin is the only one who isn't super bigger than me. They all do construction, but they also specialize in different fields. Heul, my eldest brother, wanted us to do something together so this was what we settled on."

"A twin?" He smiled. "How much older?" Her gaze lowered, and he began to frown. "What's wrong, Gwyn?"

She took a deep breath. She couldn't lie. She had never been able to lie. And she didn't *want* to lie to Taylor. "I don't know," she admitted softly. She released the bluebird and watched it fly away. "I'm adopted. They found me when I was nine and took me in as their sister. I have amnesia. I have no memories of my life before they found me. Joseff and I share his birthday since we know we're the same age. Owen can 'sense' minds. He was able to pick out that I was nine and my birthday was in May. Joseff's birthday is in May, so we share it. I might even be older than him, but there's no knowing. I hope I'm not. He likes not being the baby anymore."

"Have you ever gone looking for your family?" he asked quietly. His heart ached for her. He had a painful childhood of his own that he had often wished to forget, but it suddenly seemed as if never knowing his origins would be worse.

"I never felt a need to." Her fingers moved unconsciously to her hip and then away, the movement so brief it wasn't noticeable. "I don't even know my real name. Joseff picked Gwyn for my name because of the color of my hair. I looked like their—our—grandmother, who was named Gwyn, too."

The lost note in her voice tugged at him. He gently reached out and ran his fingers through her hair. She looked at him in surprise and was caught by the rainbows in his eyes. Her entire body came alive all at once, a flush of heat spreading across her skin. Her pulse began to throb everywhere. In wonder, she reached out a hand and touched his face, her fingertips reacting with delight at the feel of his skin. Was this why he had never left her mind? The feelings inside her were so right that she knew they were truer than anything she had ever known before.

"I thought it was just me," he murmured huskily, his breath caught at the naked longing in her eyes. "I thought I was the only one."

"I thought there was something wrong with me, that I never felt this way for anyone." Her voice was just as soft and just as husky with desire. "But I see, now, that it was because I'd never met you."

He eased his hand more fully into her hair and cupped the back of her head as he drew her toward him. Her lashes fluttered closed, and his muscles knotted with painful desire. "Gwyn," he murmured, their lips barely touching. His heated breath made her shiver softly with wonderful pleasure.

"Hey!" a sharp male voice snapped. "What are you doing to my sister, you ass?"

He released her as if his hands were on fire. She didn't look surprised, but she certainly looked annoyed as she turned a fierce glare on the one who had spoken. "He was going to kiss me, thank you very much, Seisyll! And, I'll have you know, I wasn't exactly fighting!"

Taylor hastily straightened as the man approached them. When he drew even, Taylor, at six feet tall, felt short for the first time in his life.

Seisyll may have been one of the younger Trahern brothers, but he was still bigger than the average man. His eyes carried equal doses of annoyance and discomfort. His short-cut hair did nothing to disguise the strong lines of his face. Taylor half expected him to put on a horned helmet and go looking for a village to plunder.

Gwyn was distinctly dwarfed by her big brother, but she was also distinctly not intimidated. She glared fiercely at him from her perch, which still didn't have her on eye level with him.

"Who is he?" Seisyll asked her, eyeing Taylor intently. He seemed decent enough, but Seisyll distrusted any man that came near his baby sister with lust in his eyes. It didn't matter if she was willing or not. She knew nothing about men and could too easily get her heart bruised.

"Our client, Seisyll." He gaped at her, and she blushed. "I couldn't help myself," she admitted. "I know it's improper." When he glared at Taylor, she smartly smacked his arm. "Go away! Stop being such an overprotective ninny!" She glared at him until he gave in and walked off.

"Don't touch my sister," he muttered at Taylor as he went past.

She sighed and gave Taylor a sheepish smile. "Sorry. I told you my brothers were overprotective." She lowered her gaze. "But he's right. We probably shouldn't let our hormones get the better of us." A bit helplessly, she said, "I'm not handling this well. I don't know how to flirt or be coy. I just . . . am me. Everyone says I'm naïve."

"I think you're wonderful," Taylor said honestly as he reached up to help her down off the pilings. She went into his arms with a trust that shook him deeply. It was a miracle her brothers were still sane. In fact, he suddenly sympathized with them. Protecting someone so innocent would be terrifying.

"Really?" Her hands rested lightly on his shoulders as he slowly lowered her to her feet. Their bodies brushed and pressed together in places, making their hearts beat a little faster, a little harder.

"Really." The temptation was too strong. Her scent was like fresh snow, sweet and pure. He drew her even closer, and his hands curved around her small waist. "Gwyn," he murmured.

"You shouldn't," she whispered, but her hands were moving of their own will, her arms winding around his neck. His breath tasted like coffee and was so hot that it sent a wonderful shiver through her body. She wanted his kiss. Wanted it with a vengeance.

"May I kiss you?" he whispered, something about her compelling him to ask rather than take. He would be willing to beg; he was losing himself in the storm clouds of her eyes. For the first time, he truly understood his soldier's obsession with his magically inept faerie princess. He was obsessed, too, and hopelessly enthralled.

"Please." She held her breath as his lips brushed across hers. She waited in agony for him to deepen the kiss, but it didn't happen. Disappointment filled her as he eased back. "That's it?"

"For now." He rubbed his thumb over her cheekbone. "It occurs to me that it is very tacky to kiss a lady I haven't taken out to dinner." He stepped back and lifted her hand to his lips with a courtly bow. "Have dinner with me, my faerie princess. I would be honored. I think I can scare up reservations for a suitable restaurant for a princess."

Her color rose. "I'd like to but . . . oh, you'll laugh!"

"Try me."

"I don't have anything to wear." She fumed as he did, indeed, laugh at her. "Jerk!" She blew out a quick breath. "We all draw

paychecks from the company. I won't let them coddle me financially no matter how hard they try. I can live well, have a nice place, whatever I want to eat, but I can't afford to get fancy clothes." She glowered. "Do you have any idea what a fancy, stylish cocktail dress costs these days?"

"I can imagine." He smiled. "Suppose you had a dress. Would you go out with me?"

She laughed and shook her head. "Sure. Let me just find my magic wand and conjure a cocktail dress. Thank you for the offer, though. If you wanted to take me to some place casual, I might be willing. I just can't do fancy." No matter how tempting the thought of him in a formal suit was. No matter how badly she wanted to see him in any and every venue. Her craving for his presence was growing and growing. "I'll see you later. I should be going."

He pulled out his cell phone as he watched her walk away. Magic wand, no, he thought in amusement, because his faerie princess couldn't cast to save her life. Thankfully he knew a few elves who owed him a favor or two.

By the time she got home, she couldn't resist the urge to dig in her closet. She knew it was an exercise in futility, but she looked for anything that might pass as a dinner dress. Her fanciest outfit still walked the edge of being casual, unless she counted her suit, which she didn't. Damn it.

When her phone rang, she picked up to say, "Yes, he kissed me. Go away." She promptly hung up again.

Depressed, she sat down on the edge of her couch and stared at the wall across the room. She was beginning to know how the faerie princess felt: wanting someone so badly it hurt, but knowing it was near impossible. She groaned and fell over on her back. "Why," she asked the ceiling, "do I have to suddenly discover lust at my age? I'm already partway toward being an old maid. I could have happily gone along without wanting sex!"

There came a choked sound from the doorway, and she opened one eye to see the shocked look on her twin's face. It was a comedic twist of features, and she rolled onto her side with a shriek of laughter. "Oh my god, Joseff!" she managed to gasp. "Your face!"

He scraped his hands over his face. "Where do you keep the cleaner?" he mumbled. "I need to bleach my brain!" Because she was still laughing, he walked over to the couch to tweak her ear. "Brat!"

"You," she countered, wiping her eyes, "are the one who just blindly walked on in!" She fell over on a fresh peel of laughter. "If I'd known I could get to my brothers like this before, I'd have gone looking for the right guy sooner!"

He pinched his nose between his fingers. "Okay," he said. "Let me get this straight. You have the hots for the client we acquired just yesterday and Seisyll caught him kissing you."

"No, Seisyll stopped him from kissing me. Taylor sort of kissed me after Seisyll walked away." When he eyed her, she explained, "Sort of kiss. Not a real kiss. No tongues or anything. Just lips. It was really annoying because I wanted him to really kiss me."

"I'm not having this conversation," he told himself. "I'm not." She giggled and he caught her in a headlock. "Was that all?"

"Yeah. He asked me out too, but I turned him down."

"Why? Thought you had the hots for him."

"I do. But he wanted to go somewhere really fancy, and," she glared, "I don't own a dress good enough." She kicked him in the bottom as he fell off the couch with laughter. "Stop it, meanie." Her doorbell rang and she got to her feet. "Anyway, I told him that I'd go out only if I had a dress." It was a deliveryman outside her door, and he had two packages. Puzzled, she signed for them.

"Bet he was annoyed," he decided. "You're so beautiful, and everyone loves you."

She smiled. "Thanks. Still," she sighed as she opened the larger of the two boxes, "it makes me wish I *did* own a dress. I could probably fall for him, Joseff." Her words stumbled to a shocked stop as she stared at what was in the box. "Oh," she breathed. "It's stunning."

"What is?" His brows shot up as she pulled out of the box an evening gown in rich golden yellow. It was a color that most women would never be able to wear but would perfectly compliment Gwyn's skin and hair. "Wow," he managed to say. "That must have been a small fortune!"

"It's beautiful!" She gave in to the urge and held it against her body as she turned in a circle to admire the flow of color and light. "Like something for a princess!" It dawned on her, and she put the dress down. She rummaged in the box again and shortly found the card.

My faerie princess:

You promised if you had a dress, you would join me. Here's the dress and I can't wait to see you in it. I'll pick you up just before seven.

Signed, *an adoring soldier*

"Taylor," she murmured. Her face softened as she ran her fingers over the simple white card. He had done this, she thought, holding the card to her heart. How could she say no? She wanted to see him more than anything.

Joseff watched her face and his stomach gave an odd quiver. His sister, he realized painfully, was a woman. An adult woman, and she was falling in love. It hurt a little because she had always belonged to them and no one else. He almost didn't want to give her up. It was only the glow in her cheeks and her eyes that gave him the will to share. "Well," he finally said.

"Well!" She pulled out the shoes that had been sent as well and set them to the side. She didn't question how Taylor had known her sizes. She was just going to accept the magic. "I guess I have a date," she said laughingly. "Maybe I'll finally get my kiss. He's a good man," she murmured softly. "He does his own art and writing. He knows his employees by name." She smoothed her hand over the dress. "He was like a little kid when he saw the designs. I could see the dreams in his eyes. I want to make them all come true."

Joseff was silent. Then, "Are you in love with him?"

Startled, she looked at him with wide eyes. "I . . . I don't know."

"Then weigh it."

She closed her eyes and envisioned scales in her mind. It was her special gift. She could mentally produce a scale in her mind and put evidence on the two sides. Whichever was heavier was the verdict. She had never been wrong, even in situations where the evidence was nearly balanced.

She weighed out all the evidence. Her emotions and reactions compared to her experiences and the way she normally acted. The answer was immediate, and there was no question to the verdict. If the scale had been physical, it would have hit the table with an immense clang.

Wonder filled her, and she began to smile with delight. She was in love. Love at first sight. "I didn't think it was possible," she whispered. "I thought it was supposed to be hard. People work so hard to find love and I walked blindly into it."

"What about him?" he asked softly.

"I don't know." Her smile turned sad. "I know he likes me. And he's definitely attracted to me. It hurts, a little, to think that I'm in love and the man I love might never feel the same. But I can't stop it. Whatever he wants of me, he can have."

He walked over and hugged her tightly. He could barely remember his life before knowing her. In every way that counted, she was his twin sister. Their minds automatically brushed together if they were near. If he couldn't feel her in his mind, it would drive him nuts. "He'd be an idiot not to love you," he said firmly. He released her and cleared his throat. "So, have a good dinner. And, uhm, be careful. You know."

She blushed as the meaning sank in. "Joseff!"

"I had to say something!" he retorted defensively, and hastily ducked when she took a swipe at him with the box. "I'm going, I'm going!" He moved quickly toward the door to get out of range. He looked at her for a moment, sighed, and finally gave up as he left. He might as well go tell the others and get it over with. They would kill him if he didn't.

She didn't even remember her other package until she was trying on her dress that evening. It gathered at the front and fell in slim lines to her ankles. Her back was left mostly bare and she felt like a princess as she turned in front of her mirror. There was no hope for her hair though. She tried pinning, tying . . . none of it looked right.

Frustrated, she went back into the living room and spotted the other package. There was no return label and she opened it curiously. Inside, on a bed of tissue, she found a beautiful comb set with yellow stones that perfectly matched her dress.

Delighted, she pulled it out and wondered if Taylor had sent it as well. Her doorbell rang and she hurried over to open it. He was on the other side, wildly handsome in a black suit, and she didn't fight the happiness bubbling inside. She jumped into his arms. "It's incredible!"

He managed to hold the flowers he was carrying with one hand and caught her close with the other. Dazed, he stared at her. Incredible was not the word for her. It was too pale a word. She was stunning, more beautiful than any dream he had ever had. "Wow," he said, "that's a fine greeting."

"I'm happy." She closed her eyes and rested her head on his shoulder. "I wanted to see you so much." She released him and smiled as he set her on her feet. "Oh!" she suddenly remembered. "My hair."

"I like it," he murmured huskily. A tempting image teased his mind of seeing it tangled across his pillow. "Leave it down."

"I have a comb for it though." She waved the comb at him. "See?" She caught her hair and began to twist it up, but he snatched the comb from her fingers. "Taylor!" Giggling, she tried to reach for it. "Give it back!"

"No." He held it out of her reach, and she pressed up against him trying to grab it. Her breasts rubbed against his chest and he caught a breath as desire slammed into his bloodstream. She went on her toes without thinking, and his arousal suddenly pressed against the notch of her thighs. She froze.

Their eyes locked, and he tossed the flowers onto the side table to free his hand. He curved it around her bottom and drew her more firmly against him, his eyes burning into hers. She gave a little gasp and her fingers gripped his jacket tightly as her skin flushed with desire. Pleasure radiated from the contact and her body began to throb with need. "Taylor," she managed to whisper.

He shuddered and held her closer, his head bending to take her parted lips. The comb slipped from his hand and fell onto the floor with a small clatter. Even before he heard it starting to hum, he felt his hands beginning to burn. The familiar feeling was one he had learned to associate with danger. He instinctively wrapped Gwyn in his arms and moved back sharply. His eyes narrowed on the comb.

The comb hummed and quivered around on the floor. The spines abruptly fired like spikes out of the body, as the body itself shot backwards just as hard. The spikes hit the molding around the floor and imbedded themselves several inches. Gwyn's startled gasp turned into a little shriek as the comb, itself, exploded and sent pieces everywhere in a three-foot radius.

Shaking, she clung onto Taylor tightly and buried her face in his shoulder. Shaking no less, he wrapped both arms around her. "God," he managed to say. "If I hadn't stopped you . . ." Fury bubbled up and he jerked her back. "Where the hell did you get that?!"

Her teeth chattering slightly, she stammered, "I-it came in the mail. A gift. Arrived with the dress. I thought it was from you." She shook her head quickly when he froze. "No, I don't think you did it. You would never hurt me." Her trust was in her eyes as she rested against him and curled her fingers into his jacket.

He let out a ragged breath. "Thank you," he whispered. He held her close for long moments until her shaking began to ease. He only then reluctantly released her to kneel next to where the spikes had hit the wall. It took a great amount of force to finally pry them out. "If this had gone off while you were wearing it," he said grimly, "you'd be dead."

She tried to smile. "And here my brothers said I had a hard head."

Sensing her need to keep the tone light, he didn't argue with her flippant words. He gathered up the debris and put the pieces on the table. "We should call the cops."

"I'll call them later." She set her chin in a stubborn line. "I refuse to let this ruin my evening."

He looked at his watch and sighed. "Unfortunately, we'll never make it to the restaurant in time. I had to promise we'd be there at precisely 7:30 to get a table."

"Then stay here." She took his hand with hers and smiled. "Have dinner with me here. I can cook something or we can order in."

He shook his head. "I can order something. You set up a place to eat. Leave the food details to me."

"Alright." She released his hand and headed out onto her small patio balcony. The sun was setting in the distance as she unfolded her bistro table and two chairs. A tablecloth and two slipcovers turned the patio set from casual to formal. By the time he came looking for her, she had set out candles and wine glasses and was pouring cider for them both.

His breath caught in his chest. The setting sun illuminated her in a beautiful golden glow and haloed her skin and hair. She looked like his faerie princess. His. No one else's. He wanted her to be his alone, to have her at his side where he could always turn and see her smile. He wanted to be surrounded by the utter rightness of being near her and to spend the rest of his life with her.

His breath unraveled slowly. He had written it, drawn it . . . and now he felt it. Love at first sight. From the moment he had looked up in that crowded lobby and seen her smile, he had been lost for all time. "Gwyn," he said softly as he came up behind her.

She turned and smiled as he pulled her into his arms. She softly rested her hands on his chest. "What?" she asked.

"Nothing, I just wanted to touch you." He heard the doorbell and smiled. "Dinner has arrived." He released her and headed for the door, leaving her to light the candles and wonder what he had arranged.

When he returned, she took one look at the pizza box and burst into laughter. He grinned and served them both slices. "I knew you'd appreciate the humor."

"Twenty minutes is pretty quick, I must say."

"Little place down the road. They deliver within fifteen if you live within three blocks. They have a branch near my apartment." He held her chair for her until she sat down. "You're one in a million." He moved his chair closer and sat down beside her.

"A good thing for the world. Two of me would be frightening." She watched him without shame, admiring the lines of his face and the color of his eyes. "Well, you know all about my sordid family history. What about you? Do your parents live in NYC?" He went very still, something painful and cold moving in his eyes, and her smile faded. "I'm sorry," she said quietly. "It's none of my business." She reached for another slice of pizza. "Tell me about your company instead."

His hand closed over her wrist and he drew her fingers to his lips. "No, I can tell you. It's just hard. Painful." He closed his eyes. "I've never told anyone else what I'm about to tell you. I trust you, Gwyn."

"Don't if it hurts you," she countered. She smiled. "You don't have to tell me anything you don't want to."

He searched her face in wonder. She would accept him as he was, never asking for details. Yet, somehow, the clarity in her eyes and the unwavering sense of rightness drew the story out of him like the morning drew the sunrise. He *had* to tell her. She would understand. Any judgment she passed would be the final one. "I *need* to tell you. You're important to me. I don't want there to be secrets between us."

A soft glow filled her. "Alright. Start at the beginning."

He released her and got to his feet to lean on the balcony. It was easier to tell the story if he wasn't looking at her. "I killed my parents." The words came out starkly and unembellished. "In self-defense because they were making a damned hard effort to kill me first." He blew out a hard breath. "I had a best friend once. We were inseparable. When we were fifteen, he got himself into drugs. It began to destroy his life. It was tearing me up. So I went to my parents for help. They asked if my friend had said anything about a supplier. Since I fully expected them to stop him, I told them where the meet was and that I had already called the cops." His voice grew even quieter. "They found his body the next morning. An overdose."

Her hands curled into fists in her lap. In her mind, her scales silently measured every detail. "I see." She kept her voice even with effort.

He laughed sadly. "Yeah. You probably do. Hindsight makes it obvious to me too."

"And?"

"I went to my parents and demanded to know why they hadn't stopped him. They didn't even make excuses. They just looked at me like I was an idiot. Where did I think their money came from? Selling drugs was just a nice, lucrative side business. And they expected me to keep quiet. As if it hadn't just killed my friend. As if *they* hadn't just killed him. I threatened to go to the police."

"And they tried to kill you, too." It wasn't a question. She got to her feet, her arms wrapped tightly around herself.

"My father had a gun. We fought over it. In the struggle, the gun went off and killed my mother. My father went a little ballistic. He came after me again. I got my hands on a statue. Somehow I managed to hit him before he shot me in the head. It wasn't until the cops arrived that I realized I had already been shot." He rubbed a hand over his shoulder. "It was ruled self-defense."

"As it should have been."

The fierceness in her voice had him turning quickly. She was staring at the moon, tears sliding down her cheeks. "Gwyn." It was all he could say.

"Were you supposed to roll over and die? You have nothing to be ashamed of."

"It doesn't feel that way. I suppose I'll be judged when I go to hell." He made a startled sound as she turned and grabbed his arm. She stared up at him with burning gray eyes. Lightning churned in their depths and he felt an inner recognition of the power inside her. He didn't question it.

"There is no heaven and hell," she told him. "Judgment is done your entire life. The scales tip one way or another. Hear me now, Taylor Vincent, this *is not a sin*. It was justice, and you were the weapon wielded for it."

A shiver went down his back. Her inner conviction convinced him when nothing else could. He lifted a hand and cupped her cheek warmly. "I didn't expect that," he murmured. "You're so gentle inside . . . I was sure you would be disgusted."

"I am." Her eyes returned to normal and she seemed unaware of what she had done. "By their actions." She went into his arms and held onto him tightly. "No parent should ever do anything like that."

"I agree." He closed his arms around her and savored how she felt. "I didn't mean to dump all of that on you," he sighed. "Hell of a thing to say on a first date."

She rubbed her cheek against his chest softly. "I was nearly killed, and you have a tragic past. I think we can call ourselves even. Next time we need to do something tame. You know, like bungee jumping or sky diving."

He laughed at that and slowly released her. They took their seats once more, and they deliberately kept the conversation light as they made their way through the pizza. A lively game of Twenty Questions outted him as a fan of ballet and her as having a cast iron stomach—she had drunk the infamous Coke and milk combination and lived to tell the tale.

It was only when a clock chimed in the distance that they realized it was very late. Their eyes met across the table. His entire body knotted with desire as he envisioned simply picking her up and carrying her to the bedroom. The image was so powerful that his hands lifted before he could stop them. He forced himself to put them down again. "Well. I should go. We can try the restaurant next time."

"Okay." Even she could hear the breathless note to her voice. It just disappointed her that the night had to end at all. At least there would be another. That was something to cling to. "Good night," she said softly as they reached the door.

She started to reach for the knob and he caught her wrist. "We've had our date." His voice was nothing more than a rasp of male hunger. Her entire damned family could have walked up and he wouldn't have cared. He *had* to taste her. "Let me kiss you, Gwyn."

She shivered at the sound of his voice and went into his arms eagerly. She couldn't deny him, not when she needed him just as badly. She went up on her toes and met his kiss halfway, and her arms fiercely coiled around his neck. A wonderful shiver went through her entire body as his hands curved around her hips and dragged her tighter against him.

She tasted like a snow cone, fresh and pure but sweet all at the same time. It was addicting. He slanted his head, parting her lips and gliding his tongue into her mouth. The little purring sound of delight that she made went right to his head. The kiss went wild, and he backed her against the wall as his mouth devoured hers. Her hands fisted into his hair, and she twisted against him. A desperate moan coming from her throat as fire burst in her blood and tore through her body like an inferno. She was going to die if he didn't make love to her. Soon. Now. Before she went out of her mind.

When her body arched against his, he realized that things were getting out of hand. If he didn't let her go now, he wouldn't let her go at all. He forced himself to release her and took a healthy step back. Looking at her didn't help any. She was flushed and wild, just as affected by the kiss as he was. Naked desire burned in her eyes. He lifted a shaking hand and traced the line of her swollen lips.

"Stay with me."

The breathless words against his finger tore at his control. He held on fiercely and made himself lift his hand and step back again. "No. But when this is done," he added huskily, "I will take you away somewhere and throw away the key. I won't embarrass you by getting involved with you now while you work for me. I have too much respect for the work you do. I won't see your reputation ruined."

She watched the door shut behind him and slowly lowered herself down to sit on the floor. She was shaking from the inside out, so empty and aching that it hurt. By the time the project was done, it might be too late. Her hand lowered and touched her hip. She was marked for death, and someone was finally making an attempt to kill her. Unless she was careful, she would die before she ever got a chance to know what it truly meant to be complete. She didn't want Taylor to lose someone else he cared for. Never again.

CHAPTER ELEVEN

Because she knew that she didn't dare keep things a secret, she went to her brothers' home the next morning. Everyone was there and hadn't yet headed out to the site for work. She had a key to the front door still, just like they all had keys to her apartment. She walked right in and into the living room where everyone was gathered.

Seven pairs of eyes lifted, studied her, and seven faces winced. She sighed. She knew what she looked like. "I didn't sleep, okay? He was an absolute gentleman."

"Damn him," Owen said, his voice deadpan.

"Tell me about it!" The frustration leaked into her voice. "He doesn't want to risk my reputation on us being involved while I work for him." She raked a hand through her unruly hair. "But that's not why I'm here." She put down the paper bag holding the remains of the nearly deadly comb. "Someone tried to kill me last night. This comb was sent to me anonymously. If Taylor hadn't been there . . ." She shuddered.

Almost as one, her brothers went off in fury. Joseff and Gavin began to curse rather creatively. Tomos went into a near panic while Seisyll tried to get him to calm down and think straight. Arian and Heul began to argue over the next course of action. And, as always, Owen was the calm, the center of it all.

He sidled over to the couch as Gwyn sat down and tucked her legs under herself. He sat down beside her and wrapped a hand around her ankle. He could calm people through a single touch and used it shamelessly when needed. "So," he said quietly, "want to tell me more about our client?"

She felt her color rise. She was assuming he didn't really want to know about the rather interesting dreams she'd had the night before. She cleared her throat. "Be specific."

"Don't be evasive." He studied her. "I know you care for him, but are you sure he's not behind it?"

"I'm sure." She closed her eyes as silence fell in the room. "I'm sure," she said again. "He's capable of killing. I know it. But . . ." She wrapped her arms around herself. "He treats me kindly and with respect. If he was out to seduce and kill me, he wouldn't have walked away last night, even when I asked him to stay."

"Gwyn," Arian began but stopped when Heul held up a hand.

She didn't notice. "All my life there's been something missing inside me," she whispered. "Not just my memories, but something else. Somehow . . . somehow . . . if I had never met Taylor . . . I know I would have died. I don't think he's going to kill me. I think he's the only one who can save me."

Heul walked over and knelt down to study her face. She did not lie and she had an unfailing sense of right and wrong. What she said was always the truth. "Regardless," he told her quietly, "of whether or not he can, I want you to be extremely careful. Do not accept strange gifts from anyone. Don't go out at night alone. You've been marked for death since you were a child. Until that mark is gone, don't let down your guard."

"What is she going to tell Taylor when he sees it?" Tomos finally spoke up.

Heul coughed lightly. Thinking about Taylor Vincent having his baby sister naked was not a favored pastime. "Well, he's not 3rd District. No need to explain unless necessary. Let him think it's a tattoo."

"I can't lie," Gwyn reminded her brothers.

"Well, hell." Gavin shrugged wryly. "Make sure the lights are off when you jump him."

"Gavin!"

"Whaaat?"

She just sighed and got to her feet. "You guys duke it out. I'm going to head to my office onsite." She glared at them. "Since you guys won't actually let me visit, I have to settle for watching through a window."

The men watched her go and shared a long look. How were they supposed to explain that the piling cord had been cut through, and that the construction sites were walking accident zones? It would be all too horribly easy to kill someone there, especially someone as trusting as Gwyn.

Because it was summertime, the streets of the District were lined with vendors who had set their wares outside. Gwyn loved walking through and looking at the different clothing and items. She rarely bought anything because it was rare to find something she liked well enough to splurge on.

Today was an exception. As she rounded a corner, she saw a rack of laced bodices for sale. The bodices were like something out of the Renaissance, and there was one in the same golden yellow of the dress Taylor had bought her. It had white ribbons to tie it in the back, and there was a small lace ruffle around the bottom edge.

Delighted, she took it off the rack and held it in front of her body. She could almost imagine Taylor's face when he saw her in it, and her stomach quivered with anticipation. She wondered if she would actually have the nerve to seduce him. What if she tried that and maybe he really didn't want her and was just stringing her along?

No, not Taylor. It was probably just that he wasn't emotionally involved despite his tenderness and respect. She wasn't so innocent that she could mistake that he truly wanted her, and he also genuinely liked her. She could work with that. Determinedly, she carried the bodice into the store to buy it.

The store, she saw then, also carried lingerie. She debated with herself for long moments before impulsively buying a matching set of underwear and bra to go under the bodice, and a white sundress she picked out to match it. It was an indulgence but, damn it, someone was trying to kill her, so she was entitled to splurge on pretty clothes to entice the man she wanted to be her lover.

By the time she got to the trailer that was her office, she couldn't resist the temptation. She hurried over to her window and shut the blinds so that no one onsite could see her, especially her brothers. She didn't want them to tease her again, and they always teased her when she was 'acting like *such* a girl.'

She shut her office door as well and then pulled out her packages again. She felt horribly decadent and scandalous as she tried on the lace lingerie and pulled the sundress on. She tugged the bodice on over it and liked the look so much she spun in a giddy circle.

The laces in the back were hard to tie but she managed to tighten them just enough that it enhanced her figure without cutting off her air. Looking down, she blushed. Maybe a shirt would have been better because the sundress wasn't covering as much of her cleavage as she would have liked. Good grief, she actually *had* cleavage. She had never really thought of herself as having too much of a bust, but the bodice was making a big show out of what she did have.

An odd smell drifted into the office and she wrinkled her nose as she hurried over to shut the window. The door opened without warning, and she started to turn to see who had walked in unannounced. Whoever had walked in was right behind her, and they grabbed the laces of her bodice and viciously jerked them closed.

The material constricted her lungs and cut off her air as she tried to turn around to get a hold of the person attacking her. Spots swam in front of her eyes and her vision began to gray out. She gasped for air and felt the laces tighten even more as she staggered. Even as darkness swamped her mind, her lungs burning and pained, her mind screamed for Taylor. He could save her. She knew he could!

He walked into the office a second later, saying, "I had a feeling you would be here. I thought I might as well bring you flowers since I forgot the ones last night and . . ." His voice stopped abruptly as he saw her on the floor near the window. The flowers fell from his hand as he rushed across the room. "Gwyn!"

He could see immediately what was wrong and yanked the letter opener off the desk to slice through the laces. The bodice opened and he beat lightly on her back. She sucked in a breath sharply and began to cough as her starved lungs pulled in air. His hands shaking, he drew her closer. Terror choked his throat. "What the hell were you doing?" he demanded roughly. "Lacing yourself in so tightly!"

"I . . ." She began to cough again, her entire body shaking as shock set in. "I didn't do it," she managed to say. "Someone . . . someone attacked me." On a surge of terror, she threw her arms around his neck. "Oh god! Taylor, someone's trying to kill me!"

"What?!" He jerked her back by the shoulders and searched her eyes. "Are you sure it wasn't just a prank gone too far?"

Tears slid down her cheeks. "No." She caught his hand and drew it up to rest on her hip under her skirt. He felt the little raised checkmark and confusion filled in his eyes. "I'm marked for death," she whispered. "Someone contracted for me to die. It's not an accident."

"Jesus." He caught her closer again as horror flooded him. If he hadn't been so certain he heard her calling . . . if his hands hadn't been burning in the way that always meant danger was near . . . he would have lost her. His faerie princess. "You have to go away," he ordered roughly.

"I can't!" She looked at him fiercely. "I won't run away!"

"The hell you won't!" He got to his feet and lifted her into his arms in one single motion. He plunked her down on the edge of her desk and planted his hands on either side of her hips. "I'm not risking you dying!" he barked.

"I'm willing to risk it!"

"I'm not!" He snatched up her phone and began to punch numbers. The operator answered and he ordered, "Connect me to the number for Enforcers." Gwyn looked at him in shock, and he glared at her intently, daring her to argue. When the phone was picked up, he said, "My name is Taylor Vincent. A woman I know is marked for death and she's from 3ʳᵈ District."

There was a startled pause before Rhianna said slowly, "Her name?"

"Gwyn Trahern of Driven Snow Architecture. She's twenty-six years old. White hair, storm gray eyes. About five feet tall, one hundred pounds."

"Five-one! And I weigh one-ten, thank you!" Gwyn crossed her arms tightly.

"And a stubborn streak a mile wide," he added. "Someone is trying to kill her. Someone sent her a comb yesterday that not only spewed blades at us, but also exploded on impact. Just now someone attacked her in her office and tried to suffocate her by lacing her too tightly into a bodice."

Rhianna began to have a very strong feeling in the pit of her stomach and made a note to call Eric and Rayna as soon as possible. She had been suspicious about Gwyn Trahern from the moment the family had moved back into the District. "This is important," she told him, "so answer carefully. Who are her parents?"

"She doesn't know. She has amnesia. No memories before she was nine." His brows shot up. "You know her."

"Guard her *closely,* Taylor. I'm going to send my partner and his wife out to meet you tomorrow. I can't get them there any sooner. Do NOT let Gwyn Trahern out of your sight!"

"Understood." He hung up the phone and gave Gwyn a pointed look. "You're not to be out of my sight, and Ms. Taber is sending out an Enforcer tomorrow to look into things. In the meantime, you're coming home with me."

"I can't do that!" She muffled a shriek as he scooped her up off the desk and tossed her over his shoulder. "Put me down!"

Mortified color climbed her cheeks as they left the office and she saw her brothers gaping at them. "Taylor!" she wailed. "Have pity!"

He spotted Heul and figured he had to be the eldest since he was certainly the biggest. "I'm taking your sister somewhere safe. Someone is trying to kill her, and I'll be damned before I let it happen. Enforcers will be out tomorrow."

Heul cleared his throat and decided not to say anything. He recognized a very furious and very frustrated male. In that moment, he had no doubt that Taylor was as far in over his head as Gwyn. He watched Taylor put Gwyn into his car, kicking the entire way, and covered a laugh.

Joseff swung down to his level by hanging upside down from a support beam by his ankles. "Did he do what I think he did?" he asked in awe.

"Kidnap your twin? Yes, yes he did." Damned if he couldn't like Taylor for it, he thought in bemusement. Gwyn was kind and gentle, yes, but she had a stubborn streak a mile wide. It was impossible to say no to her, just as it was impossible to make her change her mind. Taylor had just done both.

Gwyn sat in mutinous silence as Taylor drove. She was too upset to even look at him. He was no less upset; in fact, he was furious she had not told him what was going on. It was only when the car slowed and pulled into a driveway that she finally began to pay attention. It was an apartment complex in an upscale part of Brooklyn, and she blinked in confusion. "Where are we?" she asked warily.

"My place." He pulled her out of the car and kept an arm around her waist as they went into the building. He didn't quite trust her not to run away from him.

"This is a bad idea," she whispered. She wasn't sure she could trust herself to be alone with him. She loved him too badly. Wanted him more than she wanted air, and she had just learned how precious air really was.

"Tough." He unlocked his apartment and ushered her inside.

He locked the door behind them again and then tossed his jacket over the back of a chair. "This is the only place I figure I can successfully keep a faerie princess, with no self-preservation skills, safe!"

"Thanks a lot!" She poked him in the chest. "Look, wise *soldier*, I'm not going to hide away! It's not right!"

"Right! Not right she says!" He caught her chin in his fingers and tilted her face back so she was forced to look at him. "It's not right either," he ground out, "that I had to find out about your death sentence by walking into your office and seeing you on the floor!"

The truth of his words felt like a physical blow, and she closed her eyes helplessly. "I know," she whispered. "But I didn't know how you'd accept it. I was sure you would back off, and I couldn't bear the idea."

"Back off?" He gave a rough laugh and caught her in his arms. "It's way too late for me to back off now. It was too late when I hired you."

"Then why did you leave me?" she demanded, furious tears burning her eyes. "If I'm going to die, I don't want to die a virgin, never knowing what it means to give myself to the man I love! Oops!" She covered her mouth with her hands, shocked she had just blurted it out.

He went very still. In a faint voice, he said, "I left you because I would be damned if I embarrassed you by making you get involved with a client."

"It's stupid!" she snapped at him. She pushed herself out of his arms. "It's not *right!*"

"No, it's not." His hand closed around the nape of her neck and yanked her against his aching body. "You're fired." Before she could protest, his mouth had come down on hers with an almost bruising force that demanded she hold nothing back.

A shudder went through her body and she stopped struggling to get away, instead throwing herself into his embrace with a wild abandon that made his head spin. The kiss deepened, went wilder and wilder, and he finally just lifted her into his arms and began to stride down the hall.

She didn't help his self-control any by racing hungry kisses over his face. She couldn't get enough of his taste. She felt as if she was starved for him. He dropped her onto her feet beside the bed and kissed her again, his hands quickly stripping the ruined bodice aside and hurling it behind him somewhere. She quickly unbuttoned his shirt and yanked it out of his jeans, just as desperate for more as he was. Why did it feel as if she had been waiting for centuries?

He trembled as her hands spread across his chest. The storm in her eyes had been unleashed and it was drowning them both. He dragged her closer and buried his lips against her throat to taste her pulse. She whimpered low in her throat as his arousal pressed against her stomach, and she went on her toes to hold him closer. "Please," she managed to whisper.

"I'll please you. Nothing's going to stop me." He lifted his head long enough to get a handful of her sundress and strip it up over her head. His mouth went dry. Little scraps of golden lace did amazing things to an already, impossibly, perfect body. "Holy hell."

She laughed suddenly, her voice husky with feminine power. "I was hoping you'd approve. I felt so . . . so sneaky when I bought it. It seemed like a trap or something."

"It worked," he managed to say. "Good god." He eagerly drew her into his arms, his lips seeking hers again. She arched her body against his and it took all of his control to not tumble her onto the floor and take her where they stood.

The room whirled around her head. She gasped as she landed on the bed and his weight sank her into the mattress. His hot hand cupped her breast, and she moaned softly as pleasure streaked from the contact all through her body. Before she could catch a breath, he opened the front clasp on the bra and his palm softly caressed her bare flesh.

She felt like silk and fire. He ran wild kisses over her neck and shoulders and moved steadily lower. He couldn't get enough of her taste and closed his lips over one nipple to suckle sharply. Her back arched on a wild cry and he caught her there, holding her as tightly as he could. Ravenous, he devoured her flesh and raked his lips down across her stomach.

"Taylor," she pleaded, terrified of how high he was pushing her senses. Her voice became a strangled gasp as his fingers slid between her legs and found her softest flesh. He caressed her until she couldn't breathe for the tension consuming her.

"Go higher," he muttered against her throat. He shuddered as he felt how hot and wet she was even through her underwear. He wanted to dive into her, to take her so completely they were one. He stripped the scrap of lace down her legs and lifted his head to survey her naked body with savage satisfaction. "You're mine," he vowed softly.

She opened her mouth to answer but his fingers moved on her bare flesh and she couldn't think, let alone speak. She clung desperately to him and twisted her body against his touch, begging for an end to the ceaseless pleasure. "Taylor!"

His lips closed over the point of one breast just as his thumb pressed against the bundle of nerves at the apex of her thighs. Her entire body jerked in shock and then came apart, wild pleasure washing over her. When the spasms finally ended, she opened her eyes to see him watching her with rapt attention.

His mouth covered hers and she went into the kiss eagerly, a shiver rippling through her body as that alone awoke desire once more. With a rough sound, he forced himself to release her, and stood long enough to quickly shed his clothes. She reached for him as he joined her again, and there was no hesitation in her touch, no shyness, as if she knew this was right. Somehow, he did too.

"I want to touch you," she whispered against his lips when he lifted his head slightly. "I want to know everything."

"Later," he promised, his hands sliding over her flesh.

"Now." She twisted her body and caught him off guard, allowing her to tumble him onto his back. She had him pinned before he could move, and her lips made hot forays across his skin. He shuddered. She smiled, delighted with the knowledge that she could overpower him. She watched her hand gliding over his muscled stomach and trembled with emotion. "I love you," she whispered as she pressed her lips to his shoulder.

She was wild as fire, her hands and lips caressing him hotly. There was only the slightest hesitation in her touch as she curled her hand around his erection to learn the feel of him. He bit back a hoarse groan, and she closed her lips over one flat, male nipple.

His control snapped with a nearly audible sound. One hand fisted into her hair, and he dragged her higher up so he could kiss her greedily. A little sound of pleasure issued from her throat. He rolled and tucked her underneath him desperately. The feel of bare skin against bare skin brought a brief moment of sanity. He caught her face in his hands. "Do you need me to protect you?" he asked roughly.

She shook her head quickly. He didn't know if that meant she was on birth control or simply trusted him, but he didn't care. He knew she had understood the question and all of its potential outcomes. He dragged her legs up and over his arms, opening her to him. "Let me have you," he pleaded, lifting his lips slightly.

"Yes." Her instinctive fear at being so vulnerable was drowned in a searing wave of fire. "Please!" Her breath caught as his hard flesh began to stretch her, and her body tried to adjust to the movement. It ached rather than hurt, but she couldn't bear the idea of him stopping. Her hips arched wildly in an effort to take him, and he shuddered and drove into her completely.

He went still and gulped air as he tried to let her adjust. He would be damned if he hurt her now. His lips raced over her face and caught the trace of tears. He nearly started to pull away but her grip tightened, and her lips found his. She clung on desperately and twisted her body against his to prove she was fine. It was all he needed to know. He began to drive into her again and again, and her breathless cries branded his heart.

The only ache she could feel was the one built from relentless pleasure demanding release. His fingers found some sensitive place along her spine, and it lit up every nerve in her body. Only his hungry kiss kept her cry of ecstasy from escaping out the open window, and her lips equally stole his hoarse groan as he, too, surrendered to the pleasure. Her arms tightened around him fiercely as if afraid he would be torn away from her now that she had claimed him.

He had enough presence of mind to catch his weight on his arms, but that was all he could manage as he kept her locked securely in his arms beneath him. He felt stunned and shaken all the way to his core. He had, in his life, experienced both sex and making love. This didn't seem to be either of those two things. It went far, far beyond the physical and into something damn near spiritual. Magical. It could only grow stronger with time.

He lifted his head and stared at her as he memorized her features. "Gwyn." Her eyes opened and she looked up at him with a questioning look on her face. He gently cupped her cheek and touched her lips with his. "I love you." Her eyes widened, and he eased back with a smile. "I knew it yesterday. How could I not? The faerie princess of my dreams landed in my arms."

Tears burned her eyes and she closed them as her lips trembled. "You fired me, you bully."

"Yes, well, I was desperate." His lips glided over her face and stole her tears. "At that point I'd have done anything to have you. There was no way I'd be able to keep my hands off you, not after your confession." He smiled at her. "How about telling me now? Really telling me, instead of blurting it out in anger."

"It's your fault." She flushed slightly. "You kidnapped me!" On a groan, she covered her face with a hand. "I'll never be able to face my brothers again." He laughed at her and she glowered. She resembled a disgruntled faerie so much that he had to kiss her. When he lifted his head again, she searched his face with an inner hunger she could not fight. "I love you," she whispered.

He trembled slightly and held her closer. "Let me keep you

safe," he said into her hair.

"I will not stay cooped up." Her chin set into a stubborn line.

"Then come with me to the office tomorrow." He grinned slightly. "I'll get you to actually model for me." When she blinked, he freed himself from her arms and left the bed to go to his desk.

She admired him without shame, thrilling to the idea of being able to touch him as she pleased. She was startled out of her admiration when he dropped a folder on her stomach. "Oof." She sat up and curiously dumped the folder open. Images spilled across the sheets, and her breath caught.

It was her. He had drawn her as the faerie princess for his game. Her heart swelled with emotion. "I'm not this beautiful," she whispered. "And I don't have wings. And I can't cast magic."

He laughed softly. "Neither can she." He skimmed his fingers through her hair. "I knew, when I saw you, that you were my faerie princess. And like my soldier, I'll do whatever it takes to keep you safe." He drew her into his arms and closed his eyes, his heart tightening with a rush of emotion as she curled trustingly against him. Come hell or high water, he would keep her safe if it was the last thing he ever did.

CHAPTER TWELVE

The day passed in a blur. What little time they didn't spend in bed, they spent either eating together or watching movies on the giant flat screen television that Taylor called his guilty pleasure. Gwyn cooked dinner for them, and after one bite, he informed her that he would be her willing slave if she cooked for him like that all the time.

Through it all, there was a growing suspicion in her mind. He would answer questions before she asked them. If she was thinking his name, he would answer as if she had spoken out loud. He somehow knew when a vase was about to fall on her and moved her out of the way well before it toppled.

If the man wasn't psychic, she was going to eat her hat. Power recognized power and having spent a significant amount of time as physically close to him as a woman could get, she was definitely recognizing the presence of power.

It wasn't until the next morning when she finally decided it was time to bring it up. They were lying together and listening to the sound and scent of a summer rain. She was sprawled over his chest, limp with contented pleasure. With her ear pressed against his chest, she could hear his heartbeat slowly steadying. She really didn't want to go to the office.

"Me neither," he murmured drowsily, his voice as lazy with satisfaction as her body felt.

She contemplated her words for a moment. "I didn't say anything."

"Yes, you did."

"Did not." It wasn't the first time they'd had the exact same conversation. She propped herself up on an elbow and studied her lover's face. "Taylor," she said calmly, "have you ever considered the idea that you might be, shall we say, psychic?"

That got his eyes open quick. He eyed her intently. "Pardon me?"

"You hear me when I don't speak. Your hands burn when there's danger. I *know* you subconsciously heard me when I called your name yesterday. I hate to tell you, but normal people don't do that." She smiled. "Am I missing anything on the list?" He hesitated and she tugged on a lock of his chest hair. "Talk, Taylor."

"Ouch. Brat." He snuggled her closer. "I guess strange things have always happened. Ever since my parents died, I've noticed odd things. Sometimes catching snippets of conversations from other rooms. Picking up on wayward thoughts. The burning hands thing is the big one. When it's directed at someone I know, it's nearly unbearable."

She hesitated. Slowly she asked, "Have you ever sweated blood?"

"Yes," he said warily. "Under extreme pressure. Why?"

She winced. "There's an ability. It's called a Plasma Sense. It's one of the more unnerving abilities to possess. It, uhm, is essentially an early warning system built directly into your blood. That burning in your hands, it's your blood burning. If you ever fully tap your power your hands might be covered with blood as your body tries to send you the warning."

"How useful is that?" he asked on a grimace.

"I'm not sure," she admitted. "The only person I know who had it said that when she looked at her hands, she just *knew* who it was in danger and where they were."

"Pleasant." He blew out a breath. He knew full well that she couldn't tell a lie. Whatever she said, she believed to be true. "What about the telepathy?" It was easier to say than he had thought it would be.

"Most people with power have some sort of mental strength. Since yours is strongest with me, it'll probably never, actually, interfere with your life." She nuzzled his shoulder softly, her simple delight in touching him squeezing his heart. "I don't really know what my own abilities are," she admitted. "But I'm not scared of them now. You'll protect me."

Her honest and innocent trust made him break out in a sweat. "Why are your brothers sane?" he muttered.

"Hey."

"Damn it, woman, you trust too easily!"

"If I waste my time distrusting everyone, then I waste the opportunity to know new people and learn new things." She shrugged one shoulder. "And I'm a good judge of character. The problem with most adults is that they learn to be cynical."

"It's safer."

"It's stupid." She cuddled closer. "If I'd been distrusting of you, we wouldn't be here, you know."

"I'd argue that." He skimmed his hands over her back. "We might not be here right now, but we'd eventually have been here. I wanted you the minute I saw you. I still want you." His fingers slid slowly between her legs and her breath caught. "You respond like you were made for me," he murmured huskily. "Are you too sore to take me again?"

"Yes," she whispered. "Damn it." She made a startled sound and held on as he lifted her into his arms and got to his feet. She almost asked where they were going, but she saw he was heading for the bathroom so assumed it was the shower. She blushed. She was never looking at a shower the same again, not after his idea of washing her.

He gently put her on her feet and ran water in the tub. He smiled. "You take a bath and soak some of the soreness out. I'll make some breakfast."

She eyed him balefully. "Can you cook?"

"Yes, princess." He tweaked her nose lightly. "Not like your gourmet self, but I can cook." He was beginning to understand why her brothers had fought to keep her from moving out. Dear god, the woman could put professionals to shame with her cooking.

"Okay." She sank into the tub on a little wince as he left the room, and then closed her eyes and tilted her head back. She felt just a little sore, but it was understandable, she thought impishly. As demanding as his passion was, hers more than matched it. "So that's why waiting makes it worth it," she murmured to herself

She lingered for a long while until she noticed her fingers wrinkling. Contented, and less sore, she got out of the tub. She could smell bacon and eggs even from the bathroom. She wrapped herself in Taylor's robe and just sighed as the sleeves flopped well past her hands. She cuffed them several times to find her hands again, and she had to hold the bottom, like the train of a skirt, in order to walk safely.

He took one look at her and burst into laughter. She wrinkled her nose. "So I'm tiny. It's not a crime."

"No, but it's cute as hell." He helped her to her seat and bowed deeply. "My lady." She swatted at him and he grinned as he went to get their food. "I like spoiling you," he decided as he sat beside her. "I keep trying to give you flowers, too."

She smiled shyly. "I don't need to be spoiled. I just need you. That's enough to make me happy." She took a bite of her food. A smile tugged at her lips. "You burned the toast."

"Then you make breakfast from now on," he answered casually.

Her heart gave a wild leap of joy that she didn't bother to temper. Riding with it, she threw her arms around him and almost knocked them both over. "Does that mean I can stay with you longer? Sort of . . . live with you?"

"No." He framed her face with his hand. "Gwyn, I don't want you to just move in. I want . . ." He broke off as the phone rang. "Well, hell. Wait here."

She watched him go to the phone, giddy delight in her heart. Was he going to ask her to marry him? She hoped so! She would ask her brothers to give her away, and Joseff could be her maid of honor. Or something like that. Male of honor? Was there a proper term? The best man was for the groom. Brother of honor, maybe.

He hung up the phone and looked at her, his face set. "That was the office. They just got a call that an Enforcer has contacted them and will be there within the hour. We should be there to meet them."

"Okay." She got to her feet and started to clear the table when he touched her cheek and drew her gaze. "Yes?"

"When this is over, we'll talk again," he murmured softly. "Promise."

A warm glow filled her. "Okay." The glow stayed with her the entire way to the office, and it was visible to everyone who looked at her. There wasn't a single person there who doubted she and Taylor were lovers. There also wasn't a single person who doubted that that was the way it should be. Something just always seemed to be right about Gwyn. She didn't judge anyone, so why judge her?

Melissa seemed to have come to a similar feeling because she was waiting outside Taylor's office for them. "Miss Trahern," she said hesitantly, "may I talk to you? I want to apologize. Maybe we could go to the cafeteria or something?"

Gwyn could never carry a grudge. She smiled. "Of course." Taylor smiled at her, and she knew he was fine with it as long as she didn't leave the building. She fell into step beside Melissa. "You don't need to explain or anything," she told her. "It's just nice that you don't hate me anymore."

"It was jealousy!" Melissa lightly waved a ringed hand as they sat down in the cafeteria. There was no one else there but the cleaning men and they were sharing a cup of coffee. "I was horribly jealous of you," she admitted.

"Me?!" Gwyn stared at her in shock. "But, why?"

"I'd been working on getting Taylor to notice me for years, and

he was oblivious. You came in and he was worse than a tomcat who caught the scent of a female in heat." She leaned back with a smile as Gwyn coughed and blushed. "Sorry."

"It's okay." Gwyn smiled. "I'm just glad everything's okay now."

"Me, too. Hey, you hungry? I interrupted your breakfast this morning, didn't I?" When Gwyn waved a hand as if to say it didn't matter, she smiled. "Well, I want a snack. Sure you don't want an apple or something?"

Feeling it would be rude to decline, Gwyn nodded with a smile. "Sure." She watched Melissa go to the counter and get two apples and felt a sense of relief that she was going to be able to get along with Taylor's assistant. "I was worried," she admitted as she took the apple and bit in. "I mean, Taylor and I seem to be getting pretty serious. I wanted to be your friend first."

Melissa nibbled at her own apple. "You're such a good person."

A sudden dizziness hit Gwyn. Her head began to spin and the room tilted like a funhouse. She tried to lift a hand to her forehead, but her muscles were growing heavy. Her entire body was starting to feel like dead weight. She tried to get to her feet, but it was almost impossible to move. She fell to her knees, the scales in her mind tilting wildly. "You," she managed to say. "You drugged me."

Melissa caught her by her hair and dragged her head back. "You're such a good person," she repeated with a sneer in her voice. "Too good. Friends? What a laugh. We'll never be friends, little girl, and once you're dead everything will go back to normal. I'll be the most beautiful woman in the company and Taylor will come to be mine."

Gwyn managed to look up into her eyes and pity filled her heart. "I'm sorry," she whispered.

"What for?"

"That you're so empty inside."

She slumped over and Melissa released her in fury. The two cleaners approached quickly and she snapped at them, "Take her somewhere she won't be found! Preferably somewhere I can be sure she won't wake up!"

His hands were burning. Taylor lifted them and stared at them. They had been at it for the last five minutes, and it was steadily growing in force. His skin felt as if it was on fire. Someone knocked on the door, and he looked up quickly. "Yes?"

The door opened and he got to his feet as a tall man with ash brown hair winged with white and a slender young woman with silvery hair entered. The woman bore such a powerful resemblance to Gwyn that he sucked in a sharp breath. They could have been twins; they looked that much alike. "My god," he managed to say. "Who the hell are you?"

"My name is Eric Mason." Eric gently placed a hand on Rayna's shoulder. "This is my wife, Rayna. We're from Enforcers. We're here about Gwyn Trahern." Taylor was still staring at Rayna in shock, and he felt his heart clench. "I take it Rayna resembles your Gwyn."

"Yes." Taylor sat down quickly. "My god," he said again. "You've got to be related to her." His eyes shot to Rayna's. "Were you ever marked for death too?"

"Yes." She lowered her gaze. "My sister and I both were. There was a car accident when I was four and she was nine. She was flung from the car just as I was, but no one ever found her. I didn't wake from my coma until a year ago."

"And you're safe now?" he demanded.

"Yes, because of her contract with Enforcers." Eric dropped a stack of paper on his desk. "Mika Carmichael's contract is still open. The event that was supposed to occur to save her life never happened. Until this contract is fulfilled, she will be at risk. Where is Gwyn now?"

"She went to lunch with my assistant."

Rayna stared at Taylor's hands. "Your hands are burning."

"Yes." He stared at her. "How did you know?"

"We can explain later," Eric said urgently. "Where is Gwyn?"

Taylor was beginning to feel more than a little panicked. When he heard a noise in the office beside his, his stomach clenched. "Melissa!" he barked. He went over to the office door connecting his area to hers and flung it open. She looked at him in alarm and he demanded, "Where is Gwyn?"

"I don't know!" She seemed taken aback by the sight of Rayna, almost as much as he had been. "What is going on?"

"Taylor," Eric urged as he grabbed the younger man's shoulder. "Think! If Gwyn is in immediate danger, you can know if you just open yourself up! You have a very powerful gift for being not of the District!" He narrowed an icy blue gaze on Melissa. "When did you leave Gwyn?"

"We had lunch and then she decided to go out for a bit. I haven't seen her for a while now. Geez, back off! I don't know what happened to her."

Rayna's head jerked toward Melissa. Horror filled her eyes. "Riku!"

Eric didn't hesitate. He lifted a hand and cast wind magic that flung Melissa into her chair and bound her. He didn't need to know what truth Rayna had heard to understand it had to be terrible.

Taylor was barely aware of what they were doing. He was concentrating fiercely on his burning blood. He didn't care what kind of power it was. He needed it. He needed it to save Gwyn. It was the only thing important to him. He could not lose her now!

"What did you do to Gwyn Trahern?" Eric demanded of Melissa.

"Nothing!"

"Lie." Rayna's voice sounded amazingly cold coming from a face so delicate and eyes so naturally giving. "She's trying to kill Gwyn." Her head tilted slightly. "Has *been* trying to kill Gwyn. Thrice attempted."

Melissa stared at her in growing horror as she realized the other woman could see through lies. She looked at Taylor for help and went pale as she saw blood beginning to cover his hands. "What is that?" she managed to whisper.

Taylor stared at the blood. It seemed almost like a projection screen. He could see glimpses of Gwyn's pale face in the red color. She was lying at the bottom of a hole with rain beating down on her. The view seemed to shift and he saw steel and concrete. His head jerked up as the blood disappeared. "I know where she is!"

"Go!" Eric snapped. "We'll stay here. For god's sake, Taylor, hurry!"

He wasted no time as he raced through the building, taking the stairs because the elevator would be too long. He drove faster than was legal but somehow didn't get stopped. Lights changed miraculously for him so that he made the trip in a quarter of the time. Even before the car was fully parked, he leapt out and ran for the site.

No one was there because of the rain. He ran toward the foundation and slid on the mud when he didn't step right. "Gwyn!" he shouted. "Gwyn! Answer me, Gwyn!"

Nothing came back but the sound of his own voice. He slid down into the foundation itself and headed for the four holes where the first structural beams would be placed. Cement spouts were poised over the holes and tarps thrown over the entire thing to keep out water and debris.

Terror choked him as he went to the first hole to yank up the tarp. Nothing. He found her lying at the bottom of the hole under the third one. She almost looked as if she was taking a nap. "Gwyn! Wake up!" There was no response and he looked around sharply. He found a ladder and used it to swiftly climb down into the hole.

His heart only started beating again when he heard her breathing, but it was shallow and she was pale. Cold. She was so cold to the touch. He dug out his cell phone and dialed 911, praying that he wasn't too late. Why wouldn't she wake up?

He discovered the extent of the Enforcers' power quickly. As soon as he mentioned Eric's name, the paramedics prepared to transport her to the Enforcers-owned hospital in the 3rd District. He rode along with them in the ambulance, his fingers desperately entwined with Gwyn's.

At the hospital, he was forced to remain behind as she was rushed into Emergency. He was only dimly aware of when Eric and Rayna arrived. He felt numbed and battered from the inside out. He couldn't say anything as Rayna took him to the waiting room and made him sit down. All he could do was stare blindly at the floor, not even conscious of her gently tucking a warm blanket around his shoulders.

When the Trahern brothers arrived, they rushed into the waiting room and came to sharp stops as they saw Rayna. "Holy hell," Seisyll managed to say. "There're two of them."

She glanced between him and his identical twin but didn't comment on the irony. "I'm Rayna Mason," she told them softly. "Sit down. Gwyn is in Emergency. Riku, that is, my husband, Eric, is with her. I'll tell you what I know, okay?"

Eric remained in Emergency with the doctors and oversaw everything. It came as no surprise to him that Gwyn had been drugged with the same insidious venom that had tried to take Rayna just a month before. It also came as no shock that Gwyn did not wake even after the venom was gone.

When she was moved to a regular room, he gently tried to reach out to her mind. Her brain waves were vastly different from the rest of the world, even among psychics. Like Rayna, she had a built-in defensive system designed to protect an exceptionally powerful mind from outside interference.

He couldn't get a lock on her. The only thing that he could be sure of was that her power was rising rampantly as it tried to find the power Rhianna and Eric emitted. Her contract was trying to fulfill itself, but with Rayna awake, the clause in Gwyn's contract that dictated the length of her coma was completely nulled.

It was the hardest thing he had ever done to walk into the lobby where Taylor and the Trahern brothers waited. All looked as if they had been devastated.

Taylor spotted him first. "Well?" he demanded roughly. "Why won't she wake up?"

Eric wrapped his arms around Rayna when she curled against his side comfortingly. "Seventeen years ago," he began, "Lucas Carmichael came to Enforcers to tell us that his daughters had Bloody Contracts issued against them for their deaths. Contracts were formed to try to negate the effects until the girls came of age. For Rayna, she entered a coma that was to last until her twenty-first birthday. Mika was to enter a coma during her twentieth year and awaken when Rayna did. Once awakened, their power would merge with the powers of the Enforcers and nullify the Bloody Contracts."

Eyes shifted to Rayna in sudden understanding. She nodded slowly. "Gwyn is my sister, Mika Carmichael." She bit her lower lip. "Things got out of control. I accidentally awakened too soon." She covered Eric's hands when he held her closer. "It took Riku a lot of effort to keep me alive until I was twenty-one. Once I was, my contract fulfilled. My Bloody Check disappeared."

Taylor took a quick breath. "So because your contract is completed and Gwyn's isn't, there are loose threads."

Eric looked at Joseff. "No matter how much you wanted to protect her, the minute you saved her from that accident six years ago, you threw everything off balance. She has gone along largely unawakened in power and that means there's nothing to merge with the Enforcers."

"So . . ." Heul swallowed hard. "So there's no telling when she might wake up. She *might* wake up in six years, because that's how long she should have slept, and yet she might not because the contract is partially voided."

"It could be six years, sixty years . . . or six hundred years." Eric lowered his gaze. "We're not gods. There are limits to what Rhianna and I can do. All I can say with certainty is that when she finally awakes, her contract will complete. Her power will join with Enforcers and her Bloody Contract will be nullified."

"Why were they targeted?!" Arian shouted as he leapt to his feet. "Why?! Why would anyone put a mark of death on two girls like Gwyn and Rayna?"

"That," Eric admitted, "is something only they can tell us. And unless Gwyn awakens, we may never know." He released his wife and walked over to where Taylor stared blindly at the wall across the room. "Taylor." When his gaze lifted, Eric said quietly, "I've been here. I know what you're going through. Wake Gwyn. You're the only one who can. She will answer if you call her. She has to. Your mind can tune itself to hers where no other can. Help her find her way back."

Taylor didn't know what he could possibly do, but he knew that he could not bear the idea of living without Gwyn. He painfully got to his feet and went down the hall toward the room where she was being held. The guards let him in, and he felt a punch of pain as he saw the stillness of her body. She looked like she was asleep, but it was worse. It was so much worse.

He drew the visitor's chair closer and reached out to take her hand in his and link their fingers together. He remembered the blood on his hands, and knew he would never fight his abilities again if it meant keeping her safe. He should never have ignored that burning sensation. "Gwyn." He watched her face for a sign of response. "If you can hear me, I'm so sorry." He closed his eyes. "I didn't do a good job of protecting you, faerie. You must hate me so much now."

There was no answer and he moved closer. He pressed her hand to his cheek. "You were right, you know. I am psychic. Scared the hell out of me when my hands were covered in blood, if only because I could see your face and what had been done to you. I went a little mad, I think, when I saw where you were.

"You have to come back to me, you know. How else will I propose to you? I was going to do that this morning but we were interrupted." He looked at the clock and laughed softly. "Okay, it was yesterday morning. It's after midnight now. But it's true. I want you to marry me, Gwyn. In three days you have become more important to me than anything."

He closed his eyes and pressed his lips to her hand. "Please, come back to me," he whispered. "I swear I'll do a better job of protecting you this time, Gwyn. Just trust me again, the way you did before." He stood and looked down at her, his free hand lifting to cup her cheek. "I love you. I'll love you until the end of time. Even if you never wake, I'll never love another. I'll wait for you, forever." He leaned down and touched her lips softly with his, pain almost choking him. He couldn't bear it! Three days before, he hadn't known her. Now, facing a future without her, it was like his worst hell. He couldn't live without her.

She drew a deep breath suddenly. He straightened in shock, hope rushing through him. "Gwyn?" he whispered.

Her eyes opened and she looked up at him with a shy smile on her face. "Good morning," she whispered back. "I heard you calling me. I felt you, in my mind. I couldn't stay away." Her arms lifted to curl around his neck as he gathered her close in his arms, and their lips met with almost desperate longing. The painful burn that had always lingered in her hip where the Bloody Check was located seemed to fade away. As if sensing it, his fingers slid down to her hip. "It's gone," she told him softly. "My contract is complete."

He straightened in shock. "How did you know?" He searched her eyes. "Is your memory back?"

"And then some." A soft note of steel echoed in her voice, that he had never heard before. "My memory is very, *very* old, Taylor." Her eyes met his. "Millennia old." She pressed her lips softly to his and then let him go. "Hold my hand and you will see. I'm going to link with my sister."

He gripped her hand tightly, though he was rightfully puzzled. He could see the rise in her power, and it was power that was fully under control. He could literally *see* her reaching for her sister's mind. And because he was linked to Gwyn, and Eric to Rayna, he could even see Eric's presence as a shadow in Rayna's mind.

Rayna, Gwyn called mentally, *link with me, little sister.*

Rayna's head jerked up and her eyes went unfocused. The violet color seemed to overtake her pupils until they disappeared. Power rose inside her so strongly that it crackled in the air. Eric held tightly to her hand, his mind's eye observing what was happening. The two erratic wavelengths of the sisters merged seamlessly . . . and fused.

At the same time, their heads fell back as a pair of tiny wings emerged from under their hair right behind their ears. Taylor didn't fully understand what he was seeing. Eric did. All the pieces fell into place as he finally understood the critical importance of Rayna and Gwyn's existence to the District and the world. He was already calling Rhianna mentally as he followed Rayna down the hall toward Gwyn's room.

"Gwyn!" Rayna burst into the room, rushed over to her sister's side, and threw her arms around her on a sob. "You scared me!"

Gwyn held her sister fiercely close. "I know." She began to sniffle too, her breath hitching on a sob. "Oh, Rayna, I missed you!" The pain bubbled out of nowhere on the heels of her memories. Her mother was dead. "Oh god," she whimpered. "She didn't deserve to die!"

Taylor felt helpless as he watched the two sisters grieve, and he looked at Eric as the older man tapped his shoulder. Eric inclined his head, and Taylor reluctantly followed him into the hall and closed the door.

The two women clung together as they shared their grief. After a few moments, Rayna finally eased back and looked up at her sister's face to search her eyes intently. "Why didn't you come looking for us? Didn't you want to be with us?"

"I didn't remember." Gwyn wiped her eyes with her hand. "I lost all of my memories in my fall down the hill, and the amnesia stayed until I awoke just now. Those men you saw in the lobby are my brothers. They took me in and raised me. They're some of the finest men I've ever known."

"I like them." Rayna rested her head on her sister's shoulder. "And I like your Taylor. He's kind of like Riku in some ways."

"Yeah." Gwyn found a smile for the first time. "How did you manage to catch a two thousand year old elemental master anyway?" She had sensed him even from her sleep, but she just hadn't cared enough to respond. Only Taylor had reached her heart.

Rayna giggled a little. "I was in a coma," she explained, "for sixteen years after the accident. Riku woke me too soon and my contract was affected. To protect me until my birthday, he came to spend time with me. We fell in love. I ended up in another coma, after Uncle Larry attacked me. Riku called me back, like Taylor called you."

"Does Riku know what we are?" Gwyn asked softly.

She nodded. "I think he does now." She smiled. "Riku knows almost everything. I'm actually holding one secret from him, and I'm really, really proud of it."

She leaned up and whispered in Gwyn's ear, and her sister giggled softly. "Can I watch you tell him?"

"No!" Rayna giggled too.

Out in the hall, Taylor turned to Eric and asked, "Can you explain that, Mr. Mason?"

"Eric or Riku. We're going to be in-laws." Eric leaned against the wall. "Congratulations, by the way. Not many men can claim to have taken goddesses for lovers like we have." He watched Taylor choke on the bottle of water he had pulled from a vending machine. "This surprises you."

"No shit!" Taylor stared at him. "I'm going to assume you were speaking in a metaphorical sense."

"It was literal. Rayna and Mika Carmichael are the Goddesses of Truth and Justice, reborn." Eric looked at him intently. "That's why they were marked for death. There is something evil on the loose, and it is attached to their aunt and uncle. As soon as they awakened, they would track and destroy the evil. That's why Rhianna felt they were critical to Enforcers. We, too, exist to destroy evil."

"How?" Taylor asked. "I noticed Rayna has an ear for hearing lies, and Gwyn has always been firm on right and wrong, but . . ."

"Rayna is Truth. She literally hears the truth over someone's words when they tell a lie. And, if she's touching them, she hears the truth without a word. She can tap the truth of someone's soul and expose it. Sometimes it transforms the body into a shape befitting the soul.

"Gwyn is Justice. When she looks at someone, she can see the balance of their life thus far. One side is the good, one is the bad. What they've done, and what has been done to them. She treats everyone fairly, judging only on the basis of her scales. If one side is tipped too far to either side, she can balance the scales by administering justice. She has to work in conjunction with her sister because some crimes are so heinous they must be exposed as truth before justice can be properly served."

Taylor blew out a hard breath. "Not an easy existence. Explain about this 'evil' thing."

"Do you know what evil is?" Eric asked quietly.

"Yeah." He thought of his childhood. "I grew up with it. I was forced to destroy it."

Eric wasn't surprised. "That's what needs to be done, Taylor. True evil can only be destroyed. And that's what Larry and Yvonne Carmichael contracted with to put the Bloody Check on their nieces. It was prophesized before the girls were born that their mother—a Faeriekin princess, by the way—would give birth to two exceptionally powerful beings. No one knew what the girls could do, precisely, but you can be sure the evil attached to Larry did. It influenced him to arrange for their deaths. The people Rayna saw during the accident were its minions."

"Then you stepped in," he summed up. "Well, fine. That explains the why. But, and I really hate to point this out, the aforementioned uncle and aunt are still out there somewhere, and I don't see them giving up if they know our goddesses are capable of destroying them."

"That's why," came Gwyn's voice from the doorway, "we're going to go gunning for them for once." She stood side by side with her little sister, their hands tightly laced together. "We'll expose them for the murderers they are, and then justice will be served. For now, we'll start with Melissa. She does not deserve to get off without being judged."

"It's going to be hell living with you, isn't it?" Taylor complained. She stuck her tongue out at him, and he felt his heart ease as he saw that nothing had really changed. Goddess or not, she was still the same impish, faerie princess who had stolen his heart. "While all of you talk to Melissa, I'm going to go back to the office and see if I can't find a paper trail for us to use. Normal mortals wouldn't understand this whole situation."

"He's starting to sound like one of us," Eric noted dryly, and made his wife giggle softly. "Let's get to work."

CHAPTER THIRTEEN

When Gwyn walked into the lobby, her brothers were staring at the floor. She propped her hands on her hips. "Man, you'd think someone had died."

Seven heads jerked up. "Gwyn," Heul breathed.

With a whoop, Joseff shot across the room to scoop her up in his arms and swing her around exuberantly. "I missed you!" he said into her hair. "Man, you scared us!" His mind automatically searched for hers, felt her touch, and his shoulders relaxed. But, curiously, he felt something more. He looked at Rayna. "You're mentally linked?"

She smiled. "Seems so."

He considered that. "I can handle that," he decided. "That is, if you don't mind that Gwyn and I are like twins too."

"I think it's wonderful." She rose up on her toes to kiss his cheek. "I envy her a little." She smiled a little sadly. "My father and I are still not comfortable with each other. Riku and Rhianna are my only family other than Gwyn."

"Ah, wrong answer." Gavin scooped her up and hugged her. "Now you have seven brothers." He gave Gwyn a pained look. "Geez, I wish I'd been warned that there was more than one of you."

She stuck her tongue out at him. Arian glanced around but didn't see Taylor. "Where's your boyfriend?" he asked.

"He went back to his office to try to find a paper route to help explain what happened," she said dryly.

Something dangerous moved in Eric's eyes. "In the meantime, the girls and I need to go talk to Melissa Washburn."

"Don't worry." Gwyn hugged Heul tightly. "We'll come over later and tell you everything. I'm not suddenly going to stop being your sister just because I no longer have amnesia. Really, I'm not Mika Carmichael anymore. I'm Gwyn Trahern." She smiled impishly. "Until I and Taylor marry anyway."

"Oh alright," Seisyll groused. "We'll go blow up concrete and pound on steel until we feel better."

As the seven trooped out, Gwyn realized Rayna was staring at her with wide eyes. With her truth sense, she knew Seisyll hadn't been lying. Giggling, she hugged her sister. "They're construction workers. I'm an interior designer." She contemplated that. "Actually, not anymore." She looked at Eric. "I think I've been recruited."

"Hopefully," he admitted. "Enforcers needs you, Gwyn. You and Rayna both." He deliberately sighed. "And Taylor too, I guess. He has some use. But he can be a part-timer. Hate to waste all his creative talent."

"How gracious of you," she murmured drolly.

Rayna giggled as she cuddled against Eric's side. "Don't mind him. You'll get used to him." She rubbed her cheek against his chest softly. "He's not nearly as terrifying as he wants to pretend to be."

"Only for you," he promised softly. "Now let's get going."

Melissa was being held in the dungeons of the Enforcers' headquarters. Rayna, upon learning that, frowned at Eric and asked, "You have a dungeon?"

Gwyn giggled. He just sighed. "Kindly recall that I am old, and this company was founded before what is now considered civilization." He ran a hand through Rayna's hair, and skimmed his fingers over the little silver wings almost hidden within her thick locks. Most would never notice them. "Don't tease."

She shared a smile with Gwyn. "We're honor bound to tease you," she giggled. "Gwyn especially. I have dibs on Taylor."

"With my complete permission," Gwyn added impishly. "My brothers are going to have fun with you, Riku. They've adopted Rayna, so now *she* has seven big brothers."

"Gavin was right. You two should definitely have warning labels," he grumbled. He held the door in the dungeon cell for them so they could enter ahead of him.

Melissa heard the door and turned from the barred window to demand her release only to realize who was in the doorway. The color drained from her face, and she slowly sank down to the ground with her back pressed against the wall in shock and terror. "No," she managed to say. "You're dead!"

Gwyn leaned a shoulder against the doorframe. "No, very much alive. I can't die before I get married, you know. It wouldn't be fair."

"Fair! Fair! What do you know about fairness?" Melissa screamed at her.

Eric couldn't resist the humor. "Gwyn is the fairest woman in the land. Only her sister is her equal."

"Sister!" She saw the pint sized silver haired woman walking toward her and shrank back. There was something terrifying about her, as if she saw straight into her soul and exposed every truth.

"Rayna," Eric warned, "watch your thumb."

"What on Earth does THAT mean?" Melissa got her answer as Rayna's small fist suddenly landed on her jaw and snapped her head around. She hit damned hard for such a tiny thing. Melissa stared at her in shock. "The hell!"

"That was for Taylor, since he said he can't hit a woman." She rubbed her knuckles and walked over to Eric with a frown. "That hurt."

"I'll take you to Kienan to learn to make a proper fist." He kissed her fingers and watched over the top of her head as Melissa got to her feet. The other woman was visibly shaking. "We have a few questions. Truth will determine the value of your answers, and Justice will administer punishment." When she said nothing, he asked, "Did you help contract for Rayna and Mika Carmichael's deaths?"

"What?! No!"

"Truth." Rayna looked at her sister. "She wasn't involved that far."

"Yeah, I can see it." Gwyn frowned. "Why did you try to kill me then?" The scale was heavily unbalanced to the point of needing punishment administered, but it seemed a bit odd when Melissa's worst trait was jealousy. There had to be more.

"I didn't try to kill you!"

"Lie." Rayna's hair rippled lightly with power. "The truth shall set you free." Her quiet voice sounded as firm as steel. Her violet eyes flickered with bits of lightning. "You will tell us the truth, starting from the beginning when you tipped the scales."

An odd sheen settled over Melissa's eyes as the power took hold. "I hate beautiful women who get more attention than me." Her voice was without inflection, her eyes staring straight ahead. "In college, I arranged for a girl to be attacked because I wanted her boyfriend. I got an employee at another company fired when she won an in-company beauty contest instead of me. I hate Veronica too. I was planning to arrange an accident. Gwyn was more important. Taylor wanted her. I wanted to ruin her name and make her look like trash."

Sometimes the evil wasn't far under the surface. Sometimes it could be in human flesh. Eric felt exceptionally violent and crossed his arms. Softly, Rayna asked, "When did your plans change to murder?"

"When the snake bit me. I woke up in the morning and felt very clear. If Gwyn was dead, then Taylor would look at me. I used to build bombs for fun when I was a kid, so I disguised one as a comb and sent it to Gwyn. It didn't work. I loitered at the construction site, hoping that I could drop something on her. I saw her trying on that stupid outfit and tried to suffocate her. Finally, I just decided to drug her." She held up her hand where she wore a ring.

Eric walked over and took the ring away. When he twisted the face, a little needle extended. A quick sniff told him that it was the same venomous drug used on both sisters. "She must have used this to drug the apple." He studied the ring. "This has the Carmichael family crest." He looked at her. "Where did you get this?"

"The snake dropped it."

"Snake." It finally registered, and Rayna looked at Eric in horror. "Uncle Larry?"

"Uncle Larry?" Gwyn echoed.

"I exposed his true self when he tried to attack me," she explained. "It turned him into a cobra. Whatever evil we are facing must take the form of a snake. It latches onto those easily converted to true evil." She took a sharp breath as a memory from the distant past filled her mind. She grabbed Gwyn's hand. "Sis . . ."

"Yeah." Gwyn put an arm around her shoulders. "Nahga." She looked at Eric. He didn't seem surprised. "Did you suspect it was the Snake God?"

"I had a suspicion," he admitted. "It's his style, and snakes seem to be cropping up everywhere." He studied both their faces and saw fear mixed with determination. "Are you sure you can face him again? You're stronger now, but what happened back then is sharp enough in your minds that I can see it from Rayna." It made him feel slightly ill.

"We can do it," Rayna said softly. Almost achingly, she asked, "Do you think he corrupted Uncle Larry and Aunt Yvonne?" She couldn't bear the thought of the beloved aunt and uncle of her childhood being so horrible.

He crossed to her and pulled her into his arms. "I'm sorry, sweetheart," he said into her hair. "I'm sorry. He couldn't have latched onto them without something to latch on to. Larry Carmichael formulated the plan to destroy Lucas long before Nahga entered the scene." He offered his hand to Gwyn and pulled her close as well. Their belief in the goodness of mankind was their greatest weakness as well as their greatest strength.

Gwyn eased back after a moment. "What do we do with her?" She pointed at Melissa. "Even without being poisoned, she's done some terrible things. What she told us wasn't everything. I can see the evidence in my mind." Because she was unfailingly fair, she didn't say what she had learned. The disgust in her eyes made it unnecessary, though. "The scales need balancing."

"Let's get the poison out of her first since, I presume, death is not what is needed." Eric held up a hand and water magic surrounded Melissa. He began to increase the heat until she started sweating and then used her opened pores to allow his magic into her skin. The poison from the snake's bite was forced out through the same wound on her ankle it had entered through, and it took the form of a snake as well.

It slithered toward Gwyn but was repelled violently by an invisible barrier around her. Her contract was complete. Evil could not kill her while she was under Enforcers' protection. With a vicious hiss, the snake slithered out the door.

Melissa collapsed onto the floor. Gwyn walked over to kneel beside her. "For one who acted out of jealousy and vanity," she murmured, "I take from you the one thing you covetously horde." Power rippled through her eyes. "Let justice be done."

Even Eric flinched when her beauty melted away to leave nothing but a horribly grotesque appearance behind. He doubted anyone would ever look at her and mistake her features for anything except a reflection of the cruelty inside her heart.

The scales balanced once more, Gwyn walked over to her family. "Where is the snake going?"

"It has to know it has lost," Eric muttered.

"It does." Rayna's eyes slowly widened. "It will want to strike back at us. It will want to hurt Gwyn." She took a sharp breath as Gwyn paled. "It'll go after Taylor!"

Taylor logged onto Melissa's computer and began to go through the files and programs, his ire rising as he saw that she had been documenting her actions. It was annoying to think anyone would be so stupid as to keep an electronic diary on their work computer detailing her plans to kill someone. It was more annoying to think she worked for him. She hadn't even used passwords to close access to the files. Was she *trying* to get caught?

His hands began to burn.

He lifted his hands and stared at them. "What the hell? Gwyn is safe now." He heard knocking on his office door and left Melissa's to cross into his own. "Come in," he said curtly. "But I'm afraid I'm a bit busy right now."

The man and woman that walked in just smiled at him. "You have time for us, I'm sure," the woman said, and she lifted the gun in her hand to aim it at his chest. "We're going for a ride, Mr. Vincent."

He felt himself oddly unsurprised. He lifted his hands and studied the blood that quickly covered them. The answers were there, and the blood faded as he lowered his hands once more. The woman was staring at him, and he shrugged. "Sorry. Strange psychic ability that I can't yet control. It's supposed to warn me when I'm in danger, but it seems to delay in doing so until said danger has already arrived."

She couldn't help but wince. "Pleasant."

"Meh." He came around the desk calmly. "You can put the gun away. I'm not an idiot. You don't want someone to be suspicious." He willingly walked with them from the office as if there was nothing at all odd going on. He would *not* risk his employees' lives. Blake kept a sword at his desk, and he would probably try to use it. "Mind introducing yourselves?"

"Larry and Yvonne Carmichael." Yvonne was doing all the talking, which didn't surprise Taylor since he had to assume it took a lot of concentration for Larry to maintain a human appearance. When he breathed out, the tip of his tongue could be seen, and it was distinctly forked. "You ruined things," she hissed softly. "The girls are gunning for us, and so we're going to hit them where it hurts."

Taylor got into the car that waited at the curb and linked his hands behind his head as he leaned back. "Are you going to just kill me, or are you going to make them watch?" he asked conversationally.

"Oh we want them to watch." She smiled at him. "But we're not stupid enough to have them be there in person. We're going to let a few friends of ours have their way with you and then we'll bleed you out slowly. We'll film the whole thing."

"Ah. Gotcha." He closed his eyes as if he didn't care, but his mind sought Gwyn's. Even across miles, their minds were meant to touch. The bloody vision had shown him what to do, and it was wonderfully easy to let his mind merge with hers. Between his danger sense and her ability to track evil, their mind link provided a trail more accurate than the best GPS device. "Live feed or recorded? I'd hate to have your bandwidth cut out in the middle."

"Very cute." She watched his face and felt a flicker of frustration that he didn't seem to care. Either he was an idiot or he was stupidly expecting to be rescued. She couldn't wait to see his smug and cocky attitude wiped away.

The place they went to was a normal looking house in the suburbs. No one seemed to pay any attention, and a few neighbors even waved cheerfully. Taylor mentally applauded the wisdom of hiding in plain sight.

The house felt almost unbearably hot. Yvonne fiddled with the thermostat while Larry opened a window. An obedient breeze blew in the room and Taylor wondered if anyone had noticed there was no wind in the front of the house. "When do the games begin?" he asked. "This whole hostage thing is really not frightening me."

Larry abruptly turned into a large cobra and lashed at him on a hiss. Yvonne hurriedly stepped between them. "Don't kill him yet!" she ordered. "If he dies now, it defeats the whole purpose." She shivered as the wind turned biting cold. "What is this?"

"Got to watch out for those unexpected blizzards." Taylor closed his hand around a vase. "They come from out of nowhere!"

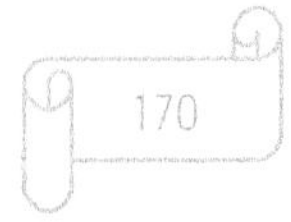

He hurled the water into her face and the wind froze it solid, preventing her from seeing or breathing. She struggled wildly and dropped to her knees as she clawed at the ice. Her struggles became weaker until she blacked out entirely. The ice melted as her body hit the floor with a thump.

Taylor ducked as the cobra tried to hit him. "What took so long?" he demanded.

Eric swung in the window. "Traffic."

"Gee thanks!" He ducked again and dodged around the edge of the hall. "Not that I'm complaining, but, damn it, were you waiting for them to shoot me?"

"I didn't have an open shot! You could be more grateful, kid!" Eric fired a stream of fire at the cobra that had it recoiling in pain. "You're still alive!"

He ducked as the cobra's tail slammed into the wall where his head had been and sent plaster flying everywhere. "That's looking debatable!"

"Stop arguing!" Gwyn and Rayna had come in through the back door of the kitchen and were at the edge of the living room.

"Release Yvonne!" Eric ordered Rayna. "Hurry! Unless they're both exposed, neither can be destroyed! Nahga split himself into two pieces, and we have to destroy them both together! Don't hesitate, no matter what!"

Rayna nodded once and looked at her aunt intently. "And the truth shall set you free!"

"Rayna!" Gwyn grabbed her sister and they dropped to the ground as Yvonne transformed into a cobra the same size as her husband, and both snakes lashed at them. They stayed low to the ground as the two cobras merged into a single being so tall it nearly burst through the roof. Venom dripped from its fangs and burned through the carpet. Its tail lashed around and hit both Eric and Taylor, sending them flying into opposite walls as they tried to get to their lovers.

"Nahga," Gwyn whispered. She remembered him. A memory

of a far distant past where evil had overcome the light of truth and justice, and plunged the world into darkness and despair. No hope. There had been no hope.

"Gwyn." Rayna's voice shook. "Kill it, quickly!" She remembered as well, and it ripped her in two. She couldn't bear the memories.

Gwyn took a breath to release her power but the cobra was prepared and blew a scalding blast of hot breath at her and Rayna. They both went flying into the kitchen and crashed into the sink. They painfully tried to get to their feet as the cobra advanced.

"Hey!" Taylor had gotten his hands on the gun and fired without hesitation to draw the cobra's attention. Eric started firing bullets of ice, and Nahga tried to snap at them with its jaws. Too late, it realized it had turned its back on the real threat.

"And justice be done!" Gwyn shouted, the wings on her head opening fully and radiating her power in a searing wave that washed across the room like a tidal wave and slammed into Nahga.

There was no ceremony with its death. It was obliterated so fast that there was a popping sound as air rushed in to fill the space left behind. Silence fell on the house as Taylor dropped the gun on the floor and Eric lowered his hands.

Gwyn took a deep breath. For the first time, she felt as if she could truly breathe. The weight of the past was gone. She could live, truly live, and without fear. No one wanted her dead. She gave a glad little cry and raced across the floor to leap into Taylor's arms.

He caught her close and buried his face in her hair, needing her soft scent and warmth to banish the terror of the last few days. It was over. Finally, it was over. Into her hair, he asked, "Is this the part where someone says 'they lived happily ever after'?"

"You're the writer," she said into his shoulder. "How does your game end?"

"The faerie princess gets a hundred lifetimes with her soldier for every year she spent in fear." His lips curved. "So, presumably, she would be stuck with him forever. For them it's a happily ever after."

Her eyes closed as she smiled. "It sounds like one to me, too."

CHAPTER FOURTEEN

Rhianna heard the giggling long before she heard the footsteps. She didn't look up from the file in front of her as she smiled to herself. "Come in," she called. The door eased open, and two of her favorite people peeked around the door at her. She smiled. "What are you up to?"

Gwyn and Rayna crossed the room quickly, the latter not hampered by her sixth-month pregnancy in the slightest. The former was carrying a gaily-wrapped package that she held out with a smile. "A little bird told us," she said cheerfully. "Happy birthday!"

Rhianna glanced at the door that joined her office to Eric's and snorted as she heard him whistling like a bird. "I can imagine." She took the package and unwrapped it curiously, only to start laughing as she saw the game within. "This faerie looks familiar."

Gwyn's color rose slightly. "I tried to convince Taylor to change it, but he's very stubborn."

"A good quality in the right man. And it's entirely accurate. You are both Faeriekin princesses." She opened her CD drive and popped the disc in to let it load. She loved the games from Memories; this one wasn't even supposed to be released for another month.

"Now that you have your gift, we have a favor to ask," Gwyn announced.

"Oh?" She arched a brow.

"Yes." The sisters exchanged a smile. "We want to 'help' our brothers." Rayna's voice was solemn.

Rhianna began to smile. "What's good for the goose is good

for the gander?"

"What goes around comes around. Turnabout is fair play. Pick your metaphor." Gwyn linked her hands behind her back. "We have plans, you see, and we're going to need you and Riku to help. We were thinking a contract. You know. Just to make sure things go the way we want them."

"Have you got someone in mind?" Eric asked from the doorway. He had been wondering what they were up to. He had seen them talking and giggling together for a week.

"Oh definitely." Rayna's eyes twinkled. "We've been learning by watching you," she added innocently. "Everything should be in place by Gwyn and Taylor's wedding next week."

"You two *definitely* should have warning labels." Eric went back into his office with a shake of his head.

"I must agree," Rhianna noted dryly. "But I will be quite happy to help however I can. The happiness of those in 3rd District comes first. Let me see what I can come up with."

"You're the best!" Rayna said happily as she went around the desk to hug her tightly. When she eased back and let go, she met Rhianna's eyes very seriously. "Is *he* trapped too?"

Her leader, and surrogate sister-in-law, went very still. "I'm sorry?" she asked softly.

"The one you're waiting for. Is he trapped, too?"

She was silent for long moments before she sighed softly and rested her arms on her desk. "I don't know," she admitted with simple honesty.

"I hope you find him." Rayna gave her a kiss on the cheek and then headed for Eric's door.

Gwyn likewise started toward the main one. She stopped there and looked back over her shoulder. "You're not a bad person, Gon, no matter what you think you've done so far. The scales are balanced. You'll find him."

Rhianna watched both doors shut and leaned back in her chair with a little smile. Having Truth and Justice around was often unnerving, but it was very comforting as well. Gwyn had just given her a sense of peace she hadn't had in a long time.

She studied the contract on her desk, wrote some notes on the bottom, and closed the folder. It promptly flashed the word 'Complete.' She swiveled and slid it into the drawer with its twin. She smiled as the drawer started to flash the word 'Finished' but changed its mind and remained blank instead. Things weren't done *quite* yet.

Status: File ~~Complete~~ In Progress
Analysis: To balance the scales of love, you just need to be the fairest in the land.

Folder Three
TRAHERN

CHAPTER FIFTEEN

Of all the people in the wedding party, and all the people attending the reception, only the bride and groom were calm. Their friends and family ran a gauntlet of emotions that swung between excited and nervous. On the groom's side of the immense garden, Taylor was greatly amused to see his friends and employees acting like they were the ones getting married. On the bride's side of the garden, Gwyn was fascinated at watching her normally levelheaded brothers act like they were readying themselves for a noose. "Guys? You do remember I'm the one getting married, right?"

Her sister giggled softly. "Stop moving, Gwyn! I'll smear your eyeshadow."

"Sorry, Rayna." Gwyn obligingly turned back to her little sister so that she could continue applying makeup.

Rayna smiled and deftly swiped shadow over Gwyn's eyes. Neither sister normally wore makeup, but the fantastical setting had demanded more than lip-gloss. It had taken Rayna two weeks to perfect her technique, and another two for Gwyn to decide on the look she wanted.

The shimmering glitter across Rayna's cheeks matched the shimmering threads in her violet dress. She figured it was probably her husband influencing Taylor that had resulted in her costume making her look like a living flower. She liked it. It seemed fitting that a faerie bride have a flower spirit for a matron-of-honor. "You're not mad at me, are you, Joseff?" she called across the room.

He stopped yanking on his collar and turned immediately to

smile. "Of course not! Gwyn's enough of a sadist to have tried to put *me* in that dress, and it looks much better on you."

Gavin snorted softly. "Gwyn wouldn't do that," he said solemnly. "Would you?"

"Mmm. Maybe." Though her eyes were closed, it was a sure bet her eyes sparkled. Rayna's certainly were, and the passing time had only made them act more and more like twins. Gwyn felt quite blessed to be able to say she had two twins.

Rayna studied her new brothers from the corner of her eye. Though mostly Welsh in blood, they looked much like Vikings that had been dropped in the middle of New York. Half had pale blond hair, the other had yellow blond. All eyes were different shades of blue. All were almost lethally handsome. They were giving, loving, and brilliant on top of it.

And every last one of them was single. It had been the bane of Gwyn's life and was now Rayna's puzzle. How did seven such spectacular men manage to escape matrimony for so long? Ah, well. The sisters shared a smiling look. They wouldn't escape much longer.

The door opened and Rhianna peered around the side. "Ah," she said in satisfaction. "Good. Looking like that, Taylor would have to be an idiot to try and escape."

Gwyn grinned. "I'd just chase him down."

"That's my girl."

As the door shut, Rayna looked at her brothers and giggled as she saw all were standing at attention with something akin to terrified fascination on their faces. "She doesn't bite! Rhianna is *really* nice. She's like my sister-in-law, so you have to like her, okay?"

"She runs one of the largest companies in the entire country," Tomos noted in awe. "She and Eric are almost *always* in the newspapers. It's like meeting a celebrity!"

"She's just Rhianna," Gwyn said simply. She got to her feet and smoothed out her voluminous skirts. The wedding gown was a pure romantic indulgence. Designed to flatter her graceful figure and snowy white hair, its creation had been nearly slaved over by her soon-to-be-husband. He was *such* an artist sometimes; it wasn't perfect until he couldn't find anything left to pick apart.

The garden in front of the newly opened Memories building had been transformed into a fantasy garden for a fantasy wedding. All guests wore elaborate costumes, and many wore masks. Since all seven brothers were giving Gwyn away, they were all wearing specially designed, formal uniforms that made them resemble princes. Tall and slightly intimidating princes, but princes regardless.

"Riku's feeling guilty," Rayna informed Gwyn, almost impishly. When Gwyn tilted her head, Rayna giggled. "He married me so quickly that we didn't have a real wedding. Now he feels like he cheated me or something."

"You want one?" Gavin wrapped his arms around her to hug her snugly. "We could step in to give you away. Or would your father want to do that?"

She shook her head. "He doesn't leave his house anymore." She smiled, genuinely. "He did what he needed to do. He couldn't live without our mom unless I and Gwyn needed him. Now that we've found our places, he can let go." She sighed softly. "He's normal, but he loved a Faeriekin. That 'mating for life' thing is pretty cross species when power is involved."

Matching looks of wariness crossed seven faces. The sisters hid a shared smile. "Now then." Gwyn picked up her bouquet of sunflowers. "I feel like getting married. Let's get this over with so I can kidnap my husband for our honeymoon."

When they got to the end of the aisle that she would walk down, they could see Taylor waiting near the arbor with the priest. Even the priest had gotten into the spirit of things and was dressed like a wizard out of medieval times. Taylor wore what looked like an elaborate dress uniform for a soldier. Eric, dressed like a rather intimidating warlock, was beside him as his best man.

In age order, the Trahern brothers moved down the aisle to take a spot. Joseff remained with Gwyn and Rayna. A small body in a tiny pink dress appeared out of nowhere and squeezed up between the three adults. She tugged firmly on Rayna's skirt. "Rayna!" Nicole Germaine asked plaintively. "Can I go throw flowers?"

Rayna knelt down and firmly fixed her skirt and wings. The flower girl looked like the perfect little faerie. At five, she was almost frighteningly intelligent for her age, thinking and acting on a much higher level, but she was still very much a little girl. The idea of being the faerie flower girl had tickled her pink. "There," Rayna said, "now you can go."

Nicole brightened happily, her vivid green eyes filled with delight. The crop of rusty red curls on her head bounced merrily as she turned and began to skip down the aisle, throwing flower petals with great abandon. Sadly, few made it onto the aisle itself. Most ended up on the Traherns.

By the time she reached the end where Heul waited, her basket was empty. She looked up at him and her lower lip quivered. "I ran out."

He brushed the ones off his jacket into her basket. She waved at him and he knelt down as close to her height as possible. She planted a big kiss on his cheek and then scampered over to the arbor to enthusiastically throw her last handful. Every last person in the audience was either snickering or grinning by that point, including Rhianna.

The priest blew a petal off his nose and tried desperately not to smile as he looked at the young woman on the piano. Since both Gwyn and Taylor hated organ music, they had compromised on a piano. The pianist was, in fact, an aunt to the audacious little flower girl and had the same rusty red hair. Her eyes were turquoise green instead.

Rayna waited for her cue before walking down the aisle serenely. She did her best to not giggle at the sight of her big brothers covered in flowers, but it was hard. Gavin winked at her as he bowed, and she bit her lip. She managed to make it to the arbor without mishap—she had been terrified she would trip—and she took her spot. As she looked at Eric, his smile warmed her from the inside out. She didn't need a ceremony. She had him.

Joseff escorted Gwyn to Seisyll, who took her to Tomos, who took her to Gavin, who took her to Owen, who took her to Arian, who finally took her to Heul. They were a marked contrast, the eldest and youngest, but there was enough of a resemblance in their coloring and features that no one had ever questioned whether she was a Trahern.

He escorted her toward the arbor, and Taylor walked forward to meet them. "I will care for her," the groom said calmly. His eyes never left Gwyn's face.

"Will you love her?" Heul was proud of himself for not forgetting his lines.

"I can do no other."

"Then I give her to you." He offered Gwyn's hand to Taylor. He bent to kiss his sister's cheek and then moved back to his place, hoping like hell his eyes weren't as damp with tears as they felt. Damn it, she wasn't supposed to grow up that soon.

Taylor escorted Gwyn to the waiting priest, and they were finally wed. When the priest said Taylor could kiss the bride, he was more than happy to swing her up into his arms enthusiastically. The cheering became whistles and clapping as it became quickly obvious the couple wasn't in a hurry to stop. Eric kicked Taylor's ankle. "Young eyes," he warned softly.

Taylor let go of Gwyn to see Nicole watching with wide eyes. He burst into laughter and scooped her up in his arms. "You did great," he told her. As he escorted Gwyn down the aisle, he passed the small child off to another woman with dark red hair. "Thanks, Remy," he murmured.

Remy smiled. "Anytime. Rayna and Gwyn are both dear friends."

The reception was held inside the lobby of the building. It, too, had been turned into a vast storybook scene. Many smiling glances were sent toward some of the artwork on the wall. It was no secret that Taylor had used Gwyn as a muse for his recent game.

Joseff liked parties as much as the next person, and the people in attendance were nice, but he didn't know how to dance and was really bad at mingling. He sidled his way toward the side exit, slowly but surely seeking escape. No one was looking, and he ducked into the hall. Letting out a little breath, he sent a mental apology to his sister. She just snorted at him in response.

The hall led to a side exit where another garden resided. Hands in pockets, he headed toward the doors. He needed to be outside where it was open. The evening closed around him peacefully, and he took a deep breath.

A sound caught his attention, and he slowly made his way toward the side of a large gazebo designed to offer relief from the sun in the summer. He cautiously peered around the side . . . and found himself face to face with the most shockingly beautiful young woman he had ever seen.

Her rusty red hair was pulled up so that ringlets cascaded around her fair features. Her eyes were a deep, turquoise green and framed by almost ridiculously long lashes. She wore the costume of an old-fashioned bard, and the laced corset flattered a distinctly curvaceous body. They both straightened up, and he discovered, to his everlasting delight, that she was clearly shorter. If she was taller than Gwyn, it was only by a thin margin. "Hi." He recognized her suddenly. "You played the piano."

"Hi." She smiled. "Yes I did."

Freckles. She had freckles. He was enchanted. "I'm Joseff Trahern." He offered a hand.

"Lexie Germaine." She shook his hand solemnly and felt her heart flutter wildly as he then brought her hand to his lips and bowed deeply. She had been staring at him since she had seen him the first time. He was so gorgeous! She had actually been afraid to speak to him; she tended to trip over her tongue when she was nervous. He looked like every girl's secret prince charming, and the way he smiled at her had her pulse going faster than an Irish fiddler's bow.

"Lexie." He liked it. "Is it short for anything?"

She took a breath. "Brace yourself. It's Alexandriana Genevieve."

He shook his head slightly and rubbed his ear. "I'm not sure I heard that properly, let alone could attempt to repeat it. Lexie, it is." He kept hold of her hand, unable to make himself let go. "I want you to know now," he informed her, "that if I do not ask you to dance, it's because I can't dance and I'd embarrass you."

"Well, if you did ask, I'd have to decline because *I* can't dance, and I wouldn't want to embarrass you, either."

They shared a conspiratorial grin. "How about a walk?" he offered.

"See, that I can do. I've even been doing it for twenty-one years. I'm an expert." She let him tuck her hand into the curve of his elbow. "So you built this building with your brothers? It's beautiful."

"I do mostly windows," he said with a smile. "We're all adept builders, but we also specialize. Like, I work with glass, and Tomos does landscapes. What about you?"

"I work with my sisters. We own an interior design company. We all specialize in different styles and have other special talents. Mine is Traditional, and I'm a stained glass artist."

"Sisters? How many?"

"Uhm, six."

"Six!" The name finally registered. "Wait, Germaine. You're Remy's little sister, right? Kingdom Design?"

"Yup!" She smiled. "I'm the baby. We're *this* close to getting Remy to join us. She's wasted on working with numbers at that budget company." The music from inside drifted out suddenly and curled around her. "I love this song." It was a slow song designed to entice couples to sway together. "The singers are from 3rd District like me."

"Me, too."

Their eyes met and both fell silent. Two hearts beat far faster than normal. When he brushed a stray curl out of her face, her hands lifted to rest over his chest. He was so strong that she felt deliciously small and delicate. Something stirred along her mind like a soft voice. The voice of his heart. It was a voice she had been waiting to hear.

They moved together without words, her head tucking onto his shoulder as he wrapped his arms around her. You didn't need steps to slow dance. Just a willing heart. There were two between them. Two hearts beating as one.

When the song ended, they didn't move. After a moment, she asked, "Joseff?"

"Mmm?"

"Is it supposed to be that easy?"

He didn't need to ask for clarification. He knew. "I never thought so, but I saw it happen to Gwyn." He looked down at her. "Let's test if we're right. There are supposed to be fireworks if I kiss you, correct?"

Breathless, she stared up at him. "Please. Test. I'm always happy to experiment." His head lowered and his lips brushed hers. Sparks seemed to leap. Her blood heated wildly. Brushed again. Her entire body began to ache. She looked into his eyes, and they were as dark and hungry as she felt. She wound her arms around his neck and rose onto her toes to kiss him with all the unleashed emotion in her soul.

When they finally parted for air, her careful hairdo had been completely demolished by his fingers. Feeling them buried in her hair, however, was worth every lost pin. "Fireworks?" she whispered.

"Is it the Fourth of July already? I'd swear the celebration was right over us."

Her lips curved even as his did. A bit guilty as she remembered something, she sighed and reluctantly released him. "Joseff . . . I need to tell you something. A locket in my family had a gift for us seven sisters. We were each given a wish. All of us, except Remy, wished for true love." She looked up at him in worry. "Maybe what we have is because of that wish."

"Is that supposed to be bad?" he wondered. "I mean, you didn't ask for *my* love, specifically. Maybe the wish's power just helped us find each other." His brain belatedly began to connect the dots. "Wait. This is a little coincidental."

"There is no such thing as coincidence in 3rd District," his love reminded him.

"That's my point. Seven sisters. Seven brothers. Six sisters who wished for love. One just *happens* to find that love with one of the brothers. Youngest to youngest." Her eyes had slowly widened and he was beginning to grin. "What did Remy wish for?"

"She didn't. It was right after she got divorced. Then Chase died a year later. She still cared for him, so it was hard. I think she's afraid to upset Nicole's life more. Poor thing doesn't even remember Chase."

"Heul needs family. Sounds like Remy does too. And Heul *loves* kids." He grinned. "Let's go find Rayna and Gwyn. We're going to need help."

She held tight to his hand as he hurried toward the door. "Help with what?"

"Nudging those wishes along. Remy and Heul might be harder because she didn't wish, but I'm sure it'll be perfect! C'mon, Lex."

"My legs are shorter than yours. Yikes!" She grabbed his shoulders as he swept her up into his arms. "Wow." She stared at his profile. "That was . . . that was really romantic. Do it again any time you like."

"Man, you're perfect for me." He put her down on her feet when they reached the other door and both slipped into the reception. Muffling giggles, they made their way across the room to where Rayna and Eric were sitting with Gwyn and Taylor. Both sisters had taken off their shoes briefly and had their feet on their husbands' laps.

When Joseff and Lexie reached them, four pairs of eyes went to where their hands were clasped. "Well," Taylor said.

"Ha! Told you so!" Rayna told Eric almost gleefully.

Gwyn's eyes twinkled. "Hi, Lexie."

"Hi, Gwyn." Lexie's eyes were twinkling too. "Can I keep

Joseff?"

"Sure. Feel free."

"And there's something else." Joseff pulled over two more chairs and sat down with Lexie beside him. "We want to set up her six sisters with our six brothers. There's this thing about seven wishes, and a locket, and coincidences."

"There are none in 3rd District." Eric glanced across the room at Rhianna, and she just smiled. He wasn't surprised.

"Wish I'd known that," Taylor groused.

"Wouldn't have done you any good," Gwyn apologized. "Now then." She leaned in and so did the other five. "To be honest, Rayna and I had already thought of it," she admitted softly. "And we've got things in place to begin making the dominoes fall. We're not taking chances. And since Taylor and I won't be here, I'm going to have to rely on you and Lexie to take our place. Rayna and Eric and Rhianna will help out, definitely."

"What's the plan?" Joseff asked.

"Arranging situations," Rayna offered. "We're just going to set up the right circumstances and see what happens."

"Details please?" Lexie asked.

By the time Rayna and Gwyn were done explaining, Joseff and Lexie were both grinning. "That's . . . that's diabolical," Joseff finally said. "But it's so simple. So perfect. If anything will happen, that's the scenario to set it up in." He glanced around the room. "And we've got the right start."

The others followed his gaze. It was fairly easy to pick out the Trahern brothers because all were tall and blond. Likewise, the Germaine sisters were easy to see for they were also on the tall side, except they were red haired. The red hair ran from dark to rust and all eyes were different shades of green.

Without fail, someone was staring at someone else. If a Trahern wasn't staring at a Germaine, a Germaine was staring at a Trahern. The very distinct, pointed, difference lay with Remy and Heul. They seemed quite determined not to look at each other at all.

"Hey, Eric?" Taylor asked absently. "How good is your control of that wind?

"Absolute."

"You're just horrible," Gwyn decided solemnly. She gave her husband a contented kiss. "And I absolutely love you."

The reception continued. Gwyn danced with all of her brothers. The cake was cut and served. And, finally, it was time for the bouquet and garter. While Gwyn was trying to find her precarious footing on a chair, Lexie and her older sister Jennifer descended on Remy. "You!" Lexie scolded. "Come on."

"Oh come on!" Remy sighed as she found herself dragged toward the cluster of single women. "I'm a mother!"

"And you're single. Ergo, you're eligible. There is no law that says previously married women can't catch a bouquet. Half the men here have been ogling you." Jen shoved Remy forward. "Give one of them a thrill, geez."

Gwyn hid a smile and chucked her bouquet over her shoulder. As if carried on the wind, it sailed through the air over outstretched hands and landed in Remy's arms. "That's great!" another Germaine sister, Samantha, said as she hugged Remy. "I'm not even upset I didn't catch it because you did!"

Remy had nothing she could say to that. And her daughter was watching with rapt adoration and delight, so she couldn't really argue either. She just sighed and moved out of the way. It was just a myth. No one really believed the people who got the garter and the bouquet would marry. She genuinely didn't even think that lace and flowers could predict future weddings anyway. That was pushing it, even for the District.

As the bachelors lined up to catch the garter, a plaintive voice said, "Tall people in the back! That's not fair."

Obligingly, the Trahern brothers minus Joseff moved to the back. Really, they didn't need to be in the front. They already had an advantage. Gavin, being Gavin, couldn't help but shout, "Taylor, stop flirting with my sister and just get her garter!"

Amid the laughter, Taylor retorted, "Her skirt is attacking me."

"You wanted it poofy!" Gwyn giggled like crazy. "And stop tickling me!"

"I'm about to try to catch my sister's garter," Arian said warily. "Isn't that blasphemous?"

"Shush!" Taylor straightened and smoothed Gwyn's skirt back into place. Without looking away from her face, he chucked the garter over his shoulder

Magically, mysteriously, it flew across the top of the crowd and landed in Heul's hands. The most interesting thing was that he hadn't even been reaching for it. He had lifted his hands to avoid bumping into someone. As he stared at the scrap of lace and silk in his hand, it dawned on him. His eyes narrowed toward his sister, who merely smiled angelically.

"You have to dance with Remy!" Lexie grabbed his hand and began to draw him toward the floor. "Come on! It's tradition!"

Joseff and Tomos were pointedly escorting Remy onto the floor at the same time. When Heul and Remy found themselves face to face, neither found a word to say. Heart pounding, she struggled against an urge to run. Why did this man get under her skin? One look at him and she was sixteen again, discovering the joys of the male of the species. He was so strong. Masculine. Everything she could ever want. "Uhm."

"They won't leave us alone unless we comply," he murmured softly. He handed off the garter and then took the bouquet and handed it away as well. He tugged her closer and stepped forward. She automatically stepped back and the dance started before she was even conscious of it.

For him, it was an exercise in self-torture. He had wanted Remy Germaine since he had laid eyes on her. She was so strong emotionally, holding together her family in a way he had held his own. He respected and admired her, and the way she looked in a slim, black. sorceress dress made his body hunger and ache in entirely new ways. Just looking at a woman had never made him burn before.

"Oh man," Jen whispered to another sister. "Look at how he's looking at her!"

Henrietta, Rie to her friends and family, sighed gustily. "Yeah." Her eyes drifted across the room to where the Trahern twins were standing. One of them, she wasn't sure which, just seemed to be more handsome to her than his brother. It was curious because they were quite identical except for hair length. Her eyes met the blue eyes of the one with short hair, and her toes curled in her shoes at the way he slowly smiled. "I think it's genetic."

By the end of the dance, the entire room was at least ninety percent sure that the myth might be more than just that. When the music ended, Remy and Heul hastily parted and went to opposite sides of the room. They didn't look at each other at all for the rest of the reception. In fact, their determination to ignore each other was quite clear.

"Let the games begin," Josef murmured to Lexie.

She just grinned.

CHAPTER SIXTEEN

When Joseff walked into the living room one morning a few days later, he discovered Heul deep in thought as he stared at a letter. "Problem?" the younger brother asked.

"Your sister."

"Which one?"

"Your twin!"

"Ah." He sat down on an armchair and threw his legs over the side. "What did she do? Oh," he added. "I have a date tonight. I won't be home until late."

Heul eyed him intently. "Correct me if I'm wrong, but haven't you gone on a date with Lexie Germaine every single night for the last five days?"

Politely, he asked, "Is that a problem?"

"No," Heul muttered as he went back to the letter. He liked Lexie, but her oldest sister haunted his waking days and sleepless nights. Then, too, there was Joseff. Heul had always felt more like a father than a brother. He knew that he had lost Joseff to Lexie. His family was slowly drifting into their own ways.

"So what did Gwyn do now?"

Heul sighed and handed over the letter. "See for yourself. If you read between the lines, you can all but hear her giggling when she wrote it. It's a very nice, very polite letter of resignation. Enforcers has offered her a full time position as a consultant. She and Rayna are going to work as a team."

"Yikes. If they walked into a boardroom together, I'd panic."

Joseff could indeed hear his twin's giggles in the letter, and he didn't need to read it to know the contents. He handed it back over. "I guess that means we're without an interior designer for Driven Snow." Casually, he added, "You know, Lexie's sisters own an interior design company, Kingdom Designs. She mentioned they were thinking of finding a construction firm to partner with, to share the burden of the economy."

Heul slowly narrowed his eyes on his baby brother. "You and Gwyn are doing that creepy mental thing again. She mentions the exact same thing in here."

"Probably because she and I talked about it first." He shrugged one shoulder. "She felt guilty about abandoning us. I think we ought to give it a trial run. See what happens. I mean, do *you* want Gwyn to come back all happy from her honeymoon only to be filled with guilt?"

"Not at all." Heul stared at the letter for a moment. Abruptly he asked, "Does Remy work there now? I know you said Lexie and her sisters were trying to convince her."

"She does indeed. She got fed up with stifling her artistic side. And she wants Nicole to grow up thinking you can chase your dreams, so she decided to chase her own. She joined Kingdom Design and the other six put her in charge." Blithely, he continued, "She's pretty much the same level as you. When Gwyn and I were talking, we were thinking, for the trial run, that we'd see if we can work together on any type of project. We'll just match up brother to sister on the basis of what they do individually, rather than shared."

Heul grunted softly as he sat back on the couch. "And you just happen to specialize in glass blowing, and Lexie is a stained glass artist."

"That's what gave us the idea," he admitted readily. "The fact that I'm in love with her is moot. We'd have worked well together despite it. If two people, two *specialists*, can work together, then builders can work with designers. We aim for the hardest scenario so that the easiest is, well, easy."

His big brother stared at him for long moments and then stared out the window. Finally, with a distinct sense of impending doom, Huel said, "Fine. Call Lexie. If she can convince her sisters, then we can convince our brothers." Sourly, he added, "Unless you two have already planned all of it out."

"Not *all* of it," Joseff denied. He smiled. "But we definitely have a good start. Let's go find the other guys."

Kingdom Design was run from a smaller building in 3rd District. The seven co-owners were all born of the District and had lived there for their entire lives. After their parents died, when Remy was twenty-two, she took on the task of raising all six of her siblings, even eleven-year-old Lexie. She had forced herself to take a desk job so that her sisters were provided for. Then, years later, she'd had Nicole to care for as well.

Now, at thirty-two, she found herself a divorcee and a single mother to a five-year-old. She and Chase hadn't loved each other enough to stay married, but he had been a good man and one of her dearest friends. He had wanted to help raise their daughter. Now he was gone. She had stopped grieving, but the effects lingered.

She had finally settled into her life. Perhaps that was why it was so frustrating to stand at the window in her office and find her thoughts consumed with Heul Trahern. "Men are not supposed to take over a woman's mind," she muttered.

Behind her, Lexie said cheerfully, "The right men are!" She tossed herself down in a chair with a suitably dramatic flair. Her upswept curls bounced merrily. "Joseff is on my mind *constantly*. I'm going to marry him."

Remy had to smile as she turned around. "Really? Hadn't guessed." She sat on the side of the desk, one ear open toward the hallway where Nicole was chasing a remote control car all over the place. "He's a good man."

"Indeed." Lexie linked her hands behind her head. "Anyway, I want to talk to you. You know how we were talking about combining with a construction company? Well, Joseff says that Driven Snow just lost their interior designer. Gwyn got stolen by Enforcers."

One side of Remy knew it was a brilliant match. The other side had been seduced by a pair of blue eyes and a smoldering dance in a storybook room. "Lex . . ."

"You're such a chicken!" She sighed dramatically. "Remy, I'm not asking you to sleep with Heul. Though it'd do you both good, I'm sure. I'm just asking you to work with him. Joseff and I were thinking of a trial run. Y'know, matching artist to artist. If we can do small projects together that focus on us and our specialties, then we can work together as a collective group."

"And naturally, you and Joseff would work well together."

"I ain't denying that that is definitely what made us think of it, but we'd work well together even if we weren't nuts over each other. We were comparing his brothers to my sisters and we found lots of ways this could work. Yeah, unfortunately, you'd have to work with Heul, but you guys are the oldest. Actually," she laughed, "it was pretty funny how it broke down in birth order. Someone had a field day when they planned our families."

Remy let out a long breath. "Let's ask the others. If they're up for it, we can try it. We've got nothing to lose."

"Awesome!" Lexie hopped to her feet. "I'll go round them up!" Whistling softly, she headed out of the room.

Ten minutes later, all seven sisters were crowded into their conference room. Remy, as was her way, sat as far from the front of the table as she could. Next to her was Lexie. On Lexie's other side was Jennifer, the next oldest to Remy. She was thirty and five-eight with rust red hair and peridot green eyes. She tended to be the quickest to temper but could also be the quietest when she was thinking.

Across from Jen was Samantha, the next oldest. She was five-eight as well, twenty-eight, her hair was dark red, and her eyes were lime green. She wore thick glasses, much to her annoyance as no one else wore them. They suited her quite well, however, and enhanced her eyes.

Next to Sam was Tabitha. Tabby was twenty-six, five foot nine, rusty haired, and her eyes were pine green. She was the quietest of her family. She rarely touched anyone and had to be coaxed into opening up and laughing. Her powers were not comfortable for her, or anyone.

Next to Tabby were Belle and Rie. Identical twins with dark red hair and teal green eyes. They were twenty-three years old and five-seven, and Belle was the fractionally older. Rie wore her hair to her hips. Belle's hair was shorter and riotous with curls. Rie could be the more outgoing, Belle was the not-so-closet romantic. All seven sisters shared a similar beauty, and they had more than once caused a double take if they went out in public at the same time.

"So." Jen leaned on the table. "What's up?"

"I have a proposal for you." Lexie hopped up to sit on the side of the table. "Driven Snow Architecture is in need of an interior designer or two. We were thinking of joining with a construction company. Joseff and I think we ought to try a trial run." She outlined the plan briefly and followed up with, "We all have to be willing to do this, so if one person doesn't want to, then we won't."

"I'm for it," Jen decided. "They're decent guys. And," she grinned, "like it'd be a hardship to work with guys who are that hot."

Lexie looked around the table and saw all her sisters in agreement, even Remy, though hers was more reluctant. She gleefully bounced to her feet. "Great! I'll call Joseff!"

The Germaine sisters arrived a few hours later at the Driven Snow Architecture building. Like their own building, it was in two parts. The front was the actual business, and the back was where the Traherns lived. Almost everyone who worked in 3rd District lived in homes attached to their place of business.

The fact that they were all District-born, and therefore subject to the mystical laws of their home, was in the back of everyone's mind as they all marched into a large conference room. The males sat on one side of the table, the females on the other. Amusingly, perhaps unintentionally, they sat in order of birth. For Remy and Heul, it was a study in frustration. They carefully avoided looking into each other's eyes.

"Well," Joseff said cheerfully. "This ought to be fun!"

"I bet." Gavin tried his level best not to stare at the quiet redhead across the table from him. There was something in her large green eyes that tugged at everything inside him. And she was tall. He liked tall females. She appealed emotionally and physically, and he couldn't have been more delighted at the chance to get to know her. His sharp eyes hadn't missed, however, that she didn't shake hands or even touch her sisters. He longed to know why. "How is this working?"

Lexie hopped up and began to hand out contracts. "Rayna gave these to me. Since our businesses are overseen by Enforcers, they will be keeping an eye on our potential merger. So here's how it'll work. Joseff and I went over everyone's skills and came up with a game plan."

"First up is Remy and Heul." Joseff looked at his notes. "Since her specific talent is in designing buildings, and Heul builds 'em, we figured they could work on a small building. A dollhouse for Nicole's birthday or something."

Remy had to smile. "She'd love that."

"Then next are Arian and Jen." Lexie paused beside her sister. "Since you both work with wood as a carpenter and woodworker, respectively, we found a client who wants a hand-crafted bed made. Here's his information." She handed over a card to Jen.

"Then Owen and Sam." Joseff found a set of drawings in his

folder and gave them to Lexie to pass down the line. "Owen specializes in turning drawings into blueprints, and Sam is a 3D modeler. They can work on turning those drawings into a full set of blueprints and 3D models."

Sam looked down, trying not to show that she was as happy as she was. Owen was by far her favorite of the Trahern males. There was just something about him. If he turned out to be half as attracted to her as she was to him, she would have him. It was that simple.

"And next," Lexie continued, "we have Gavin and Tabby. Gavin specializes in electrical work and Tabby is awesome with mapping and diagramming things that need fixing. We'll have you guys work on this project." She handed a card to Gavin. "An old building that needs rewiring. It hasn't been touched in fifty years."

He grimaced. "Good god, who knows what will be in those walls."

Tabby smiled at him almost shyly. "Don't worry. If it's in there, we'll find it."

Joseff covered a smile. "Annnnd next are Tomos and Belle. Both of you are landscapers."

"Gee, are we landscaping something?" Tomos asked dryly. He grinned at Belle and she grinned back. Inside his chest, he felt his heart clench. Though Belle and Rie were identical, he found only Belle to be attractive. She took his breath away. Working with her, getting to know her, was something he had wanted since he had seen her at the wedding.

"Good guess!" Lexie handed Belle some documents. "The guy who wants the hand carved bed wants his mansion garden redone. Hey, he's got the money, we got the talent. It works for me."

"And lastly, Seisyll and Rie. You both work with metal. Seisyll is a welder and Rie is a metal sculptor. We couldn't find any special projects for you together, but we thought you could give each other's job a try. Mutual respect would be just as effective." Joseff was sitting next to Seisyll so he handed him the papers he needed. "A building needs some work and a chick from the Bronx wants a statue. Pick the order you want to do them."

"Does everyone feel okay with things?" Lexie asked.

"And what will you two be doing?" Owen countered dryly.

"We have a project, too." Joseff smiled. "We got a special order for a detailed stained glass piece. It'll take both of us to do it. We figure if we haven't killed each other by the end, we'll pick a wedding date."

There was a moment of silence before Sam decided, "I'm in." She signed the contract in front of her and slid it across the table to Owen. He paused for a moment and then signed as well. In a matter of moments, everyone had signed their contracts, even Remy and Heul, although they showed much more reluctance.

As Lexie collected the contracts, her eyes met Joseff's across the table. They both began to smile.

CHAPTER SEVENTEEN

By mutual agreement, the teams met the following morning at one or the other's preferred place of work. For Arian and Jen, that meant meeting at Jen's woodshop. It was a small room converted from a garage attached to Kingdom Design's building.

Arian wasn't in the best of moods as he headed for the shop early in the morning. He hadn't slept a minute the night before, haunted by a pair of peridot-colored eyes. Jennifer Germaine was long-legged, willowy, and beautiful. He would have expected her to be a model instead of a woodworker, but he had seen her hands. They were elegant and shapely, but marked with the little scars and calluses that showed she had paid the price for her work.

His own hands showed the wear and tear of almost twenty years of hard work. He could build, construct, and arrange steel beams with the best of them, but his first love was lumber. When Driven Snow built a building, no matter the size, once the steel frame was done, he took over with internal woodwork. If they worked on a house, he was in charge almost from the start.

The sweet and fresh scent of recently shaved pinewood filled his nose as he headed toward the open door to the shop. He could hear the very busy sound of a saw of some kind. Wisely, he didn't say anything as he stepped into the doorway; he didn't want to startle anyone with a saw. He cautiously looked in the room and quickly forgot everything he might have said.

Jen stood at a workbench, her unruly red hair tied on top of her head. She wore goggles to protect her eyes, and they were the only spot on her body not covered in sawdust and woodchips. She was bent over the table and delicately cutting out a curved line in the piece of wood she held. Her long legs were wrapped with well-worn blue jeans and a snug tank top flattered her upper body.

She was breathtaking. He could only stand there staring at her. It felt as if he had been punched in the gut. There wasn't supposed to be such a thing as the perfect woman. Yet, in his book, Jen was perfection personified. Was there any man alive who could resist a redheaded artist who could make sawdust look sexy?

She turned off the saw and straightened up. When she saw him, she smiled and put her goggles on top of her head. "Good morning," she said cheerfully. As he continued to stare, her heart began to beat faster. Self-consciously, she brushed at the sawdust on her face. "What?"

"I think you're sexy," he finally said. "I want that stated now."

"Oh." She cleared her throat. What was she supposed to say to that? Was she supposed to admit that she thought he was God's gift to female woodworkers? In blue jeans and plain t-shirt, he was over six feet of mouthwatering muscle and breathtaking beauty. She had been hoping they wouldn't be paired together. How was she supposed to concentrate? She had been ogling him since the wedding!

"So." He walked into the shop and took a deep breath. "I love that smell."

She grinned. "I'll give you five bucks if you can name each one."

He lifted a brow and then grinned as well. "Pine, maple, oak and . . ." He sniffed the air. "Cedar."

"Ooh." She pulled out her wallet and handed over five dollars. "You have a nose like a bloodhound." She removed the slat of wood she was working on and carried it over to another table. "I saw from our instructions that the bed was supposed to be in a more traditional style, so I've been working on some details."

He walked over and leaned over her shoulder to look. The

wood was beginning to shape into something that might have been a curved part to a headboard. The true detail would be her hand carving. "So if I need help, I know you know your way around a jig saw."

She sniffed. "And a circular one, thank you." She could only hope a bit desperately that he hadn't noticed how fast her pulse was racing. He smelled like cherry wood. It was her absolute favorite. And he was so big and hot. For one of the few times in her life, she felt small as he moved closer.

Belatedly, he realized he was crowding her. He started to step back when his eyes lowered to the delicate line of her throat. Her pulse tripped as hard as his did. Relief made him lightheaded. He wasn't the only one feeling the madness. He moved closer and lifted one hand to lightly rest on her hip. "Question."

"Sure." The word was almost a squeak, and she cleared her throat. "I mean, sure."

"Are you afraid of me, or attracted to me?"

She considered lying. Then she considered being evasive. She even considered losing her temper. Finally, she just sighed. "I think it might be a rather intimidating combination of both." She looked up at him with a frown. "I'm not the type to just look at a man and start lusting after him. I'm out of my depth. I saw you at the wedding and was terrified you'd talk to me, and I'd act like an idiot."

"So far you're not acting like an idiot." He wiped a smudge of sawdust off her face and his hand lingered warmly. "In fact, I like how frank you are." He eased back.

Her quick smile was rueful. "So he says now. Wait until I *really* get comfortable with you. Remy blames every single swear word that Lexie knows on me. The sad part is that Lexie only knows half my vocabulary. I have a tendency to be, uhm, vocal with my temper."

"Me too." He grinned. "And I yell."

"Loudly?"

"'fraid so."

"Good. So do I." She grinned, too. "And I think this may work out after all. I think I'm starting to really like you."

"It's mutual." He looked at the clock. "Wasn't our client supposed to come by this morning to go over the details?"

"He was indeed." She looked down at her clothes. "Hopefully he won't take offense that I've already gotten started." She brushed at the wood chips and sawdust but it didn't help. "I must look like I was rolling in the bin."

He refrained from mentioning that that was part of why she seemed so sexy to him. Instead, he began to move around the shop, examining the equipment and supplies. She was as fully outfitted as he was. He felt as at home here as he did back at his shop.

A man cleared his throat and drew their attention toward the door. There they found a rather portly man in a suit staring at them. He seemed pleasant enough in appearance, but there was something in the corner of his eye that Jen didn't like. The feeling compounded when his eyes slid over her, very slowly, and lingered on her breasts and hips.

Before she was even fully conscious of her discomfort, Arian suddenly stepped slightly in front of her and shielded her with his body. "May I help you?" he asked pleasantly.

The man had to tilt back slightly to meet his eyes. A lip curled in slight disdain. "My name is Davis Harkin."

"Assemblyman Harkin?" He lifted a brow slightly.

"None other." Harkin swept his gaze over the shop. "I was told I could find Jennifer Germaine and Arian Trahern here. I presume you are they?"

"Good presumption." Jen kept her hands in her pockets. She didn't like the way Harkin looked at her. In fact, she didn't like the way he looked at her shop. He felt slimy and disgusting, and she refused to even shake his hand. "I'm Jennifer, this is Arian."

He offered a hand to her but Arian took it instead. Pointedly, Arian applied subtle force. "Nice to meet you, Assemblyman Harkin," he said pleasantly, but his blue eyes were cold. "I will assume you are our client?"

Harkin wasn't stupid enough to try to get into a pissing contest with Arian Trahern. He looked like he ate nails for breakfast and had steel girders for lunch. "Yes, yes I am." He flicked a glance over Jen again, something covetous in his eyes. "I felt it was time to upgrade my furniture, and I wanted to start with a new bed. Something fancy and handmade. I assure you, I can pay for it."

"Traditional, I believe I heard mentioned." Jen stayed slightly behind Arian; he felt like a protective shield. Chills ran down her back and she felt sick to her stomach. "Four posters, full headboard and footboard?"

"Indeed." Harkin got his hand back from Arian but all his fingers were numb. It was vaguely alarming, because he didn't recall Arian applying force. He tried to step to the side to see Jen better, but Arian shifted his weight and continued to block his full view. "I need it within two days. Tomorrow afternoon if possible."

Jen looked up at Arian as he glanced over his shoulder. He nodded slightly in agreement and turned back to Harkin. "Done," he said. "King size?"

"Yes. Room for two."

The way he said it nearly made Jen gag. Her fingers curled unconsciously into the back of Arian's shirt. He shifted back only the slightest bit, but it made her feel enveloped in his strength and heat. Safe. Protected. "We'll get started right away." She was proud of her even tone, though her stomach rolled worse than a marble on a ship deck.

Harkin paused, looked at her, and sensed, more than saw, Arian's alertness. "Very well. I will return tomorrow." He took his leave quickly, backing out of the shop without taking his eyes off Arian. He somehow felt that turning his back could be lethal.

As soon as he was gone, Jen bolted for the garbage can and proceeded to throw up all of her breakfast. While the spasms wracked her body, she was only vaguely aware of Arian gently holding her and giving her whatever support he could. When the attack ended, she had no strength to stop him as he lifted her into his arms and carried her over to the couch against the wall. He put her down as delicately as glass and went to grab a bottle of water from the cooler.

He knelt in front of her to offer it, and she found a wan smile. "I suppose this would be the ideal time to mention my gift. I'm a...barometer, I guess is how we've classified it. The higher the reading of one of the 'seven deadly sins,' the more sick I get." She took a sip of the water and then saluted lightly with the bottle. "Greed and sloth seemed high on his list."

"I do not want you to meet him alone. Ever." His voice was hard, even though the hand resting on her knee was gentle. "Do you hear me, Jennifer? Do *not* ever see him alone. I don't trust the bastard, and I'd hate to have to kill him. Killing a politician would be bad publicity."

"Depends on which paper ran the notice." She lifted a brow slowly. "And I will agree on the grounds that I am a fully grown and intelligent woman, not on the grounds that you have just ordered me to do something. You have no authority over me."

He leaned in suddenly, and they were nose to nose. Her pulse and heart kicked into overdrive. Breathless, she stared at him. There were little flecks of darker blue in his eyes, like chips of the sky. It took considerable effort not to lean forward and press her lips to his.

"How's that barometer of yours around me?" His voice was little more than a rumble of male desire.

"Silent," she managed to say.

"Then it's not as accurate as you think. Right now, your 'lust' sensor should be on full alert." He nipped at her full lower lip before backing up and straightening. "I'm going to start cutting out the frame. Once your stomach settles, you can help me or start the detailing."

Her stomach didn't need settling anymore. It was her libido that needed help. She let out a long breath. She had the very sneaky feeling that she had fallen in love. Sure as hell, there couldn't be any other reason for why he jerked at her heart and soul as strongly as her body. She watched him almost helplessly. She had once wished for true love. Did wishes really come true?

Steadier, she got to her feet, and walked over to her detailing table where smaller tools were laid out. She grabbed a sketchpad and began to draw quickly, outlining what she thought the bed should look like. It was to her credit that she didn't jump when Arian's arm suddenly slid around her shoulders and he tugged her against him so he could see over her head. "Well?" she asked.

"I like it." He ran a finger over the line of a poster. It was inlaid with beautiful details. "Which is easier? To carve a poster, or to carve a casing for a poster? I can make a poster to scale and you can carve into it, or I can make a smaller one and we can attach details."

"For stability sake, we should carve into the poster. But, frankly, I don't see his bed getting that much usage, no matter what he infers."

He decided he was absolutely crazy for his red haired partner. If he wasn't looking at her, he was thinking about her. And when he was looking at her, all he could think of was pulling her into his arms and tasting her lips. It was more than that, though. She was acerbic and strong willed in ways that he loved. When she smiled, he felt like he was looking into paradise. He would go crazy if he couldn't have her at his side, always. "Let's go with simple. I'll make the posters smaller."

They settled into an easy rhythm. She put on the radio in the background after a while, so they had something to listen to other than the whine and whir of power tools. She narrowed in and focused on her detailing. Under her skillful hands, the little accents started to bloom. As he worked, the entire bed frame began to come to life. At first there were planks of wood. Then there was the rough outline of a bed. He only gave it a temporary assembly, because it needed to be taken apart for more detailing later.

As the sun was setting, he was beginning to sand and smooth in preparation for stain. She still worked on details. The pain in her lower back finally got to her, and she put down her tools to stretch largely. The clock cheerfully said it was nearly one in the morning. "I think we need some sleep."

He watched her hungrily. The way the light rippled over her when she stretched had done dangerous things to his already aching body. "Don't suppose you'd mind if I fell asleep on the couch."

"Not at all." She got to her feet carefully. "I'll probably only sleep a few hours then come back to do more work. Is that okay?"

"Sure." He busied himself with cleaning up anything they wouldn't use the next day while she closed and locked all the doors. Finally he just couldn't take it anymore.

When she turned from locking the door, he was right behind her. Breath lodged in her chest, she backed into the wall as he loomed in dangerously, seductively close. This time her barometer seemed to be going off the chart, but it didn't make her stomach sick. There was a deep difference between selfish lust and a lust born of deeper emotions. She just couldn't tell if it was his or hers that had her sensors spiking.

His head slowly bent until his breath was hot on her lips. He stayed there, his eyes keeping hers captive. He waited with the stillness of a predator, and his body seemed to vibrate with desperate hunger. She knew, was certain, that he would back off and not press the issue if she told him no. She couldn't do it, not when she wanted him just as terribly. She slid her arms up around his neck, rose on her toes, and met his kiss with aching desire.

The kiss turned into the most devastating experience of her life. He didn't just kiss her; he *consumed* her. Despite the blatant carnal nature of his tongue tangling with hers, he kissed her with a famished need, long, and deep, and drugging. It seemed as if he was imprinting her taste inside him. Her entire body went hot and weak, only his arm around her waist keeping her on her feet.

He lifted his head, and his eyes burned. She couldn't even find her voice or her mind. In fact, she wasn't sure she entirely remembered who she was or where she was. The best she could get her jumbled thoughts and riotous hormones around was, "Wow."

His teeth nipped at her lips and her knees shook. He shifted, and pressed closer so she couldn't mistake his body's desire for her. The languid, slumberous darkening to her eyes made a shudder rip through his body. If merely kissing her was hotter than foreplay with other women, how the hell would he survive if she was in his bed? Or hers. The couch was also looking appealing. "Are you going to stay with me? Or invite me in?" His voice was a purr against her ear as his teeth nibbled enticingly.

She wanted to. God, she wanted to with every fiber of her being, but she hadn't gotten to thirty without learning who she was and what she wanted and needed. She had decided on an 'all or none' commitment, knowing only that would make her happy. "Not yet," she managed to say. Not until she knew she could keep him.

He slowly released her, his hands sliding over her body with a possessive touch. "Okay." His lips quirked. "But know that I only have the strength to release you because you said 'yet' and not 'never.'"

"What, am I stupid?" She shoved her hair out of her eyes. "Are all of you Traherns alike?"

"To our knowledge."

"Then no wonder Lexie lost her mind." She pressed against his body for a moment to find his ready strength. His arms curled around her, and she let herself soak in his comforting embrace. As she did, she acknowledged what was inside. She loved him. Her wish had come true. But did he love her? Well, if not, then she would change it. "Good night, Arian."

He released her and watched her go into the building through an attached door. He let out a long breath and eyed the couch. He would never fit, but perhaps the cramped corners would help distract him from his body's cranky messages.

When Jen walked into the house, she saw Lexie looking at her gravely. "Not a word," she muttered as she stomped past. "I need a cold shower." Ignoring her baby sister's distinct giggles, she went upstairs.

She only managed to get a few hours of sleep, and what few

hours she got were not very restful. She had never realized before how cold and lonely it could be to sleep by herself. She should have offered to share her bed, she thought, as she stared at the ceiling. Arian had the bedrock decency to sleep with her but not seduce her unless she wanted it.

A little guilty that he was sleeping on the couch, she got out of bed and got dressed. When she walked into the shop and saw him sprawled on the couch, his legs hanging over the arm, she had to bite her lip to hide a smile. She walked over and leaned down to brush his lips with hers. "Wake up, sleeping beauty," she murmured.

Drowsily, he said, "That's my baby sister."

"Snow White?"

"T'other sister."

She shook her head affectionately. "You have the most fascinating family, Arian."

One eye cracked open and then closed on a groan. "It's not morning."

"Afraid so. It happens every day in fact. Usually around the same time of day." She moved back hastily as his hands lifted. "Don't you dare." He swung his legs around and sat up, and she held out the coffee she was holding. "Careful. Rie made it, and I could use it to clean my saw."

He gratefully accepted the cup. The coffee was hot, strong, and could have etched steel. He drank half the cup in a single gulp. His sleep hadn't been any more restful than hers; the small couch had done nothing to distract his mind or body. "How much work do we have left?"

"If you'll take over using the jig saw to cut out shapes, not much at all. A few hours." She rolled her shoulders and neck. "The nearly all-nighter helped. Oh god." The last was added as his hands settled on her neck and began to rub. She relaxed under his hands as his fingers found and firmly removed every knot. With a soft whimper of pleasure, she braced a hand on the table.

The little sound went through him like lightning. He bent his head to brush his lips over her ear. "When we're done," he breathed softly, "want me to get rid of all of them? All over your body?"

"Yeah." She leaned back against him, her head finding the perfect spot on his shoulder. "But I won't promise to sleep with you."

"I wouldn't expect you to." He feathered a kiss over her cheek and slowly released her. "It was an offer made without strings, Jen." He contemplated her. "Why Jen instead of Jenny?"

She lifted a brow. "Do I look like a Jenny?"

"No. It's too . . . perky."

She opened her mouth but closed it without protest. She laughed. "Damn, it's hard to be offended at the truth." She turned to lean up and brush his lips with her own. "Let's get this thing finished."

With him focusing on cutting, she was able to focus on the detailed carving. Sure, there were machines to do that kind of work, but it really wasn't the same as doing it by hand. While she finished the last piece, he attached everything together.

When the bed was finally done, they both stepped back to survey their work. "Damn," he said.

"I'll see your 'Damn' and raise you a 'Holy Hell.'" She ran a hand over the footboard. "This is definitely the best thing I've ever made. I *hate* the idea of giving it to that slimy worm. He doesn't deserve something this nice."

"We'll make another one," he decided. "Even better than this one."

"Deal."

He tossed his goggles onto the table. "I don't know about you, but breakfast didn't stay long. There's a restaurant a few blocks away that does dine-out. I'll pick something up. What do you want?"

She thought about it. "Anything edible. I'm not picky." She smiled as he dropped a casual kiss across her lips before heading out the side door. Arian, she had learned, was a very physical man. He showed affection with touch. A hand on the shoulder, a skim of his fingers through her hair, a kiss on the lips or cheek. A woman would never question his feelings for her, and she was beginning to think her handsome Viking was the tiniest bit infatuated with her as well.

She busied herself with starting to put away tools. All the doors were shut and the radio was playing, so she danced her way around the tables. A knock on the side door had her brows lifting, and she walked over to open it. Her stomach instantly rolled and she was on her guard. "Assemblyman Harkin, hello."

Harkin glanced over her shoulder, saw no sign of Arian, and couldn't have been more delighted. He had already had a bad morning and didn't want to deal with this Trahern brother, too. "Hello, Miss Germaine. I came to see progress."

She reluctantly stepped back and mentally prayed for Arian to come back quickly. If needed, she thought Lexie and Joseff might be in Lexie's shop on the other side of the building, but she wasn't sure she could call them in time if Harkin pulled something. "We're done, in fact."

He spotted the bed and his mouth fell open. "Well." Astonished, he walked closer to see it better. He had never seen finer craftsmanship. "This is impressive work by both of you. Every penny is well spent."

She sat down at the workbench. Her hand rested on the top, ready to reach for a sharp tool if needed. Her stomach rocked and rolled. "Arian and I haven't discussed price," she said, though she was filled with disgust at watching him touch the bed. "He just stepped out, so why don't we wait for him to come back?"

"Nonsense. Name your price." He moved closer to her. "I assure you, I can meet it." His eyes slid over her. "Any price."

Temper began a slow boil and alleviated the sickness. "I am not for sale," she warned, her voice clipped. "And I do not appreciate the way you look at me or address me. Harassment is a strong word, Mr. Harkin, but I'm not afraid to use it."

"Don't be silly. Who would believe you?" He put a hand on her leg and slid it up her thigh. "It's your word against mine. Now, name your price."

Just as her hand curled around a carving tool, a dark shadow filled the doorway and blocked the sunlight. Arian was on Harkin in a blink, his hand closing around the other man's and prying it off Jen with little effort. "You don't touch a woman without permission," he snarled. "Especially not mine!"

"I'll have you arrested for assault!" Harkin squeaked. He couldn't feel his arm, and his fingers were a blaze of agony.

"Before or after I send security tapes to the press?" He applied force and drove Harkin slowly back toward the door. His entire body vibrated with rage. "There are cameras in this shop, Assemblyman. And even your money couldn't buy your way out."

"Wh-what about your job?" Harkin was nearly doubled in pain, the words a gasp. If his fingers weren't broken, they were assuredly going to be dislocated.

"We're firing ourselves. We don't want your money, and you certainly don't deserve our work!" Arian shoved him out the door so hard that he landed on his ass on the cement, his useless arm hanging at his side. "Good day." He slammed the door hard enough that the walls shook, and then turned his gaze on Jen. Something volatile and deadly churned in his eyes. "You let him in."

"Was I supposed to let him rot outside?" she snapped. She dropped the tool she had grabbed. "I was trying to stall for you to get back!" She fiercely rubbed a hand over her leg. "He *touched* me!" Despite her anger, her voice hitched. "His hand felt slimy!"

He crossed the room swiftly, and his hand brushed hers aside. As his hot palm swept over her leg, even the lingering remnants of Harkin's horrible touch faded. When he snatched her up off her seat, she threw her arms around his neck and kissed him with all the pent up fury in her heart.

Just as fast, his anger turned to hunger, and he tumbled her down onto the floor of the shop. "He touched you!" he said against her lips. His fingers rushed over her work shirt, unbuttoning it as fast as he could. He had to have her naked. Had to touch her. Love her. "Damn you, Jennifer!"

It only barely crossed her mind to stop him. Barely. For a split second. It was, after all, the middle of the afternoon and they were on the sawdust and wood chip covered floor of her workshop. The pungent scent of wood combined with his own ripe, wonderful scent and any protest died. She needed him. Wanted him. And, damn it, she was going to have him.

The next time she found any energy or will to think or speak, she was lying sprawled underneath him. Her body was still quivering and shaking in the aftermath of ecstasy. Her legs were locked around his hips and her arms around his shoulders. Against her chest, she could feel his heart still hammering as hard as hers. "Wow," she managed to say.

His lips curved against her neck. "I'll see your 'Wow' and raise you a 'Holy Hell.'" He carefully lifted his head. "Am I too heavy?"

"Not really. But the wood chips are digging into my back." She held on with a laugh as he rolled and pulled her on top of him. She sat up, straddling his hips, and shook her hair back. Their bodies were still joined, and she felt the sudden leap of his arousal slowly stretching her again. It sent off streamers of pleasure, and her lashes dropped. "It's a good thing there aren't really cameras in here," she said huskily.

"Yeah." His voice was just as rough as he stared up at her. She was rumpled and flushed and covered in sawdust and wood chips. She was the most stunning thing he had ever seen. "Jen, I think we're just going to have to get married. I can't seem to stand the idea of you rolling over wood chips with any other man."

"I suppose that's fair." She flexed her hips for the sheer torture of seeing his eyes darken. "I'd hate to find you rolling on sawdust with any other woman. What do you suppose we keep the bed for our honeymoon? We can reinforce the posters. I'm sure we'll give it a *lot* of use." Her breath caught as his hands slid slowly up her body. "I don't suppose I could get a vow of everlasting love, could I?"

His fingers tangled in her hair, and he drew her down until their lips met softly and sweetly. "Yes to all of it," he breathed. He kissed her again, deeper and sweeter. "Hell yes I love you, Jen. I think I have all along."

Tears burned her eyes. "I love you, too," she whispered. "I wished for true love once. I never expected the powers-that-be to give me someone like you." She slowly straightened and stretched, knowing it did wicked things to him when she did. "Now make love to me."

"I thought that's what I had already done."

"Do it again."

"As my lady wishes." His lips curved. "After all, when you wish for something, you apparently have to have it."

Her eyes smoldered with love, and laughter, and desire. "Of course."

Listening on the other side of the door, Lexie and Joseff shared a grin and a high five. One down, five to go.

CHAPTER EIGHTEEN

Owen and Sam decided to meet at Kingdom Design as well, since Sam's computer lab hiding on the second floor of the building was better outfitted. First thing in the morning on the day after the meeting, Owen knocked on the front door. It was opened by a rather harried looking Belle. Or Rie. He wasn't sure which was which yet. "Morning . . .?"

"Belle. Sam's on the second floor. Gotta go, bye!"

He moved aside as she zipped out the door. He smiled wryly to himself. Tomos had better watch himself. He knew full well that his little brother was smitten with Belle, and if she was half as charming as she seemed, Tomos was a doomed man.

As he climbed the stairs, he contemplated his own future. From the moment he had laid eyes on Samantha Germaine, he had been fascinated by her. She was by far the most outgoing of the Germaine sisters, but there was a hint of vulnerability inside her large green eyes that tugged at his nurturing heart. She wore extremely thick glasses, and he had the feeling they weren't the run-of-the-mill kind. They added to the hint of vulnerability and seemed oddly appealing.

Was he attracted to her? With every fiber of his being. She was lush, and sultry, and the kind of tempting siren who would, very easily, lure happy sailors to their doom. He was practical and levelheaded. He understood the lack of coincidence in 3rd District, and he understood symmetry. His startling hunger for Sam Germaine would, no doubt, turn into affection and then to love. He was prepared for it. Even fascinated by it.

He was not prepared to walk into her computer room and have the floor drop out from under his feet so fast and sharp that he was falling before he knew he had stepped off a cliff. She was curled up on a window seat next to a bay window and reading a thick book. The morning sun turned her dark red hair to the rich, lush color of red wine, the kind that lingered on his tongue and was the embodiment of flavor.

Her skin was flawless like porcelain, and freckles scattered across the top of her nose and her high cheekbones. Her lips were tempting red, carnal and inviting. Her body was shapely and made as if from his fantasies. She sensed his gaze and looked at him. And she smiled.

Owen hit the ground. Hard.

The gut punch nearly knocked him back a step. Reeling, he could only stare. Every thought of being calm and practical dissolved. *It wasn't supposed to be that easy!* But it was. Between the slam of desire at seeing her to the heart wrenching beauty of her smile, he had fallen in love.

He very carefully hid it inside until he was more ready to deal with it. Even as his practical mind said it had to be mutual eventually, his heart was going ninety miles an hour with agitated ponderings. How was he supposed to handle Sam now? He knew she was hell on wheels; he could sense she was like Gavin, and god only knew that Gavin was a terror. If she knew she could have anything she wanted just by smiling, he would be doomed.

"Owen?" Sam tilted her head as she got to her feet. "Something wrong? You're just standing there." And making her pulse dance like a drunken frat boy at Mardi Gras. The way his cerulean eyes had darkened as they swept over her face had stolen her breath. She hoped it was a sign he wanted her as badly as she had wanted him since she had first seen him.

Unfortunately, his eyes cleared, and he smiled in a way that seemed only friendly. "Not at all. I was just surprised, because I didn't realize you were as big a book geek as I am."

Her back teeth clicked together. "I am not a geek."

"I didn't mean it to be offensive," he protested. "I see it's a sore spot, so I'll let it be." He walked further into the room and smiled. Though the computer desk and set up was totally high-tech and modern, the rest of the room was as feminine as it could get. "I feel much like Gallagher must have felt encountering the Lilliputs."

She smirked. "Suck it up, and be a man about it." She walked over to the drafting table and easily adjusted it. "There. Now you'll fit. Should I find a chair more suitable to your frame, Mr. Gallagher?"

This time it was his back teeth that clicked together. It took considerable effort not to let his temper flare. It seemed surprisingly quick, for once. "I think I can make do." He put the case he was carrying down on the top of the table. "I have the drawings here. Let's work on the first blueprint for the outside and then move inward. As I work on them, you can do the modeling."

"Fair enough." She pulled another chair over and sat down beside him. Deliberately, she leaned in, so he was sure to notice her presence. He didn't even bat a lash. "How does this work for you?"

"I have to calculate the rough dimensions of the drawn buildings and translate them to a blueprint." He wished like hell she would back up. Her perfume made his mouth water. And, damn it, he wished she would button her shirt all the way. The tempting swell of her breasts made his fingers itch.

"Oh so you're not all brawn. Sometimes it's hard to tell." Her eyes widened innocently. "I mean, you know all the stereotypes."

"Like the one about redheads having a temper?"

"It's not a stereotype if it's true. All us Germaines have a temper. Bad ones. And did I mention that most of us tend to yell?"

"No wonder you aren't married."

That stung. She straightened up and crossed her arms. "I'll have you know," she retorted stiffly, "that we all set our standards very high and no men have ever held up to them. I haven't met a single one yet."

Equally stung, he nodded sagely as if he didn't want to give her a good shake. "I know how that feels. We Traherns set our standards pretty high as well. I don't think I've ever met a woman who could compare. I always leaned toward short brunettes, personally." It was a lie, but he couldn't resist the dig.

She got to her feet with a sharp motion and went over to her computer to start booting it up. It was as much to keep from getting mad as it was to hide how much that had hurt. So she wasn't the perfect woman. There was no such thing as perfection. So what if she was tall and red haired? So what if she wasn't some kind of meek little mouse that he could boss around? He would be bored. Quiet and practical as he was, he was still too strong a man to be happy with a woman he could run roughshod over.

Things were quiet for the next two hours. Neither spoke except to make preliminary decisions about building materials, room dimensions, and other details for her to plug into her modeling program. It was homegrown and specially made to suit her needs. She didn't even want to know how Tabby had fused so many different program elements into her 'Modelmaker 2000.'

When the silence finally got to her, she asked, "How did you lose your parents?"

"Car accident. You?"

She had to smile. "Our ever-so-practical parents decided to go mountain climbing. When Dad fell off a cliff, he was hooked to Mom for safety. They both fell all the way down the mountain. We've always thought that it was just like them to go out together and so spectacularly."

"You were only eighteen," he murmured.

"Small 'only' margin. I was halfway through my degree. Remy held us all together. Jen and I helped however we could." She looked at him to see him watching her, his eyes dark with shared empathy. Her heart lurched and stopped for long moments. When it started again, it was no longer her own.

A little shaken, she turned back to her computer. She hadn't been expecting that. She hadn't expected to fall in love. Was he the one she had wished for all along? When she had made her wish for true love, she had never truly expected to get it, let alone with a man like Owen Trahern.

Silence fell once more. He handed over the first set of blueprints, and she got to work. His handwriting was very precise and his calculations were fabulous. She didn't have to question anything. She could simply lose herself in the construction of the delicate flower shop. She loved modeling. Seeing a building spring up with a few mouse clicks was her favorite thing.

However, as the day became evening and then turned into night, her eyes became strained. It was only when his hands settled on her shoulders and pulled her back from the monitor that she realized how close she had gotten. "Oops." She rubbed at her eyes. "Sorry."

"Don't be sorry. I didn't notice either. I think my neck is permanently stuck sideways." He rolled his shoulders. "Let's close up shop and start again in the morning." He peered at a clock. "Hmm. Amended. Let's start again later."

She squinted at the clock. "It's not midnight."

"Afraid it is."

"Ugh." She pulled off her glasses to better rub at her eyes. "See you later then."

"Good night, Sam." He hesitated, brushed a hand over her hair, and then left the room. He headed down to the first floor and unexpectedly found Lexie sitting on the stairs. He quirked a brow. "And here I thought you'd be with Joseff."

She smiled at up at him. "He went to get a bag. Remy told him to just stop being wishy-washy and spend the entire night. We'll be trading back and forth until we get our own place." She eyed him shrewdly. "You like Sam, huh?" Before he could speak, she continued on blithely, "In case it wasn't mentioned, I can read people. I hear the voice of people's hearts. And yours? Yeah. LOUD."

He smiled. "No wonder you've got Joseff hooked."

"He says it's because I'm a good kisser." She nodded sagely. "He said he was addicted."

He bent and gave her a quick kiss like he would give either of his sisters. "Nah, not that impressive."

"Hey," Joseff complained as he came in the front door. "Lips off my girl. Get your own." He studied Owen's face but said nothing about what he saw. "How's the project?"

"Moving along." He hesitated, then asked Lexie, "Why does Sam wear glasses?"

Her gaze lowered. "It's her decision to tell if she wants to."

Sensing the sadness, Owen let it be and left for the night. He went home and went to bed, but he wasn't entirely surprised when he couldn't go to sleep. He was fairly sure that he and the others were being set up, and he didn't know whether he wanted to yell at his meddling Enforcer family members or thank them.

He headed back over to Kingdom Design the next morning. When he got there, Sam was leaning on the open sill of her window. She looked as lovely and fresh as a storybook princess. Owen, a closet romantic, couldn't help but be charmed. "Good morning," he called up to her. "Sleep well?"

She looked down to answer, and her glasses slipped off her nose. He tried to jump forward, but he wasn't quite fast enough. The glasses hit a large rock in the garden and promptly shattered. "Shit!" he cursed. He quickly gathered up the pieces and looked up. She hadn't moved, and there was horror in her eyes.

He took the stairs two at a time and went into her room. She hadn't budged from the window. "It's okay, Sam," he urged. "We can make this work." He looked closer and realized her shoulders were shaking. "Come over here," he added gently. "It's not the end of the world."

"I can't," she whispered.

"Why not?" He began to frown. "If you're near-sighted, then . . ."

"I'm not." She turned around very carefully, her hands gripping

the wall. Tears slid down her cheeks. "I'm legally blind, Owen. All I see right now is a blurred wash of color. No details. Nothing." More tears slid free. "I can't even see where you're standing. I could be in front of a cliff and wouldn't know."

He moved toward her carefully but her eyes didn't blink. He waved a hand gently in front of her eyes and she didn't flinch. Her gaze was completely unfocused, unable to grab onto anything. "Do you have spare glasses?" he asked as calmly as he could.

"No. Th-they're so expensive. Experimental glass. They're fragile but they allow me to see. I'm better with 3D than 2D, so computers are okay for me, but I have trouble reading on paper. I make myself do it anyway because I love books." Her lips trembled and she reached out a hand blindly. "Where are you?" Her voice quivered.

He caught her hand and drew it to his heart. "Here," he said softly. He eased her away from the window and took her over to the couch. "Sit." When she had, he sat beside her. He never once released her. His heart was breaking. His sassy, confident, and rather aggravating partner seemed more fragile than her glasses. "What happened?" he asked softly. He stroked his thumb over her cheekbone. "Was it from birth?"

She shook her head and desperately held onto his hand. Her other hand covered the one on her cheek. Even with him right beside her, she saw nothing but a blur. The blur was so extreme that not even movement penetrated it. Sometimes she thought she saw something shift, but she could never be sure it wasn't just her imagination. Only color could move across her sight but it never had form. She wanted to crawl into Owen's arms and make everything go away, but she was terrified of moving.

As if sensing it, he pulled her into his arms and pressed her head to his shoulder. "Close your eyes," he said softly. "Then you won't see anything because you want it to be that way."

She closed her eyes and everything steadied. Her body relaxed against him. "You would think I ought to have great eyesight, considering my gift," she murmured. "I'm a pentachromat. I have five cones in my eyes for receiving color, unlike normal humans who have three. There's so much color in the world, Owen. I can't even describe it."

He rubbed his cheek against her hair. "No wonder you're an artist. How did you lose your sight?"

"When I was five, my kindergarten class was attacked by a psychotic woman. I don't remember the exact details of what set her off. She planted a bomb in my classroom and kept us all hostage while she screamed at the police. The others were eventually released. I wasn't."

He went very still. "I remember that event. I remember watching it on the news. I was nine." He took a sharp breath. "God. I do remember that event. She detonated the bomb while you were both inside the room."

"It was faulty. It wasn't as big as she thought it would be. It killed her." Her lower lip trembled. "All I remember was seeing this immense fireball of heat. The next thing I know, I'm waking in the hospital and I can't see anything except a permanent blur of color. The explosion damaged my eyes in ways that even surgery could not fix."

He flinched harshly. With a soothing murmur, he pulled her closer and sought to use his power to keep her calm. "And the glasses?"

"Pure experimentation, but they work for me. It'll take me a few months to save for a new pair." She tried to smile but it wobbled. "Maybe I can call on my distant family relation through Lexie to Gwyn or Rayna, and Enforcers can help me out."

"You're not alone, honey. We'd all help chip in."

"But what do we do *now*?" She wiped her eyes on his shirt. "I can't uphold the end of my bargain. I can't see, so how can I use a computer?"

He took a long breath. "If you are willing to trust me, there is a way. My primary abilities are of the mind. I can sense and read things about people. I have, on occasion, merged my mind with one of my brothers so we could share data. When we did, we could see out each other's eyes as needed."

She didn't lift her head but she was suddenly alert. "Would that work for me?"

"It can't hurt to try. But here's the thing." He framed her face with his hands. "Doing this means that there will be no secrets between us. You're going to see everything inside me and I'll see everything inside you. And if you don't trust me, it'll never work at all. Your mind will reject me."

He would see everything. That meant he would see all her desperate love and desire. She lowered her head. He would have known anyway. Eventually he wouldn't have been able to mistake it. "Okay," she said softly.

She didn't really know what to expect. There were all sorts of stories and legends about mind merges and what they were like. Much to her surprise, she at first didn't feel anything at all when he merged his mind to hers. Then, without warning, it hit her. Like a shot of straight whiskey to her blood, the rush flooded her head. The tidal wave of memories and thoughts and feelings dragged her under so fast that she nearly panicked and pulled out. But then she saw something. Something beautiful and wondrous. It was his most cherished memory, most cherished emotion.

Her.

She saw herself reflected in his eyes. She saw his acceptance of what might happen and his shock for what did. His vulnerability. And his hunger. Her breath shortened as his hunger whipped up her own. And there, surging at careful chains, was his love. He loved her.

Owen, reeling from the onslaught of her emotions and thoughts, hadn't realized she had clamped onto his most carefully hidden secret, until he noticed she was swinging her hand blindly. "What are you doing?"

"Trying to find you so I can hit you!" she shouted. "You gave me no clue that you were attracted to me! Or that you were in love

with me! I was going nuts trying to get you to notice me, and you were pretending like it was nothing! Hold still so I can hit you!"

An absurd urge to laugh rose inside him. Her emotions were laid bare before him. It was fairly obvious, now, that they were both idiots. "I knew at the start that this was bound to happen, and yet I stupidly kept it inside, never thinking that your sharp tongue might be because you were feeling rejected. So much for my being the levelheaded one."

"Steady as a rock," she retorted waspishly, "but about as dense! Oooh! Damn you, Owen Trahern! I ought to kick you!"

"You can't even see to hit me," he pointed out practically. "So kicking is out."

She lowered a hand, patted forward, and found his chest. She pinched sharply and was rewarded by his yelp. "Yeah, but I fight like a girl!" She opened her eyes reflexively and the room spun eerily on its axis. Everything abruptly settled, and it was in crystal clear, sharp detail. An explosion of color surrounded her like the inside of a prism. She took a sharp breath in shock. "That's not possible."

"I told you that you could use my eyes." His face was impossibly tender as he looked down at her. His blue eyes seemed to be made of a million flecks of other colors. "That doesn't just mean you see what I see. It means you can literally borrow my *ability* to see." He framed her face with his hands. "You have the most amazingly complex and beautiful mind I have ever seen or touched. It's going to tear out a piece of me when we let go."

"Then don't." She smiled up at him. "I'm in love with you, and you're in love with me. That seems to be a good reason to keep this mind merge. I mean, you don't have to. People in love don't *have* to be together, so you could walk out the door." She paused, then added deliberately, "Of course, I'd have to chase you down. I may be blind, but I'm sneaky."

He rubbed a hand over where she had pinched him. "I'd noticed." He cupped the back of her head and drew her up so that her lips met his. The kiss was soft, and sweet, and wonderful. His feelings and hers; they were a jumbled mass that fueled both. Hunger rose sharply and burst into a firestorm. Ravenous for him, she threw her arms around his neck and kissed him wildly as her body arched against his to relieve the pressure.

He twisted and tumbled her down onto the couch. As his mouth devoured hers, his hands slid under her shirt and began to memorize every inch of her soft flesh. Old scars marked her body from the explosions and he lingered over each to erase the memory. "You better stop me," he muttered against her lips, "or I'll take you right here!"

An out-of-control Owen was the sexiest thing she had ever experienced. "Don't you dare stop!" He rose over her, his eyes burning, and she lifted her hands to frame his face. Very seriously, she asked, "Owen, will you marry me? If I waited for you to ask, your practical mind would wait *forever* for 'the right moment.' This is it, and I'm not waiting. I love you, I want to marry you, and eventually, I want to have your children."

He slowly began to smile. "You are the most incredible person I have ever met." He kissed her again, slowly, with a famished heat, until she seemed to melt underneath him with a purr of pleasure in her throat. "Yes," he said softly. "I'll marry you, Sam Germaine. I'll share my eyes with you if you share your heart."

"I just want *your* heart."

"It's yours." He feathered kisses over her face softly and began to slowly make his way down her body as he tugged her shirt up and out of his way. "How's that wishes coming true thing working for you? Am I a suitable choice for a girl who wished for true love?" Her answering emotion nearly took all the strength from his arms. On a groan, he gathered her fiercely close. "Out loud," he rasped. "Say it out loud."

"The girl who wished for true love," she whispered, "could never have dared imagine you. The woman who wished for true love could ask for nothing more." She muffled a giggle suddenly. "Owen, aren't we supposed to be working?"

"Later." He buried his face between her breasts. "Much later. Maybe this afternoon."

They didn't get much work done that afternoon, either. Eventually they gave up and snuck down to her bedroom. As they cuddled together, she rested her head on his shoulder and listened to his heart. She had stopped using his eyes but was no longer so afraid of being blind. She wasn't alone inside her rainbow world anymore. "When do we tell the others?" she asked idly.

He linked his hands under his head. "We'll tell them as we see them, and they no doubt guess, but I think we won't be the only ones with news. Coincidentally, we both have five other siblings paired up. And this makes us two for two of matched couples."

Her lips curved. "But, Owen, there's no such thing as coincidence in 3rd District."

"Exactly."

CHAPTER NINETEEN

When Gavin got outside the meeting room, he saw Tabby walking down the hall ahead of him. He hurried down to catch up with her. "Hey," he said as he fell into step beside her. As he did, he didn't miss the way she edged away. He also didn't miss that she wore long sleeves and jeans despite the heat outside, and her hands were in her pockets. The only bit of skin showing was her face.

It was a beautiful bit of skin, tempting and alluring. His eyes ran over her face eagerly. She seemed so delicate compared to her sisters. She was, by far, the most slender and had the most fragile feeling to her. She would glance at him out the corner of her eye, and the wary flashes of pine green were stirring up every urge possible to go out and slay dragons for her.

She really wished he wouldn't stare at her. It was making her entire body heat and long for things it could not have.

Her hands were in her pockets as much for his safety as her own. They wanted nothing more than to get into the thick mop he called hair and to trace the strong line of his jaw, to feel the scrape of the neat goatee on his chin.

Dear god, her partner was *hot*. HOT. Capital letters, bold, underlined, italics. His voice fluttered along everything feminine inside her whenever he spoke. When they got outside, she finally asked softly, "Can you not stare at me?"

He shot her a lethal grin. "Well, I *can* but I don't want to. You're really pretty, Tabby." He stopped walking and turned to face her. Deliberately, he held out a hand. "Let's be formally introduced. I'm

Gavin Trahern, computer hacker extraordinaire and electrical wiring genius."

She looked at his hand but didn't take it. "Tabitha Germaine, or Tabby to most everyone. I'm a computer programmer and programing specialist. I design diagnostic programs on the fly, tailored to situations."

He started to lift his hand to her cheek and she flinched back sharply. He dropped his hand. "Okay," he said quietly. "This could be difficult. I'm from a very physical family. We show affection with touch, and I like you, so I'm inclined to want to touch you in passing." *There* was an understatement. The way he wanted to touch her had nothing to do with family, and nothing to do with casual. "You want to tell me why you're afraid of me?"

She looked up swiftly. "No, it's not you. I'm not afraid of you." Miserably, she said, "My 'gift' for being 3rd District born can be painful to other people and to me. It's transmitted via physical contact. So please don't touch me."

There was a long silence. Then, "When was the last time you were hugged, Tabby Cat?"

Her eyes widened slightly at the nickname. "Tabby Cat?" she echoed. He just smiled and she frowned, choosing instead to focus on the question. "I don't remember," she admitted. "Probably when I was a kid. The problem kicked in when I was five."

"What would happen if I touched you?" Because he had to. Needed to. Craved to. The ache in his body paled when compared to the ache in his heart. His kitten desperately needed someone to hold and cuddle her. Belatedly, something dawned on him and his eyes slowly widened. "Tabby . . . you've *never* been able to touch *anyone*?"

She looked at him miserably, knowing well what he was really asking. "No, I haven't." She let out a long breath. "You don't have to be delicate around me, Gavin. If you tell bawdy jokes, you're not going to offend a fragile virgin. Just because I've never been kissed doesn't mean my mind isn't an adult's."

The sheer fact that she blushed slightly seemed to argue with her words, but he didn't push it. He was still reeling that she had been entirely isolated from any physical contact for that many years. The injustice of it churned inside him. She was so beautiful, and sexy, and sweet. She had known idiots in her life. He would have happily risked anything to have her for his own.

Would risk anything.

The thud inside his heart was not entirely unexpected. He had landed in love. Falling? He had been doing that since he had looked across a conference table and seen a pair of haunted green eyes watching him. Being Gavin, he didn't bother to hide or evade the situation. "Okay, Tabby cat," he said. "We need to talk. Follow me."

Puzzled, she followed him around the side of the building to where there was a small garden. He sat down on a bench, and she sat down as far from him as she could. "What's wrong?" she asked. "Are you . . . offended?"

"Hell, no." He turned to face her. "Here's the thing, Tabby Cat. I'm in love with you. I just realized it about thirty seconds ago." As her eyes widened, he continued on, "It's not really surprising, actually. I've wanted you since I saw you, and you were pulling on my heartstrings with more skill than a concert violinist.

"That being said, what would happen if I touched you? Would it kill me?" When she shook her head, he scooted closer. "Just be exceptionally painful?" Sparks seemed to almost literally leap between them as he leaned in. His entire body was heavy with desire to touch her. He bent his head, intent on claiming the soft pink lips luring him to his doom.

She hastily shot off the bench and moved out of reach. "You are *dangerous!*" she blurted. Her pulse was scrambling and her lips were tingling, and he hadn't even touched her! He stood and began to stalk toward her, and she backed up quickly. "No!" she said sharply. "Gavin, please! I don't want to hurt you! If-if we're going to work together, you're going to have to get over this."

He grinned. "How does one get over being in love, Tabby Cat?"

"Stop calling me that!" she demanded in exasperation.

"No. It suits you. You're sleek, and feminine, and you could really do with a good dose of petting from the right man." His blue eyes smoldered. "Like me."

"My abilities won't magically turn off," she whispered. "Don't you think I've *tried*?"

"What are they? Tell me and maybe I can find a way around them." She shook her head, and he shook his head in return. "I get the feeling you're a little bit afraid, Tabby Cat. Not just of me, but of yourself. What idiot blamed you when you accidentally hurt him with your powers?" She was silent. "Clearly there was one."

"I didn't say that."

"You didn't have to." He hooked his thumbs through his belt loops. "Okay. I'll try to be patient. I can't promise to succeed. I have a tendency to grab what I want, when I want it. And I want you. Let's meet at the project tomorrow, and we can get to know each other. And if you decide to trust me, then you can tell me what your gift is."

She took a deep breath. She wanted to run away as fast as possible, but she couldn't do it. She wanted to be with Gavin. She wanted to see his quick smile, to see his midnight blue eyes lighten when he was amused. And dear god she wanted to kiss him. Her entire body throbbed with heat. Her breasts ached, and she crossed her arms quickly. His eyes lowered and his lips curved as if he knew. She decided on the coward's route. "See you tomorrow." She turned and hurried away as fast as she could.

He sank down to sit on the bench and put his head in his hands. When he sensed Joseff sit beside him, he said ruefully, "You have my sincerest apologies for the hell I gave you the last few days over Lexie."

Joseff cleared his throat. "Apology accepted. I take it you like Tabby?" He got a sideways look from wry, and warning blue eyes. He grinned. "Ah."

"Great understatement there." Gavin straightened up with a sigh. "There must be some mystical compatibility between our two bloodlines. And our children are going to confuse the hell out of everyone." He scrubbed his hands over his face. "Boy, aren't I the optimistic one? I haven't even kissed her."

"You know," Joseff said, "Lexie told me that Tabby and Sam were the two with the biggest handicaps but they had responded in polar opposite ways. Sam is outgoing and blunt. Tabby is shy and soft-spoken. And no," he added, "I don't know what their handicaps are. But Lexie said that Tabby's one, and only, attempt at having a boyfriend ended up with him hospitalized. She was fourteen at the time."

He winced. "Yeah. I can see why she's been a bit traumatized." He got to his feet. "I'm not without my own skills," he mused. "If the world wants to be so 'coincidental' as to match seven brothers with seven sisters, then there *has* to be a way. And I'm damned well going to find it."

His confidence lasted only as long as it took to get to the project site. He got out of his car, took one look at the dilapidated house, and began to curse rather creatively.

To say the house was falling apart would be putting it politely. It was decades old and hadn't been upgraded once. The last owner had moved out years before and had left it alone. When she had died, her granddaughter had sold it to a real estate company to be refurbished and resold.

"Are you kidding me?" Tabby complained behind him. "There's got to be rats in there. And bugs. Did I mention I dislike rats and bugs?"

"They won't bite, I'm sure," he promised her. He turned with a smile, but the smile slowly faded as he looked at her. Hunger rose and rattled at the bars of its cage. He hadn't slept all night, aching and frustrated in body and heart. And now she stood there looking so beautiful that it was pure torture. His hands started to lift, and she took a slight step back. He forced himself to put his hands down. "Good morning."

As his rough voice swept over her, she felt like the cat he had

called her. Every pulse point began to throb, heat surging in her blood. Aching, empty, her body made its demands known. It was doubly frustrating because she had always been able to ignore her body before. There was no ignoring her desire for Gavin. "Morning."

The slight rasp to her voice didn't make it any easier for him to keep his hands to himself. She wanted him as badly as he wanted her. It was *deeply* tempting for him, especially because he knew she didn't have any real idea of what kind of pleasure they could share. He really wanted to replace her loneliness with joy. "Tabby Cat."

She held her laptop in front of her like a shield. "Let's go inside and see what it's like in there."

He took a deep breath. "Good idea." He gestured her ahead and fell into step behind her. His lips curved slightly as he watched her hips. She was slender but she was shapely in all his favorite places.

"Are you staring at my butt?" she asked with a slight dryness to her voice.

"Your hips," he admitted candidly. "But now that you mention it, your butt is quite nice, too."

"How kind." She felt the heat in her cheeks and wished it wasn't so telling. She simply wasn't used to men, or teasing them and being teased. It had always seemed so much easier to just stay away from them entirely than to accidentally tempt someone with something they couldn't have. She had the feeling that she could sneeze and it would tempt Gavin.

The house had been gutted. All plaster and drywall had been torn down. All that was left standing were the wooden beams, and they were showing signs of rot. The wiring and plumbing also remained, and he eyed some of the cords. "That is not code."

She smiled wryly. "Sure it is. It's 1958 code."

"Mmkay. It ain't 1958, babe." He looked at her suddenly, askance. "Er, sorry. I didn't mean to offend."

"Calling me 'babe'?" She shook her head. "I'm hard to offend. It's just a nickname and you don't mean it in a derogatory manner.

It's no different than 'dude.'"

"Dude."

"Dude." She nodded sagely. "One of my college friends was from California. Her lingo rubbed off on me. For an entire year, I couldn't seem to get that word out of my dialogue. And it's androgynous. It works for men and women."

"Dudette."

"Nope!" Her eyes began to sparkle. "Hasn't been 'in' since the 1980s."

Enchanted by her all over again, he offered, "Make you a deal. You take no offense if I call you babe, and I take none if you call me dude."

"Deal." She looked around at the floor and found a spot she wasn't afraid to sit on. She settled down and unpacked her laptop. While it was booting, she pulled out a sensor and tossed it to him. "Attach that to your meter. It'll hook you to my laptop."

"Cool." He studied the sensor, and then opened his meter's back and attached the cords. He put the cover back on and knelt to begin inspecting an outlet. "It's not grounded." He began to take readings. "Ugh. It's spiking somewhere."

She typed on her keyboard swiftly. "Start checking all the outlets. We can create a diagram of the house, and I can track down the short." She watched her computer as he moved from outlet to outlet. "Based on the image I'm getting, there is only one outlet per room."

"Seems like it. Make a note that we need to add more outlets. Ideally, we'd want one per wall per room. Grounded, of course."

"No hairdryers killing lights?"

"Not unless the owner wants to go to work with an afro."

She bit her lip as she made notes. "So what got you into wiring?"

His lips curved as he began to check light switches. "Well, I was always into trouble. All I ever heard was 'you're grounded.' I finally took it as a sign and specialized in electrics and electronics. That way if I was told I was grounded, it was a compliment." He enjoyed the sound of her soft giggles. "What about you, Tabby Cat?"

"Hmm." She studied her laptop screen. "Hard to say. It was one of the few things I could do safely. And it's fun for me. Being able to build and design security protocols helps with our company. A lot of people like to have homegrown security systems that dig right into the wiring."

"Damn. Wish I had thought of that." He began to check the wiring itself. In more than one place, the wires were corroded or worn. "I want a closer look." He made his way through the beams to where the breaker box was located. He double-checked that everything was off before heading back to the wires. Using pliers, he began to pull them apart. "Yick."

She found herself deeply amused as the day progressed. His choice in words was steadily getting more creative as they found the extent of the damage. "You know," she finally said, "at this point, we ought to just tear it all out and start over. We've got a list of faults, breaks, frays, and corrosion. The time and cost it would take to repair and play patchwork isn't worth much when it'd have to be done again later."

"I think you're right." He straightened from where he was stripping the end of the wires in an outlet to see their current state. A scuttling nose had him looking down, and he saw an immense rat running between his feet. He hastily stepped back. "Company."

She looked up and blinked as she saw the rat. So long as it didn't come near her, she had no issue. She looked at Gavin's face, and a smile began to blossom. "Gavin?"

He backed up as the rat came closer. "What?"

"Are you afraid of rats?"

"No!" He hastily back-stepped again. "Damn thing is taunting me!"

She put her laptop aside and got to her feet. She couldn't help the smile on her face or keep it out of her voice. "Gavin, you do remember you're over six feet tall, right? And it's only a rat."

"It's a mangy football with feet!"

He shot her a look of such helpless horror that she felt her smile reaching all the way into her heart. The warm glow seemed to melt all the cold loneliness inside. With a breathless sort of wonder, she could only memorize his face with her eyes.

She was in love with him. This impossible, stubborn man who could rewire a house in his sleep but was afraid of rats. This over six foot tall linebacker of a construction worker who was so gentle with her that she wanted to cling onto him in a way she could not dare do.

Pushing it where it couldn't be found, for she knew he would take ruthless advantage, she walked over and used her shoe to nudge the rat. It scampered off, and she shuddered. "Yuck." Still smiling, she looked up at Gavin. "Chicken. Your 'Tabby Cat' had to scare off the big, terrible rat."

He looked at her for long moments, then grinned. "My hero," he said gravely. Without thinking, he lifted his hand to touch her cheek.

She backed up so sharply that she tripped over the meter on the floor. She backed into the wall and her hand connected with the wires. An immense electrical flare went up, the light sharp and blinding, and every wire in the house shorted and blew apart. When the light faded, the smell of burned plastic and copper filled the air. Smoke drifted up from the wiring, and anywhere the wooden beams were near the wires, the wood was charred and blackened. She looked completely unharmed, but her eyes were filled with misery, and her rusty red hair had frazzled at the ends.

Gavin was silent for long moments. "Okay," he finally said after a minute. "Let's talk, honey."

Shoulders slumped, she moved away from the wall and kept almost two feet of distance between them. She walked over to a window and stared outside. It was easier than looking at him. "I have a very powerful electric field around me. You know how you can build up a static charge with your body? Mine's about the five million watt version. I experimented once. I sat in a chair for *hours* without moving. I discharged the field beforehand. At the end of the time, I touched some wire. It blew apart. I guess I absorb it from the air and not the ground."

"How did it start?"

"It was dormant until I electrocuted myself." She sighed. "By the way, when parents tell you not to stick a penny in an outlet, *listen to them*." She caught sight of her reflection in the glass and scowled as she tried to smooth down her hair. "After that, no one could touch me without getting nasty shocks. We thought it was the length of time between shocks, but the jolt never seemed to get better between discharges. But it definitely got worse the longer between them."

"And the accident that made you give up?"

Her lower lip quivered. "Jackson Sanchez. Cutest guy in ninth grade. Nicest guy in the school. He asked me out. I wanted to believe that my curse wouldn't ruin my life. He was okay with me not touching anyone. Everyone knew I was different. But he really wanted to kiss me." A tear slid down her cheek. "All he did was take my hand. And I electrocuted him. He ended up in the hospital for a month. He didn't blame me, Gavin. I blamed me. Other kids blamed me. I went into home study. It was easier."

"So for twelve years, you've had no other physical contact. No wonder you blew out the wiring here."

She braced her shoulders. He sounded more musing than mad, but she was still braced. She slowly turned and found, in surprise, that he was right behind her. She backed up, but the window was right behind her, and she couldn't move. "No!" she said sharply. "Don't touch me!" His hands lifted toward her, and she flinched, her eyes squeezing shut. "I don't want to hurt you!" she nearly wailed.

His fingers softly skimmed her cheek and threaded into her thick hair. Nothing happened. Her eyes flew open as his other hand closed around her wrist. It slowly slid up her sleeve so that his warm hand could caress her flesh. Shaken to her core, she stared at him. "How?"

"You didn't notice?" he asked softly. He smoothed down her hair, erasing the static clinging to her rusty-colored locks, so that they fell back into place. He then curled that hand around the back of her neck. Tenderly he stroked her skin. "Hadn't you wondered why I wasn't wearing gloves to work with the wires? Even with the breaker off, it's not a good idea."

"I . . . I hadn't noticed." Her eyes closed with helpless pleasure as his hot hands softly stroked over her skin. She could feel the line of his fingerprints. Just those little touches on her arm and neck were wildly arousing. Her entire body was heating and aching until she almost couldn't breathe.

"Damn, you're sensitive." There was wonder in his voice. "I wonder what'll happen if I kiss you, Tabby Cat." He eased closer, his body pressing to hers. The feel of her curves molding to his body was wildly erotic, especially when she nearly purred at the sensation. She seemed to go entirely weak, only his weight and his hand on her neck holding her up. "God, Tabby Cat," he said roughly. "We were made for each other."

"What are you?" she managed to whisper. She couldn't think, couldn't speak. He was so hard and hot. And safe. Dear god, the feel of him was safety, and security, and the seductive promise of comfort. Someone to hold. Someone to hold her. She felt starved for the feel of his arms. Her lips trembled. "Is it prosaic to ask for a hug at this moment?"

He yanked her into his grip as his arms fiercely banded around her. "Never!" he vowed hoarsely. "Jesus, when were you last hugged, Tabby Cat?" He buried his face against her neck as he lifted her off her feet. "I'm never letting you go!"

She carefully wrapped her arms around him. It felt . . . odd. But it was a wonderful odd. A beautiful odd. His strength seemed to sink into her and suddenly she was holding onto him just as tightly, wishing she could absorb herself into him. Her body arched to press closer.

He dragged her head back and took her mouth with his. There was no first kiss hesitation. He kissed her as if he had the right, his lips almost bruising as he eagerly devoured her, his tongue tangling with hers hotly, daring her to meet him halfway. And when she followed his lead, brazenly but hesitatingly stealing the kiss, he felt as if he would go up in flames.

He tore free and gulped in air. "We have three options," he rasped. "We can try to sneak into your house. We can try to sneak into my house. Or we can find a hotel."

"Where's the 'try to ignore this and get back to work' option?" she asked breathlessly. She clung onto his shoulders for support, because her legs felt too weak to hold her up. Only his arms kept her upright.

"You think we can?" he demanded incredulously. "Damn it, woman, are you mad?" He gave her a little shake. "I'm in love with you. And if you tell me you're not in love with me, I'm calling you a liar."

"What makes you so sure?"

He lifted her higher. "Wrap your legs around my hips." When she had, he turned and began walking for the door. He kept one arm around her waist and bent to pick up the laptop. That in hand, he went out the door. "I know you love me," he finally said, "because you have to. I won't accept anything else. It might not happen right now. But I'm going to make it happen. I want your love, Tabby Cat, so I'm going to have it."

She took a deep breath. "Hotel."

He didn't waste a second in putting her in his car and getting into the driver side. In minutes they were on the freeway. "I should feel guilty," he decided, "but I don't. I want you to myself. We can deal with our giggling siblings later. Much later. Like next week."

"Gavin." She smiled at him. "We still have a job." She poked his arm, a little thrill inside her that she could touch him. "Now explain yourself."

"I have a dampening field. It's the easiest way to explain it. I could grab a live wire and it wouldn't do shit. I could get hit by lightning and *possibly* singe my hair. I'm a friggin block of rubber for all intents and purposes." He shot her a grin. "Insults bounce off too, just a warning. So anything you might be putting out, I'm absorbing. We're a perfect match, Tabby Cat. And no matter how long it takes, I'm going to make you see it, too."

She thought about it for long moments. Her eyes closed as she settled back in her seat. "Gavin, will you marry me?"

"In a heartbeat," he responded instantly. "God knows I'll be miserable without you."

"And you'll be my lover?"

"Every chance I get."

"I might not be able to have kids," she warned him. "I mean, we can't know how my power will affect a baby."

"So we spoil our future nieces and nephews."

She took a deep breath. "Will you love me forever?"

"Haven't you been listening?" he demanded. "I'll love you until I die. Hell, I'll love you after that. We'll have to be buried together, and some day three hundred years from now, they'll unearth us to find two happily fused skeletons. Or we'll be cranky old ghosts and haunt badly wired houses while chasing each other around the attic."

She began to laugh almost helplessly. "Oh, Gavin! That's so horrible!" She leaned over and pressed her lips softly to the corner of his mouth. "I love you," she breathed softly.

"You'd better," he said, his voice strained. "And keep your lips off me, Tabby Cat, or we'll never make it to the hotel."

She settled back in her seat once more. "You just want me around to scare off rats."

The smile he gave her was tender and teasing all at the same time. "I was always a cat person."

CHAPTER TWENTY

The morning after the meeting, Rie went to wake her sister before she left to meet Seisyll. Not to her surprise, Belle was a lump under the blankets. She walked over, turned on the timer of the clock, and walked out.

The alarm went off ten seconds later with all the bells, whistles, and banging of a fire truck running through a Fourth of July parade. Belle jolted awake so hard and fast that she almost tumbled out of bed. Blearily, she peered at the clock. Her eyes popped wide open as she saw what time it read. "Crap!"

She hastily scrambled out of bed in a flurry of dark red hair and silk nightgown. She rushed down the hall to the bathroom, rushed through a shower, and then also rushed through her room to get dressed. Her hair was still damp as she skidded down the stairs. A plate with toast and scrambled eggs was on the counter. Grateful to her twin, she gulped down breakfast.

The doorbell rang and she hurried over to open the door. She found Owen Trahern on the other side, and he blinked at her. "Morning . . .?" His voice trailed off.

"Belle. Sam's on the second floor. Gotta go, bye!" She ducked around him and ran down the sidewalk toward the car she shared with Jen. Her sister didn't need it that day, so she was in charge. She could have kicked herself. She hated being late! She also really hated keeping a hot guy waiting.

She wasn't sure what it was, but there was something about Tomos Trahern that had instantly gotten her attention. Staring across the table at identical faces, she had found her eyes fixed to Tomos. His ponytail seemed to beg to have a woman's fingers in it, and there was something soft and dreamy in his pale blue eyes. Her heart fluttered when he smiled. Oooh. The man was dangerous to any woman's sanity, let alone a romantic woman's sanity. He looked like a man quite happy to find a white horse and rescue a damsel in distress.

When she pulled into the driveway of the old manor, she saw fairly quickly why the place needed work. The front area alone was in desperate need of help. There were more weeds than flowers. Barren dirt patches seemed like missing teeth in the garden's lopsided smile.

She got out of the car with a grimace. Bemused, she studied the beat-up pickup truck she had parked beside. It took character to own something like that. She wondered who it belonged to; she doubted it was a man. Few men would admit to owning a white truck with a series of faerie bumper stickers.

The front door was standing open. The entire manor was over eight thousand square feet, and there was a centralized atrium that also needed work. She blew out a quick breath when she found it. It wasn't as bad as the rest, but it needed help. It definitely seemed that the owner of the mansion didn't know anything about plants. The rest of the place was well designed and excessively luxurious.

Curious, she made her way through the rest of the house toward the back. There was no backdoor on the first floor so she headed up. A little turned around, she finally went through a bedroom toward a balcony. She could just shimmy over the side. Her sisters teasingly called her Trinity since she could jump off buildings a la *The Matrix*. Their best guess was that she could lower the force of gravity around her body.

She stepped onto the balcony and got a perfect bird's eye view of the vast back garden. It was *huge*. A large hedge maze took up the majority, but there were other areas, as well. Something that had likely once been a pond, and dilapidated flower rows. It was a bit depressing to say the least. She mentally began to catalogue what needed to be done. She and Tomos would need to call in backup. Thankfully, she knew a few workers she could call on. He probably did too.

Something rustled. She looked down quickly to find Tomos standing under the balcony and looking up at her. In the morning sun, he seemed like a golden god. A Viking prince there to carry her away. There was something in his eyes, something hot and soft all at the same time. Something that made her heart flutter and her pulse spike. "Hi," she managed to say.

He felt gleeful talons of desire rake his body at the breathless sound of her voice. When he had seen her on the balcony, he had been irresistibly drawn toward her. He had wanted her since the first time he had seen her. She smiled almost shyly at him, and he found himself falling helplessly in love. This stunning, red-haired princess was the woman of his dreams. He was sure of it. "Hi." Prosaic as it was, it was all that came to mind.

Silence fell for long moments. Finally, she said, "I can't figure out what to say. I feel like I ought to say something from *Romeo and Juliet*, but I hated that story."

"You and me both," he agreed with feeling. "Give me happy endings or give me nothing at all. It should've stayed a comedy." He moved closer, hands tucked in pockets. "How about this? Rapunzel, Rapunzel, let down your hair."

She grabbed a handful of her hair and studied it. It was wild with curls and only hung to just past her shoulders. "No, I don't think that'll work either." She leaned on the balcony rail. "I can't think of any other balcony scenes though. At least, not with a meeting sort of theme. I've seen plenty of princes scale balconies, but *that* is definitely a faerie tale quirk. I've never met a man strong enough to scale a balcony."

He lifted one blond brow. "Really now." Feeling slightly challenged, he looked around.

Warily, she asked, "Tomos . . . what are you doing?"

"Proving you wrong." He studied the wall next to the balcony. It was brick and mortar and just uneven enough to make climbing it plausible.

"If you fall on your ass, I reserve the right to laugh at you before helping."

"I'd expect nothing less." He got a grip on the brick and began to climb. It wasn't a question of strength. It was the actual amount of surface he had to grab. Luckily for him, there were plenty of bricks protruding just enough to allow him to climb fairly easily.

Eyes wide, breathless, she stared at him as he pulled himself over the side of the balcony. "Well." It was the only thing she could say.

He grinned at her mischievously. "Thank you, milady." He gave a courtly, sweeping bow.

She could only look at him in bemusement. Princes weren't supposed to be wearing torn blue jeans and a scruffy t-shirt saying '*I'm the GOOD twin. Really.*' They weren't supposed be wearing mud caked boots and a faded bandana. And they sure as hell weren't supposed to be so lethally male and overwhelming.

Yet when she had once wished for true love, she had wished for her perfect match. Not *the* perfect man, but the perfect man for *her*. And here he was. Her secret prince, her romantic fantasy lover, who could climb balconies and go muck around a garden with her.

She was in love.

She realized belatedly that he had stepped closer, and his pale blue eyes carried all the answers to her secret dreams. Striving for even ground, she held out a hand. "Let's get this back on track. I'm Belle Germaine and I am a hopeless romantic who likes playing with flowers."

He took her hand with a matching smile. "I'm Tomos Trahern and I am also a hopeless romantic who likes to play with flowers." He brought her hand to his lips softly, simply because a handshake didn't feel right on a balcony with a woman he would happily climb any tower to find. "Does Rie kill plants like Seisyll does?"

She nodded sagely. "Sadly, yes. She says I hogged the genes related to growth. It's just as well. She hogged the genes related to time and direction."

"Uh oh. Let me guess. You'll get us lost *and* we'll be late."

"In a nutshell? 'Fraid so." She tugged lightly at her hand. "Can I have that back now?"

"If you insist." He released her slowly, his fingers caressing the soft skin of her palm. Watching her as intently as he was, he saw the soft flush that rose high on her cheeks and the telltale beating of her pulse in her neck. Elation filled him. He could work with attraction. He could make her love him the way he so desperately needed.

He stepped forward and she forced herself to hold her ground even though he was looming deliciously over her. At five-seven, she had never felt particularly small before. Caught in the shadow of his body, his heat curling around her seductively, she felt positively tiny. Of course, the way he was looking at her didn't help. She felt as if he was a hungry wolf eyeing a particularly tasty bunny.

"I think we need to clear the air." His voice deepened without his control. "One, we need to work together. Two, we're both hopeless romantics. Three, I've wanted you since I saw you. We're going to have some serious tension at times. We're going to have to try to be practical."

"I agree with all of the above." She took a deep breath but it wasn't the smartest thing she had ever done. He smelled like rich, wild nature and the promise of earthy sensuality. "And I want you, too. When we're done with this job, we need to look at where we stand."

The irony of the romantics of their families being practical wasn't lost on him, but he also understood that they, more than anyone else, needed to be sure they weren't deluding themselves. At least, she needed to be sure. He already was. He had waited twenty-eight years to give his heart and he had recognized the event when it happened.

He eased back a step. "So. Let's go examine this sorely

neglected garden. Our client is supposed to come by after stopping to see Jen and Arian."

"Okay." Unable to resist, she ran at the side of the balcony and leapt over. She landed as gracefully as a tiger on the grass and turned to look up at him. His jaw was hanging open. She promptly burst into laughter. "Your face!"

Deciding to show off as well, he sniffed slightly. "Why jump when you can fly?"

Before her fascinated gaze, his body began to twist and contort, feathers blooming over his skin as his face lengthened and his overall shape began to shrink. In seconds, there was a large falcon in his place. He flew into the air and over the side of the balcony and then zoomed for her head.

She ducked with a shriek of laughter. When he came at her again, she took off running. She looked over her shoulder to see where he was, but saw no sight of him. She ran right into his warm body a second later. His arms snapped around her waist to keep her from falling. "Gotcha!" he said.

She grabbed his arms for balance, still laughing. "So you can shift?"

"Nothing smaller than a large bird," he confirmed. "I can't quite compact myself enough to become a mouse." He released her and stretched. "As it is, I always get a little cramped in smaller bodies."

"I can't imagine why," she murmured dryly. She grabbed his hand. "C'mon. Let's start looking around." She pulled out her iPhone and stuck a stylus over her ear. "You talk, I'll take notes. My memory is selective."

"What does it select to remember?"

"I can quote every great romance novel, movie, or play known to mankind dating back to the 1600s. I cannot, however, name any presidents other than the current one, and if you ask me where China is, I *might* find it on a map with some clues."

"Isn't that the big country near France?"

He asked it innocently enough that she blinked for a moment before grinning. "You flunked Geography too, huh?" When he grinned back and winked, she realized that she truly liked him just as much as she loved him. "Did you swap with Seisyll to cheat in class?"

"Never!"

He denied it so vehemently that she knew he was lying. The twinkle in his eye was a giveaway as well. "And I never swapped with Rie," she said staunchly. "Now, let's get to work."

Hip to hip, they made their way through the sorely neglected garden while she took notes. More than once, one or both of them muttered the phrase 'low maintenance.' They didn't even bother to tackle the hedge maze. It just needed a decent pruning.

A sudden chill went down her back. Before she was even fully conscious of it, Tomos was at her side. His broad shoulders sheltered her protectively. "What is it?" he asked in a low voice.

"Someone's staring at me." She moved closer to him without thought.

He wrapped an arm around her waist and looked around. His eyes fell on an affluent looking man walking toward them. There was something in his eyes as he looked at Belle that made Tomos' hackles rise. "Play along," he murmured so softly only she heard. She gave a nearly imperceptible nod. Lifting his voice, he said, "Hello. I'm Tomos Trahern. This is my fiancée, Belle Germaine. I presume you're our client." He offered a hand.

The man looked at his hand as if it was a snake before very carefully accepting the handshake. His eyes never entirely strayed from Belle. "I am Assemblyman Davis Harkin. I just came from meeting your brother and your sister."

Tomos hid a grin. If Harkin had looked at Jen the way he was looking at Belle, he had a good idea why he had been so wary of shaking hands. Arian wasn't very subtle with his abilities sometimes. "I'm sure they will do a good job for you," he said pleasantly. Unable to resist, he applied subtle force to the hand he held until Harkin's eyes swung toward him warily. "She's beautiful, isn't she? I can't take my eyes off her either."

Belle had never considered herself the type to need rescuing, but there was definitely something thrilling about having someone stand up for her. She watched their hands in fascination. If Tomos was exerting effort, it didn't show. On the other hand, Harkin's knuckles were white.

"Yes, she is." When he got his hand back, Harkin stepped back quickly. Thank *god* he didn't have to deal with more than two of the Trahern brothers. If it hadn't been for the fear of retribution from Enforcers, he would have destroyed their reputations. How *dare* they treat him like this? "So, I apologize for the state of the garden. It went to hell long before I moved in, and I lack any sort of gardening skills. I intend to hire a gardener, however, so don't worry about making sure I can't kill it. The grander the better."

His eyes had strayed back to Belle again. She pointedly leaned against Tomos' arm and smoothed a hand over his wrist in a tender gesture. "We can make it very grand. Do you have any preferences? Cottage style? Tropical?"

"Whatever will best suit the house." He looked at her hand, slightly offended. What did this Viking have that he didn't have? These women had no taste at all. "I leave it in your hands."

"Why don't we take our leave now," Tomos offered, "and we'll start designing something for your land. Do you have all the notes, *mon belle amour*?"

She almost lifted a brow. She should have known he would speak French. "I do."

"Then we'll see you later, Assemblyman." He kept her safely tucked under his arm as they walked away, but he was well aware that Harkin was staring at Belle very intently. If it had been a look of simple desire or attraction, he wouldn't have minded it much. The look in Harkin's eyes, however, was greedy and cold and disgusting. When they were out of earshot, he murmured, "Did we have an escape clause in the contract?"

"Not that I remember," she said regretfully. "Let's go back to

your HQ and get to work. The sooner we're done, the better. I'm willing to pull an all-nighter if you are."

"Done." He released her as they reached their cars. "Meet you on the backside of Driven Snow's building." He hesitated for a moment and then leaned down to lightly brush her lips with his. "He won't touch you," he breathed softly. He released her and went to his truck.

She lightly touched her lips as she watched him get into his truck. The whimsy made her smile. Her prince wore mud-caked boots and drove a white truck decorated with faeries. Only she would have such an unlikely hero.

She followed him back to the building. It was quiet inside since everyone else was out working on their own projects. Curiously, she followed him upstairs. "Where is your lair?" she quipped.

He sent her a smile. "In my room. I hope you don't fear I have dastardly purposes."

She gave a gusty sigh. "And here I was hoping for some sort of romantic ravishment. You disappoint me, Tomos."

"Don't tempt me."

The low mutter was nearly a growl. It reverberated through her nerves until her entire body heated and softened. Despite his light attitude, he wanted her as badly as she wanted him. She let out a soft breath. Damn it, she was sure. Why couldn't he be sure? She didn't think she could wait until the project was done.

She followed him into his room and promptly smiled. To call it a disaster would be polite. Clothes were strewn everywhere, and bookcases filled with books on landscape and plants were crammed together with romantic movies and novels. The bed was nearly a lake and took up a good portion of the room. Taking up the rest was an armchair for reading and a desk with a high tech computer set-up. "Maid's year off?" she asked politely.

Dull red climbed his cheeks. "Er, yeah."

"We must have the same maid."

Their eyes met, and he smiled. "Dust bunnies under the bed?"

She snorted softly. "I have colonies. Jen swears they're going to come to life and invade the city." He unearthed a corner of the bed for her, and she sat down comfortably. She kicked off her shoes and crossed her legs. "Okay. Let's do this."

With him manning his landscaping program and her manually looking through books for ideas, they fell into an easy rhythm. Ideas were punctuated with movie quotes, and Latin plant names were deliberately mangled until both were laughing.

They had so much fun that it was after midnight before he looked at a clock. "Damn. Is it that late?"

She rubbed at her eyes. "My internal clock says it is." She covered a massive yawn. "Sorry."

"No don't be." He rolled his shoulders. "I'd say we've got a solid plan. We can present this to Harkin tomorrow and arrange for him to buy the plants needed. Normally we'd pay for the purchase and invoice the cost, but I do *not* trust that man."

"Me neither." She rubbed at her eyes again. "Give me some coffee and I'll be good to drive."

He smiled. "Sure."

As he walked out of the room, she got to her feet to stretch. She peered at the computer, adjusted a retaining wall in their design, and sat down on the bed again. It felt soft and comfortable, and she couldn't resist lying down on her side. She would just close her eyes and get her second wind.

When he walked back into the room with two cups of coffee, he found her dead asleep and curled up on his bed. It was a toss-up whether his body or his heart ached harder. He put the coffee aside and walked over to look down at her. Almost reverently, he ran a finger down the freckles on her cheek.

She snuggled into the pillow with a sleepy mumble. He knew he should wake her, but he just couldn't bring himself to do it. Instead, he saved their design, closed the program, and shut down the computer. He cleared off the rest of the bed, closed the door, and turned out the light.

He got onto the bed as carefully as he could. He tugged Belle back against him and cuddled her against his chest. She snuggled closer but did not wake. He draped an arm lightly over her waist and savored having her in his arms and his bed. If he could do nothing but hold her like that forever, he would be a very happy man.

She awoke the next morning when the sun got into her face. She rolled over to get away from it and found herself snuggling into a hard male body. Startled, her eyes opened wide. She was curled against Tomos' chest and his arm was draped over her waist. He was still fully dressed and just as asleep as she had been.

Her heart quivered. She must have fallen asleep while he was getting coffee. And instead of waking her, he had just snuggled up beside her and gone to sleep as well. She lifted a hand to softly touch his face. His chin was just a little rough, stubble scraping deliciously over her palm. His eyes opened and she felt suddenly shy. "Hi," she whispered.

"Hi." He memorized her face and the soft flush to her cheeks and glow in her eyes. Dear god, she was beautiful! "You know," he said softly, "I know you have an identical twin, but I just don't find her as beautiful as I find you. From the moment I saw you, I couldn't tear my eyes away. I must be attracted to your heart and soul. God knows I'm attracted to your body, but there has to be more."

Her breath hitched as he turned his lips into her hand and softly kissed her palm. "I have the same problem," she admitted softly. "I just don't find Seisyll as attractive as I find you. You take my breath away, Tomos."

His hand slid slowly up her back to cup the back of her neck. He drew her toward him slowly, giving her plenty of time to get away, but that was the last thing she wanted. She sighed softly and lifted her chin to meet his kiss halfway, craving the feel of his lips on hers.

The kiss was soft and tender, drugging and consuming. Her lips parted on a second sigh and he deepened the kiss to let his tongue softly tangle with hers. Heat rose without hurry, the pleasure long and luxurious. Even the hunger of their bodies had softened to give way to the hunger of two hearts and one shared soul.

He shifted and tumbled her onto her back. He braced himself over her, still drinking from her in those consuming kisses that stole her thoughts and her breath. One hand cupped the back of her head. The other smoothed slowly over her body to memorize her curves and leave an indelible imprint.

Both were breathing hard when their lips finally parted. Quivering with need, she couldn't find any strength to move. She was going to die if she didn't feel his weight on her, feel his hot skin. Her hands pressed against his chest and her fingers kneaded sensually. "Tomos."

"I should stop." The words were breathed against her lips as he began to softly trail kisses over her face. "Imagine the embarrassment if one of my brothers walked in." He teased her ear by nibbling lightly. "Stop me, *mon belle amour.*"

She cast around in her mind for something, anything, that might stop him. And finally only one thing came to mind. "I'm a virgin."

His head came up quickly. "What?"

She cleared her throat. She knew she was blushing. "You heard me." She gave him a helpless look. "I'm a romantic, remember? I never felt compelled to experiment just for the sake of my body. And, frankly? Until I met you, my body was always easy to ignore. I wanted to wait until I met someone I couldn't ignore." She sighed. "You'd never get it."

"Yes," he said quietly, "I would."

Her eyes met his and everything inside seemed to melt as she saw the steadiness in his gaze. "Oh." The word was almost nothing but a breath. "Really?"

"Really." He lightly kissed her again. "There was never any ignoring you, Belle." He pressed his forehead to hers. "Let's go over to the manor and get the meeting done with. Then we can chase each other through the flower aisles at the nursery." He took another kiss, unable to resist her softly swollen lips. "And then, when we're done with the project, we'll see where we stand."

"Or lie."

His lips curved. "That, too." He released her and rolled to his feet. His jeans felt far too tight but he ignored his clamoring body to the best of his ability. "You want to go home for fresh clothes?"

She pointedly kept her gaze on his face as she sat up. "And listen to my sisters harass me? Mm no thanks." An idea occurred to her. "Let me borrow a shirt."

"A shirt."

"Yes, the article of clothing that goes on the top of the body, often worn over a bra if you're a woman." She grinned a little when he sighed. "Well, I don't mind wearing the same jeans again, but a different shirt is a subliminal message that I probably changed clothes. People notice tops before they notice bottoms. And if I'm wearing *your* shirt, it looks more like I spent the night with you." She added smoothly, "Actually, it would appear I did."

"Body armor against a pervert. Sounds good to me." He rummaged in his closet. "It'll be too big."

"So?" When he handed her the dark blue shirt, she contemplated it. "I like your taste in color." She stripped off her t-shirt without embarrassment. She pulled on the loaner shirt and was amused because she didn't even need to unbutton it. Listening to his breath break was wildly arousing. She wanted him to want her. She needed it.

Of course, she was left to stare at his bare chest when he pulled his shirt off. Mouth dry, she watched helplessly as the muscles of his chest rippled in the morning light. Even after he pulled on a fresh shirt, the memory had burned in her brain. Gravely, she said, "You do realize I will forever look at you and remember your bare chest, right?"

With equal gravity he said, "It seems fair. I'll forever remember that bit of lace and silk that you call a bra. Is that even legal?"

"Assuredly." She paused, then offered, "Wait until you see what's hiding in the back of my dresser."

"You're an evil woman," he groaned. Putting it forcefully out of his head, he booted the computer and got the designs printing. "We can grab breakfast on the way out."

They were arriving back at the manor within the hour. They were both riding in his truck this time since there was no need to waste gas on two vehicles. She found it hard not to snuggle into her borrowed shirt. It smelled wonderful, as if it had absorbed the essence of his skin.

They knocked on the door but there was no answer. Together, they headed around to the back. Still no sign of Harkin, but the patio doors were open. "I'll go inside," Tomos said. "I'll be right back." He disappeared into the manor as he called Harkin's name.

Belle wandered a few steps into the maze. It was just high enough that she couldn't see over the top. A familiar chill went down her back and she turned to see Harkin staring at her. He had come up from the side of the building. Without conscious thought, she fled into the maze. All she knew was that she couldn't bear to be near him without Tomos.

Ironically, her ability to get lost served her well in mazes. She found the center within a matter of moments and ducked down behind the gazebo, her heart pounding. Mentally she called for Tomos over and over, unsure if he could hear her. He had never said whether he was mentally strong like most District people were, but she was hoping her own power might be enough.

Harkin walked into the center and clicked his tongue. "Now why did you run? Don't you know that just makes it better?"

The ugly anticipation in his voice made her stomach roll. He was only feet away. She said nothing, wishing she could make herself invisible. His hand suddenly closed around her arm, and she swung her free hand with all her strength. He jerked back and the blow missed, but it also freed her. She darted away. "Don't touch me!"

"Do you really want to cause trouble?" he asked her. "I can make your boyfriend's life very uncomfortable."

Fury filled her eyes. Before she could say anything, there came

a low and menacing growl. Her eyes slowly widened and she stopped breathing. At the look on her face, Harkin slowly turned around. Behind him was an immense lion, crouched low and ready to spring. Sharp teeth were bared as it snarled softly. Its tail lashed furiously, and its mane bristled and lifted warningly.

Harkin screamed like a girl and ran out of the center just as the lion tried to pounce on him. He didn't stop running until he was out of the maze. It had to have been an illusion, though he was damned if he knew how it had happened. Those people from 3rd District were *weird*.

Belle stared at the lion. "Tomos?"

It shifted and changed and reformed into the man she loved. His eyes were no less furious. "Are you okay?" He framed her face in his hands. "Did he touch you?"

She shook her head. "I'm fine, thanks to you."

"Scared me half to death." He scooped her up into his arms. "Okay, Belle. I think it's time for some honesty." He headed deliberately for the exit of the maze. "I think we both know we're in love. We're the victims of love at first sight and we're too hopeless of romantics not to know it. We've both been acting like it was just lust."

"I concur," she admitted. She rested her head on his shoulder. "At the risk of raising the romance factor, I made a wish on a lucky locket once that I would find true love with the perfect man for me."

"You're right. That definitely raises the romance factor. Did you ask for a happily ever after too?"

"Of course. I hate sad endings." She snuggled closer. "Let's go home, Tomos. We'll worry about finding a contractual loophole to get out of the job later."

"Much later," he concurred. "Right now, I just want to be with you. We've both waited long enough to find each other."

She looped her arms around his neck with a happy sigh. And they said there was no such thing as perfection.

CHAPTER TWENTY-ONE

After the initial meeting, Rie was on her way down the street toward a café when she heard her name being called. Surprised, she stopped and turned to see Seisyll hurrying toward her. She could be sure of his identity for two very simple facts: he kept his hair much shorter, and she was attracted to him.

It was a curious situation, being attracted to a man with an identical twin, but she simply didn't feel anything for Tomos. She found him to be good looking but without feeling any sort of interest. On the other hand, when she looked at Seisyll, she had the unnerving sensation that all her hormones were standing at attention and saluting the wonder that was testosterone-induced male physique.

She wasn't quite sure what to do about it. When their eyes had met across the dance floor at the wedding, she had half expected to find slag on the floor from the flying sparks. All the Trahern brothers shared this 'look.' It was a way of looking at a woman that made her feel as if she was the *only* woman in his universe.

Seisyll stopped in front of her, and she felt something low in her belly heat and clench. He was definitely looking at her as if every other woman in the world had disappeared. The little curve to his lips and the smoldering heat in his eyes seemed to invoke images of tangled sheets and heated skin and long, lazy desire.

"Where are you going?" he asked her.

"Uhm, café. Felt like some coffee."

"May I join you?"

"Sure." She tucked her hands into her pockets as he fell into

step beside her. "So you're the younger twin too, huh?"

He smiled wryly. "Yeah. Ten minutes."

"Thirty." She grinned. "Your twin doesn't let you forget it either?"

"Ha. He's counted the seconds." He tilted his head curiously. "Thirty minutes? That's a long time."

"I wasn't in the right position." She shook her head. "They ended up doing a C-section." She walked into the café and took a contented sniff of the coffee-laden air. She would happily breathe coffee if possible. "But everything turned out okay. Mom was fine and so were Belle and I."

He contemplated her as they ordered their coffee. From the moment he had laid eyes on her at the wedding, something inside her had drawn him. His eyes had wandered to her repeatedly, nearly devoured her appearance in her fire elemental's dress. He had deliberately tried to focus on Belle, but he simply hadn't been attracted. Then, when he had looked at Rie again, it was as if he could see no one else. A curious phenomena, to be sure, but one for which he was grateful. Tomos had a serious thing for Belle.

But what was it about Rie that was different? She was beautiful and shapely, sure, and she possessed the same porcelain skin as her sisters mixed with the same scattering of freckles over her nose. He had looked carefully at the meeting, but there had been no difference in freckle pattern over Belle and Rie's faces. Now *that* was fascinating. Her hair was dark wine red like half of her sisters, and her eyes were an interesting shade of teal green. She was taller than average, which he definitely appreciated, and she was lively and witty.

So what was it that tugged at him? Hell, he could practically see the ropes yanking him toward her. It wasn't just physical, though God only knew that he felt slightly ravenous for her. If he didn't get his hands on her at some point over the next few days, he would go stark raving mad. He *burned* hotter than the welder he used at work. There was something more here. Something less clear. Something that ached when she smiled. Something that was just as hungry, just as longing.

She grabbed a seat at a table out of the way and smiled as he sat across from her. "Is this the 'getting to know your partner' thing?"

"Definitely." He grinned a little. "You have to know my first question."

She sighed. "Yeah. It's usually the first question. 'Rie' is R-I-E. It's short for Henrietta." Even saying it, she winced. "My options for a nickname were Etta, Henri, Hen, or Rie. Rie won."

"And you were named this because . . ."

"Belle is named for our mother's grandmother. I was named for our father's grandmother. Those nice, old-fashioned, colloquial names that torment modern children." She grinned at him. "Not that you'd know about that."

"No kidding!" He leaned back in his seat and studied her. "Rie is a good choice. You absolutely don't look like a Henrietta. Are you the only one with a nickname that she uses because her full name scares her?"

She stuck her tongue out a little for the teasing. "Sam and Jen use their nicknames by choice because they can. If you call them Samantha and Jennifer, they don't mind at all. No Sammy or Jenny though. My companion in name-dom would be Lexie."

"Alexis?"

"Nope."

"Alexandra or 'dria'?"

"Nope." She grinned. "Alexandriana Genevieve."

He choked on his coffee.

She grinned and propped her chin on her hand. "Named for our grandmothers' mothers. Both of them. But she was Lexie from the day she was born. Mom 'n Dad were always good about understanding that they gave us the name and thus gave tribute. It was up to us how we handled it."

"If I have a kid," he decided, "he or she will go without a name until they talk. At that time they can pick their own name."

She kicked him under the table. "You will not! You'll just spend a lot more time thinking about it." As it fell naturally on the ends of the statement, she asked casually, "What does your girlfriend think?"

"I don't have one." He gave her a slow smile. "Until a few days ago, I really hadn't been attracted to anyone enough to contemplate pursuing a serious relationship."

"What happened a few days ago?"

"I saw you at my sister's wedding."

The words fell between them. She almost stopped breathing. He was giving her that look again, the look that said he had tunnel vision and she was the light at the end. His hand slid across the table to cover hers, and before she could blink, he shifted his chair closer so that he was looming close. "Uhm."

"Are you single?" he asked softly, his breath brushing against the skin of her ear and cheek.

"Uhm, yes." She took a deep breath but all she got was the alluring scent of male combined with the aromatic scent of coffee. It was a potent combination.

"Are you attracted to me?"

"Are you nuts?" Her voice was as shaky as she felt. "I'm going out of my mind here. You're *lethal*. Get away from me before I do something really stupid." She turned her head and they were nose-to-nose, almost lip to lip. Her gaze dropped helplessly. He had one hell of a kissable mouth. She had never been happy with kissing before. She had a feeling that he would make her *very* happy. "People are watching."

Without looking away, he drew a veil down around them. "No they're not. As far as anyone can see, we're just sitting here having coffee." He curled one hand around the back of her neck. The other hand rested hotly on her thigh. He couldn't stop himself. With a soft rasp in his voice, he said, "I'm going to kiss you, Rie."

Shivering from just those two little touches, she knew she was doomed. When his head tilted and his lips glided across hers, she was trapped. And when his lips settled, when the heat and power of the kiss poured into her, his taste as wild as the coffee they had been drinking, she knew she was lost.

Her lips parted under his, and a soft sound of desire slipped free as he deepened the kiss and curled his tongue around hers. Her entire body was beginning to ache and yearn. She lifted a hand and splayed it over his chest. Her fingers kneaded sensually. He was so wonderfully big. Hot and hard and masculine.

He carefully lifted his head. Little shudders ripped through his body. Her taste was so unique that he knew he was addicted. He slowly slid his hand up her leg and savored her supple flesh. "Do you have any idea how badly I want you?" The words were little more than a rumble. His breath hissed out as her hand slid down into his lap to rest as light as a butterfly over his straining erection. "Rie, I think you're a tease."

"I think I might be." Her fingers tingled as she lightly tormented him. "You started it. Your hand is almost in the danger zone." His hand was so close to where she ached most that she felt the heat of his skin, even through her clothes. "I don't think I've ever been groped outside a date before."

He forced himself to pull his hands away. Her hands lifted, and he wisely put a few feet between them. "Okay." He drew a long, bracing breath. "Okay. We have a job to be done together. We both know that we're probably a few kisses away from falling in bed together."

"Or on the floor."

He had to smile at that. "Or on the floor. So . . . let's call the job a date. It's a long date to get to know each other. We can evaluate where we stand after that. Why don't we give your metal craft a try first? I have no artistic sense though," he warned.

"That's okay." She smiled. "We'll find some." She got to her feet and looked around. The corner felt cushioned where they were. "What did you do?"

"I can cloak and shield," he admitted. "I blocked our presence from other people. They see what they expect to see." He looked up

at her. "What can you do?"

Her smile was sultry and enticing. "You'll have to find out on our date." With a toss of her long hair, she broke past the veil and headed for the exit.

He watched her leave and felt a smile tugging at his lips. He had finally realized what it was about her that pulled at him. It was very simple, actually. He wasn't entirely surprised, based on the evidence. In fact, he was quite content.

Loving Rie was possibly the easiest thing he had ever done.

The next morning, Rie made the effort to ensure that Belle would wake up on time and then went downstairs and left out a plate of breakfast. Honestly, she found it highly amusing that the 'younger' twin was the only one with practical brain cells.

Her practicality seemed to have taken a hike, though. She hadn't slept well thanks to a mind in a state of fluctuation and a body in a distinct state of frustration. She was more than happy to go to her shop and lose herself in the crafting and shaping of metal.

She was so lost in her work that she didn't realize she was no longer alone until she straightened and lifted her safety visor. She promptly saw Seisyll leaning against a table nearby. Her pulse kicked into overdrive. "How long were you standing there?"

"Only a little while." He smiled. "You looked so intent that I didn't want to distract you."

"And you didn't want to be hit by flying slag." She walked closer with a matching smile. "You want to give it a try?"

"First thing's first." He reached out a hand and curled it around the back of her neck to draw her closer. She melted against him happily. Her body aligned perfectly to his as her hands splayed across his chest. He bent his head to kiss her without hurry, contentedly lingering over her taste. When he finally eased back again, he murmured, "Good morning."

Feeling much like every muscle had melted in pleasure, she could only lay against him. "Good morning," she said dreamily.

"You know," he looped his arms around her, "I have to apologize to my brother-in-law."

"Which one?"

"Taylor. I gave him hell when I caught him almost kissing Gwyn."

She nodded sagely. "It would probably be wise, as you seem to be determined to kiss me at every opportunity."

He stole another kiss. "I'm not a hypocrite." He slowly, and very reluctantly, let her go. "Show me how this works. I know the mechanics, but I warn you, again, that I am not very artistic."

She was a patient teacher. She took him through the process of trying to find inspiration and how to make what was in his mind get to his hands and then to the welder. It didn't take long, though, before she realized he was right. He was *really* bad at art.

Biting her lip, she studied the pile of metal he was glaring at. "It's, uhm. Unique."

He shifted his glare to her. "Sure." He scowled and crossed his arms. "It's like the time Joseff tried to show me glasswork. I didn't do bad with blowing glass. When it came to shaping it? Yeah. I made the Picasso of unicorns."

He looked and sounded so sulky that she bit harder on her lip. He shot her a warning look that was a combination of embarrassment and annoyance. Giving in, she covered her mouth as she began to laugh, her eyes dancing as he made a rude noise. "You look like the little boy who can't build anything but a lopsided kite!"

"I never made a lopsided kite." Grudgingly he muttered, "That couldn't fly anyway."

Something shifted and settled inside her as she studied his face. Contentment rose and spread. Love. Finally. She had wished for true love, prayed for it, and had hoped that the magic of her grandmother's name and locket would bring it to her. And it had.

She framed his face and rose up to kiss him softly. His arms curled around her, and his pale blue eyes darkened with hunger and something more. Something that made her heart ache as badly as her body did. "I can't make kites either," she said against his lips.

He snorted softly. "It's an art, according to Gavin." He studied the misshapen piece of metal he had been trying to work with. "Why don't I let you handle this, and you can come help me with the building. It's basic welding work from what I saw this morning."

"You went by before coming over?"

"I had a feeling we'd be going there soon," he muttered. "I told you I had no artistic sense."

She smiled. "Okay. Let's get going. You get to drive. I share a car with Lexie and I promised she could use it today just in case she had to go somewhere."

"Sure."

They cleaned up the shop together and then made their way to the building that was in need of their work. Somehow, she wasn't surprised to see it was an old industrial building. It was all steel beams and little else. Nothing was very appealing about it. "And we're doing what again?" she asked as she got out of the car.

"The building was just bought by a couple of people who want to convert it into an artist workshop. Several of the ceiling beams need repairs and we also are to install some pieces of art."

"Install?"

"Weld 'em to the ceiling."

"Now *that* will be cool." She nodded decisively. "Let's get to it. You point me at something and tell me to weld it shut."

"Would that work on my brothers' mouths?" he asked wistfully.

"No more than it works on my sisters."

They shared a conspiratorial grin. He was much more in his element here, and not needing to worry about aesthetics helped lift his mood. She just laughed at him. They started at the base level and sealed anything that was easy to reach and repair. Once all that was left was the ceiling, he went to get the ladder. When he came back in, he got the shock of his life to see Rie hovering near a beam, welding competently. *Hovering.* "Rie!"

She yelped and lost her concentration. She also promptly started to fall. He was thankfully fast enough to catch her before she could hit the ground. Heart racing, he clutched her close. "You scared the hell out of me!"

She shoved back her visor with a glare. "*I* scared *you*?! You're the one who distracted me! I have to concentrate to stay in the air! It's not easy, thank you!" She crossed her arms in annoyance. "Now put me down and I'll get back to work."

He forced himself to put her down. He set up the ladder and she gracefully floated up to the ceiling again. Side by side, they worked together easily to first repair all the mishaps and tears caused by poorly done deconstruction. Once that was finished, they got to work with hanging the art pieces. That part of the job started with having to decipher the layout drawings they had been given. It was only her eye for art that at last clarified the rather jumbled instructions.

They started welding the work to the beams. He used the ladder to hold the pieces in place while she hovered and secured them. After hanging the first piece, he went to check the drawings. She finished welding the last part and moved back to make sure it was level. Unfortunately, she burned her hand on the beam and lost her concentration. He hastily caught her again. He could only sigh and put her on her feet again.

An hour later, after the fourth mishap, he had had enough. When he caught her, he didn't put her down. He instead headed for the doors. "Alright," he said. "That's it. We're going back to your shop."

"But we're not done!" she protested.

"I've had enough scares, thank you. If you're so determined to give me gray hair, I'm going to give you some by making you teach me to be artistic."

She snorted. "It'll take you fifty years to be artistic."

Easily, he countered, "Fair enough. I'm willing to hang around that long."

Her heart began to beat harder. "Are you now? Well, I suppose Lexie and Joseff will be married for a nice long time, so we'll have plenty of good reasons to see each other."

He put her down slowly and let her body slide along his. Firmly he trapped her against the car. His fingers pulled down her ponytail so that they could get lost in her hair. "That was not what I meant," he said softly.

"Then what did you mean?" She met his eyes evenly.

His free hand smoothed over her cheek before framing her face warmly. "I know it's tacky to propose on a first date, but I can't seem to stop myself. Marry me, Rie. I fell in love with you when I looked at you. Give me a chance to make you fall for me."

She framed his beloved face with her hands. "You can't make me fall for you, Seisyll. I already did that by myself." She leaned up to kiss him softly. "I'll marry you." She smiled. "Did I tell you there was an enchanted locket from my grandmother that gave us sisters each a wish? Seven wishes for seven sisters."

"The grandma you were named for?"

"Mmmhmm. And all of us except for Remy wished for true love. I wished for my perfect match . . . but I could never have imagined you. I wouldn't have dared wish this big."

He had to kiss her for that. When he released her, he asked softly, "What did Remy wish for?"

"She didn't." Sadness moved in her eyes. "I think she's afraid. But Heul . . . he's so perfect for her, Seisyll."

"There's no such thing as coincidence," he murmured.

She eyed him warily. "What are you thinking?"

His smile came slowly and wickedly. "I'm thinking we were set up." He scooped her up and carried her around to put her in the car. "I'm taking you home." He leaned in to kiss her, but she tasted so wonderful that he lingered longer than he intended. He finally broke free and muttered thickly, "Taking you home, *fast*."

She took a deep, trembling breath. "Good idea. I don't think I'll be able to concentrate unless you do, and we both know what happens when I lose my concentration."

He grinned and stole another kiss. "That's okay. I'll just keep catching you." He got to his feet and went around to get in the driver's side. As they were heading back toward where he lived, he asked, "What do you think about all of us, sans Remy and Heul, getting together for a meeting? Working together won't be enough for them. They're going to need another push. We're going to have to waylay them at every turn. We need to get Remy's weaknesses to Heul, and vice-versa."

"Well, Lexie and Joseff set all of us up, so I don't see why we can't get them to help again. But you know who we *really* need? We need Nicole. If she doesn't approve of Heul, our opinions won't matter." She tilted her head. "Let's let things stand for a few days. Finish our projects. On Friday, we'll call everyone together and see where we are."

He shook his head. "I'm never letting you near my sisters. You'd take over the world."

She grinned. "I'll take that as a compliment."

CHAPTER TWENTY-TWO

The morning that Remy was supposed to start work with Heul didn't get off on the right foot. She and Nicole had the entire fifth floor of the building to themselves, and it was on its own air conditioning and heating; she refused to let her sisters pay even part of her own living. Sadly, that meant that some mornings the air went out. It was eighty degrees and climbing when she woke.

She hastily adjusted the thermostat and made a note to call for someone to come fix it. Again. She then went to get coffee, but the timer hadn't gone off, and there was none waiting for her. With a sigh, she went down three flights of stairs to beg coffee off of Lexie. That in hand, she went back upstairs. *Elevator.* They desperately needed an elevator on this side of the building.

She kept an eye on the clock. When it was closer to seven, she went down the hall to Nicole's room. "Rise and shine, baby," she said as she went into the room. She automatically looked at the small bed, but Nicole wasn't there.

Before panic could set in, she heard her say, "Mommy?"

She looked around quickly and saw Nicole sitting in the rocking chair. Her red braid was coming undone and she looked hot and miserable. She was holding a raggedy stuffed dog that she'd had since she was born. "What're you doing up?" Remy walked over and knelt down. "Too hot?"

"I dun' feel good."

Remy gently pressed a hand to her forehead. Alarms went off mentally. She was very warm and it wasn't a sweaty heat from the air. It was a dry feverish heat. "Uh-oh. Stay here, Nic." She went down the hall quickly and came back with the thermometer.

Nicole sat still while it was pressed to her ear, but it was a stillness born of exhaustion and not behavior. She was never still unless she was sick. While Remy waited for the thermometer, her sharp eyes spotted Nicole scratching surreptitiously at her stomach and arms. "Has anyone been sick at school?"

Nicole rubbed at her eyes and scratched her arm again. "Benji Greeber has been out. Ms. Woodrow said he's got . . . uhm . . ." She wrinkled her nose. "Turkey spots."

Remy closed her eyes. "Chicken pox?"

"Yeah, that."

Remy studied the thermometer as it beeped, but she was already resigned to what she knew. "One hundred degrees. C'mere you." She scooped up her daughter and stood her on the bed. Gently she tugged off her sweaty nightgown. On a sigh, she studied the little spots forming across Nicole's stomach and arms. They would be full-fledged pox within a day or two. "You and Benji play together before he got sick?"

Nicole nodded. "We feed the class hamsters together. He pulls on my braid, so I kick him."

"Well, it looks like you got chicken pox too."

"Nooo! Luis from fourth grade sez that if you get chicken pox, you turn into a *chicken*!" The last word was a wail as she burst into tears and grabbed onto Remy's neck. "I dun wanna be a chicken, Mommy!"

"You won't be a chicken! You're going to be hot, and itchy, and miserable for a while, but you won't be a chicken." Remy carried her down the hall into the bathroom. "You get to have a nice cool bath, and then you're going back to bed."

It was a testament to how bad Nicole really felt that she didn't argue with her mother. She didn't splash or make a peep as Remy bathed her gently. She was still quiet when Remy dressed her in a fresh nightgown and tucked her in bed. As Remy re-braided her hair, she asked in a quivering voice, "No chicken?"

"No chicken." Remy handed her the flop-eared dog she loved. "I'll bring my TV in here, okay? You can watch movies and sleep lots. And I'll make you lots of nummy things to make you better in no time."

Her lower lip quivered. "Pudding?"

"I could be persuaded." Remy gently kissed her forehead, her heart aching as always. She loved her daughter more than anything. "Now rest, baby."

She wasted no time in moving her small TV into Nicole's room and hooking it up with the DVD player. She put on Nicole's favorite Disney movie, then headed down the hall to their living room. She could only sigh as she grabbed the phone and dialed the school.

"Golden River Kindergarten."

She braced a shoulder on the wall. "Hello, Ms. Woodrow. This is Remy Germaine, Nicole's mother."

"Good morning, Ms. Germaine!" Ms. Woodrow's voice had her smile in it. "What can I do for you?"

"Warn your parents there's an outbreak of chicken pox. I have a very miserable little chicklette in bed right now."

"Oh dear." Ms. Woodrow sighed. "I was hoping Benji hadn't infected everyone. He's already been out a week. I'll notify the other parents immediately. Once is an occurrence. Twice is an epidemic. Especially among five-year-olds. You tell Nicole that we'll be looking forward to seeing her get better. I'll have someone drop off her lessons for the next two weeks, just in case."

"Thanks, Ms. Woodrow." Remy sighed again and hung up the phone. Her reflection in an antique mirror seemed to smirk at her across the room. She looked flushed and tired and frazzled. In faded sweatpants and a camisole, she looked like a particularly unappealing housewife. "How the mighty have fallen," she groused.

There was a light knock on the wall, and she looked over quickly to see Heul standing at the top of the stairs with a lifted brow. She stared at him for a moment until her memory kicked in. "Oh!"

She groaned. "Oh." She covered her face with her hands. "Oh damn."

"Good morning to you as well," he said gravely. "Bad time?"

"I have a five-year-old with chicken pox, and a broken air conditioner that may give out any minute," she retorted crossly. "What do you think?"

He thought she would hit him if he told her that she looked like an invitation to sin. He had never seen her without her self-defensive styled hair and well selected clothing. Seeing the woman underneath her protective shield was highly alluring. The flush to her cheeks made him want to kiss her and make her more flushed. Her hair was haphazardly pinned up with curls sticking out everywhere, all but begging for his hands. Her camisole and sweats did nothing to disguise that her body was all woman.

Carefully hiding it, he said, "I think we should work from here today so you can be on call for Nicole." He grimaced. "I had to get Joseff and Gwyn through a double dose of chicken pox. They were ten. I threatened to have Arian tie them in bed."

Oddly, it made her feel better. Impulsively, she asked, "You want to see Nic? She likes you a lot."

"I'd love to." He kept his hands in his pockets as they headed down the hall. He mentally told himself that he would just peek in, say hello, and step out. Professional. Calm. Distant. He needed to keep himself from being tangled up by these two dangerous Germaine women.

Every thought of being distant left his head when he looked into the small room decorated with yellow and cream. Two miserable green eyes looked at him, capped by a mop of rusty red hair, and he lost his heart. "Hey, baby," he said softly as he walked across the room. He knelt next to her bed. "Gonna be a chicken for a while, huh?"

Nicole's lip quivered. "Will I grow feathers?" She held out her arms.

He gently lifted her up and cuddled her in his arms. She felt small, and delicate, and tugged on every heartstring. He loved all kids

but this one got to him the most. "Only a few," he told her solemnly. "But you'll never even see them. They'll just make you itch for a while, and then they'll go away." He rubbed his cheek over her hair softly. "In the meantime, you get to take time off from school and watch movies."

Her lashes drooped. He felt so nice and safe. Like a daddy. She had always wanted a daddy. Someone to make her mommy smile and to make her feel safe. He could beat up that mean Luis from fourth grade. "Mmkay." She looped her arms around his neck and hid her face. She was asleep in seconds.

Remy felt something in her heart twist as she watched them. Nicole never trusted strangers, but she clearly trusted Heul. It made her heart begin to crack open. She didn't want to love Heul, but with every passing minute, she was more afraid that she would. "Want me to take her?" she asked softly.

"No, it's okay." He gently tucked Nicole back into bed and smoothed the covers over her. He waited until they were in the hall again before saying, "We can work from here, Remy. I don't have a problem. The first part is simply planning anyway."

"I suppose so." She tugged on a lock of hair nervously. "If you'll give me a chance to change clothes, I . . ."

He pulled her hand away from her hair. "You look fine," he told her. "Stop worrying so much."

"Ha." She turned and headed down the hall to the living room. "Have a seat. I'm going to go grab my sketchpad. If you want something to drink, there's soda and juice in the fridge." She had taken two steps when she heard the thump that was the thermostat failing. She groaned. "Not now."

"Go get your sketchpad." He nudged her down the hall. "I'll deal with the thermostat." He stepped over to peer at the temperamental device. The cover popped off easily when he took his pocketknife to it. The problem was apparent: one of the wires wasn't staying in place where it belonged. He jimmied it into place again and closed the panel. "Hey, Remy? It's no big deal. I'll ask Gavin to come fix it. He'll have it taken care of in minutes."

"Really?" She stepped over with her sketchpad under her arm. "Last time I had someone out, they said it would need to be replaced entirely."

"Well, eventually, I'm sure it will. But it's just a short in the system. Gavin can handle it." He sat down on the couch and offered a smile. "I don't bite, Remy. Let's sit down and work together. We're both adults. We can stop being such idiots just because we're attracted to each other."

She opened her mouth to deny it but could only sigh. "Yeah." She walked over to sit down across from him. "It's awkward for me," she said carefully. "The last man I was attracted to was Chase, and it didn't work out."

"Want to talk about it?"

Oddly, she did. She had never really talked about things with anyone other than her sisters. "Okay." She began to lightly sketch out the basic shape of the dollhouse. "I met Chase in my last year of college. He was funny, and smart, and we had good times hanging out. We were attracted, thought we were in love. We got married. Yet almost from the honeymoon, we realized the attraction wasn't strong enough. We gave it a year, but it just didn't work. We decided to get a divorce before we ruined our friendship. But then ...I discovered I was pregnant."

"Did you try to make it work?"

She shook her head. "We refused to chance becoming the sort of parents we hated. We went through with the divorce, but we stayed friends. Chase was *ecstatic* about being a father, as much as I was about being a mother. When Nicole was born . . . oh, he loved her so much. We had it all worked out. Visitations and how he'd spend time with her. He'd come over just to watch her sleep. I loved him," she added softly. "I wasn't *in* love, but I loved him."

He wanted to reach out, but knew better. Any jealousy he might have felt was drowned in pain for Remy, and for Chase. "What happened?"

"He loved to go water skiing in the summer. He was really good at it, but there was another skier out there with a less skilled driver. The two boats nearly collided and jerked apart. It jerked Chase and the other skier together. The collision," her voice broke briefly, "the collision was so strong that their heads cracked together. Both fell unconscious. And tangled together, they couldn't be pulled from the water in time. Both drowned. A freak accident."

"Does Nicole remember him?"

"No, thankfully. It's horrible of me, but I'd rather her not remember, than remember and grieve." She took a deep breath. "And you're the only person outside of my family that knows the whole story."

"I'm practically family," he reminded her.

"I suppose so." She contemplated the drawing that was emerging. "How detailed can you get?"

"How big will it be?"

"Probably about four feet high."

"As detailed as you want me to be. I might delegate the tiny carving to Arian or Jen though." He grinned swiftly. "The key to being in charge is to delegate."

"No kidding!" She grinned back at him, in that moment understanding him completely. She added a few more details. "So, turnabout is fair play. Why haven't you taken the fateful plunge?"

"I've never been in love, or thought I was in love." He scooted over so he could see what she was drawing. He was fascinated by the way she could draw and talk at the same time. It was as if two different parts of her brain functioned simultaneously. "And . . ." He hesitated for a moment. "And I've always been . . . lucky to know whether or not something will work. To know exactly what I want."

"Your gift?"

"Mm. You?"

It was her turn to hesitate. "I'm . . . a medium, of sorts."

His brows went up. "Ghosts."

"Ghosts."

"As in Casper and Slimer."

"As in the old guy who used to sell bagels still stands on the corner of the District and wonders why no one can see him."

"He doesn't know he's dead?" He eyed her. "I thought that was just bullshit from *The Sixth Sense.*"

"Not hardly." She shook her head. "Sudden death can be as disorienting to the dead person as to the people left behind." She bit her lower lip, hard, but decided not to tell him the rest. Aiming for humor instead, she said, "I've figured out how to crack up my sisters. I just do an impersonation of Haley Joel Osment."

"Reasonable?"

"Darn reasonable."

"You'll have to show me sometime." He plucked the sketchpad from her hands. The dollhouse looked like a miniature version of an old-fashioned Southern manor. It didn't look like it was backless, however. "Hinged sides so it can open and close?"

"I think so. Gives her double the space but can be stored easily." She took the pad back and began to lightly draw the inside on a fresh sheet of paper. "Do you have moral or religious objections to pink and yellow?"

"I raised a baby sister," he said dryly. "And she's as girly as they get."

The mental image of him trying to take his baby sister shopping made her cover a grin. The Viking in a girl's department store. It might as well be a bull in a china shop. "Good. Nicole loves them."

"Mommy?"

Both looked up instantly to see Nicole standing at the entrance of the room. She was rubbing at her eyes. "Can I have breakfast?" She itched at her arms in agitation. "The feathers are *itchy.*"

"I'll take her," Heul murmured. "If you want to handle the food."

It was foreign to lean on someone other than her sisters, but she trusted him implicitly. "Done." She walked over to Nicole and

lifted her up. "You want pancakes?" she asked. "I could be persuaded to make some."

"'Kay." Nicole was happy to be passed over to Heul. She snuggled in close, content to be held by him. "Whatcha doing?"

He held up the sketchpad. "We're building a dollhouse for a cute little girl."

"Oh. Will you build me one, too?"

"We might be able to do that. You like this one?"

"Uh-huh." She scratched at her arm again and then at her stomach. "Will it have flowers?" Almost on the heels of the question, she complained, "Being a chicken *itches*! I don't wanna be a chicken anymore!"

"Got a damp cloth?" he asked Remy. She tossed him one over the breakfast bar, and he gently began smoothing it over Nicole's skin. "Here we go," he said softly. "This will help some. Your mommy will get some lotion that will help. But now you know."

"Know what?"

"Why chickens are always running around clucking." His grave voice barely covered the humor in his eyes. "They itch too. And they don't have fingers to scratch with."

Remy bit down on her lower lip to keep from laughing at the wide-eyed look Nicole was giving Heul. She carefully concentrated on flipping the pancakes lest she give him away. Itchy chickens. He was *incorrigible*.

"Do they havta use lotion, too?" Nicole asked. In her fascination, she had forgotten her itchy skin.

"Yep. Farmers will catch and pluck them and dump on lotion. The ones that keep complaining end up getting sold to supermarkets where they're put out of their misery." He nodded sagely. "But little girls who get chicken pox are special. They get to complain all they need to. And your feathers won't grow back once they're gone. Right, Remy?"

"Leave me out of this!" The laughter was in her voice. "It's your story." She carried the plate of pancakes over to the table. "Bring our chick over here and let her eat her mush. I mean breakfast."

Nicole giggled as Heul carried her over to the table. "What's your name?" she asked him.

"Well, where are my manners?" He shook her hand solemnly. "Heul Trahern. I'm Joseff's big brother."

"Ohhhh." She dug into her pancakes happily. "'Kay."

Letting her be, Remy and Heul went back over to the couch. She elbowed him as they sat down. "I can't believe you," she said softly. Laughter made her eyes merry. "That was so bad of you."

"She stopped thinking about the itching, didn't she?" He grinned. "I'll pick up some calamine lotion for you before I come over again tomorrow morning." When she opened her mouth, he narrowed his eyes. "No arguing. Just say 'Thank you, Heul' and we'll move on."

She closed her mouth to smile in bemusement. "Thank you, Heul."

When Nicole had finished her breakfast, she was tired again. This time it was Heul who took her back down the hall to her room. As he was tucking her into bed, she asked, "Why don't you have kids?"

"Hmm." He knelt beside the bed to study her face. "I haven't met a woman I wanted to have kids with."

"What about Mommy?"

Warning bells went off in his head. "What about her?"

"You watch her lots." Her eyes were drooping closed. "An' she watches you."

Out of the mouths of babes. He gently smoothed her hair out of her eyes. "Would you be happy if I was interested in your mom?" It was, to him, one of the most critical aspects of any relationship he and Remy might have.

"Uh-huh. You'd be an awesome daddy." She rolled over and snuggled into her pillow. "Will you come over again tomorrow?"

"Mmm."

"'Kay."

He waited until he was sure she was asleep before he left the room. As he shut the door quietly, he thought of his 'gift' and the things it could and could not tell him. When Joseff had asked him if he was interested in the merger, he had seen the potential outcomes of going ahead or holding back. It had come down to his brothers' happiness weighed against his. Going forward meant that his brothers would find true love . . . and that he wouldn't.

Nothing was set in stone, he reminded himself as he went downstairs. If he wanted, he could fight against what he was shown and change things. He had changed things before, but at a great cost to himself. He wasn't sure yet if he wanted to change things, though. If what he and Remy had was just attraction, then there wouldn't be any problems.

The problem would only be if he was falling in love. And as he looked at Remy across the room, saw the concentration on her face as she sketched, he had a strong feeling that he was.

CHAPTER TWENTY-THREE

Over the next few days, Remy and Heul alternated between working at her home and working at his. Nicole was taken with them to both locations and snuggled into either her bed or a couch where she could be pampered by her six aunts and six future uncles.

The status of her new uncles also came to light over the next few days while Remy and Heul worked on the dollhouse. Every last one of the other partnerships finished their project and came out a couple. In many ways, neither Remy nor Heul was surprised. In many other ways, it just added to the stress of their own relationship. They *knew* their siblings were waiting for signs of orange blossoms.

If anything was flying, it was sparks. Remy was going out of her *mind*. She had stopped being able to sleep at night; her dreams were feverish and plagued by the masculinity that was her partner. He hadn't even kissed her and she burned for his touch. She had never considered herself overly sexual before, but now she was being forced to re-evaluate.

While she was trying to fasten on a pair of earrings Friday morning, she scowled at her reflection. "What the hell is wrong with me?"

"It's called passion, Rem."

She very slowly straightened. There was nothing in the mirror, but when she turned around, there was a very familiar young man sitting on the side of the bed. His tousled black hair was as unruly as she remembered. His face was as handsome, and his eyes as blue. "Well," she finally said.

"Hey."

She rubbed the bridge of her nose. "Sane women do not have conversations with their dead ex-husbands."

Chase Crowley just grinned. "Women who are mediums do." He got to his feet and looked as fit and healthy as he had before he had died. He walked over to take the earring from her and competently fasten it to her ear. "Talk to me, Rem. We were friends. We sucked at being married, but we were awesome at being friends."

"I am not talking about my sex life with you!" she muttered.

"Why not? I'm dead. Who am I going to tell?"

She opened her mouth, then closed it. Bemused, she said, "You still make the absurd sound so . . . reasonable. Tell me, is there an afterlife? No one else has ever said."

He contemplated that. "Well, I haven't played chess with the Grim Reaper, and I sure haven't seen any pearly gates or barbeque pits of doom, so I can't be sure. Mostly it's just a fuzzy gray area. I don't see color now. And you look hot with gray hair, by the way."

She gave a long sigh as she sat down on the side of the bed. When he sat beside her, she gave in. "I'm so confused, Chase. What we had was . . . nice."

"And nice just isn't enough. What have you got with Heul Trahern?"

"Intensity." She pressed a hand to her heart. "He has this way of looking at me that makes me feel like he just stripped me naked and enjoyed every minute. With you, I never . . . I mean . . . it didn't . . ."

He nodded. "Which is as much my blame as yours. You can't blame yourself if I didn't turn you on, Rem. We were *friends*."

"But that's why I'm so confused." She pressed her fingers to her eyes. "Heul is a friend, too. And I want him more than I want air. How can my body crave something it hasn't ever experienced?"

"Nature," he intoned gravely. "Animals wouldn't reproduce if both males and females didn't enjoy sex. Humans just happen to be programmed to have sex for reasons other than reproduction."

"You sound like an anthropologist, Dr. Crowley," his ex-wife muttered.

"Perish the thought!" He crossed his arms. "Let me see if I can reason this out. You have felt inadequate because I couldn't turn you on enough. A combination of bad chemistry and not enough effort, to be sure, so we're equally at blame. And, also, you're wary of giving your heart because you don't want to be hurt again, and you don't want Nicole hurt. On the other hand, you have Heul. You're so attracted to him that, given five minutes and a bottle of syrup, you'd strip him naked and dive in like a secret chocoholic. This is an oddity to you because you've never before had that urge, more's the pity for *me*. At the same time, you're confused because you consider Heul a friend and you're convinced that friends can't be lovers." He paused. "How am I doing?"

"Stay out of my dreams."

"Ah. I'm doing well. I'll continue. Now then. I'm going to point out one simple fact for you: the couples who have lasted longest together are the ones that are friends as well as lovers. It's not the intimacy of making love, Remy, it's the intimacy of sharing your thoughts and your feelings. Not just your body. If you're not comfortable enough with someone to share your every thought, then why be comfortable enough to share your body? Or vice-versa."

"I was comfortable enough with you for both, and it didn't work."

"Mm. That's where we pull in the phenomena of nature known as 'mating for life.' Some animals, like wolves, mate for life. They are chemically programmed by Mother Nature to have one perfect match. Wolves will leave their family pack to find a mate and have their own pack. Many other species are the same way, and humans can be counted among them. Some men and women simply don't respond chemically to any but their perfect mate. There's nothing wrong with them any more than there is anything wrong with someone who does respond chemically to others beyond their natural mate."

"And how do emotions play into this, Dr. Crowley?"

"Oh, those things? They make a mess of *everything*."

She ran both hands through her hair. "For God's sake!" She blinked. "Is there a god?"

"You think I'm telling if there is? Ha. I'm dead, not stupid." He took her hands and held them tightly. "Remy. You can't live your life in the past. You're not living. The ghosts in our bedroom were as much my making as they were yours. You couldn't banish them, and I couldn't make you want to. But your Heul is different. Follow your heart. And be happy."

She took a deep breath and asked the question she had wondered about for years. "Chase . . . do you hate me?"

He shook his head with a smile. "No. If I was meant to know her, I'd have lived longer. I'm her birth father, but I'm not her dad. I don't regret helping create her. I'm proud to have given such an amazing little girl to an amazing woman."

"Now you're sounding a little oogie-boogie for my tastes. You'd think you believed in destiny."

"Who me? I'm just a dead anthropologist who thinks his ex-wife needs a good kick in the rump. Or to get a good tumble in a bed. Sadly, I can't provide the second, but I can give the first." His eyes flickered to the door and back. He smiled. "Bye, Remy."

When Jen opened the door, all she found was Remy glaring at the bed. "Problem?"

"No," Remy muttered as she got to her feet. "Not at all."

"Well," Jen said casually, "we decided to do you a favor. We're taking the midget over to Driven Snow so that you and Heul can relax. I'm letting Heul have command of my shop, so there shouldn't be any trouble. It'll be just you two and you can finish your project quicker. Taking care of Nicole has been taxing you."

"I . . . hmm."

"No secret motives," Jen assured her. "We need this project done so we can hammer out the details. I think we all know the merger is sound. Orange blossoms aside. So you and Heul don't get together. Big deal. There is such a thing as irony."

"Well . . . okay," she reluctantly said. "I know Nicole loves her new uncles. She'll like being over there."

"Yup!" Jen's eyes were completely without guile. "So you have a good day." She pulled the door shut again and looked down the hall to where Arian was standing with Nicole in his arms. She gave them a thumbs-up and both, even Nicole, returned the gesture.

An hour later, Remy found herself in the shop with Heul. They were working on the details of the dollhouse. She was also a painter and color specialist, and she was handling that aspect. While he cut, and carved, and constructed, she added color to small pieces.

When he happened to glance over at one point, he had to hide a smile. "Remy, do you want a headband?"

"Huh?" She blinked at him.

"You're pushing your hair out of your eyes."

"So?" She looked at the mirror across the room and saw instantly what he had. "For crying out loud." She scowled at the smears of yellow and pink on her cheek. "I haven't done that since I was ten. Jeans are fair game, but not my face."

He got a wet cloth and walked over. "Here we go." He stepped close and bent to begin removing the smears. It was self-inflicted torture. He couldn't breathe for wanting to taste her. He couldn't think for thoughts of her. He had stopped sleeping. He was barely eating. His body was in a state of desire that was agony if their skin so much as brushed. Standing this close, she was a tempting offering. Her scent was pungent, and her body seemed wildly seductive in paint stained clothes.

Their eyes met, and he saw the darkening of her hunger for him. She was trembling softly, nearly vibrating with frustration. He could hear the soft struggle she made to keep her breathing even. "How much longer can we ignore this?" he asked softly, his voice a rasp. He tossed the cloth aside without looking. His hands sank into her thick hair and he bent his head to close his teeth lightly over the line of her jaw. "Let me kiss you. For god's sake, Remy, let me kiss you before we both lose our minds."

On a desperate groan, she turned her head and found his mouth with hers. She wound her arms around his neck and dragged him as close as she could. His hands tightened, and he pulled her up into him so that she was nearly bent backwards while he devoured her. Lips clung and burned, teeth scraped. It was madness. Insanity.

She had never been kissed with such famished intensity, and she felt herself sinking into a heated pool of surrender. It was her teeth that nipped at his lip when he moved as if to release her. He groaned and sank into her again, his fingers moving convulsively in her hair as his tongue wildly dueled with hers to gulp in her taste and scent.

Then, suddenly, the embrace went from wild to tender. His fingers softened and so did his kiss. She opened her eyes slightly to find him watching her, his blue eyes as soft and dark as velvet. Something churned inside, something stronger and hotter than desire. He watched her as if she was his entire world.

The thud was painful and hard inside her heart. It seemed to wrench her entire soul. Terrified, she broke free of the kiss and tried to push him away. She was in love with him. Had been in love with him but too terrified to admit it. She could pinpoint the exact moment it had happened. She had walked in to find him rocking Nicole to sleep in the rocking chair. She had looked at him and seen everything she could ever want in a mate.

He loved children and was brilliant with them. He was strong enough to take charge when needed, but not afraid to step down when someone knew more. He gave of himself to his family without thought or consequence. And he watched her as if she was the only woman in his world. This man who was blessed to know what he wanted . . . wanted her.

She tore herself out of his arms and fled out of the shop toward the house. He paused only a moment before following her swiftly. Things were about to come to a very critical point. There were two outcomes before him, and the next five minutes would decide which he chose.

Blocks away, at the Driven Snow building, Nicole was cuddled onto a couch, and watching Sam and Seisyll beat the heck out of Tomos and Jen at a video game. She was happy. She liked her new uncles. She liked to see her aunts be happy, especially Tabby, because Tabby smiled lots now that she was with Gavin. And if she was touching Gavin, she could even hug Nicole. That was Nicole's favorite part. She never got to hug Tabby 'cause Tabby had electric veins, or something.

But there was a blip on her happiness. Thinking it made her frown to herself. She was absolutely, positively certain that she wanted Heul to be her daddy. She loved him *lots*, more than her uncles. As much as she loved her mommy. And he loved her mommy. She was sure of it 'cause he watched her mommy like her uncles watched her aunts. And since her mommy watched him the way her aunts watched her uncles, then her mommy had to love him, too.

"Uh oh," Belle murmured. "She's thinking."

"This is bad?" Owen asked curiously.

Rie jerked a thumb at her niece. "Machiavelli's reincarnation."

"What's up, kidlet?" Gavin sat down next to Nicole on the couch. He had to smile as he looked at her. Her face was lightly colored with spots that made her resemble a pink Dalmatian. She had stopped scratching, though; Arian had wrapped her hands in soft mittens. Keeping her distracted helped too. She was starting up the slope toward being healthy, and that meant she was getting fidgety.

"I want Heul to be my dad." She nodded decisively. "I want him to marry Mommy."

The adults exchanged looks. Then, carefully, Lexie asked,

"What if they don't feel that way?"

She rolled her eyes as if adults were too dense to get it. "'Cause they watch each other like you and Unca Joseff look at each other. Or like Unca Gavin and Aunt Tabby. An' 'cause you love each other, that means they gotta love each other, right?"

"Nothing gets past her," Tabby apologized to the men.

"Yikes."

"Well," Joseff said, "we're working on it, Nic. We want them to be happy, too. It might take a while though."

She nodded. "'Kay. I can wait." She contemplated that. "Until Christmas. 'Cause there's a party and I wanna go with my new daddy. He can beat up mean old Luis!"

Seisyll suddenly went pale. "Dear god. What do we do when she's a teenager? Gwyn was bad enough."

The Germaine sisters exchanged a grin as the Trahern brothers all began to look horrified. "Welcome to the family," Sam said drolly.

Remy took the stairs two at a time until she was in the attic. Once surrounded by the familiar scent of dust and time, she was able to release some of the panic. She walked on trembling legs across the room to the large wooden trunk under the window. Heart pounding, she opened the lid and looked inside. There, resting on top, was the gold locket.

She carefully picked it up and turned it over. Tiny little engravings of initials were clear on the back. Seven sets of initials, and six of them darker than the surrounding gold. She lightly touched where she had engraved her own initials but never made a wish.

"Well!" an old woman said suddenly. "A fine kettle of fish you're in now, Remy Germaine!"

She slowly turned her head to see a familiar old woman sitting in what had been, only minutes before, a broken rocking chair. The old woman was knitting competently, her needles clicking and flashing. Her short white hair framed a wrinkled face that still retained its freckles. Her eyes were meadow green and sharp as ever.

All Remy could say was, "You couldn't knit."

"I've been dead for fifteen years. I've had time to learn." Grandma Henrietta watched her oldest chick intently. "I was quite content to chase your grandfather around fluffy clouds. I'm not entirely happy I have to come down here and smack you."

"Then there is a heaven?"

"For me," she said easily. "For others there may be something different. There's a . . . cycle, Remy. We're all a part of it. What we do after death is entirely dependent on our beliefs and our desires and our sins." She waved a hand and almost lost her knitting. She scowled. "I dropped a stitch."

Remy sank down and looked at the locket in her hands. "What do I do?" she whispered softly.

"You could wish for his love. You would have it."

She shook her head quickly. "No. I will not wish for something that I might never get naturally." Her lower lip trembled. "I'd live with the knowledge for my entire life. If he loves me, I want it to be because of me."

"Well of course you do."

Remy eyed her grandmother. "Of course?"

"Naturally. Everyone in 3rd District has the internal workings to mate for life. Some call it chance. Others call it magic. Me? I call it damned lucky and leave it there." She resumed her knitting. "Chase came along in your life when you needed him. He gave you Nicole, and we both know he couldn't be happier for it. If you hadn't had Nicole when you did, you might never have had a child at all."

"And how do I tell Heul that?" she asked achingly. "Tell a man who loves children so badly that if he wanted to be with me, he might never have a child of his own blood?" She got to her feet. "An aberration, they called it. Just a fluke. Some women stop ovulating but don't stop menstruating."

"Frankly, if nature was going to turn off one, she ought to turn off the other." Grandma put down her knitting. "You could wish for that, Remy. That locket has the power to grant anything you wish."

Remy thought of love. She thought of having more children. She loved children as much as Heul did. She thought of a life full of laughter and joy and passion. And she thought of Nicole. Softly, she said, "I wish only for Nicole to be happy. Whatever is needed for her to be happy in her life."

The locket glowed and the initials on the back darkened. Grandma nodded sagely. "A worthy wish. I see Nicole as having a nice, long life. But never forget your own happiness, Remy. She'd be miserable if her mother was sad."

"I'll do my best."

Outside the door, Heul leaned against the wall. His heart ached for Remy. Life was cruel to give her only one child when she had enough love for many. And it hurt him as well for he knew she would never get over what she felt were her own shortcomings. He loved her. He finally knew it for what it was, and only one outcome lay before him.

When Remy stepped onto her floor, she found him waiting for her. "Sorry," she said. "I just . . . I've never felt desire before," she admitted. "Not like that."

"I want to make you an offer." He got to his feet and walked over to her. "It's an offer I don't make lightly."

Her heart began to beat harder. "What kind of offer?"

"We have a one-night stand. We're alone today. Let's be lovers once and see what happens. Afterward, we'll see where we stand, if we want to continue the affair. It's not just new territory for you, Remy. This is way out of my league. I'm in over my head, too."

"You won't want to stay with me," she whispered miserably. "When we step into that bedroom, you won't want to stay."

"Try me."

Before she could blink, he had reached out with that shocking speed of his and literally swept her off her feet. His mouth came down on hers with desperate hunger holding something wild and feral but tender. A helpless moan echoed in her throat as she surrendered. She loved him. Wanted him. If only once, she wanted to live.

He walked into her bedroom and came to a sharp stop. His head lifted. A chill went over her skin as she heard the soft feminine whispers flowing through the room. Shaking, she looked around to see the wispy forms of several women standing at the edges of the room. All very different, but all lovely in some way. Different ages, different ethnicities. All they had in common . . . was Heul.

Touching Remy as he was, he saw them too. "What is this?" he asked her softly.

She braced her shoulders. "The downside of my gift," she said flatly. "Welcome to the ghosts of lovers past. And welcome to one of the big problems Chase and I had. There were only two ghosts to stand around and stare at us, but they were enough. Add in that I just couldn't want him that way . . ."

"Did you even try to banish them?"

"How can I?"

"Easily." He set her down on her feet and began to strip off her clothes. His hands were hot and deliberate as they caressed her slightly chilled skin. "You make me forget they ever existed. Replace their presence with yours. And I'll make you forget they ever existed, too." He lifted her off her feet and pressed his lips to her throat where her pulse was rapid.

"I can't," she started, but the words strangled off into a gasp as one of his hands closed over her breast and sent sensation streaking through her body.

"Yes, you can." He tumbled her down onto the bed and began to slowly kiss and caress his way across her body, leaving no inch untouched, no secret unfound. "God," he said roughly. "I don't know how you found them. How could they ever compare to you? I didn't even remember their faces!"

She opened her eyes slightly to see all but one ghost was gone. The one that remained was smirking at her. Something wild and fierce rose inside her, as hot as her desire and potent with feminine power. Heul was *hers*. She wasn't going to turn him over to anyone, especially not ghosts of the past!

He almost staggered when she suddenly threw herself into his arms and her mouth sought his. She seemed to simply pour herself into the kiss. Her body moved erotically against his, and her hands fluttered over his skin, sensitizing it to a fever pitch. Aching, throbbing, he fell onto his back as her sensual assault continued. "Remy." It was all he could say.

The rough rasp of his words was a physical caress. She knelt across his hips and rushed to open his shirt. She was naked and he wasn't. It wasn't fair at all. With a murmur of wordless delight, she rubbed her hands over his chest and bent to nuzzle her nose through the soft blond curls.

He wasn't a passive participant. His hands swept over her, kneading her breasts and lightly scraping her nipples. He skimmed his hands down her stomach, teased the small stretch marks that were evidence of her child, and then slowly his hands slipped between her legs. He shuddered. She was hot and wet, and as he stroked her softly, he watched her face intently.

She shuddered. A whimper left her lips as the need built. Those rough fingertips were making her entire body throb for more. Helplessly, her hips began to follow his touch. Her head fell back as the heat rose inside until she felt as if she were burning alive. "Heul!" His name was nothing more than a choked cry of desperation.

She found herself on her back a second later. She pushed and shoved at his jeans, almost sobbing with every breath as her body dangled, enticing, on the edge of something . . . on the edge of *something*, and she needed that something more than air.

When he was finally as naked as she was, he dragged her legs over his arms. "Look at me," he managed to say. Her eyes met his and he plunged into her deeply. Fire raced up through his entire body. She was tight and wet and hot; they fit so perfectly, her muscles eagerly clamping down on his aching flesh. Her groan of agonized pleasure seemed to sear him. Brand him. "Do you see any ghosts?" he demanded harshly.

She forced her eyes open. There was no one in the room but them. "No," she managed to whisper.

"That's because there's only you inside me. Only me inside you." He pulled back and thrust forward again. "You never tried to banish them, Remy! Never wanted to. You had to want me enough to make them go away."

"Stop talking," she begged, grabbing at his shoulders for balance.

After that, there were no words for either of them. There was nothing but the driving hunger for each other's body until they couldn't take any more and fell together into a shocking ecstasy that neither would have ever imagined. No ghosts. No inadequacy. There was nothing but them, burning together in a velvet paradise.

Some indeterminable time later, he muttered into her hair, "Your bed is too small."

She smiled against his shoulder. "You're too tall." He lifted his head and she framed his face gently. "Thank you," she said softly.

"You're welcome." He rolled off her only to tug her up against his side. "In case it escaped your notice, I was going absolutely *mad*. I haven't been eating or sleeping." He gave her a fierce glower. "I had never even kissed you, and I wanted you until I was close to insanity. I'm shocked that I lasted as long as I did once I got my hands on you."

She lifted her head to look at the clock. "An hour is an aberration?"

"I prefer three."

"Three!" Her eyes went wide. "Can a body *survive* three hours?"

His smile was slow and lethal as he leaned over her, his hands suddenly gliding over her skin with an intent other than comfort. "You're going to find out."

She awoke much later in the afternoon to find herself alone in bed. He had made good on his promise and she felt like an overcooked noodle. She ached in some muscles, but the others were melted down to puddles of satiated flesh. She had never felt so loved. She had just needed the right man. She had needed Heul. She really hated when Chase was right.

She carefully sat up and looked around. She knew without asking that Heul was not there in the building or anywhere close. A note sat on the nightstand and she picked it up with trembling fingers.

Dear Remy,

Thank you. Thank you for giving me something so precious. Your trust and your body, but something more as well.

I know you're probably mad to wake alone. I'm sorry. But if I stayed, I'd ask for more than you can give. My gift is to see future outcomes. The one I saw . . . it gave you happiness, but it would take you from me. I choose your happiness. I knew all along that in the end I would never have you, no matter how I wanted otherwise.

The dollhouse is done. Nicole ought to love it. If you wish, the merger will go forward. Don't worry about me. I won't demand more of you. But never ever doubt that you are a warm and sensual woman, and that you'll make the right man very happy.

Heul

She crushed the note in her hand as her temper flared. He was walking out for *her* own good? Bullshit. Furious, she got out of bed and got dressed. He thought he could make love to her and leave? Over her dead body. Did he think she didn't love him? Well, he was a damned blind idiot! If his note was any indication, he loved her too, and if he did, what the *hell* was he doing walking out? He saw the future, saw her walking away? They would see about that!

At Driven Snow, Heul was sitting in his office with twelve males and females glaring at him. "What?" he demanded. "I'm not in the best of moods, so kindly take yourselves out of my office."

"You *walked out*?!" Belle planted her hands on the desk. "You idiot! Why didn't you tell her you loved her?!"

"She'd never believe me!" he shouted.

Silence fell. No one was sure of what to say. As it happened, no one had to try. The door suddenly slammed open to reveal a tall redhead who was so mad that her eyes were like green flames. "Heul Trahern!" Remy shouted. "What the hell do you think by leaving me alone in bed?"

The others stepped back quickly en masse. "Holy shit," Lexie managed to whisper, eyes wide. She had never seen Remy that mad before.

Heul grabbed onto the edge of the desk before he grabbed Remy. She stalked over and planted her hands on the desk and leaned across to get in his face. "You are an idiot!" she told him. "A big one! In fact, I've never met another idiot who was bigger! You want to tell me what the meaning of this note is?" She leaned back and threw it at him so that it bounced off his head. "What kind of crap is this? You saw me walking away so you walked away first?"

"You think I don't see that you're afraid to love me?" he countered harshly. "That you're afraid to make another mistake?"

"And it didn't stop me from falling in love, did it?" she shouted. "We're both idiots! *You* thought I was so fragile that I wouldn't believe you, and *I* was sure I'd screw things up! Well I'm not fragile and *you* were the one who screwed up!" She gestured sharply at the door. "Tell me you want me to walk out, and I will. If you want me to stay, then I'm staying! If you can handle a woman who sees ghosts—including her dead ex-husband—then I can handle a hardheaded precognitive who doesn't know destiny when it bites him on the ass!"

"Stay." The word came from the deepest part of his soul. "You have to know I love you, Remy. I can't seem to function without you."

"Then you'll have to marry me." She crossed her arms. "If you can handle the fact that I might never have any more children."

"Then share Nicole with me," he said simply. "You know I'll love her as if she was mine. If we want more, we can always adopt." He carefully got to his feet. "Now tell me you love me without shouting at me."

"I love you." She smiled as she said it. The words were easier than she had thought they would be. Oddly, she wasn't worried anymore. How could she make a mistake when everything was fitting together perfectly? Yes, he was her friend, but he was her lover as well. She didn't think she could ever envision having one with him and not having the other. "It's not a mistake this time."

"Well." Gavin cleared his throat. "Does this mean we're going ahead with the merger?"

Remy and Heul glanced at their grinning siblings. To be honest, they had forgotten they were there. Heul coughed. Remy cleared her throat. "Yes," she finally said. "I believe we are." She held out a hand to Heul. "What do you say we call it Seven Wishes Design?"

He took her hand. "I think that sounds perfect." And with easy strength, he yanked her across the top of the desk into his arms and kissed her with all the love in his heart while their brothers and sisters clapped and whistled.

Out in the hall, Nicole carefully closed the door and grinned cheekily. She absolutely *had* to be flower girl for her mommy and daddy. A little skip in her step, she climbed down the stairs to where Rayna and Eric were standing near the door. "Here, Auntie Rayna." She held up the seven contracts she was carrying.

Eric took the contracts while Rayna snuggled Nicole. Satisfied, he watched all seven contracts glow and the word 'Complete' appear. "Perfect," he said softly. "I think Gwyn will be quite happy when she gets home."

Rayna smiled up at him. "Seven wishes for seven sisters and seven happy endings. You can't ask for more."

"Can I ask for a baby brother or sister?" Nicole asked. "'Cause

I want one."

Eric and Rayna exchanged a grin. Remy and Heul were in for a quite a shock. Remy had wished for Nicole's happiness, and if Nicole needed a baby sibling to be happy, then that's what she would get.

After all, a locket made from a golden apple of Aphrodite *always* kept its word.

EPILOGUE

When Rhianna was handed the seven contracts, she read them closely. She smiled. "I'd say young Joseff and Lexie did a fine job, wouldn't you?"

"They're naturals," Eric concurred. "Now can we get out of the matchmaking business?"

She slowly lifted a brow. "What are you talking about? We're not in the matchmaking business. We're in a business to ensure the happiness of the people of 3rd District. We've issued thousands of contracts over the years but only half of them deliberately had anything to do with finding someone love."

He stared at her. She stared back, her black eyes guileless. On a mutter, he stalked to his office. They both knew he couldn't prove that she was doing anything on purpose. All he had were hunches and suspicions because, despite her words, anyone associated with a contract from Enforcers—of any type—somehow ended up finding true love.

He stopped at his door and looked at her. "Rhi . . . where did you get the golden apple you made the locket from for Henrietta Germaine? The elder one, I mean."

She arched a brow in the maddening way of hers. "I found it lying around."

He looked at Rayna inside his office, and she made a helpless gesture. Rhianna was telling the truth. "*Damn* it," he groused and stalked into his office. The door shut firmly.

Covering a smile, Rhianna made some notes on the contracts

and put them into their proper folders. She slid the folders into the drawer labeled 'Carmichael.' When she locked the drawer, the word 'Finished' appeared. This time she knew it was for real.

She settled back in her chair contentedly. She had indeed told Eric the truth. She really wouldn't call herself a matchmaker. Mostly she just liked to meddle. Was it her fault if happiness and love tended to be synonymous? Of course not. It just happened to fall that way, and she just took advantage of things.

She couldn't help but look forward to what was next. She loved her job.

Status: File Complete
Analysis: Whether you wish for love or happiness, for yourself or others, your wish will only come true when you believe in yourself.

Keep going for a bonus story from Mirage where another pair of lovers are 'coincidentally' brought together, but the one Enforcing their contract is someone entirely new . . .

Bonus Folder
JERAN

CHAPTER ONE

People often see wavering images of things on hot days. As they draw closer, the images disappear and prove they never existed. But they did exist. They existed in another world that lies parallel to Earth. That world was known as Mirage.

When it drifted too close to Earth many centuries ago, it got stuck to the River Styx and thusly stayed connected. Unlike Earth, which drew its magic only from the River Styx, Mirage consisted entirely of magic. To Earthlings, it would be a world of faerie tales. To those of Mirage, Earth was the world of tall tales.

Although only the people of the place known as 3rd District within New York City knew about Mirage's existence, Mirage knew completely about Earth. Many citizens had crossed to Earth to stay, and some had come home with mates. It was always kept a secret if they did.

Some of the 'lower class' people of Mirage thought of Earth as only a faerie tale. Some, like Jeran Windwalker, figured it was just a story parents used to make sure their children didn't go wandering at night. 'Be careful,' his father had often said, 'or an Earthling might kidnap you.'

Jeran was a good boy and often seen as simple-minded. He obeyed his father without question. It was why he still lived at home even though he was nineteen years of age and more than old enough to have gone seeking his fortune in the world.

He was a handsome young man with lavender hair and purple eyes, although he was of slightly shorter height than most males his age. Regardless of his height, farm girls for miles around were smitten with his good looks and the honest and kind heart he had. He was a young man who, almost literally, had his choice of women.

His elder brothers, Jared and Jonah, despised him for it. They were of ages twenty-two and twenty-four, and they were equally handsome, with similar coloring to their youngest brother. They were taller than their brother by five inches, and they had gone out into the world to make their fortunes, only to fail and return home to wait for their father to name his heir and die.

Their father, Julian, loved his boys, but it was Jeran he loved the most. As he lay in his sickbed and watched through a window as Jeran patiently filled a bucket with cool water, he thought again how much he wished that his two eldest were as kind as their brother, or that Jeran was as smart as his older brothers. None were currently suitable to inherit.

Jeran saw his father grimacing as he returned and rushed to his side. "No, don't overdo yourself, Father." He smiled and brought a cup of the cool water he had fetched. "The more you stress yourself out, the sooner you'll die."

Julian regarded his son. "You don't want me to die?"

"Not at all." He busied himself straightening the bed and fluffing the pillows. "You're my only father, so of course I'm loathe to lose you." He smiled, little sparkles appearing in his eyes; the sparkles were just one of the many things the girls loved. "If I had two fathers, then maybe it wouldn't be so bad."

Julian sighed fondly. "You're a brat." He held out a hand that Jeran took tightly. "Tell me, what have your brothers been doing lately?" He had no reservations about taking advantage of Jeran's open nature and quick-to-speak-before-thinking tendency.

"Jonah spent today visiting all of the neighbors, seeing if any of them were looking to sell any time soon. Jared spent his time trying to go courting amongst the girls. He came home quite furious since he couldn't find them." Jeran's voice was puzzled. "I can't understand how he missed them. They were visiting with me while I tended to the horses."

Julian hid a smile. "Ah, well. He is not nearly as open-minded as you. How did Jonah's time go? It's quite a fine idea, actually, seeking to merge our lands."

"Not well, either. None of the other farmers want to deal with him." Again, Jeran was confused. "They're always so open with me and always happy to talk and haggle prices."

Not for the first time, Julian wished with all his heart that Jeran had just a slightly harder personality. If Julian could be surer that he could defend himself on all fronts, he would have named him his heir in a heartbeat and gone to make funeral arrangements.

He was at a loss. All of his sons had flaws. He had no way to decide amongst them. With a sigh, he settled back against his pillows. "I want to rest for a little while, Jeran. I'll call when I wake."

"Alright." Jeran smiled and leaned down to kiss his father's cheek. "No dying in your sleep."

"Yes, yes," he said gruffly. Jeran's open and honest love was humbling. He cherished his son more than anything. "Off with you."

Jeran left the room and shut the door behind him. His smile immediately turned into a frown. Sometimes he wished he had the courage of his brothers. If he did, then he would have been able to tell his father that it had not been Jonah's idea for the merger but his. It was just the most recent in a series of similar events throughout his life.

To be truthful, he was not as simple-minded as most thought. He was simply too nice, and too shy, to speak up for himself. For his entire life, his brothers had been taking his ideas and promoting them as their own. At this time and date, he highly doubted anyone would believe him anyway.

It was evening when the front door slammed open and Jonah and Jared staggered in, both so drunk that Jeran could smell the alcohol from where he stood on the stairs. His nose wrinkled. "Keep quiet. Father is resting."

"Oh suuuure," Jonah slurred, "we'll be quiet. Real quiet. Right,

Jared?" He gave his brother a sloppy punch in the arm that sent the already-off-balance male staggering across the room where he crashed into a table. "Shhh!" he said with an exaggerated gesture. "We gotta be quiet. Wouldn't want to scare the geezer to death."

Jared lurched up to his feet and narrowly missed cracking his head open on the closest door. "Right you are. No need to make noise." He walked woozily toward Jeran. "Still baby-sitting, kid? I'd say you ought to get a wife but what woman'd have you?"

Jeran nimbly stepped to the side and watched his brother smack into the wall. He told himself he didn't care. Then he sighed. "I'll make something to get rid of your headaches." It would also sober them up, but he was smart enough not to mention that at least. The first and most important ingredient in the cure was apples. He got out the apple basket and headed out into the back orchards to start gathering.

The apple orchard was an acre in size and the apples the trees produced were the best in the country. They came in every color under the sun from red to white to yellow to green. The ones he wanted were the green apples, and they grew on the trees toward the back. He looked over the orchard as he walked. He didn't need a kingdom. Just this little farm.

There was a loud and indignant squawk from up ahead followed by a feminine shriek. Startled, he dropped the basket and hurried toward the sound. "Hey! What's going on?" As he rounded the corner, he got his answer; the moonlight was bright enough that he could see clearly as the day.

There was a young woman crouched on the ground with her arms thrown over her head to protect herself as a large golden bird tried to peck at her. She wore the plain and simple clothing of a farm girl, so he had to assume she lived nearby. "Cut it out!" he shouted as he ran forward. He scooped up a rock and chucked it at the bird.

His aim was true and he struck the bird in the side. With an outraged cry, it flapped its wings and took off into the sky, shedding golden feathers as it went. He ignored the feathers and knelt beside

the girl quickly. "Are you okay, miss? Oh, you're bleeding!" he exclaimed, noticing her arms had been pecked at viciously.

She lowered her arms to look at them and then looked up at him. He took a sharp breath, his eyes widening. He had never before seen such a beautiful girl in his life; her features were too impossibly perfect to be real. Her hair was thick and black, and her eyes were the same, but there were little golden flecks caught in the blackness of them that he likened to stars in the sky.

A long silence descended. Abruptly, he realized he was staring. He flushed. "I'm terribly sorry." He sat down beside her and reached for her arm. He tugged it closer gently so that he could see the marks. There were three of them, all of them deep enough that blood welled up slightly. "They must hurt."

"Very much so." She lowered her lashes and watched him from under them. "I can tend to them myself. I was trespassing, so I'm hardly worth your time."

He gave her a shocked look. "Trespassing or not, I'm not going to walk away." Because injuries were par for the course on a farm, he always carried one or two first aid supplies in the satchel around his waist. He pulled out a strip of bandage and began to gently wind it around her arm. "Besides," he told her, smiling, "I don't worry about trespassers. You were chasing that bird, right, so it was an accident."

"What if I told you I was here to steal some apples, and the bird got in the way?" she asked softly.

"Well, then I'd pretend I hadn't heard. There are *plenty* of apples in this orchard." He finished wrapping the bandage and tied a jaunty bow on the top. "There you go." He smiled at her, his eyes sparkling. "My name is Jeran. I live here. What's your name?"

"Michaela." She searched his face intently, feeling her heart beat harder inside her chest. She had never before seen such a handsome man, and he wasn't a giant like so many others. She was very small herself, and she always hated males who towered over her. And, more importantly, he was honestly kind. Was he the one she needed? "I'm from far away. I was visiting."

"That's okay." He pulled her up to her feet easily and his eyes widened. "You're so small!" he blurted happily. She was only slightly over five feet in height, and therefore he was several inches taller. Since the average height of a female on Mirage was anywhere from five-six to six feet, he was delighted.

She was no less surprised to find her head fit just under his chin. Warmth filled her heart. "Maybe we're destined to be," she laughed as she looked up at him.

"Destined to be what?" he asked curiously.

He really was sweet, she thought. Kind of naïve, but she really liked it. "Never mind. If we are, then you'll find out." She reached up to frame his face and then went on her toes to kiss him quickly.

His eyes widened as she released him. He touched his lips and felt them tingle. He wasn't *that* naïve, and he recognized that there were some potentially potent sparks between him and his starlight beauty. "Promise I'll see you again," he told her.

"Oh I'm sure I can promise that. Thank you, Jeran," she added softer, "for giving me hope." Without another word, she hurried off out of sight. She didn't go very far, though. She ducked down and hid behind a tree so that she could watch him. If he was the one . . . well, she would soon know for certain. She hoped so, with everything she was. She could easily fall in love with a man like Jeran.

Jeran was puzzled but knew he distinctly looked forward to seeing Michaela again. He had never considered courting any girl before because he had never met one that he honestly took a fancy to. Michaela was perfect for him.

With a sigh, he started to pick some apples for the cure for his brothers. As he was carrying them back to the basket, he noticed some of the golden feathers had fallen in as well. Curious, he picked one up. Much to his shock, he realized it was real gold and not just golden colored.

Delighted, he said, "I'll give it to my father. He'll love it. Perhaps it will help him live longer!" He held the basket close and hurried back toward the house. He would share his gift bright and early in the morning. He needed to make the cure for his brothers right then. Gold could wait.

Michaela watched him hurry off and felt tears begin to slide down her cheeks as she slowly sank down to her knees. He was, she thought in dim shock and relief. He truly was the one destined for her. She had thought she would never find him, and realizing she was soon to fall in love was a little terrifying. With a little sigh, she rested her forehead against the tree beside her. "Oh, who am I kidding?" she asked on a wry smile. "I already fell."

Jeran could barely keep the feathers a secret, almost bursting at the seams to tell someone. But because he had already promised, he got to work with the apples and other ingredients needed and made the hangover cure for his brothers. It was no easy feat to make them drink it, but they were so drunk that he finally just poured the concoction down their throats.

He awoke the next morning with the dawn. He quickly hurried into his clothes and went to get the chores done. Once they were completed, he made breakfast. By the time that was done, his brothers were awake and staggering into the dining room. They were sober and not hungover, but both were clearly exhausted.

Jared gave an earsplitting yawn. "Once I'm more awake, I intend to go wife-hunting again. I have no idea where all the women were yesterday, but maybe I scared them off with my dashing good looks."

Jonah snorted over his cup of coffee. "More like they were hiding in abject terror."

Jared opened his mouth to retort and Jeran didn't hesitate to rap him smartly in the back of the head with the spatula. "Ow!" Jared glowered and rubbed his head but couldn't argue with his baby brother; if he did, he wouldn't get fed. Jeran might have been stupid, but he was stubborn.

When breakfast had been cleared, Jeran hurried to his father's room with a tray. "Good morning!" he called cheerfully.

Julian looked over with a smile as he came in. "Good morning, son. As you can see, I decided to live another day."

"Good." He set the tray down and smiled. "Because I brought a gift. They fell off a bird in our orchard." He held out the feathers. "Gold, father. Real gold! Aren't they beautiful?"

Julian stared at the feathers in his hands in shock. Greed churned inside him. "A bird you say? Which direction did it fly?"

"North."

"Jared! Jonah!" he called. When the two other young men had joined him and Jeran, he held out the feathers. "I want you to travel to the north. Find me the bird that shed these feathers! I must have the whole bird!"

Jared stared at the feathers. "Real gold," he breathed.

Jonah was no less stunned. "Well." He snorted. "So what? I don't want to go on some weird journey, thanks. I'll stay here."

Jeran frowned and said softly, "But Jonah, Father seems very insistent. Perhaps having this bird will cure him."

"All the more reason not to go, I think," his brother muttered back.

Julian beetled his brows together. "I will give my farm to whichever of my sons brings back that golden bird."

"Sold!" Jared took off for the barn as fast as he could.

"Hey, you asshole!" Jonah was hot on his heels. "I won't give up that easy!"

Jeran eased down until he was sitting on the side of the bed and took the feathers away from his father. "Don't stress yourself out, Father, please." He studied the feathers and wondered to himself if perhaps there was a spell of some sort over them. He had never before seen his father act like this. Perhaps it would be best if his brothers never found the bird.

Time passed, and days became months. Spring faded into summer, and two months went by. Julian's health stayed steady, and Jeran continued to run the farm as he always had. Still, he would watch the north every evening, waiting for his brothers. Finally, he knew they likely would not return.

"I'm sorry, Father," he said softly.

Julian frowned intently. "I refuse to believe such a thing! I must have that bird, Jeran, understand? I feel as if I will die if I do not."

"Then I will go," he said. "I will find this bird for you." Even as Julian shook his head, Jeran took his hand. "Please, Father! I will have the neighbors watch over things while I am gone, and I will find my brothers and the golden bird, I promise!"

"No, Jeran." Julian felt his heart quiver. Losing Jonah and Jared was not as frightening as losing Jeran. "You're my dearest son, I would never risk you." That and he was worried Jeran was not smart enough to find the bird, but he kept the thought to himself.

The longer he argued, the more he realized Jeran's stubbornness was rearing its head. His mind and heart were set. With a heavy heart, Julian finally gave his blessings and watched out the window the following morning as Jeran set off toward the north with a big backpack full of supplies.

He sadly picked up the feathers sitting on the table beside him and studied them. But, to his utter astonishment, they turned black in his hands like the feathers of a raven. If they were enchanted, he had no idea what the enchantment was, but he did have to wonder just why they had chosen that moment to change. Was it Jeran? What gift did his son have that he did not know about?

CHAPTER TWO

The road was long and dusty, but the sun was bright and warm. As he walked down the trail that led into the woods, Jeran realized he was happier than he had thought he would be. He had never been far from home before, and it was like an adventure to consider seeing so many new things.

He began to whistle as he walked, and there was an added spring in his step. The only thing that marred the niceness of the day was the knowledge that he still didn't know where to find Michaela. He had been scouring the town since the night he met her, but no one had seen or heard of her. A part of him wondered if he had conjured her up.

"Hello."

He stopped in surprise and looked down to see that there was a little golden fox sitting next to him. With a smile, he knelt and patted the small animal gently. "Hi, yourself." Talking animals were as common on Mirage as skyscrapers were on Earth. He didn't find it odd at all to have the fox speaking to him. "Need some help?"

"Actually, I am here to help you." The fox circled him slowly and studied him. Yes, this one would do just fine. Sitting in front of Jeran again, he said, "I understand you are looking for the golden bird."

"I am!" Jeran smiled. "Can you help me?"

"I certainly can." He pointed with one paw down the road. "Down this road, two days hence, you will find a small resting place. It has two inns. One of them will be bright and lively. The other will

be dark and gloomy. Whatever you do, stay at the gloomy one."

Jeran thought about that. "I suppose that makes sense. I mean, you can't sleep well at a lively inn."

"Exactly. Now, beyond the rest stop, another couple days away, you will find a kingdom. This is where the golden bird lives. I will tell you how to catch him, but you had better pay close attention!" he scolded. "The bird is kept in its own pen at the back of the palace. Sneak into it and put the bird into the *plain* cage. It will remain quiet and you can escape with it."

Jeran committed the information to memory. He wanted to be sure he did this right. He wanted to prove to his father that he was not simple-minded, and that he could be trusted to run the farm. "Okay," he promised. "Is there any way I can repay you?"

"We can talk about repayment when you are done with your journey," the fox promised.

He straightened. "I understand." He smiled and dug into his bag. He came out with a cookie and offered it to the fox. "As thanks for now." With a renewed spring in his step, he turned and hurried down the road once more.

The fox sniffed the cookie and then nibbled on the edge. It was really quite tasty. He supposed it was a good thing Jeran knew how to cook. Michaela could burn water.

It was indeed two days before Jeran reached the two inns, and it was close to sundown as well. He was exhausted. His feet were sore, and he was dusty and grimy from the road. The idea of being able to sleep in a bed, a real bed, was a haunting lure as he stared at the brightly glowing inn.

He abruptly remembered the fox's advice and realized that resting at a lively inn was not going to allow him to sleep. He turned away from the sight and headed to the slightly gloomy looking inn. Much to his surprise, the interior was not gloomy at all. It was warm and welcoming, and it felt as if all his troubles faded away.

The desk clerk smiled as she saw him. "Good evening! Will you stay for the night?"

"Yes, please." He laid a few coins on the counter and sniffed the air. "Is that food I smell?"

"Naturally. If you'd like to go up to your room, I'll send someone along with a complimentary tray."

"Thank you." He gathered his backpack again and trudged up the stairs slowly. He was hoping very much for a bath before bed. He was used to being dirty because of farm work, but he didn't like wearing dirt overnight.

With much delight, he discovered there was a copper tub filled with hot water waiting for him. Hooray for modern convenience! He eagerly dropped his backpack on the ground and rummaged in it for a change of clothes. There was soap and a towel near the tub so he wasted no time in stripping off his tunic and vest.

He had just reached for his belt when the door opened. In shock, he and Michaela stared at one another. The latter was carrying a tray of food. The moment was broken when they realized what had happened, and he ducked behind a bookcase even as she whipped back out into the hall and out of sight.

There was silence. Then, "Er, hi, Michaela."

"Hi, Jeran." Oh my god, she thought over and over again. He was short but he was *gorgeous*. Though Nature had not given him much in height, it had taken full advantage of what inches were present. Clothes had hidden very nicely that his arms and chest were corded with sleek muscles. Her fingers itched to touch.

"What're you doing here?" He was embarrassed, but only because he had panicked. She was the prettiest girl he had ever known. He wanted to be at his best when he saw her, not sweaty and dirty from days on the road.

"I brought food. I'll just leave it out here."

"Okay but . . ." He grabbed his courage. "Come back later, okay? Like in thirty minutes?"

"But you need sleep."

"I want to see you more."

Her color rose even as her heart fluttered in her chest. "Oh.

Well . . . okay." She bent and put the tray on the floor and pushed it around the edge of the door without looking. Quickly she pulled the door shut and hurried down the hall. She needed to do her hair or something. She wanted to be her best when she saw him again.

He wasted no time in stripping and jumping into the tub. He wanted to get as clean as possible and look his best when she got back. He wanted to know where she lived, and why she was working here. His hunger to know everything was matched only by the hunger he felt to hold her in his arms.

Thirty minutes later, he was dressed in clean clothes and finishing his meal when there came a knock on the door. He smiled and went to unlock it. "Hi, Michaela," he said as he opened the door. His voice stuttered to a stop, and he stared at her. She had put her hair up and done something to her face. Some strange female thing that made her already impossibly beautiful features even more unforgettable.

Self-consciously, she patted her hair. "Is something wrong?"

He was bemused. He had never realized that seeing her hair up would make the urge to get his hands into it worse. He had to fight to keep from taking it down for her. "I was just surprised." He stepped back to let her in and shut the door behind her. "Do you work here?" he asked as he walked over to the table and pulled out a chair for her.

"No." She smiled as she sat down. "I befriended the clerk recently. I offered to bring the tray up so she could rest herself." She folded her arms on the table as she studied him curiously. "You're so far from home." She had begun to think he would never start down the path leading to her.

He sighed. "Well, remember the golden bird?" He gave her a quick rundown and summed up by adding, "I just want to prove I'm not stupid."

She straightened, the golden flecks in her eyes snapping like sparks. "That's ridiculous! You're just too nice, that's all." She contentedly studied the lines of his face and his purple colored eyes.

"So you're the baby in the family?" she asked.

"Yeah." He was no less content in admiring her black eyes with their golden flecks. "I turned nineteen a few months ago. How about you?"

She smiled. "I'm the spoiled brat since I'm an only child. I turned twenty a little while ago."

His eyes widened. "You're older than me!"

She frowned. "Is . . . is that bad?"

"No, but why aren't you waiting for a prince, or something? I mean . . . you're just the kind of girl they'd want!"

Her lashes lowered slightly. "Am I?"

"Well . . . sure." He gave her a puzzled look. "You're beautiful and funny, kind and gentle. You're also intelligent and strong. What prince wouldn't be smitten with you? I mean, I know I am, and I'm no prince." It belatedly dawned on him what he had said as he saw her wide eyes. "Oops."

"You're . . . smitten with me?" she asked softly.

"Yeah." He smiled. "I was really disappointed, you know. I went looking for you the next day but no one had seen you or heard of you." He reached out and took her hand. "I want to court you, if you'll let me."

"Court me?" She was nearly breathless. "For . . . for marriage?"

"If you'll let me." His eyes crinkled at the corners as he smiled. "I'm falling in love with you."

Michaela, in her twenty years of life, had seen dozens of princes. She had been romanced by some of the best. She had heard every flowery word, every pretty compliment, and been given every rose. As Jeran pulled a wildflower out of a vase and tucked it over her ear, she realized that his honest and simple nature was exactly everything she had ever wanted. "I'm glad," she said softly, her eyes glowing. "Because I'm falling for you, too."

His smile faded. "But . . .?"

She closed her eyes sadly. "There are . . . complications."

"Another suitor?" he asked in dismay.

"No, not at all." She got to her feet to pace away a few steps, her arms tightly crossed. "Jeran, I'm not what you think I am. I'm . . ." Her voice stopped sharply and she felt an impotent frustration. She could never talk of it. She was free to walk at night, but her curse stopped her voice if she tried to speak of it.

"You're what?" He walked over to her. "If there's something wrong, I want to fix it if I can." He took her hands with his and held them tightly. "Michaela, please. Tell me what's wrong."

"I can't!" On a sound of despair, she pressed against his chest and pulled her arms free to wrap them around his waist. "I want to, but I can't! Promise me! Promise me you'll keep looking for the golden bird."

He felt his heart flutter suddenly. "Michaela, are you cursed?" Fear and anger mixed inside him. His gentle Michaela . . . the idea of anyone cursing her, in any way, made him furious. If he found the person, he would probably hurt them.

"I can't talk about it!" She held him tighter. "Just hold me for a moment!"

His arms went around her, and he lowered his head toward hers. "Okay. I'll hold you as long as you need."

She drew a deep breath and got a grip on herself. Reluctantly she pulled out of his arms. "You should rest. I'm so sorry."

He just as reluctantly released her and watched her go to the door. "Michaela?" When she looked back, he smiled. "When I see you next time, I'm going to kiss you, okay? I wanted to this time, but you're scared."

Her lips trembled as her broken heart mended a little. She loved him so much. She would have loved him even if he wasn't her destiny. "I'm going to hold you to that, Jeran Windwalker. And I'm never scared when I'm with you."

He quietly locked the door behind her. Determination filled his heart. He would find the golden bird to save his father, and then he would find a way to save his Michaela as well. Protecting them was more important than anything.

A few days later, he found himself staring at the high brick wall of a castle courtyard. He was stumped. He could not figure out a single way to get himself up and over the wall without attracting the attention of everyone in the courtyard.

He took off his backpack and began to pace restlessly. He wished that he could have his brothers' intelligence just once or that he could think in complicated ways. The only idea he had at all was walking up to the gate and asking to look around.

He blinked and looked at his backpack. He knelt and dug inside it and came out with a book. It was half-full of sketches he had done of things he had seen. They weren't great sketches, but he wanted to remember everything clearly.

Wondering if it would work, he went over to the gate and up to the guards. "Hi. Can I come inside to draw the castle?"

The guards shrugged. "Sure," one said, and moved his axe out of the way so he could enter.

He scuttled past them, wondering why people called *him* stupid. It was a nice castle, he saw, and wished he really had the time to draw it like he wanted. Maybe later. He was in too much of a hurry to get the golden bird and give it to his father. More than that, he didn't know how, but he was sure the bird would somehow lead him to Michaela.

The pen was on the backside of the courtyard, and he snuck inside quickly. He immediately spotted the bird. It was sleeping on a perch at the back of the room. He quietly crept toward it. A look around revealed the plain wooden cage. As he was reaching for it, he realized that a bird this spectacular deserved something better. There was a golden cage nearby so he scooped it up instead.

The bird was silent as he picked it up, but the instant he tried to put it in the cage, it woke up and began to complain very loudly. He dropped the cage and grabbed the plain one. The bird silenced but it was too late. Guards were already bursting into the room with weapons drawn. "You! Boy! Drop the bird!" one barked

He opened his hands but the bird seemed to have taken a

fancy to him and began climbing all over his shoulders and head. "I can't," he said. "I tried, sorry." It was kind of a cute bird. It was plump like a chicken but it was plump with feathers and not fat. It had a rounded beak and the tips were sharp for pecking. It had a long sweeping tail and its wings were sturdy. Since it wasn't much bigger than a housecat, it was really extra adorable.

"Bring them both." The guard grabbed Jeran's arm and dragged him along as he went into the palace proper. The bird obediently followed in their wake.

Jeran was mortified as he found himself shoved to the floor in front of the king's throne. The king was an older man with a long graying beard and beady black eyes. Jeran had no idea what kind of ruler he was, but he was terrified regardless.

The king studied him. "Name?"

"Jeran Windwalker, majesty." He took a quick breath and blurted, "Please, please, let me go! My father is sick and dying and I have to bring the golden bird to him or he might die anyway! I'm the only one left to run the farm, and my father needs me very badly, and there's a girl that I'm in love with who is cursed, and this bird might help her, so please!"

The king studied him for a few moments. "You seem like an honest lad. More importantly, the bird seems to have taken a fancy to you, and lord knows it hated all of us."

Since the bird was on Jeran's shoulder and cooing happily, he could hardly argue the point.

"Here is what I shall do," the king decided. "You will go to the neighboring kingdom and fetch me their golden horse. I have wanted it for a long time. When you return with it, I will give you the bird to save your father and your love. How is that?"

Jeran leapt to his feet. "Oh thank you! You won't regret it!" He plucked the bird off his shoulder and handed it to the nearest guard despite the bird's annoyed squawk. "I promise! I'll return as soon as I have the horse!" He whirled and ran out quickly, determined not to mess up again.

As he went, everyone in the throne room looked at the floor where golden feathers had fallen from the bird's wings. It was obvious the minute Jeran was gone. The feathers turned to black.

Outside, Jeran hurried to pick up his backpack. The neighboring kingdom was close enough that he could see it from there, so it was easy to get onto the road and start walking. He felt like the idiot that his brothers called him. He had been given specific orders and he had messed them up. He just couldn't help it. He hated seeing anyone, animal or human, not being given what they truly deserved. Still . . . he supposed he was lucky the bird liked him. It would make going home much easier.

"Did you mess things up?"

He looked down swiftly to see the fox walking beside him. His color rose. "I know, I know! Don't berate me, please," he said miserably. "I'm already feeling like enough of an idiot. I just . . . I just thought it deserved better."

"Do you think that gold is so important?" the fox asked.

He frowned. "Well, no. I don't really think money means that much to me. But it was a royal pet. It's much more than common. And it deserved better. Anyone deserves better. I mean, if I'm going to make it live on a farm, it ought to have something special for itself."

"I am going to tell you something important, so listen close." The fox glanced up at him. "You think you are common and have nothing to offer, but you have something inside that is more special than anything. I am not telling you what. I *will* tell you that because of what is inside, that golden bird will see any cage it is ever put in as being beautiful as gold . . . as long as you are the one who chose it."

He frowned thoughtfully. "It didn't want the golden cage because the king chose it."

"Exactly! Now, as to your new problem . . ."

Jeran looked down. "I know I have no right to ask, but if you can help, please do. If only for the people counting on me."

The fox smiled. So typically Jeran. He had no idea of his own

worth. "Alright then. Here is what you do. It is the same situation, really. The golden horse has refused any owner. All those who have possessed him have wanted him only because his mane sheds golden threads. But as long as the heart is greedy, the threads are useless."

"That poor horse." Jeran frowned. "I almost don't want to give him to that greedy old king. He figures if the bird is gone, he needs more money."

"The bird is useless to him for the same reason, actually. Anyway, what you need to do is find the horse and put the plain bridle on him. You have to ride him out of the stable and the guards will not notice. Once you are outside the walls, you will be safe."

He nodded. "Right. I'll try not to mess this one up." He smiled as the fox snorted softly and wandered off. He supposed good faeries and helpful spirits came in all shapes and sizes.

When the sun finally set, he was not very far from the next kingdom. He stopped to set up camp and sat down with his back against a tree. He wasn't very tired. He was hopeful. He had no idea what Michaela's curse was, but he was fairly sure she was only able to roam at night. He hoped she would come to him again. He wanted to see her more than anything.

An hour passed, then two. It was dark, and he was hungry. Regretfully, he began to make something to eat. He guessed Michaela wasn't able to find him now, just like she hadn't on those other nights on the road. He finished his dinner and got to his feet to go put the scraps out for the animals. As he was straightening, he heard a sound.

He turned quickly but only just in time to have someone plow into him and take them both down to the ground. When the dust settled, he found himself on his back in the dirt with a familiar female sprawled over him. Despite the moment, he smiled. "Hi, Michaela."

She cleared her throat. "Hi, Jeran." She carefully pushed herself up into a sitting position and then realized she was pinning him down. She blushed and scrambled off him. "I'm so sorry! I was hurrying to see you and tripped over some pesky little animal."

He propped himself up on his elbow, content now that she was back with him. "I didn't mind. I was wishing to see you, and I guess I got my wish." He sat up fully and looked at her sadly as she sat beside him. "I messed up, Michaela. I'm so sorry."

"Messed up?" She frowned. "How?" She listened as he told her about the bird and wished she could reassure him that what he had done was actually a good thing. "You're still working hard, though. And you befriended the bird. That's the first important thing."

"What else do I have to do?" he asked simply. He reached out and framed her face gently. "I want to take you home with me, Michaela. We could run my father's farm together. In the morning, the orchards are always so beautiful. You could help me work the fields, or work in the house, or whatever you wanted. We could have a family ourselves, to pass the farm to when we're old."

Tears slid down her cheeks, and her lips trembled. It was a dream. A wonderful dream. He was offering her the most basic and simple of lives, something she wanted more than anything. "I can't cook," she whispered.

He smiled and brushed her tears away, not noticing how dark they were against her skin. "That's okay. I can." He moved closer and his hands framed her face. "May I kiss you now?"

In an answer, she slid her arms around his neck and drew him closer. She rose up slightly to press her lips to his. He tasted like dreams. Like a dream she had waited so long to find. "I love you," she whispered softly.

He trembled slightly and caught her closer as he bent his head and deepened the kiss. In this he knew exactly what he was doing. The knowledge was inside his mind and stamped in his heart. Because it was Michaela, he knew everything. Her taste, like golden strawberries, went through him powerfully. Desire tightened his body in a rush.

She shuddered as the kiss went even deeper and her body awakened with wild passion. She eagerly met the kiss headlong, her tongue tangling with his as he darted it into her mouth. She was too hot, her skin feeling too sensitive. More. She needed more of him. She couldn't get enough. She had been waiting so long for him.

She made a startled sound as he suddenly scooped her up onto his lap. The sound turned to a soft whimper as he pressed his lips to her shoulder and nudged aside the edge of her bodice strap. She almost couldn't breathe; her laces felt too tight. Her breasts ached for his touch and she wanted to beg him to touch her.

"I think I should stop." Even as he said it, he was rushing his hungry mouth over the upper curves of her breasts. He had been right from the beginning. What was there between them was more than powerful; it was downright *explosive*. It took a considerable amount of willpower to not tumble her onto the grass and drive her as crazy as he felt.

"Don't, please." She caught him closer, her fingers digging into his shoulders. She felt the light edge of his teeth scrape over her sensitive skin, and her nipples tightened in a rush, sending ricochets of pleasure through her body. "Jeran."

He lifted his head carefully and drew her closer, holding her tightly until he could get a grip on himself. "Not here," he told her, a slight rasp in his voice that thrilled her. "It's not safe, and you deserve better."

"Do not," she said against his shoulder.

"You do, too. And, besides, it'd probably be uncomfortable with rocks and sticks poking us, and we'd both get filthy."

She sighed. "Do you have to be so practical?" She lifted her head, wryly resigned to discovering she wanted him to the point of frustration but unable to help that same frustration. "If I took off my clothes and wrapped myself around you like a coat, would you be able to stop?"

His purple eyes turned almost black and raw hunger for her moved in his gaze. "No," he told her softly. "But I'd hope you would be willing to wait until we're married."

She made a soft sound of frustration and got off his lap. "What if it doesn't happen? What if you can't save me, Jeran?"

"I will." There was no hesitation in his voice. "You know how important gold is to other people?" When she nodded, he cupped her cheek. "Well, that's what you are worth to me. You're worth *more* than gold. You're everything. I love you, you know that."

She found a smile even though it trembled. His ironic use of words was not lost on her. "I know." She wrapped her arms around him and held on tight for a moment. "I trust you, Jeran. I know you'll save me. And when this is all over, we'll go back to your farm and give your daddy grandchildren to dote on so he has a reason to live a long time."

He smiled and held her closer. "It's a deal."

CHAPTER THREE

Jeran awoke the following morning to a dead campfire and the dawn sliding over his face. He carefully sat up and looked around, a bit puzzled as to where he was and what he was doing there. Memory returned with the sound of a bird calling, and he scrubbed his hands over his eyes swiftly.

Michaela had left him around midnight over his protests. He knew she couldn't stay but he had at least wanted her to know that he wanted her to be with him. He had wanted to kiss her again but he hadn't trusted himself to stop.

All he could do was keep on going. With a little sigh, he got to his feet and cleaned up his campfire. It took only a short amount of time until the area looked as if it had never been disturbed. He got something to eat out of his bag and munched on it as he began to walk down the road toward the next kingdom.

A shiver went down his back suddenly as he hit the main road and left the forest. It was possible to see for quite a distance, and when he glanced to the north, he could see the outline of a dark and forbidding castle.

It was black and gray, and the sky was dark above it. It was clearly a cursed place, and malevolent energy seethed around every tower. He felt a chill just looking at it. It was scary to think that somewhere, someone had done something to be cursed, whether it was earned or not. Worse still was the tiny smidgen of fear in his heart that he might have to go there himself.

He stopped dead in his tracks and stared at the castle. Maybe

Michaela was a member of the castle. Maybe she was one of the servants and she was cursed by proxy. If the entire place was cursed, then she was an innocent bystander. His heart firmed. If that was the case, he would storm the walls until he found her. She belonged to him, damn it.

"You know," the fox said conversationally as he materialized at his side, "your simple-mindedness is a good thing sometimes."

Jeran looked down. "How so?"

"It makes you more possessive." He smiled. "And when you know something is yours, you will fight for it." There was, for a moment, sadness in his eyes. "Many a man with a complicated mind or personality would envy you. They have to learn the hard way to fight for love."

"Like you?" Jeran asked softly.

"Ah, there is that surprising astuteness!" He shook his head. "Never mind about me. This is about you." He pulled a rolled up piece of paper from out of thin air and placed it at Jeran's feet. "This is a contract. It is a binding document. When you free Michaela, you both need to sign it."

Jeran picked up the paper and studied it. He couldn't read a single word as it was in a language he did not know. "What is it for?"

The fox smiled. "When you and Michaela are together, you will be able to read it. I will pick it up once it is signed. Good luck, Jeran."

Jeran frowned and watched the fox wander off. More curious than alarmed, he tucked the contract away safely in his bag and continued down the road toward the kingdom where the golden horse was located. Plain bridle, he told himself over and over again. Don't be stupid!

It was evening by the time he found himself outside the castle. This time he didn't think the guards would be stupid enough to let him in on the premise of drawing. He put down his backpack and began to pace back and forth as he thought.

Something tickled his leg. He glanced down absently and realized that some of the feathers from the golden bird had gotten

stuck to his bag. He picked them up and studied them intently. Crossing his fingers, he blew hard and sent them flying through the air at the guards.

"Hey, are those golden feathers?" one asked his partner as he watched the items in question flutter past.

"Quick, grab 'em!" The other made a grab, but the feathers were fast enough to get beyond his reach.

While the two guards chased after the feathers, Jeran quickly shot forward and snuck around the gate and into the courtyard. His heart pounded in his chest, and his palms were slick with sweat from nerves. As quietly and stealthily as he could, he made his way to the stables where he was sure the golden horse was held.

The stables were warm and dry as he entered, and he spotted the horse immediately. It had a stall all of its own. It was an average sized beast with a white coat and a mane and tail of pure golden strands. He hesitantly approached as the horse watched him warily.

When he was a foot away, the horse stepped forward and sniffed at him. It liked whatever it smelled, since it snorted and butted against his chest. He let out the breath he was holding and rubbed a hand between the horse's ears. "Good boy," he said softly.

He swiftly looked around and spotted the plain bridle. His nose wrinkled. It was plain material, but it was covered in gaudy accessories. Annoyed, he took off the excess decoration. "You don't need diamonds on a bridle," he muttered. "It would hurt the horse's skin!" He dropped the valuable gems on the floor where they bounced uselessly.

The golden horse nodded its head as if in agreement, and he swiftly slipped the bridle on and adjusted the bit expertly. Not worrying about a saddle, he went to swing onto the horse's back when he saw the bandage wrapped around its ankle. He stopped and knelt to look. The golden horse had hurt itself somehow, and the wound was only just mending.

He *knew* he was breaking the rules he was under, but riding a horse when it was wounded was one of the cruelest things he could think of. He had medicines in his backpack. Maybe he could sneak out and back in as easily as he had the first time.

Before he could move, the stable doors flew open and guards surged in with weapons drawn. He ducked as the guards lunged forward, but to his surprise, the golden horse gave a furious whinny and planted itself in front of him, stopping the guards cold. "Wow," he said softly, shocked. "Thank you."

"Let's take him to the king," one guard muttered. "If we harm him, the horse will attack us."

And so, much to his dismay, Jeran once more found himself escorted to the king. The entire castle was nonplussed, however, for the golden horse followed him the entire way and right into the throne room. "Get that horse out!" the prime minister ordered.

"We can't," the guard said apologetically.

The horse, happily nibbling on Jeran's hair, snorted softly. Jeran felt his cheeks heat slightly. "I'm sorry," he said apologetically. "Your neighbor told me to get the horse in exchange for a bird I need."

"Damn it!" The king was more resigned than annoyed. "Not again! He's always after this horse!" He studied Jeran intently. He could not doubt that the young man was good at heart and a decent person. Not when the golden horse was so visibly smitten with him. The horse had hated all of them and had turned to black the instant any touched it. Jeran had a hand on the horse's neck and it remained gold.

He made his decision. "Here is what I shall do. I will give you the horse if you will fetch me the princess from the neighboring kingdom. Her father gave her to me in marriage, but I have yet to retrieve her. The kingdom is cursed, and I cannot enter. You, however, could."

Jeran's stomach flipped. "Can't I opt for the community service option?"

"No. Fetch me my bride, and I will give you the horse."

He sighed. "Okay." Reluctantly, he turned and left the throne room.

The horse was forced to stay behind. As it watched him go, its coat and mane turned to black as it laid down sadly in despair. It would not sleep nor eat until its true master returned.

Jeran retrieved his backpack, and morosely headed into the forest to find a place to camp since it was dark. It took an hour before he found a hidden pathway between some bushes. He curiously followed it as it wound around scenery until he heard the sound of water. It sounded like a waterfall.

As he rounded the edge of thick trees, he beheld what he sought. It came out of a tall cliff and fell into a pond that drained via a small stream. Judging by the steam, it was a hot spring of sorts. He thought of a bath and was delighted as he put down his bag. Belatedly, he heard soft singing, and his eyes went to the waterfall. His eyes widened even as the singing stopped abruptly.

Michaela. Michaela was bathing under the waterfall, and she was gloriously naked. His entire body heated, and desire knotted his muscles. Her eyes were wide as she stared at him, and he couldn't stop himself from hungrily devouring her with his eyes. It suddenly dawned on him what he was doing, and he quickly ducked around a tree. "Uh, hi, Michaela."

"Hi, Jeran." She ducked behind the waterfall, arms around herself. Her entire body was flushed and not from the hot spring. The single encompassing look he had given her out of his beautiful, purple eyes had been more potent than a thousand compliments from other men. It took considerable willpower to not go wrap herself around him and bring him into the spring with her.

"Sorry for peeking. I didn't realize." He kept his back turned, even though his hands were fists at his side to keep from going to her and snatching her up in his arms. If what he felt for her was even marginally like what people felt for money, then he was beginning to understand what the greedy people of the world went through.

"It's okay." She dried herself swiftly and yanked on her clothes. "I guess since you're here, you didn't get the horse."

"I couldn't ride it, not when it was wounded." He sighed. "And now this king wants me to fetch his bride from the cursed kingdom."

Temper sparked in her eyes. Like hell she was any man's bride but Jeran's! She had never been engaged to that greedy bastard. Her father had sold her in exchange for land, but before she could be taken away, the kingdom had been cursed! "I see." She kept her voice neutral as she walked over to where Jeran waited.

"You sound angry." He guessed it was safe and turned around as she reached him. He couldn't stop himself from reaching out and gently cupping her cheek in his hand. Her skin was so wonderfully soft. If the rest of her was as soft as she looked, he was going to be addicted. Heck, he already was. "What's wrong?" he asked softly.

"The princess doesn't want the king." She crossed her arms in agitation. "She was sold by her father for land. All she wanted was to fall in love, and then that happened. I guess either someone took pity on her, or was mad at her father, but the kingdom ended up cursed until she could find a man to love. A man whose heart was as pure as gold."

He studied her face. "You're from the kingdom."

"Yes," she whispered, her eyes closing. "And you're a man whose heart is as pure as gold."

"Then the curse has to stay." He framed her face as her head came up in shock. "I love you, Michaela, not some princess. We'll find another way to break the curse. I don't care if I'm the only man she can love. I only want *your* love."

Tears slid down her cheeks as she turned her face helplessly into his hand. She couldn't tell him. She couldn't tell him what she was without the curse binding her voice. "I love you!" she whispered fiercely. She threw her arms around him. "Remember that! I loved you the minute I saw you!"

"Good. Because I loved you too." He eased her back and bent his head to take her lips with his. He kept the kiss tender at first, but the taste of her seared his nerves with delight, and he caught her closer.

She trembled as the kiss deepened, and she buried her fingers

in his hair. She wanted him so terribly! A low moan echoed from her throat as his hands slid down to cup her breast and rub sensuously. Pleasure radiated through her entire body. "Jeran," she whimpered softly as he released her lips to taste the skin of her throat. She prayed to every god she knew that he wouldn't stop this time.

He drew her closer, wanting to feel all of her curves pressed to his body. A shudder went through him, and he eased back to study her face with a hunger he couldn't fight. She was so perfect that he couldn't believe she was his. "Michaela."

"Don't you dare stop," she whispered huskily. "Or I'll do something drastic."

"We have to." It took considerable willpower to release her and let his hands rest on her hips. "I want us to be married first."

She dropped her head onto his shoulder. "Fine, let's go find a preacher and get married. Like *now*. Curse or no curse, I'm going to be your wife if it's the last thing I ever do!" She shot him a fierce look. "I've never known a man who was so perfect for me. I've been offered kingdoms and fortunes, but it means *nothing* compared to that simple life you offer. I've dreamed of such a thing my entire life!"

He caught her closer again and buried his face in her hair. "The minute the curse is lifted, we're getting married," he promised. "I want to return home with you as my bride." He eased back again and smiled. "Then we can go on a honeymoon and lock the doors behind us."

She leaned up to kiss him hard. "Good!" She released him with a sigh and walked a step away. "Do you know how to break the curse?"

"Not yet. Do you?"

"Yes." She looked at him. "You must go to the princess' room and call her by name. She will wake only for a man with a heart of gold. Once she wakes, you must take her from the palace. Once she is away, the curse will break."

He frowned. "I'll go right back in for you, Michaela. I promise. I won't leave without you."

"I know." She smiled. "But I'm sure everything will be fine. I believe in you." She leaned up to kiss him again, lingering over his taste and the way it felt to have his arms around her. He made her feel safe and cherished. She was doted on by her kingdom, but she had never felt loved until she had looked into Jeran's purple eyes and seen his love for *who* she was, not *what* she was. "If you hadn't met me," she asked, "would you have wanted the princess?"

"I don't know." He smiled. "If she's like you, sure."

"And what if I was a princess and not some simple farm girl?" She held her breath. It was as close to telling him the truth as she could without being silenced.

He rolled his eyes. "Michaela, I love *you*. Your wit and your kindness, your humor and your strength. I love all the funny little quirks that make you up, including the way you chew on your nails when you're nervous."

"I do not!" She belatedly realized she was indeed nibbling on her nails and swiftly put her hands behind her back. "So, even if I was a rich girl, you would want me?"

He pulled her snuggly against him for the sheer torture of feeling her curves. "Michaela," his voice was tender with amusement, "I want you right now. You could be ugly, and I'd want you. I don't care what you're wearing, or how much you own. Let's look at it this way. If you *were* a princess, would you stop loving me? I'm just a farm boy."

"Of course not!" She was indignant. "Any woman worth her salt, let alone a princess, would be willing to be your bride simply because of who you are." He poked her nose gently and she had to sigh with a smile. "Okay. You made your point." She leaned up to kiss him again, but his taste was so tempting that she lingered longer than she intended.

His hands tightened for a moment before he set her away firmly. "Be good."

"But you make it so tempting to be bad," she complained. Obligingly, and feeling wonderfully desired, she moved back a few steps. "I should be going anyway. You need rest." She hesitated, wanting to kiss him good night, but knowing that they were both at the edges of their control. "Good night," she whispered, then turned and fled into the trees.

He let out a long breath and looked longingly at the hot spring. He was beginning to wish it was icy cold. He had been observing all kinds of animals in mating season his entire life, and for the first time he was beginning to understand why it was always such a frantic time. If he didn't get his hands on Michaela soon, he was going to go crazy.

A thought occurred to him and he realized he had no ring for her. He went swiftly hunting through the trees until he had found the perfect piece of wood. He took it back with him and got out his knife from his backpack. He would just make her a ring. One that was completely and uniquely hers.

It was mid-morning the next day before he was heading back onto the road. He had stayed up late to finish the ring and so had slept late as well. Now, as he stood facing the gloomy kingdom in the distance, he felt the beginnings of nerves all over again. There was so much riding on this!

Firming his heart, he started walking. It was evening before he entered the domain of the kingdom, and he knew the instant he had. The land went from lush and green to dead and brown. The sky went from blue to malevolent gray. Dangerous power seethed like shadows around the towers and around the base of the walls.

All the farmlands had been cursed as well. Everyone in the kingdom had been cursed. He saw the extent of the curse as he walked. People were unconscious wherever they had been working last. Even the animals had been affected.

Letting out a careful breath, he continued toward the castle even though it was steadily growing darker. There was no way he was going to camp out in this place. He was going to break the curse, find Michaela, and get the hell away. The princess would just have to go with them and deal with the king herself.

The castle gates hung partially open. He carefully pushed them apart and walked inside. It was even gloomier and more dangerous inside the courtyard. He had no idea where to look for the princess, but as he studied the surrounding turrets and towers, he noticed that the energy was the worst around one particularly high tower.

He took a deep breath and entered the castle proper to head toward the tower. He was nervous again. If he was the one who could wake the princess, then she might wake and fall for him or something. He didn't want to hurt her feelings, but he was in love with Michaela. Maybe whoever had cursed the kingdom had accounted for that. He hoped so.

The guards outside the tower had fallen in front of the door, and he gingerly stepped over them to enter. He slowly climbed the stairs, listening to his steps echo hollowly off the brick walls. When he reached the closed door, he took another deep breath and braced himself. Slowly and carefully he pushed the door open.

The tower was a bedroom. It was decorated the way he imagined any princess' bedroom would be, with elaborate furniture and little charms and baubles. The bed was a big four poster with gauzy curtains. Through them he could just make out the form of the princess. Something was familiar about her, and he went still in shock.

Dropping his backpack, he rushed to the side of the bed and pulled back the curtains. His eyes widened and his throat closed. He could not speak. *Michaela.* It was Michaela that lay before him, her face as serene as a tranquil pool. Unlike the times he had seen her before, her hair was not black. It was gold. It was the pure rich color of gold. She wore a white dress edged in gold trim and there was a golden pendant around her throat. His Michaela was the princess. Her words of the night before made much more sense now, and the reasons why she had never been able to speak of the curse short of how to break it.

His eyes ran over her face eagerly. She looked precisely the same to him. Only her hair color had changed, and he thought that this was as beautiful as her black hair. She deserved so much more than a simple farm boy, he thought, gently reaching out a hand to touch her cheek, but in her own words she had said she loved him and wanted the life he offered. He was going to hold her to it.

He leaned down until their lips were a breath apart. "Michaela," he said softly. "Wake up. I'm here now."

Her lashes fluttered and slowly lifted. Delight filled him as he saw that her eyes were the same black pools as always, still scattered with golden flecks. His golden princess. He had always seen her as such even before knowing it was literally true. Her lips slowly curved, and she lifted her hands to frame his face. "Hi, Jeran," she said huskily.

"Hi, Michaela." He kissed her softly and then simply gathered her close in his arms. "I don't deserve a princess," he said softly.

"That's okay," she said just as softly, holding him tight. "I'm a farm girl at heart." She reluctantly released him and let him pull her to her feet. With a touch of defiance, she removed her pendant and chucked it out the window. "I refuse to wear that again!"

He thought of the golden bird and its golden cage, and the golden horse and its golden bridle. He could only smile, thinking of the ring he had made her. "Let's get out of here." He took her hand and laced their fingers together tightly.

They raced down the tower stairs together and back through the palace. As soon as they broke through the gates and into the surrounding city, there was a crack of thunder across the sky. He swiftly ducked down and pulled her with him around a corner to safety. Both watched the castle pensively as the clouds writhed and seethed.

Then, suddenly, the clouds were gone. The energy lifted and the storm went away. The malevolence in the land went away as well, and all around where they stood, they could see the people beginning to stir. The curse was gone. On a laugh of joy, she leapt into his arms and held onto him fiercely. "I knew you'd save me!"

He swung her in a wild circle and caught her as close as he

could. "Of course. You promised to marry me, remember? I'm holding you to that." He lifted her hand and reached into his pocket to draw out the ring he had carved. "It's not gold," he told her as he slid it over her finger.

Her eyes filled with tears. "It looks like gold to me," she whispered, treasuring this small thing he had made more than she had ever treasured anything else. He had made it for her alone, and it fit perfectly. Nothing could be more valuable in her eyes.

CHAPTER FOUR

Because the city was waking, neither Jeran nor Michaela wanted to stay there for long. They wanted to get somewhere beyond the kingdom to where they would be free. The minute it was discovered that she was gone and the curse was lifted, there would be a massive search party sent out.

As they attempted to sneak through the back of the city, he remarked, "I don't think your father will be happy."

"No, really?" she muttered. "He sold me!"

"I wouldn't mind giving him a piece of my mind about that," he muttered in return. He caught movement out the corner of his eye and turned quickly. He put her behind him protectively. She was so vividly obvious with her white dress and golden hair that anyone who saw her would recognize her.

To their surprise, they found themselves looking at an old man standing in the doorway of a brightly lit inn. He was looking at them curiously, his iridescent blue eyes oddly youthful and ancient all at the same time. He began to smile. "Come on in, children."

Jeran and Michaela exchanged a quick look. "Sir," Michaela said very slowly, "you know who I am, right?"

He chuckled softly. "You are this young man's bride, are you not?" He winked at her.

She immediately brightened. "Of course!" She held onto Jeran's hand tightly as he followed the old man into the inn. It felt so odd to her to be awake and walking freely. She had been allowed to roam at night, but she had always felt as if there was a ball and chain attached to her ankle.

The old man escorted them to a large room on the third floor and offered the key to Jeran. "Here you are, my boy. If you want a bite to eat, just ring the bell, and I will have someone send something on up."

"Thank you for your generosity," Jeran said as he put the key in his pocket. The old man walked away, and he ushered Michaela into the room and shut the door behind her. His shoulders relaxed and he let out a long breath. "We lucked out, didn't we? Umph!"

He staggered and lost his balance, falling onto the ground with a thump as Michaela literally launched herself into his arms. Desire roared through him in a cheerful wave as he stared at her caging him to the carpet. Her golden hair tumbled around her shoulders and spilled forward to brush against his skin. "I understand now," he murmured.

"Understand what?" She hadn't been intending to knock him flat, but she wasn't arguing. She felt like the most cherished being in the world if his arms were around her. Her pulse pounded eagerly, and her lips tingled with the hunger to feel his again. She was *not* taking no for an answer tonight. Not when he was hers at last.

"Greedy people." He lifted a hand and threaded his fingers through her hair. "I see now why they covet their gold so deeply. I'd kill anyone who took you from me." His other hand curved around her waist and tested the resilience of her soft flesh. The fabric of her dress was silk, and he found himself thinking it wasn't as soft as her skin. "It doesn't suit you."

She lowered her lashes, knowing precisely how his mind had wandered. "Then take it off me," she offered, her voice husky with invitation. "I want to be your wife, Jeran."

"But you aren't, not yet." He stared longingly at the curve of her breasts where they were gently revealed by the low cut of her bodice. He wanted to press his lips there and taste her heartbeat. He wanted to know every secret she possessed, but he would be *damned* if he broke his promise. "You deserve to be wed first."

She made a sound of frustration and got to her feet. "Because I'm a princess?" she asked scathingly.

He shot to his feet and caught her wrist to yank her into his arms. "Because I love you!" he shouted. "Because you're special simply by being you! You deserve to have the wedding of your dreams and everything you've ever wanted!"

"All I want is you!" She pressed against him and lifted her hands to bury her fingers in his hair. She rose on her toes and eagerly covered his mouth with hers, kissing him with all the frustration and pent up desire she felt. His taste alone sent a shudder through her body. She *craved* him.

His control snapped and he jerked her even tighter against him as he returned the kiss ravenously. He couldn't get enough of her flavor, and he curled his tongue around hers demandingly. It didn't seem to matter anymore. Nothing mattered but making her his. He tumbled her down onto the floor, not even realizing the bed was right beside them. "Michaela," he said roughly, pressing his lips to her throat.

"I will *kill* you if you stop!" She dug her fingers into his shirt and thrilled at how it felt to have his weight pressing her to the floor. "I'll go out of my mind if you don't touch me."

"Nothing could stop me." He shifted his weight so that he was beside her and began to unlace her dress with trembling fingers. It fell open with a soft rustle of sound, and his breath wedged in his chest as he stared at her. Her breasts were impossibly perfect to him, and the sight of them hidden behind a gold lace bra was more tempting than water after thirst. "You're so beautiful."

"You're noticing now?" She shivered as his finger curved down the outside of her breast and sent ripples of pleasure through her nerves. "You saw me naked."

"Just a glimpse." He drew her up to a sitting position and took a swift breath as her hair spilled down over her shoulders and nearly hid her figure from sight. "But this is much, much better. Now I can touch you."

Her only response was a soft moan as he bent his head and nuzzled between her hair, seeking the curve of her breast. When he found it, his lips trailed soft kisses over every curve as if memorizing her. His free hand lifted and curved around her other breast, his palm rubbing the nipple and making her voice splinter with a soft cry. "Jeran . . ."

"How am I doing?" he asked huskily. He felt addicted to the flavor of her skin and greedily closed his lips around the hardened nipple that begged for his touch. She tasted like strawberries everywhere and the lace in his way frustrated him. "I'm still learning," he said against her skin. His teeth scraped lightly.

She shuddered and reached behind herself for something, anything, to anchor herself. "If there's a test," she managed to whimper as his lips suckled at her strongly, "then you'll pass it!" She couldn't breathe, could barely think. Her entire body seemed to be throbbing with need. "Take your time later!" Her back arched helplessly as he tugged her bra aside and his lips were suddenly on her bare skin.

Her hand found his backpack and she curled her hand into it to ground herself. Something inside was sharp, however, and sliced her finger. The pain was shocking enough to break her out of the sensual haze clouding her brain. "Ouch!"

His head came up swiftly. "What? What's wrong?" He saw the little line of blood on her finger and swiftly brought her hand to his lips and kissed the wound. "What did you hit?"

"I don't know." She forgot the pain as she felt his tongue touching the cut and soothing it. Her breath hitched. "It was in your backpack."

He kept a firm hold on her finger with his to stop the bleeding and used his free hand to drag the bag closer. It was hard to concentrate on anything other than the half-naked woman beside him. His body was hard and hot with desire for her. Nothing short of her injury would have stopped him. "There shouldn't be anything sharp in here. The knife is closed."

The scroll the fox had given him was sticking out of the top and the edge of the paper glinted in the lamplight. He immediately realized what had happened. "You cut yourself on the paper."

"Oh." She curled her free hand around the back of his neck. "Well, if that's all . . ." She groaned in frustration as he pulled out the scroll and began to open it. "Read later! Ooh, damn you, Jeran Windwalker!" She blinked as he held the scroll in front of her face. "What?"

"This." His voice was warm with love. "It was given to me by a, er, friend. I couldn't read it before, but he assured me that when you were with me, I would be able to. He was right. Read what it says, Michaela."

She muttered under her breath and took the scroll from him. "Alright!" With a sigh she began to read, "'This contract is a binding and legal document that can and will be Enforced to the highest degree. This document is to certify that the signees below, Michaela Sandstorm and Jeran Windwalker, are hereby lawfully married and as such are entitled . . .'" Her voice broke off, and she stared at the scroll. "What!"

He took it from her with a smile. "That's the important part, but it also goes on to verify that I rescued you, and what I did to be with you. So, by signing it, we're married." He waved it in front of her face. "Willing to wait long enough to sign this? Provided you still want this farm boy."

"Give me a damn pen." She grabbed the backpack and dug in it until she found a pen he used for inking his art. "I want my farm boy!" she said, aggrieved. "My whole problem is that I want my farm boy until I'm insane, and I'm madly in love with him, and he keeps stalling!"

His grin felt like it could split his face. "That's odd. Because he seems to be equally insane for his princess and just as madly in love with her." He watched her sign the contract and then took it from her to sign as well. "You're my wife now, Michaela Windwalker. No one can dispute that."

"Good!" She took the contract and chucked it over her shoulder before throwing herself against him and leaning up to kiss him with a hunger that had not dimmed once. "Mine now," she muttered as she began to unlace his tunic as swiftly as her trembling fingers would let her. "My husband."

"Always." He scooped her up into his arms and rolled to his feet. His fingers were trembling just as much as he carried her to the bed. Desire. Need. Hunger. Love. There was no word big enough for the emotions churning inside him as he laid her down on the soft white sheets. "I love you."

She smiled up at him. "Promise?" She held up her pinky to him.

He linked their pinkies together. "Promise." His heart so full it might burst, he shrugged out of his tunic and tossed it to the side. With as much care as he could, he went to work on the rest of her dress so he could remove it entirely.

She trembled as his fingers brushed against her skin and sent little sparks along her nerves. "You could always just rip it. I never cared for it anyway."

"But then you'll have nothing to wear." He lowered his head to begin trailing hungry kisses over her breasts. He dropped the dress to the side, then removed her bra and dropped it as well. "I'm the only one who can see you naked."

"Good point." She lifted her hands and ran them slowly over his chest, thrilling at how his skin felt and delighted by every muscle. "Little Jeran. I bet the girls back home were always around when you were hard at work and shirtless."

He lifted his head, surprised. "Yes, they were. How did you know?"

She wound her arms around him on a happy laugh. "Promise me you'll never change." She pressed her lips to his shoulder to taste his skin. Her farm boy worked for a living and it showed. She remembered her sight of him when she had accidentally walked in on him about to bathe, and she realized that it was far more thrilling now that he was close at hand. "You're so beautiful."

"I am not." He curved a hand around her hip and tugged her closer as he bent his head to taste her silken skin. She was wonderfully soft! "My brothers are more handsome."

"I don't believe you." Her eyes met his, and she smiled. "And even if I did, I'd still prefer you."

There was a long silence as tension grew between them. Then, even as he was reaching for her, she was reaching for him, and their mouths met and fused in a wild kiss. With a hunger he no longer needed to fight, he began to run his hands over every inch of her he could. His hands were shaking, but he couldn't stop it. He needed her more than air.

She could only grab onto his shoulders for an anchor as his hands set fires wherever they went. Her body was hot and restless, craving more and more from him. Her skin was so sensitive that just the brush of his hair was enough to drive her wild. "Jeran, hurry!" she pleaded as his mouth moved voraciously over her breasts.

He barely heard her. He swiftly stripped her panties off and leaned back to stare at her naked body. His breath came in and stayed there as he stared at her. "There's supposed to be no such thing as perfection," he whispered huskily. "Apparently they never met you."

She couldn't form a response to that before he was kissing her again, his mouth as hungry as his hands and nearly as rough. It sent her senses spinning dizzily with delight, and she curled her fingers into his hair to keep him close.

She nearly stopped breathing entirely as she felt his hand curving over the sensitive skin of her inner thigh. She felt as if she was waiting forever before his fingers finally slid upward and cupped the heart of her. The touch was electrifying, and pleasure ricocheted through her entire system. It still wasn't enough.

He shuddered as he felt the slick heat of her against his fingers. He petted her, watching her face with rapt attention as her body twisted in his arms. Her eyes opened to meet his, and the golden flecks were more dominant than the black, as if they had gone liquid gold with her emotions.

He couldn't stand it anymore and released her long enough to strip off the rest of his clothes. If he waited any longer to claim her as his, he was sure he would go out of his mind. He returned quickly to her side and kissed her deeply, unable to resist the lure of her swollen lips. "I won't hurt you, I promise!"

She closed her eyes in sheer delight as his weight settled over her. "It never crossed my mind," she said huskily. She curled her long legs around his hips instinctively, wanting to bind him to her in every way possible. Her fingers slid up to clench in his hair and she held him close as their mouths met again.

The feel of his hard arousal pressing against her made her hold her breath. As she felt him slowly sinking into her, stretching her thoroughly, her breath unraveled on a soft moan that was pleasure and pain combined. She wanted him deeper but she felt too stretched. Her nails bit into his shoulders. "Jeran," she whimpered.

"I'm sorry." He shuddered as he raced his lips over her face. She was like hot silk beneath him, and she fit him like a glove. His breath hissed out as she clenched her muscles around him. "Don't do that," he managed to say. "I don't want to hurt you!"

"Then do something!" She clenched her nails into his shoulders and twisted beneath him. The pain was nothing. She needed him inside her to ease the unbearable pressure that made her feel as if she would be broken in two. "Please!"

A tortured sound rumbled in his chest as he gathered her close and surged into her in a single stroke. Electricity seemed to race through his body and some inner pain he hadn't been able to define seemed to ease at last. "Michaela." He caught her tears with his lips and kissed her hungrily. "I'm sorry."

"It doesn't hurt." Her words became a soft gasp as his hips flexed, and he began to slowly stroke in and out of her. The terrible tension rushed back in wildly until she was clinging onto him with all her strength, her breaths nothing but soft sobs against his shoulder as she tried to cope with the ceaseless pleasure.

Something inside seemed to shatter, and ecstasy rushed over her like a wave. She would have cried out but he was kissing her again, and he took her cry into himself. Her muscles caressed him with every pulse of her pleasure, and he shuddered as he buried himself to the hilt and let the ecstasy consume him as it had her.

His lips met hers again with a touch of desperation, needing to know her taste again. For the first time in his life, he finally felt as if he had found where he belonged. He gathered her close and held her with all his strength as he buried his face in her hair. She was his wife in every sense of the word. He would be damned if he let someone take her away.

She let out a soft sigh and burrowed closer against her husband's warmth. "Jeran?" she murmured.

"Hmm?"

"You were right, damn it." She smiled and rubbed her cheek against his shoulder. "It was worth waiting for."

He smiled. "It was very worth waiting for." He snuggled her closer, and the feel of her soft and fragrant skin was enough to make his body tighten with fresh desire. He softly tasted the curve of her ear and listened to her breath hitch. "Guess what?"

"What?" Her eyes closed slightly as she felt her body heat with a suddenness that took her breath.

"I want you again."

On a contented sigh, she drew him closer. "Good. I want you again, too."

They were awakened the following morning by a loud knock on the door. "Open in the name of the king!" a man bellowed.

"Can I refuse in the name of the princess?" Jeran shouted back in annoyance.

Michaela dissolved into giggles as she tumbled off his chest and watched him look for his pants. She fell over onto her back on a happy sigh and stretched largely. She felt incredible. Her body felt as if it was singing, and she ached in some places. The ache was just as delightful, and it was a constant reminder that she had claimed her husband as thoroughly as he had claimed her.

He pulled his tunic on and looked at where she was lying on the bed with the sunlight flowing over her soft skin. His heart swelled in his chest as he crossed to her and leaned down to kiss her softly. "Good morning, by the way," he said huskily.

"Good morning." She threaded her fingers through his thick, lavender hair happily. Another pounding on the door made her groan. "Damn it! I'll kill them all!" She scrambled out of the bed and scooped up her clothes to begin getting dressed. As soon as her laces were firmly tied, she raked her hands through her hair. "Do I look like I was just tumbling in a bed?"

He studied her and the way she looked wonderfully rumpled and flushed as if she had indeed just been tumbling over a bed with him. "Yes," he said, his voice slightly rough. "Makes me want to tumble you more."

"Good." She stalked over to open the door. "My husband and I," she said with a slight edge to her voice, "were sleeping."

The handful of guards standing outside the door in full armor and weaponry could only stare at her in shock. Then, with a slight scramble, every single one dropped to their knees quickly. "P-princess Michaela!" the leader stammered. "My lady, we did not realize you were in there as well!"

She rolled her eyes. "Well, where *else* would I be? You knew Jeran was the one who saved everyone, so obviously I had to be with him!"

The guards fidgeted nervously, clearly uncomfortable with envisioning their princess in any man's bed. "Your father presumed you had run away," the leader said. "He demanded we find you, and we thought to start with the one who broke the curse."

She looked at Jeran. "Let's go see the old man and get it over

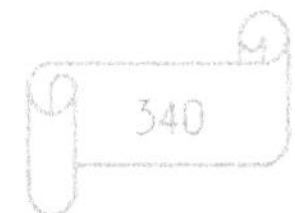

with. If he thinks I'm marrying that bastard next door, he has another think coming."

Jeran had to grin. His princess had the mouth of any farm girl. He loved her all the more for it. "As my lady commands," he said, loving amusement in his voice. He took her hand and their fingers laced together tightly as they left the room and edged carefully around the guards. "Do they always do that?" he asked her in a whisper.

"Yes," she whispered back. "It's annoying! Do you have the scroll?"

"It's in my pocket." He wasn't letting it out of his sight and didn't trust himself to not lose his backpack, which was itself over his shoulder.

The entire place seemed vastly different without the curse hovering over it, but there was something about it that he still didn't like. After a moment of thought, he realized that he didn't like it because he was viewing it through Michaela's eyes and was able to see it for the golden cage it was.

The king was clearly displeased as he stared at his daughter. "Where is your royal pendant?" he demanded.

"I threw it away." She smiled. "I have no need of it." She held up her hand where her wooden wedding ring rested. "I'm married, Father. And as such, I will be traveling with my husband to his home."

The king stared at Jeran. "And where is your kingdom?"

He straightened his back. "I have none. I can offer Michaela nothing but my love and a simple farm life."

"Which is more than enough for her," his wife pointed out to her father. She leveled a finger in the astonished ruler's face. "I want Jeran. Nothing more, nothing less. You sold me like I was a piece of property! Even before Jeran knew I was a princess, he loved me!" She smiled with feminine smugness. "And believe me, we're *completely* married now so there's nothing you can do."

A couple of ladies-in-waiting began to giggle softly. Some of the guards had to turn away to hide grins. The king could only stare in horror. Finally, on a sigh, he sat back on his throne. "Alright. I know when I'm defeated. You are married?"

Jeran pulled out the scroll and walked forward to offer it. "It is a binding contract," he said. "And I'll fight anyone who tries to take her away from me."

The king studied the scroll and looked at the bottom. "I am to sign this as well?" When Jeran tilted his head, he indicated the blank line below the couple's names. "My name is here. It is to indicate I verify this document and the events mentioned within."

"I suppose so, then." Jeran took the scroll back once it had been signed and went back over to Michaela. "We have your blessings?" he asked the king.

The king studied the two of them, and the way Michaela seemed to glow softly with happiness as she leaned against Jeran's shoulder. He couldn't find it in his heart to be upset or angered, not when they were so obviously in love. "Yes," he finally said. "You have my blessings, provided you come back to visit with grandbabies for me to spoil."

"It's a deal!" Michaela said, then leapt into Jeran's arms happily and kissed him in front of the entire castle. All who were observing began to cheer. Jeran could only smile and hold her closer. Living with Michaela was going to be a terror, but incredibly fun. His father would adore her.

CHAPTER FIVE

The following morning found Michaela and Jeran waking up in the woods not far beyond the castle of the neighboring kingdom. They were taking their time on their way back and enjoying every minute they could together. That, and they were trying to find a way for Jeran to keep Michaela at his side, get his horse, and his bird, and get home without trouble.

"Well," she said as she washed her face in the stream they were sitting beside, "disguising me is easy once we're past this kingdom. I'll get some normal clothes and braid my hair, and no one will be any wiser *despite* my coloring."

He admired the way the sunlight filtered over her face. "Only if you let me unbraid it for you at night. I like your hair the way it is."

"So I shouldn't get it cut?" she teased.

"You better not." He leaned over to kiss her. It still sent a thrill through him, and he knew it would likely never go away. "It might make me lose my temper, and I've never done that before."

Her brows lifted. "You've never lost your temper." She winced. "I hope I'm not the target when you do. You'll probably be really scary." She thought about things. "But really, *really*, sexy."

He flushed. "Stop it." He tugged her close and rested his chin on the top of her head. "I don't even want to let that greedy king see you." He smiled. "Well, I guess that makes me greedy too."

"This is a good kind of greedy." She rested a hand over his heart and sighed softly. "So who was this friend who gave you advice before? Perhaps he can give you advice now."

"You called?" the fox asked suddenly from beside them, making her stifle a yelp, and Jeran nearly sent them both tumbling into the stream. The fox hid a smile. He adored both of them very dearly. "My apologies."

"Your friend is a talking fox?" Michaela asked her husband.

"Yes, he is." Jeran smiled and offered a cookie to the fox. "I don't suppose you can help me get home, can you? I got the last task right, didn't I?" He nuzzled his nose into Michaela's hair. "I claimed my golden princess."

"And how," she murmured.

The fox snickered and nibbled on the cookie. "Mmm. I can tell Michaela did not make these. She would have set the kitchen on fire again." He dodged when she tried to swat him. "He would have found out eventually."

She glowered. The fact that he knew her biggest mishap didn't bother her as much as that he had blabbed. "Tattletale."

Jeran just smiled. "I don't mind. I can cook for the both of us. I can do the mending too as needed."

She stuck her tongue out at him. "I can sew, thank you, and quite nicely. I can manage to take care of any mending that is needed." She ran her eyes over him. "Especially if I cause it personally." She flicked a finger at the slightly torn edge of his collar. "Sorry about that, by the way."

He grinned. "I didn't mind." If there was anything sexier than his wife pinning him to the ground and stripping him, he had yet to hear of it. He loved the bold and sassy side of her more than anything.

The fox chuckled at them both. "I can see that you are indeed well suited. I knew that you would be." Before they could call him on his near admission, he continued, "Because I like both of you, I will tell you how to get home. That contract of yours will end up being the most important part."

"You mean the extra lines for signatures?" Michaela asked.

"Precisely. You see, this contract will only show the signer their role within it. In other words, you two will see the whole thing. This king who owns the horse will see only that Jeran retrieved the golden princess. Jeran, you will need to insist the king sign the contract and give you the horse before you give him Michaela. Ask to test it out first and then pull Michaela up with you."

"I see." Jeran smiled. "Once he has signed the contract, he cannot back out. He'll think he's making a trade when he's actually just confirming my work. Are we invisible when riding the horse?" he asked curiously.

"You may as well be." The fox smiled. "Only those who are pure at heart will see you until you wish otherwise."

"That will make getting away easier," Michaela agreed. She smiled. "And I think I see what we do at the first kingdom. It's nearly the same thing. You can ask for the king to sign before you'll give him the horse, then ask for your bird, and once we have it, we can take off!"

"It almost feels like stealing," Jeran remarked.

"Well, you *do* own them, you know." The fox playfully butted against Jeran and Michaela both. "It is not stealing. It is taking back what is rightfully yours." As he was starting to walk away, he added, "Oh, and when you get to the inn to rest for the night, make sure not to buy any dead carcasses."

"Ew!" Michaela exclaimed. "Why would we?"

"Just do not do it, trust me."

Jeran's nose was as wrinkled as Michaela's. "I should hope I wouldn't buy a dead carcass." He got to his feet and reached down to draw her up as well. He frowned as he suddenly noticed the little scrapes and nicks on her hands. "Where did these come from?"

She blushed. "Well . . . It's really bad but . . ." She reached into her pocket and pulled out a slightly misshapen ring made of the same wood as her own. "I tried to make this last night after you fell asleep. It's not nearly as beautiful as the one you made."

He took the ring from her and held it up to the sunlight to see it better. It was probably one of the worst carvings he had ever seen.

He loved it immediately. "It's perfect," he told her. He held it out to her. "Here. Put it on me properly."

Her face lightened with a radiant smile. "You really are something special." She took his hand and slid the ring over his ring finger slowly, delighted to discover it fit. "I was worried it would be too small."

"Looks just right to me." He threaded his fingers through her hair and leaned down to kiss her softly. "Let's go," he said softly. "And if your feet get tired, tell me. I'll carry you."

"You will not." She let out a contented sigh and leaned against his arm as they began to walk down the road. "When will you let me peek into that sketchbook of yours?"

He smiled. "Anytime you want. But you're in there too."

"What!" Her brows shot up. "Me?"

"Lots of you. They don't do you justice though."

"I'll decide that, thank you." She was secretly pleased. Her husband was probably the most incredible man in the world, she decided happily. In light of her happiness, she couldn't even really resent that darn fox for possibly having a hand in her curse.

Her happiness began to turn into trepidation as they drew closer to the castle. Jeran squeezed her hand tightly and she drew strength from him as always. Because she knew it was crucial that no one realize she wanted to be with him, she searched her memory for an idea of how a spoiled princess should act. "Quick, carry me," she told him.

"Are you hurt?" He frowned swiftly.

"No, but I want to pretend like I'm spoiled."

"Good luck with that." He tied his backpack on his hip and smiled as she climbed onto his back. He got a firm grip on her legs around her skirts so that he didn't worry she would fall and realized he enjoyed it because he could feel every one of her curves. "You're light."

"You're a smart man," she mumbled. "Never tell a woman she's heavy."

"I wouldn't mind even if you were." His stride never changed as he walked toward the castle gates, and he knew the instant the guards recognized him. They boggled at the sight of Michaela on his back and then they turned and raced into the castle.

He put Michaela down on her feet but kept her firmly behind his body as the guards fetched the king. In a whine, she demanded, "You dropped me!"

"You wouldn't stop complaining," he retorted, but it took all his willpower to resist snickering. He felt like an utter fool. As he saw the king approaching, he felt Michaela tense. "Your majesty, I retrieved the golden princess."

"So there you are, Michaela." The king glared at her. "All this trouble you caused!" She said nothing and he turned to Jeran. "Give her to me and you shall have your horse."

"Please forgive me," Jeran apologized, "but I have found myself going through quite an ordeal. I would prefer if you signed this contract verifying what I did, and gave me my horse to test, before I give the princess to you."

The king nodded. "Naturally, my boy. Let's see this contract." He took the document that was offered and read it swiftly. It stated very plainly that Jeran Windwalker had stormed a kingdom, broken a curse, and retrieved a princess. Since it was quite nicely to the point, he had no objections to signing. "Bring the horse!" he ordered the stable master standing near.

The man obeyed and led the golden horse out of the barn. Its leg was healed now, and it was wearing the plain bridle Jeran had picked. Its ears perked up as it saw Jeran, and it eagerly trotted over to butt against him. The black coat and mane turned back to gold, and it happily began to chew on his hair.

Michaela had to muffle a giggle. She couldn't help but wonder if it was just some odd quirk amongst her and her 'brethren', but they all seemed to love Jeran's hair. Perhaps because it was as soft and strong as his heart.

Her stomach fluttered lightly with desire as she watched him swing up onto the horse's back. There was something very seductive about the sight of him on horseback. It made him seem stronger and more giving and more wonderful. So much more of everything he already was. With a sense of wonder, she realized that here, truly, was the man of her dreams riding in to rescue her.

"Are you satisfied now?" the king asked, eyeing her covetously.

Jeran smiled. "I am." He walked the horse around the courtyard briefly. He kicked it lightly in the sides and it shot forward. He leaned down out of the saddle and scooped Michaela up into his arms and onto the horse before him, removing her from the king's reach.

The instant she was on the horse it was as if all three of them suddenly disappeared into thin air. Only a few of the servants could see them still, but every last person heard Michaela's delighted laughter amid the sound of thundering hooves as they took off out through the gates.

Jeran let the golden horse run at its own speed as they raced across fields and through trees. He couldn't help but grin down at Michaela as he felt her wrap her arms around his waist. "I wouldn't let you fall."

"I know." She gave a little nervous laugh. "But I'm not the best rider in the world either."

He burst into laughter. "You have no ladylike graces, do you?"

"No." She sulked. "I was feeling rebellious when the lessons were insisted on." She smiled and cuddled closer. "But that's okay. I'm sure I can learn everything I need to. I'd much rather be out playing in an orchard than sitting and sewing any day." She rubbed her cheek against him. "Your neighboring farm girls will be so disappointed, I'm sure."

"You'll win them over." He was sure of it. He looked around and began to measure the distance of the sun in the sky and the distance they still had to go to get to the last kingdom. "We should camp for the night."

"It's only the afternoon," she protested, then saw the heated look in his eyes. "Oh." It was the best she could manage. Well, who was she to argue with her husband when he had that look in his eyes?

It wasn't until much later after the sun had set and the moon was rising that she thought to ask, "Will you tell me about your brothers?" She curled more snugly against his side, content to use his cloak as a blanket. "I get the feeling that you don't like them even as you love them."

He tucked his hands under his head. "Yes," he finally said on a sigh. "You put it correctly. I love them because they're my brothers, but there are times I almost wish I could hate them. All my life they've been taking my ideas and using them as their own. I don't mind that too much, really. I suppose it's just the idea that they are willing to do such a thing."

She slowly smoothed a hand over his chest. "You said your father was ill?"

"Yes." Worry darkened his face. "I don't want him to die, Michaela. I love him more than anything except you. Even if I go home and he gives the farm to Jared or Jonah, I don't mind as long as he lives."

"You deserve the farm. You've worked so hard, Jeran." She set her chin. "He's your father, so he's not a fool. But if he does give the farm to them, then we'll go make our own and *prove* him wrong."

He smiled. "You just want to be in charge of something. It's the princess in you."

"I do not!" She tried to hold her indignation but couldn't. She smiled and held him tighter. "I think it's just that I want to be in charge of my own life and know that something belongs to me and only me."

"You have me." He rolled and tucked her protectively underneath him. "I will always be yours alone."

She smiled. "I can settle for that."

The next morning as they were getting dressed, she thought to ask, "Where will I get some normal clothes?" She fingered the silk of her dress, not wanting to put it back on. "I'd sooner go naked than wear this again."

He opened his mouth to respond when he spotted an unfamiliar bag sitting on the ground next to his backpack. He curiously knelt and opened it only to discover a set of clean clothes that looked like they might fit his slender wife. "How about these?"

She was delighted as he pulled the clothes out. There was a nice and sturdy pair of leggings with a tunic-dress and a thick cloak, all of which looked like they would be incredibly comfortable. "Oh! They're wonderful!" She held them up in front of herself. "I bet your friend did this."

He smiled. "I think so." He watched her as she changed, and his eyes lingered on the curves of her body as she did so. No matter what she wore, she was always beautiful to him. The tunic-dress reached her knees, but when she belted it around her waist, it fit precisely like it was supposed to.

"It's not a dress." She couldn't have been happier. "I always wanted to be able to wear leggings but they're a *commoner's* piece of clothing." She twirled in a delighted circle. "But now I'm a commoner too. How do I look?"

"Like a princess," he said softly, his voice tender. "You'll always be one to me."

Her eyes stung with tears for a moment. "Well, you've always looked like a prince to me, so I suppose we're going to live happily ever after." She caught her hair and began to braid it swiftly down her back. She tied the end with a piece of string and then took the hat he offered her. She pulled it onto her head at a jaunty angle. "Will I pass?"

"With flying colors." He pulled her close for a kiss before releasing her to whistle for their horse. It trotted over and stood patiently as he lifted her up before climbing up behind her. "We ought to name him," he remarked.

"Hmm." She rested against him while she thought about it. She was glad to concentrate on something. Her stomach felt a little funny

now that she was in motion. She seemed slightly queasy and it was annoying. "Let's see . . . How about Coal?"

The horse snorted even as Jeran did, both with humor. "Because he isn't, or because it's an undervalued item?" he asked shrewdly.

"Both." She smiled. "Coal is the cold man's gold just as water is to someone who is thirsty, or food to a starving man or . . ."

"You to me." He kissed her softly when she looked at him in astonishment. "Don't look so surprised." He snuggled her closer against him. "Take a nap if you like. I can see you don't feel well."

"I'm not sick," she grumbled. "I never get sick." Much to her surprise, however, she was asleep within moments, lulled by Coal's steady trot and by Jeran's easy strength and warmth.

She woke to Jeran's tender kiss. With a sigh, she curled closer. "Are we home?" she asked.

"No, we're outside the kingdom." He was loathe to wake her. He had never felt as contented as he had riding across the land with her sleeping so peacefully in his arms. He was a little worried though. When they reached the crossover town, where the inns were located, he was making her go to a doctor to be sure she was fine.

"Oh." She rubbed her eyes. "I'm awake now. What should I do?"

"Make sure I don't do something stupid."

"Sounds easy enough." She straightened as they rode into the courtyard so that she wasn't reclining against him. He would need his hands free. As she looked around at the people, all she could think was that every kingdom she had ever seen was precisely the same. It was no wonder it held no appeal to her.

The guards had gone to fetch the king the instant they had recognized Jeran. The king came out into the courtyard, and the expression on his face was heavily put upon. He had reason. The golden bird, now black in color, was sitting on his head. "Windwalker!" he barked. "Take this damned bird!"

Jeran bit his lip to hide a laugh. "Yes, your majesty, as soon as we take care of things. Would you sign this?" He leaned down to offer the contract. "It's to verify what I've done. I want to make sure everything is nice and finished."

He took the contract and studied Michaela. "Your love?" he asked.

"She is." Jeran smiled.

"Ah. Well done, lad." He looked at the contract, and it read as exactly what Jeran had said it would. It stated quite plainly that he had retrieved a golden horse from the neighboring kingdom and was thusly entitled to the golden bird. "This looks perfectly fine." He signed his name on the line and handed the contract back. "Now get this bird off my head!"

Jeran laughed. "Yes, your majesty." He leaned down and plucked the bird off the king. It gave a happy squawk and turned back to gold as it began to climb all over Jeran and Michaela both. It settled down on Michaela's lap and began to make a sound that was half a purr and half a twitter.

Before anyone could say a word, Jeran, Michaela, and Coal seemed to simply vanish before everyone's eyes. The king gaped for a moment and then had to brace himself when wind was kicked up around him as the horse and its riders took off. He suddenly burst into laughter. "Well, I suppose I earned that." They did say, after all, that the greedy men in the world were the ones who always ended up the poorest.

Jeran and Michaela waited to camp that night until they were sure they were well away from the kingdom. Not that they didn't trust the king, but they both wouldn't rest peacefully until they were home where they belonged. In fact, they didn't rest very peacefully that night anyway, because the golden bird seemed to like Michaela's hair and spent the entire night chewing on her braid.

By the time they were riding into the small town a few days later, Michaela was resigned to the bird that was attached to the end of her braid. "Maybe I'll make a new fashion style," she muttered.

Jeran, as had become habit over the last few days, plucked the bird off her braid and put it in his backpack. Eventually it would get free and zero in on her braid again, but he hardly blamed it. His fingers often got stuck to her hair too. "How are you feeling?" he asked her, hugging her lightly. She had gotten sick a few hours after setting out that morning and his worry was increased for it.

"Better now." She sighed as he stopped in front of the inn and dismounted. "Tomorrow morning before we leave, I'll go see the doctor in town and see if he has any herbs that will help. I think it's just the stress. It's been a very trying time, you know."

"I know. But when we get home we can relax all we want to." He smiled at her. "Once we know my father is fine, we can go on a trip somewhere to be alone, just the two of us. Where do you want to go?" He lifted her down easily and held her while she found her balance.

"The ocean," she decided. "I've never been there before. It's not far is it?"

"No, not far at all." He gave a coin to the stable boy standing near. and he led Coal off to the stables for the night. With an arm around Michaela's waist, Jeran headed into the inn. As ever, it was quiet and peaceful and he knew they would both be able to rest peacefully despite the golden bird—now named Lead because she was so heavy—potentially chewing on their hair.

In fact, they did sleep peacefully. They were woken rather abruptly, however, by the sounds of shouting outside. Jeran sleepily got out of bed and walked over to look out the window. There was a group of people gathered around the hanging tree. "Just a hanging," he said on a yawn.

"Ugh." Michaela raked a hand through her hair. "It's too early for that."

"Apparently not." He frowned, wondering why something seemed odd. He looked closer at the crowd and suddenly went pale. He recognized the two standing under the tree with nooses around their necks. "Oh my god! It's my brothers!"

"What?" She scrambled over to him. "Oh dear!" She could tell they were his brothers; they were just as handsome as her husband. But, as she had thought, she much preferred Jeran's shorter height and softer smile. His brothers looked hard around the edges. "What are we going to do?"

"I have to find out what they did." He gave her a swift kiss and grabbed his clothes to get dressed. "Go to the doctor and get checked over. I'll see if I can save their carcasses. It wouldn't be the first time."

She felt a sudden chill as she watched him hurry out of the room. The fox's words danced in her ears, and she couldn't shake the feeling that something terrible was about to occur. She took a deep breath and got dressed. She was going to the doctor and then she was getting her husband and they were leaving.

He hurried down to the square and over to the hanging tree. "Hey what's going on?" he asked the owner of the other inn. "What's the commotion about?"

The owner was happy to explain, "These two idiots racked up an immense bill at my inn with all their drinking and partying. In an effort to pay for it, they tried to steal from some other patrons. Then they got into a fight over it. They *deserve* to hang."

He sighed. It figured, didn't it? "What if I paid their bill and for the damages from the fight? They're my brothers," he said apologetically. "I have to help them even when I'm ashamed of them."

The owner studied him briefly. "Sure." He smiled. "You seem like a good young man. If you can cover the bill, I'll consider it a done deal."

Jonah and Jared, overhearing this, were so relieved that they nearly collapsed and hung themselves regardless. When they were cut loose and freed, they immediately hugged Jeran enthusiastically. "Jeran!" Jonah exclaimed. "We knew we could count on you!"

Jeran pushed them both away with a sigh. "Of course. I can't believe you!" he scolded. "Partying for *months* while Father and I worried about you!" He sat down on a bench near the well while his brothers got themselves drinks. "I had to go looking for the golden bird myself!"

Jared snorted. "I still say it was nothing but a joke."

Jeran smiled. "No, it wasn't." He opened his backpack and Lead instantly stuck her head out with an indignant squawk. "I found the bird. And I also got a golden horse." He pointed to where Coal was waiting near the inn. His smile brightened as he saw Michaela hurrying toward him, and he completely missed the sudden looks of greed that crossed his brothers' faces. "And I found a golden princess."

Michaela was nearly giddy with delight. She wasn't sick. She was pregnant. She was going to have Jeran's child. She couldn't wait to tell him. "Jeran!" She threw herself into his arms with a happy laugh. "I have wonderful news!"

"Tell me later, Michaela." He smiled at her. "As long as you're not sick, that's all that matters."

"Not at all." She smiled. "You sure I can't tell you now?" When he shook his head, she sighed. "Oh alright." She turned to Jonah and Jared, and her smile dimmed. She was well acquainted with the greed in mankind. She recognized it instantly inside them. "Hello. I'm Jeran's wife, Michaela."

The two brothers looked at her, their eyes lingering on her hair and figure with a greed that churned her stomach. It also made Jeran's eyes narrow sharply. He would tolerate a lot from his brothers, but never this. If they didn't treat Michaela respectfully, he would kick them both. "Brothers," he said warningly.

"Aw, it's no big deal!" Jonah took his shoulders with a big smile. "We're family."

Before he could say anything in response, Jonah had suddenly given him a shove. "Jeran!" Michaela shouted, lunging forward as her husband staggered backwards and began to fall into the well. "*Jeran*!" She fell to her knees beside the well but could see nothing. All she could hear was a resounding splash. There was no other sound.

Tearing pain welled up inside her and she leapt to her feet as black tears streamed down her cheeks. "You bastards!" she shouted. She came up short as Jared suddenly aimed a dagger at her. Ice hardened her heart and her hands moved protectively to touch her stomach.

"Here's the deal," Jared said. "You don't tell anyone the truth, and we'll let you pick which one of us you marry. Open your pretty mouth and we'll kill you."

Her eyes narrowed. A part of her didn't want to live without Jeran. She wouldn't have cared about her fate if she hadn't been carrying their child. If it was the last thing she ever did, she would have her child and let his or her appearance prove who her true husband was. "I won't say anything at all," she said, her tone almost emotionless. "I will remain silent until the day I die."

"Good. No one likes a talkative woman anyway." Jonah caught her wrist and dragged her along behind him toward the golden horse. His smile swiftly turned to a frown as he realized the horse had inexplicably turned to black. "What the hell?" He looked at Michaela. "What is that?"

She said nothing. Jared could only shrug; he had his arms around Lead to keep her from flying away. She was still a golden bird, but the feathers she shed were turning to black as they fell to the ground. Neither brother knew what to make of it. Still, they didn't care. They had all the evidence they needed to prove to their father that they had done the deed and not Jeran.

As they rode away, Michaela looked back toward the well where Jeran had fallen. Grief nearly tore her in two. Why should someone so kind be the one who suffered? She had found him only to lose him. Turning her gaze toward the sun in the distance, she closed her eyes. Her hair almost immediately turned from gold to black and startled both Jared and Jonah. It made no sense to them in the slightest. Oh well. A princess was a princess.

CHAPTER SIX

The well in the town was not shallow. It was quite deep and never ran dry. As such, when Jeran landed at the bottom, he landed purely in water. He did not strike the bottom and die as his brothers had intended. Instead, he was able to swim to the surface and tread water. His first emotion was grief. He had never imagined his brothers would betray him like that.

Then, finally, he began to become mad. For the first time in his life, he became truly enraged. He'd had enough. For his whole life, his brothers had been taking away anything that was his that they wanted. He would be *damned* if they took Michaela.

The end of a rope fell down into the water beside him. He looked up toward the top of the well to see the fox perched on the edge and staring down at him. "Get out of there," the fox ordered. "Damn it, boy! I told you not to buy dead carcasses!"

"Be more specific next time!" he retorted as he began to climb out. "Next time say 'don't rescue your brothers even though you love them, because they're assholes and will try to kill you!'"

The fox's brows shot up. "Well." It was the best he could think to say. "So, little Jeran finally loses his temper."

He began to wring water out of his clothes with short and jerky motions. "Yes, he does. I'm through with being nice." His eyes swept over the area quickly. It was easy to tell that his brothers had taken off with Michaela, as well as Coal and Lead. "Michaela is *my* wife." The idea of how much pain she must be in was just more fuel on the fire of his anger. "Any more good advice?"

The fox thought about it. "Do not tuck your thumb under your fingers."

It made little sense but he committed it to memory. "Done." With a controlled sort of energy, he picked up his backpack and slung it over his shoulder. He was going home, and he was claiming what was rightfully his: Michaela and the farm. Michaela most of all.

Julian was still alive when Jonah and Jared returned home. He was vastly puzzled by their sudden appearance and the young woman they brought with them, but he was alive. He was also deeply saddened. He was sure now that Jeran would never come home. A part of him wanted to die right there but he resisted the feeling. Charon couldn't ferry him down the Styx just yet. "Well, who is she?" he asked Jonah.

"We rescued her from a dragon." Jonah was thinking as fast as he could. "She's a princess. We haven't decided who she's going to marry. And, uh, the horse is the fastest in the land. Oh, and we got the bird too. So you need to give us the farm now."

Julian studied Michaela and the sadness that seemed to be etched into her face. The girl was grieving, of that he was sure. "What is your name, my dear?" When there was no response, his frown deepened. "Are you well?"

"She's a mute," Jared blurted. "All the trauma, you know. Go into the kitchen and make dinner, Michaela. We'll take care of the horse and bird."

She shot him a scathing look before stalking into the kitchen. She was actually glad now that she couldn't cook. She hoped they both got sick and died!

Julian wasn't an idiot. He knew as he looked at his plate of dinner that she had no domestic talent. He didn't doubt that she was a princess, but he highly doubted that she would have been destined to marry any man that was as domestically inept as she was. And there was no denying that his eldest two sons were indeed inept.

He bided his time for a day, watching her intently while Jonah and Jared argued over who was more worthy to inherit. The more he watched her, the more sure he was that she was far better suited to his missing son. He was also more and more sure that she was pregnant. She was sick every morning, and she often touched her stomach when no one was watching. He remembered his wife vividly even after many years, and how she, too, had acted.

Finally, one morning two days later, he made his way to the living room where Michaela sat at the window and stared across the land. She spent nearly all her time there, the very sad looking golden bird beside her. The bird shed only black feathers. The horse would not eat. Michaela had the look of a woman grieving for someone she loved. Julian was beginning to suspect there was more here than met the eye.

"It's a pity you're mute," he said as he sat beside her. "I'd love to hear about your family." When she said nothing, he leaned back in his chair with a sigh. "Well, I'll tell you about mine if you'd like." He watched her face intently. "I actually have a third son, you know. He was my greatest pride. So kind you had to love him."

She closed her eyes helplessly as tears welled up inside. She cried every night and yet it seemed there were more tears still to cry. On a broken sound, she buried her face in her hands. She couldn't bear to hear about Jeran, not when her soul seemed to be dying without him.

Julian sighed softly and reached out to take her hands. He lifted her left and looked at the ring resting there. He knew the workmanship instantly. "Michaela," he said gently, "I know you are Jeran's wife." He smiled when her head swung toward him. "I'm old, daughter. My eyes have seen a lot. It was Jeran who rescued you, wasn't it?"

She said nothing. She couldn't. She feared for the life of her child, and for Julian. She did not doubt Jonah or Jared's ruthlessness.

They would kill their father if they thought it would assist their own greed.

Julian didn't need her to say a word. He could see it in her eyes. "Where is Jeran, Michaela? What did Jonah and Julian do?" That they were at fault, he did not doubt. How else would they have come to be with Michaela and not Jeran? "How many lies have they told?"

"Lies? What lies?" Jared laughed but the sound was strained as he and Jonah stood in the doorway. They were terrified. Ever since they had woken that morning they had felt as if their world, which had seemed so perfect, was about to fall apart. "What are you telling him, Michaela?"

"You said she was mute," Julian noted as he got to his feet.

"She can write," Jonah defended their lies. He walked over to put a hand on her shoulder in what looked like a friendly gesture but his fingers bit in cruelly and she flinched at the pain. "Are you smearing our good names, princess? For shame."

As Julian stared at his two sons, he wondered how he could have been so blind for so long. How had he fooled himself into thinking they were good at heart? How long had Jeran been covering for them, protecting them at the cost of his own happiness? "Where is your brother?" he asked, his voice very quiet.

"What? Jeran?" Jared laughed, but his palms were sweating. "We never saw him at all."

"I see." Julian's hands curled into fists. "And how did you come to find Michaela again?"

"We, er, stormed a tower and fought a wizard, right, Jared?" Jonah was beginning to sweat as well, and he carefully took a step away from Michaela.

"You said it was a dragon." Fury tightened Julian's face. "Where is Jeran? I am not the senile fool you believe me to be! Michaela wears a ring that Jeran made, and when I mentioned him to her, it drove her to tears! What did you do to your brother? Have I raised murderers?"

"Shut up, old man!" Jonah gave him a shove and sent him

sprawling on the floor. "Do you have any idea how tired we are of Jeran? It's always Jeran this, Jeran that! We proved we were better than him, didn't we? He's a simple, stupid boy!"

"Yeah," came Jeran's voice behind them, "but he was smart enough to learn to swim."

Everyone turned sharply to see him standing in the open doorway. Michaela couldn't breathe. Almost afraid to believe, she took a slow step toward him. He held out his hands to her, and on a sob, she rushed forward and leapt into his arms. "Jeran! You're alive!" She clung onto him desperately, shaking with her emotions. "I thought you were dead!" she sobbed into his shoulder.

"I'm alive." He held her fiercely for a moment, his face buried in her hair, and then he lifted his head and looked his brothers dead in the eye. They both swallowed hard and went white as they looked at Michaela and saw that her hair was turning to gold from black like the night sky taken over by the light of the sun.

"Th-that's impossible!" Jared managed to say.

Jeran held Michaela with one arm and used his other hand to pull the scroll out of his pocket. He held it out to his father without taking his eyes from his brothers. "This contract is a verification of what has occurred. It states Michaela is my wife, and it details the deeds I have done to win her and to claim the golden bird. It is signed by three kings, one of which is Michaela's own father. The horse in the corral is also mine; I'm sure it will be just as glad to see me as my wife is."

Julian put the scroll down without looking at it. He did not doubt Jeran in the slightest. His son did not lie. He was stunned at the transformation in him, however. He had never seen Jeran sounding so forceful. He had never thought he would see it, but he was seeing it then: his little boy was a grown man. "What happened to delay your return?"

"Jonah and Jared were set to be hung for thievery and for causing immense damages in a fight. Both of these events were caused, by the way, by their racking up immense bills at an inn over the course of these last few months." Jeran spotted the bruises on Michaela's shoulder and his fury grew. "I paid their debts and freed them. In return, they shoved me into a well. A friend helped me get out."

Jonah gave a shaky laugh. He had never before been afraid of Jeran, but right then he was positively terrified of him. Jeran in a fury was something he hoped to hell he never saw again. "Father, how can you believe him?"

"Because he has never lied to me." Julian got to his feet painfully and braced himself against the table. "And because he has brought the evidence of it to me." He looked at Michaela. "What say you?"

"Everything Jeran says is true." She lifted her chin. "I am Princess Michaela of the Sandstorm Kingdom. Jeran is my husband. These two," she gestured at Jared and Jonah, "threatened to kill me if I told the truth."

"I see." He was unsurprised by the news.

Jeran set Michaela gently aside and walked toward his brothers. "You know," he said, "all my life you two have taken what was mine and claimed it for your own. It didn't bother me because I loved you. If you had never taken Michaela from me, I would have never bothered to tell the truth. I would have let you lie about why you were delayed and never have corrected you. I'm through, now, with being nice to you."

Jared snorted even though his knees wanted to knock. "What? Are you going to hurt us? You can't even hit properly."

Jeran lifted his hands and curled them into fists. Then he smiled and untucked his thumb from under his fingers. He tightened his fists and suddenly struck. The first punch knocked Jared on his ass. The second sent Jonah onto the floor beside him. "Try me," he challenged. "Get up and I'll hit you again."

Holding his bleeding nose, Jonah said, "That's okay. We'll stay down here."

Jeran turned and gave a laugh as Michaela leapt into his arms.

This time he caught her and they didn't go tumbling to the floor as usual. Holding her tightly, he looked at his father. "What do you have to say, Father? I went out into the world. I found the golden bird. I found the woman of my dreams. She's pregnant with my child."

Michaela gave a gasp. "Darn it, Jeran! I was going to tell you! How'd you know?"

He smiled at her. "I'm not completely stupid. I asked the doctor before I left. He was happy to tell me." His hands slid down to rest possessively over her stomach. She was carrying his child. Now that the anger was gone, he was able to savor the joy he felt inside. He couldn't wait to take her away somewhere private so he could study her body. He knew it wouldn't be any different, but he wanted to be able to memorize every change.

Julian eased down onto a chair with a sigh and a smile. "So I see," he murmured. "Even if you had not found all of that, what you showed me when you walked in here would have convinced me. The farm is yours, Jeran. You are the only one I would trust with it. I can die peacefully now."

"Don't you dare," Michaela scolded him. "You have a grandchild to meet and spoil." She turned her head as the other two Windwalker males got to their feet and walked silently out of the house. "I suppose there is no helping some people."

Jeran smiled as Lead flew over to land on his shoulder. "I'm not going to think about them anymore. I've got what I want."

"The farm?" Julian asked.

"Nope." He scooped Michaela up into his arms and spun her in a quick and giddy circle. "My golden princess."

Julian smiled. He supposed it would be worth living long enough to meet his grandchild, particularly if he or she turned out to be just like Jeran. Mirage needed more Jerans to help balance out the greed of mankind.

Jeran and Michaela left on their honeymoon trip the following morning. Julian assured them both that he would still be alive when they returned, and they were able to set out with light hearts. Coal seemed to be sensitive to Michaela's rebellious stomach, and the ride was far smoother than ever.

Content, Michaela snuggled against Jeran. "You were so incredible yesterday," she murmured.

"I was angry," he said. "I'm so sorry, Michaela, for being so stupid."

"That's okay." She suddenly straightened in surprise as she saw a familiar figure in the road ahead. "Isn't that the fox who has been helping us?"

Jeran looked and smiled. "It is." He stopped Coal and then dismounted and helped Michaela down as well. Together they walked down the road to kneel in front of the little fox. Jeran pulled a cookie out of his bag to offer it, as was his way. "Hello again."

"Ooh. Oatmeal." The fox nibbled happily on his treat. "Hello indeed. I am very proud, Jeran. You have learned a very important lesson."

"Don't buy dead carcasses?" Michaela asked innocently.

"Don't put golden birds in golden cages?" Jeran asked.

"Or, when rescuing a princess, make sure to get her completely out of the kingdom before her daddy sends the army to knock on the door?" his wife offered.

"It was more like a pounding than a knocking."

The fox began to laugh. "You know the real lesson."

Jeran smiled. "I do. And I promise I'll try to work harder at knowing when to be nice and when to let someone take the punishment they deserve."

"Something tells me I'm still going to be the one disciplining

our child," Michaela countered dryly.

He grinned at her. "Probably." He turned back to the chuckling fox. "I owe you," he said seriously. "Name it, and it is yours."

The fox thought about it. "I ask only that you take the contract that has been signed and give it to a Good Faerie to be delivered to Earth. She will know where to take it precisely. As I cannot take it myself, I must ask this of you."

"Consider it done." Jeran was silent for a moment, and then he said softly, "I hope you find her again, someday." At the startled look shot toward him, he smiled. "The woman that you loved that you learned, too late, to fight for."

The fox was equally silent and then smiled as well. "Thank you, Jeran." With a little bow, he turned and began walking down the road away from them. Within twenty feet he seemed to simply disappear into the sunshine as if dissolving into the light.

"Who do you think he is, or was?" Michaela asked softly.

"I don't know." Jeran stood and pulled her up to her feet as well. "But I think he'll find what we did. What everyone is looking for."

"What's that?"

"Happily ever after."

EPILOGUE

On Earth, there was a place known as 3rd District. Running directly under the district was the River Styx. It was through this mystical river that the world, Mirage, was connected. Resting over the entrance to the Styx was a building in 3rd District known as the Enforcers Headquarters. It was where the company known as the Enforcers was stationed from. They protected and defended the people of the District and also guarded the entrance to the Styx.

Rhianna Taber was one of the two co-owners and founders of Enforcers. She took care of the daily running of the place and the day-to-day business. Her partner took care of the larger processes and business deals they got into. His wife was their resident hacker.

It was for this reason that Rhianna studied the humorous image of herself depicted as a cherub, which was now her wallpaper, and turned to call at the adjoining office, "Riku! Keep Rayna out of my computer, damn it! And tell Taylor to stop being a smartass!"

Her response was a chuckle from her partner and a giggle from his wife. Taylor was another Enforcer, the husband of Rayna's sister, and he was also a game artist and writer. Only he would have drawn such a spectacular image. He and his wife had only just returned from their honeymoon, and they were already jumping into things. Taylor was only a part-timer, since he had his own business, but Gwyn and Rayna worked as a team to uncover truth. They also worked as a team to pester Rhianna.

She just sighed. She was surrounded by smartasses, but she hardly minded. She could be just as bad, if not worse. Why did like always call to like?

She turned to pick up her cup of tea when there was a shimmer, and a scroll appeared on her desk with a flicker of golden light. The scent of peaches seemed to drift gently up from the scroll, and her heart stilled inside her chest.

"Rhi?" Her partner was standing in the doorway watching her. "Is something wrong?"

"No, not at all." She picked up the scroll and carefully blocked Eric from her mind. She covered her emotions with a smile, but even she knew it was strained at the corners. "It's just a contract from Mirage. See?" She held it up. "There's a note on it. 'One for the records.'"

"Ah." Eric shut the door and looked down at the slender woman beside him. Her face was pensive. As she was Truth, he knew, then, that Rhianna had lied blatantly to his face. He just wished he knew why; she had never directly lied to him before, and the knowledge was painful.

In her office, Rhianna traced a finger lightly over the handwritten notes on the scroll. She had never forgotten that handwriting. Forcing it out of her mind, she turned and slid the completed contract into its own folder in her desk drawer. There was no use dwelling on the past, especially at her age.

There was far too much past to dwell on.

Status: File Complete
Analysis: A heart of gold can turn even the simplest of gifts into a treasure fit for a princess.

Author Notes

And thus ends the second book of the 3rd DISTRICT Series. I can already hear the cry of "What about Rhi?!" Don't worry, friends, Rhianna will have her turn! Her story lies at the heart of the District as a whole, and by the time we get there, you might just already know what faerie tale she belongs to . . .

Next in the series will be THE DEASE FILE. It will be coming out in Fall of 2016. What, two books in the same year? Yes! Hopefully that will make up for everyone waiting almost two years just for this one!

If you loved this story, or any of my stories, please leave me a review on Amazon! Reviews are the bread and butter of an author's life, and even a simple "More, please!" will keep us going.

You can keep up with me on www.facebook.com/stacyjgarrett or www.stacyjgarrett.com or follow my blog at stacyjgarrett.wordpress.com. I sometimes lurk on Twitter (@stacyjgarrett), and Tumblr as well (stacyjgarrett.tumblr.com).

I can't wait to see you again within my magical District! Until then, keep looking for those happy ever afters!

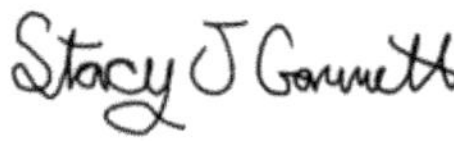

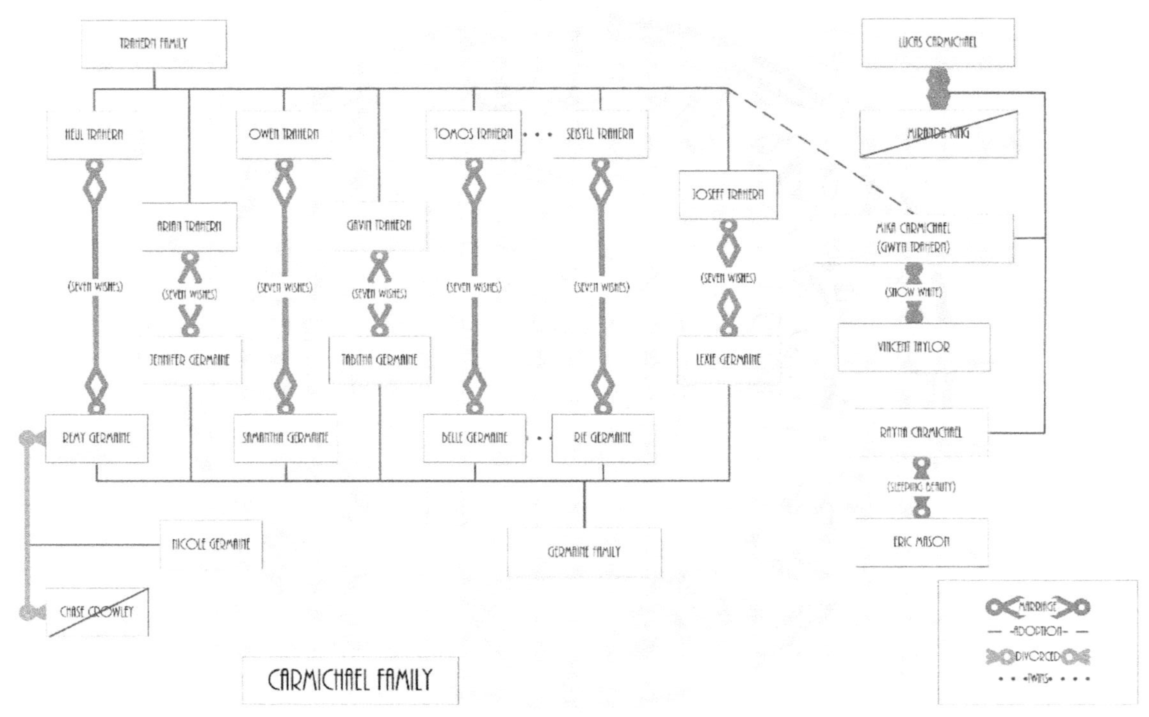

LUCAS CARMICHAEL
MIRANDA KING
TRAHERN FAMILY
HEUL TRAHERN
OWEN TRAHERN
TOMOS TRAHERN
SEISYLL TRAHERN
ARIAN TRAHERN
GAVIN TRAHERN
JOSEFF TRAHERN
MIKA CARMICHAEL
(GWYN TRAHERN)
(SEVEN WISHES)
(SEVEN WISHES)
(SEVEN WISHES)
(SEVEN WISHES)
(SEVEN WISHES)
(SEVEN WISHES)
(SEVEN WISHES)
(SNOW WHITE)
VINCENT TAYLOR
JENNIFER GERMAINE
TABITHA GERMAINE
LEXIE GERMAINE
RAYNA CARMICHAEL
(SLEEPING BEAUTY)
ERIC MASON
REMY GERMAINE
SAMANTHA GERMAINE
BELLE GERMAINE
RIE GERMAINE
NICOLE GERMAINE
GERMAINE FAMILY
CHASE CROWLEY
CARMICHAEL FAMILY
MARRIAGE
-ADOPTION-
DIVORCED
...TWINS...

SHAUGHNESSY FAMILY

KAY SHAUGHNESSY — (THE RAVEN) — RAVEN CHILDROSE

150 YEARS

SULLIVAN SHAUGHNESSY — SAMANTHA DONAHUE

TAEGAN SHAUGHNESSY
(CINDERELLA)
KALLIOPE TAVOULARIS
DIANA SHAUGHNESSY

MEL SHAUGHNESSY
(BEAUTY & THE BEAST)
AUDRA ALEXANDRIOS

KIERAN SHAUGHNESSY
(THE NIGHTINGALE)
MADELYNE WINTERS
CONNER SHAUGHNESSY

AENYA SHAUGHNESSY
(THE DANCING PRINCESS)
HIRO MICHAELS
RUTH MICHAELS

KALIJI SHAUGHNESSY
COLLEEN SHAUGHNESSY

MARRIAGE
ADOPTION
DIVORCED
TWINS

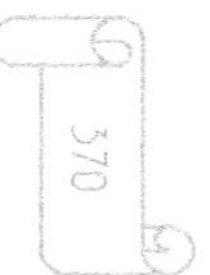

Stacy J. Garrett was made in England but born in Sacramento, California, and like the redwoods of the state, her roots have dug deep. Her destiny as a bard was somewhat inevitable. Little else can explain how she constantly told her mother tall tales so outlandish that she couldn't even get grounded for them. Her mother and grandmother had her reading by age three, and that love of a good story propelled her through so many books that Scholastic Books gave her a medal. A love of worlds created by others eventually brought out the desire to create her own, and she has never looked back.

Stacy has seen both good and evil in her life, and her stories, like life, have no half measures. Even in a fantasy world of dragons and faeries, even in a modern city where magic abounds, she knows that the constants of real emotion never change. Dreams come true, love can be found at first sight, princesses can rescue their princes, and maybe there really can be happily ever after. Her happy endings never come without cost, though, for she truly believes we can't appreciate the good and the joy without the bad and the pain along the way.

Her current haunt is a comfy house in her beloved Sacramento where she wrangles four feline fur-kids and consumes peppermints like mana in order to balance a calendar filled with more creative venues than a sane person should realistically undertake. If she's not chained to her desk, she's stomping through the scenery in search of equally fantastical photographs.